I0451976

Night to Knight

Randy Tramp

Night to Knight

ISBN: 978-1-945975-10-3

Published by EA Books Publishing a division of
Living Parables of Central Florida, Inc. a 501c3

EABooksPublishing.com

ACNOWLEDGMENTS

First, I'd like to thank my wife, Kim, and our eleven children, Kristina, Alicia, Danielle, Brooke, Alisha Dawn, Austin, Noah, Kalli, Tristan, Aaron and Aliah, for their inspiration.

JD Elliot, the best man at my wedding, and lifetime friend, helped with the section with military. JD is a retired Navy pilot.

Elaine Steffen, respiratory therapist, helped with the hospital section.

Dan Walsh, mentor, instructed me, giving me a solid writing foundation.

Believer's Trust led by Eva Marie Everson has been a place of education and encouragement, along with the annual Florida Christian Writer's Conference.

Writer's Group with, Loretta Sorensen, Marilyn Kratz, Chris Wevik, Brenda Johnson and Paula Bosco Damon has given great support with valuable critiques.

On-Line Word Weavers group with, Susan Simpson, Colleen Kastner, Jennifer Hallmark, Sandra Godfrey, Candice DuVernois also has given valuable critiques with encouragement.

My editor Dale Lipscomb with his insights and effort made this novel the best it could be.

Cheri Cowell and team at EA Books have been great to work with.

My online friends have given encouragement along the way. Tamie Dearen and Jason Fort. Both are great authors.

Given space constraints, I am omitting many people. I hope they know how appreciative I am for their advice and input. Writing a book is a team effort.

PART 1

Chapter 1

C ommander Mark Steele drew the well-worn picture of his wife and little girl from his shirt pocket. He traced the locket with his finger, kissed it, and put it back over his heart. His wife, with her curly brown hair, and his five-year-old girl, whose light brown hair framed her cherubic face, were his entire world. *Will I ever see them again?*

Steele donned his head gear to dampen the chopper's roar, then bent over and ran under the blades. Jumping into the seat, he buckled his belt and nodded to the pilot. The palm trees faded with the distancing ground as the pilot began his ascent. A vast expanse of blue water then another Philippine island came into view as the helicopter flew to the assigned destination.

A rush of adrenaline poured through Steel. Ever since he was a young boy, he dreamed of dangerous missions. When playing with his friends, they'd hide as wounded soldiers behind enemy lines, to be rescued by Mark or vice versa.

Steele, the lead of a four-man team, tested his intercom and received an affirmative response. He spotted the target beach, and his men, who were already there. The pilot pointed downward, then began the descent. Once landed, Steele ran beyond the chopper's blades. The wind decreased, and the sand resettled as the chopper lifted and flew out of sight.

"Update," Steele said as he looked at Gunner, the second in command. Two other men, both in dark camouflage, completed the group. Tracker took care of the GPS while Bill worked as the interpreter. These guys were family. They pledged, if needed, to take a bullet for each other. Hopefully, that wouldn't happen today.

"Here's the intel." Gunner pulled a paper from his pocket. "The terrorist group Abu Sayyaf is in the southern theater on an island called Sulu. Estimated at eighty men. Orders of the

President—we are to secure the release of the abducted missionaries. The Filipino military will assist us."

Steele set his eyes further up the beach. "Supplies are here—good." He walked to a pallet, opened a box and picked up a machete. "Gear up and get ready. We pull out at nineteen-hundred- hours."

The men cleaned the camp and buried the excess supplies for use when they returned. They loaded their camouflaged boat, maneuvered it beyond the sand, and pushed off the shore.

The noise from the waves and engine made it difficult to hear any voices as the vessel cut through the water. Thirty minutes later, boots hit the sand. They pulled the boat into the trees on Sulu beach, and covered it with underbrush and branches.

"In position," Steele whispered into his mouthpiece.

"Stand by."

Monkeys screeched among a forest of moving branches. Steele stood straight. His tense arm muscles filled his camouflage clothing. His eyes pierced ahead. In his ear-piece, Steele heard his commander relaying a message from the Manila command center. Steele took out a notepad and wrote numbers.

"We have new orders. The Filipino army will move in and execute the rescue. We'll rendezvous at these coordinates, where they'll have the missionaries." Steele almost added, *I hope*, but stopped. He handed Tracker the paper. "When we get the Americans, we'll bring them back here, then to home base." Steele's team was no longer in charge. Someone higher up had passed responsibility to the Filipino's. Steele didn't like it, but he was trained to follow orders. The men looked at each other with raised eyebrows.

Tracker stepped forward. "Remember what happened to Bravo Team when they worked with the Filipino's?"

"That's our orders. Get ready to move out." Steele hated not being able to execute the release of the missionaries, but he couldn't allow his men to see his disappointment. At least, not right now.

Tracker punched numbers into the GPS as the other men cleared their tracks from the beach. After several minutes of waiting, the order sounded in Steele's ear-piece. "Move out."

They cut through the trees with backpacks on and machetes in hands, swatting mosquitoes as they chopped. After a few hours, the sun began to set. They took out their night vision gear. At this time of the day, during their last mission, they nearly lost a man. Steele forced it from his mind.

They emerged from the jungle to find a rocky beach stretched out before them. Each man put his machete in his backpack as the rain began to fall.

Steele spotted a cave and pointed. "We'll stay up there until daybreak. Dry off and try to sleep. Bill, you have first watch, then Gunner, followed by Tracker. I'll take the fourth." Steele looked at his watch. "One hour each. We move at oh-five-hundred."

They lowered their heads to get into the cave, but, once inside, they stood. The air was musty and the walls moist. The sound of dripping water came from further into the cave. Steele took out his bedroll and placed it on the cave floor, then thought of his family. Since the Philippines was fifteen hours ahead of California, they would probably be just starting their day.

Every night, he told his daughter, Carina, a story. "In the castle, a lady became a prisoner. She wanted to be free. Each day she looked out her window, waiting and dreaming."

"Daddy, what was she dreaming about?" Carina asked, her eyes wide open.

"She dreamt of a young man rescuing her. From her window, she saw a field, but didn't like it."

"Why not?"

"Because she was a prisoner and couldn't run through the grass. So, she looked and dreamed. Dreamed about home, and dreamed of *him*."

"Who is him?"

"A knight who would rescue her. One day, as she was looking out her window, she had to squint really tight, and look really hard." He paused. "Can you squint your eyes, like this?" Steel smiled as his daughter scrunched her face, imitating him. "She thought she saw something shiny. You know what she saw?"

She shook her head no and pulled on her pajamas.

"You should close your eyes and dream. Can you do that?"

"If I close my eyes, will I see it?"

"Yes, if you close your eyes and fall asleep. And in the morning, you can tell me. Okay?" She nodded, closed her eyes, and pulled her stuffed Mickey Mouse closer.

Steele drifted to sleep. It seemed he had just closed his eyes when Tracker woke him. Steele arranged his backpack, and went to the cave entrance for his assigned watch. He removed an energy bar from his backpack, took a bite, and surveyed the area.

The rain had stopped, and the trees dripped with moisture. The sunlight hit the beads of water and shined like crystals with a rainbow effect. Steele looked heavenward and gave a "thumbs up." He took a deep, refreshing breath.

Kate, his wife, would be at work right now, maybe on her lunch break, and Carina would be at school. He missed them. Hopefully, after this mission, he'd be allowed a little rest and relaxation, R and R as the military called it. But for now, he shifted his attention to the present.

His eyes scanned the jungle. The enemy lurked somewhere out there. All was quiet, except for the thumps of his own raging heartbeat in his ears. He looked at his wristwatch and moved inside the cave.

"Up and at it." He kicked each man's foot then went back to the entrance. They descended the hillside and continued their trek.

The terrain was slippery from the previous night's rain. The group moved slower, with increased caution. Steele breathed a sigh of relief once the men reached the covering of the jungle. Steele signaled all stop. His heart rate increased. He motioned for Tracker and pointed to a footprint in the ground. Tracker was the resident expert in jungle warfare. He nodded to Steele, who motioned for his men to stay low. Could be the enemy. Each took a different position and extended their guns.

***

The California sun broke through the kitchen window. Kaitlyn put the dreaded bills on the counter as the phone rang. Her heart beat fast as she stood. Should she answer it? Had Mark been captured by the enemy? Maybe a phone call was better than a uniformed service member coming up the sidewalk. *If he was gone, how could I go on? Raise Carina by myself? Please no. Oh God! She needs her daddy, and I need my husband.* Kaitlyn answered the phone—wrong number. A breeze blew the curtains. In the nearby room, Carina sat in her daddy's chair. She appeared small in the huge cushions.

"You miss your daddy, don't you?" Carina nodded, and Kaitlyn scooped her up. "Want to go to the beach?"

Carina brightened. She wiggled from her mother's arms and ran to the front door.

Kaitlyn drove them to Coronado Beach. With her large white hat on and a beach bag in hand, she exited the car. Carina wanted to carry the beach bag, so Kaitlyn handed it to her. They crossed the sand and found a place to land. The smell of coconut filled the air as Kaitlyn applied suntan lotion to herself and Carina. After stretching a blanket on the beach, Kaitlyn put swimmies on her daughter and let her run to the water. She stopped short of the waves. If Mark were here, he'd never allow Carina near the water. Kaitlyn sat and wondered about Mark's over-protective personality and the arguments they created. But right now she'd welcome the disagreements.

Carina ran, fell, got up and ran again. She hit the waves and retreated, giggling as the water flowed in, then receded.

A couple walked hand-in-hand past Kaitlyn. She and Mark had walked this beach. They'd held hands, ran through the water and fell in love. She wanted his strong embrace, wanted their lips joined, and wanted his hand in hers. *I need you, Mark.*

Warm sand covered her toes. Carina had dug a hole and was making a sand mountain. The rhythm of the waves relaxed Kaitlyn, allowing her to dream deeper of Mark, his strong jaw, and piercing, deep blue eyes.

Her jaw clenched; goosebumps formed; a dark feeling assaulted her. *Something is wrong. I know it. I'm just overreacting? Letting my imagination go, right?* She prayed.

Chapter 2

Steele whispered into his mouthpiece, "In position." With less than half a mile from the pickup point, a reply came over his ear-piece to stand by.

Several minutes later, "Package secure—taking heavy gunfire," sounded.

"Prepare to engage the enemy." Steele took a deep breath. "Shoot if I give the signal." Bill, their interpreter, made the sign of the cross.

All eyes were wide, no one spoke. Their lives could be over in the next few minutes. The sound of branches breaking nearby brought goosebumps to Steele's arms. A young Filipino appeared. He wore a camouflage shirt and pants, probably five foot five, Steel guessed. He raised his M4 Carbine and spoke into his mouthpiece. "Soldier here, need confirmation."

Steele waited for a reply.

The Filipino put his hand in his pocket. Steele clicked off the safety and moved his gun upward. The wide-eyed young man raised his hands."Bill, search him."

The translator spoke in Tagalog, took the Filipino's weapon, and frisked him. "Me Reyes, Ang larawan ay mga missionaries."

In the soldier's pocket, Bill retrieved a photo of a family and handed it to Steele. "Reyes says it's a picture of the missionaries and their two sons."

Steele nodded. *Oh God, please let them be alive.*

Confirmation came over his earpiece. "Not terrorist. Repeat: Not a terrorist. He's with the Philippine Army." Steele lowered his weapon, motioned for the soldier's gun to be returned, and stuck the picture in his pocket. "Status?" said Steele.

Bill translated and listened for a response. "The missionary shot—not life threatening. A bloody fight. Terrorists escaped." More Tagalog, more translation. "New coordinates." Bill relayed the numbers to Steele; who penned it and handed the paper to Tracker.

"Ask him about the two boys," Steele said.

Bill spoke in Tagalog and received a reply. "Unconfirmed."

Tracker punched in the numbers. "Hey, Words, you sure about this last number?"

"My name is Bill, just Bill." He looked at the soldier, spoke in Tagalog, and waited for an answer. "It's right."

The Filipino ran back into the jungle.

Double timing it, they traveled to the new location and arrived ten minutes later. Steele scanned the area. An eerie silence encased him. His heart beat fast. He steadied his breathing, a technique that usually calmed him. It didn't this time.

Steele spotted a few bodies in front of a bullet-ridden building, turned and looked at his men. With his eyes, he gave the orders. They moved into position.

From behind the building, several Filipino soldiers came from the trees, followed by a man and woman. Steele signaled, and they moved in, fingers on the triggers. "My name is Commander Steele, and these are my men, Bill, Tracker, and Gunner."

"Me Cervantes, my kawal," one of the Filipino men said as he pointed at himself then the other soldiers. Steele raised his eyebrows and examined the soldiers. A few had blood stains on their clothes, all looked like they had seen hell.

"Missionaries." Cervantes motioned with his hand, "Tayo na," and walked toward the trees. The Filipino men followed, and they disappeared into the jungle.

"Kevin and Susan Hampton?" Steele acknowledged the missionary's nod. At one time, they probably wore nice clothes, but not today. Their shirts were ripped and pants stained. Susan's shoes looked as though they used to be nice, and Kevin's like they used to shine.

Susan trembled, her hands shook hysterically. "Where are our boys?"

Steele stepped toward the couple, eyes looking beyond them to the crudely constructed dwelling. A memory flashed of his own daughter, Carina. He couldn't imagine life without her.

"Joey and James." Kevin put his arm around his wife. "They were with us."

Steele signaled for Tracker to search the building. He ran, entered and after a few minutes from the front door, Tracker motioned for Steele.

Time slowed as Steele attempted to read Tracker's expression. His lips were tight, his eye contact cold. Steele turned toward the missionaries. "Please stay here."

By Steele's assumption, the place at one time was someone's home. He imagined kids running out of the hut, playing in the grass. But no kids played today. The blood sprinkled flowers, alongside the house spoke of death. He climbed the steps, lowered his head, and entered. Sunshine streamed through holes in the walls. The sour smells of urine and body odor filled the place. Steele stopped, looked around, then followed Tracker into the next room.

Tracker stepped over dead bodies, then stopped next to an open closet. He motioned downward with his eyes. Steele swallowed hard and shifted his gun to the center of his back. He could only stare at the horror before him; two young American-looking boys locked in embrace. Steele stared for a solid minute.

"Commander?"

The voice of Tracker broke Steele out his nightmare. "They're dead."

Both boys had a bullet hole in the center of their forehead. Steele imagined the boys had hidden in the closet and held each other for comfort before the bullets took their lives. Before they were executed. He hated what he'd have to do next. As they walked out, Steele wondered how the missionaries survived this blood bath. *Would the boys be alive if his team conducted the rescue?* He'd never know and needed to shut down the "what ifs."

Steele exhaled, then went back to the missionary couple. He noticed the blood on Kevin's shirt and motioned for Bill.

Bill removed the medical bag from his backpack and looked at Kevin's arm. "How long have you lived in the Philippines?"

Kevin looked past Bill and watched Steele. "Ten years. The boys were born here." Eyebrows knitted together; Kevin asked, "Are the boys okay?"

Susan stepped forward, eyes narrow, her voice trembling. "Are they in there?"

Bill wrapped Kevin's arm with bandages and turned to Susan. "Do you need any medical care?" She shook her head and stared at Steele. Bill zipped his bag.

Steele stood and struggled to speak. Realization hit them.

Susan screamed and doubled over. Kevin stared in shock, then tried to help his wife. "I'm sorry," Steele said.

Kevin held his wife as they both wept in agony. She sobbed and tried to stand.

Steele watched in horror. Mark had seen that grievous look one other time. Susan started dry heaving. She fell back to the ground. Kevin knelt beside her. After a few minutes, he helped her stand.

On his first mission, Steele belonged to a team who rescued several children. A senator's son had been kidnapped along with several other kids. The senator's son was rescued, but one didn't make it—Ramos Gonzales, a ten-year-old. Steele was present when the mother received the news of her son's death.

He felt sick himself but controlled his reaction. After a few minutes, Susan's sobbing subsided.

"How did you stay alive? That place is filled full of bullet holes," Steele asked.

"I was outside," Kevin said. "Digging a hole. A soldier grabbed me. I tried to go back inside for the boys, but he wouldn't let me."

Kevin turned and looked at his wife.

"Right after the shooting started, a soldier pulled me through a window," Susan said between sobs. "I told them about our boys. They told me they'd get them."

Steele felt the urgency to move. Any more questions would have to wait. Under different circumstances, they would memorialize the moment, possibly retrieve the bodies for a simple ceremony, but the enemy could return. Balancing safety with sensitivity, he waited a few more minutes and then asked in a soft voice, "Can you travel?

Kevin looked at his wife who also nodded. "Our boys?" she managed to say.

Kevin hugged his wife. "We can't leave them."

"Another unit will take them to the military base."

9

Terror etched on Susan's face as she wiped tears from her eyes.

"They threatened..." Kevin paused. "to kill us." Pain etched across his face. "This morning the boys were alive. I heard them."

Susan took her husband's hand. "The boys were so afraid."

"So much gunfire." Kevin looked at his wife.

"That's when they must have..." She stopped.

Steele shifted his position. "I hate to be insensitive, but we need to move."

Susan moved toward the building. "Please let me see them."

Steele put his hand on her shoulder. In anger, she pushed it off. "My boys. I have to see my boys." She continued to walk.

Steele motioned for Tracker, who ran in front of Susan, blocking her way. "Ma'am, you don't want to go in there. Trust me. It's not a pretty site," Tracker said.

"I don't care. Those are my boys and I won't leave them here."

"Ma'am, the enemy may come back. We're in danger, and I need to get you to safety," Steele said. "Please."

A distant gunshot sounded.

Kevin moved to Susan and put his arm around her. "We should listen to him."

"No, I won't do it," she said.

"I promise you another unit will get them."

"No."

More gunfire.

Steele motioned for Bill and Tracker. Bill took a sedative out of his bag, maneuvered himself behind Susan and injected the shot into her side. She collapsed into Tracker's arms, who then put her over his shoulder. "I'm sorry we had to do that, but if we stay we'll be in danger," Steele said.

Kevin didn't say a word, Steele assumed because of shock.

Steele moved to the front. "Please stay close, and if I put my hand in the air, stop."

The group traveled back to the landing point. After several hours, they stopped short of the beach. Steele motioned for Bill, and together they proceeded onto the sand while the others went to the boat, that was hidden in the trees.

Steele scanned the beach area. Too quiet. Tension simmered under his uniform as he and Bill continued toward the water.

***

At the Coronado beach, a dark cloud formed near the horizon. "Figures," Kaitlyn said. "Carina come here." With their things in hand, they hurried to the car. Kaitlyn started the vehicle and pulled out of the parking lot. The dark feeling returned. Something wasn't right.

When dating Mark, she dreamed of living on Coronado Island, but now after the dream became reality, she would give it up to be with her husband. Before marriage, Mark explained his "job" and asked, "Are you okay with this?" Back then, she was okay with it, not so today. Today she worried about Mark with greater intensity. A few minutes later, she pulled in front of the apartment and intentionally ignored the next-door neighbor, a non-military man. Two months prior police found the bodies of two women less than ten miles from the apartment. Murdered. Since then, Kaitlyn began exercising extreme caution. Too many people went in and out of that apartment complex. She entered, double-locked the door, then lowered Carina, who ran to her daddy's chair.

Rain fell for the next two days. Besides work, the daycare, and Carina's school, Kaitlyn stayed in the apartment. With Carina napping, Kaitlyn took a long hot shower. If Mark had been home, he'd join her, then they'd retreat to the bedroom. After getting dressed, Kaitlyn took one of Mark's shirts and pressed her nose into it, taking in his aroma.

A blinking light on her cell phone caught her attention. She pressed play. Lines of stress creased her forehead. It was the Commanding Officer of North Island and she needed to call him. With a shaky finger, she punched in the numbers. Only one reason he'd call—something happened to Mark.

Chapter 3

K aitlyn called her mom. "Mark... Guam... go —"

Elaine Kramer cleared her throat. "Kaitlyn, please slow down. I can't understand you." She put her hands to her head and tried to talk slower. "Mom, Mark is hurt. I need — "

"Hurt? Will he be okay?" Kaitlyn needed one of them to be calm, but that wasn't happening. The Commander at the base had told her Mark had been injured in the Philippines and flown to Guam. "I don't know." Kaitlyn tried to steady her voice. "I can't take Carina with me. Mom, can — "

"I'll take the next available flight."

"Thank you, very much." After saying goodbye, Kaitlyn collapsed in her chair. It had only been ten minutes since she had talked to the Commander, but it already seemed like days. Reaching over, she took a notepad and pen. She needed to write a to do list, but she couldn't think straight. She tossed it on the end table. Several minutes later her phone sounded. Her mom's picture appeared.

"Hi Mom."

"Do you have paper and a pen?"

She picked it up. "Okay, I'm ready."

"I'll be arriving in San Diego at 9:14 a.m. tomorrow morning. United, flight number 1150."

"I'll get you. Again, thank you." Kaitlyn clicked off the phone and sat. She couldn't control her imagination. *Who could I call?* She tried her sister's number and let it ring over ten times. It had been a while, but she could try her old roommate, Alice. Kaitlyn went to her bedroom to find her number. She opened her dresser and removed a notebook she used for phone numbers. After scanning the pages, Kaitlyn couldn't believe she didn't have Alice's number. She slammed the drawer. Afraid her thoughts would overtake her; Kaitlyn stayed active, while Carina napped. She cleaned the apartment, wrote notes for her mom and made phone calls: Carina's school, daycare provider, and her supervisor, who gave her leave from her secretary job. Kaitlyn stopped and hugged her daughter and wondered what went through her mind. How could she tell a five-year-old she may never see her daddy again? Stop it. Critical doesn't always mean fatal.

***

Hours before the sun rose, two days after the horrible news of Mark being injured, Kaitlyn prepared to leave her apartment. "Mom, let me go over this—"

"We'll be okay."

The tears broke, and Kaitlyn fell into her arms. "Mom, I can't lose him."

"You won't."

"How can you say that?" Kaitlyn stepped back and wiped the tears from her eyes. "We can pray and believe he'll be okay."

Still in her pajamas, holding a teddy bear and blanket, Carina sat wide-eyed in her daddy's chair. Kaitlyn went to her. "Mommy will be gone for a little while. Grandma will stay with you." Kaitlyn knelt beside Carina. "When I get back, Daddy will be with me." Kaitlyn restrained her tears and hoped she spoke the truth. With luggage in hand, Carina at her side, Mom driving, Kaitlyn went to the Naval Air Station North Island and stopped at the front entrance. A white-gloved, uniformed man stood by the gate. After getting out of the car, Kaitlyn leaned down to the back seat, hugged Carina, and asked her to be a good girl for grandma. Carina held out her hands wanting to be held. With tears in her eyes, Kaitlyn kissed her daughter, smoothed her hair, and exited the car. Kaitlyn stopped at the driver's window. "Thanks, Mom."

"We'll believe for daddy's recovery and your mom's safe travel, right Carina?" No response from the back seat. Carina cried, holding out her hands. "Mommy?"

"It'll be okay. You'll have fun with grandma." Kaitlyn didn't want this to be the last image of her daughter before leaving. She had to hold back the tears.

After showing her military dependent ID, Kaitlyn entered a Navy vehicle as directed. Any other day, the shine of the polished, leather seats would be impressive. But not today. For today would begin Kaitlyn's journey of several thousand miles. Six thousand, one hundred and eighty-three to be exact, according to her computer.

Kaitlyn tried to grasp the situation as a Petty Officer drove her to the airfield. Her thoughts blurred as she exited the car and went into a building as instructed. Mark, in critical condition, hospitalized in Guam, Carina at home with grandma, and herself preparing to travel, all blended in her mind.

After entering the building, a man approached her, with his hat under his arm. "I'm Lieutenant Commander Karpinski, and I'll be escorting you to Guam. I have your paperwork."

Thank God. I don't have to do this myself. She hadn't thought she'd be given a personal escort. Karpinski picked up her luggage and exited, Kaitlyn followed. The LCDR looked military all the way, tall, clean shave, perfect hair cut with all his buttons in a perfect line.

They entered another government car and went to the Passenger Terminal at Base OPS. He checked her luggage in with a Second Class Petty Officer. "We'll wait in the VIP lounge while the aircraft is loaded," he said. "Our trip has a few stops, Hickam AFB in Hawaii, then we'll get on a C-17 and fly to Kadena in Japan, then to Guam."

"Is there a long layover?"

"We'll get you there as fast as possible. Our admin department has a reputation for working miracles when dealing with military transport."

Kaitlyn looked around. She wondered if there would be a flight for her. "There are many people in the terminal." Kaitlyn rarely flew. Until her high school years, she lived on a farm where car was the only mode of transportation.

"They are trying to get to Hawaii cheap, by flying Space Available. Your orders give us top priority."

"I have to use the restroom."

Kaitlyn followed his direction. She didn't have to use the bathroom, but she needed to calm herself. Splashing water on her face helped a little. After a few minutes, pulse still racing, she moved through the crowd back to Karpinski. He looked so calm. That helped a little.

They boarded the plane in the darkness of night. Karpinski sat next to Kaitlyn. "C-40s are a military variant of a Boeing 737. It should be a smooth flight."

"Do you know Mark's condition?"

"Last I heard, it was still critical." He lowered his head.

You're not making me feel better. The pavement rolled past as the jet picked up speed and lifted off the ground. Kaitlyn's stomach rebelled. She looked around for a white bag in vain. She looked out the window hoping it would help her nausea. Lights from Navy ships dimmed as the craft continued its ascent. She saw no beauty in the miles of ocean lit up by the full moon. The words "He's in critical condition," assaulted her, and this ride terrified her. Finally, the plane leveled off.

"The C-40B is what Congress and prominent leaders use. This is a C-40A and not as sophisticated as the other C-40s. This one can seat 121 passengers, but it could be reconfigured to seat 70 passengers and cargo."

Kaitlyn tried to keep from getting angry. Her husband lay in a hospital dying and this man is talking about the plane.

"This unit costs $70 million." He continued speaking several more minutes. Kaitlyn interrupted him. "Do you have a family?"

"Yes Ma'am, my wife is the Assistant Navigator on board the USS Ronald Reagan."

"Is the Reagan deployed?"

"The aircraft carrier is pier side, Yokosuka, Japan right now. After I get you to your husband, I'll catch a hop back to Japan for a week of leave in Yokosuka."

"Your wife will be happy."

"Yes, Ma'am."

"How long have you two been separated?"

"Long time."

Kaitlyn turned toward the window. At this time of day, she would typically take Carina to kindergarten. Then, on base as a secretary, she would arrange meetings for the captain she worked for, answer the phone, and handle general paperwork. If Mark was home, she'd ride to work with him since they worked on the same base. Kaitlyn worried she hadn't told her mom everything. She hoped her replacement at work did a good job.

Kaitlyn took a deep breath and realized this was the nightmare she had dreaded. Would Mark recognize her? Ever? Would he be alive? The little information Kaitlyn received didn't give her any reassurance. She felt a strange mix of fear and excitement about seeing Mark. After an hour of flight, Kaitlyn closed her eyes. Exhaustion overtook her, and she fell asleep.

It seemed like she had just closed her eyes when she awoke to the sun beaming through the window. She stretched, pulled down the shade, then looked at Karpinski. "Did you get any sleep?"

He lowered the Sports Illustrated magazine. "No, Ma'am." Then looked at his watch. "We'll be landing in an hour."

Kaitlyn followed the ocean as the Hawaiian Islands became visible, then became larger until the craft touched down in Hickam AFB. She always wanted to see paradise, the palm trees, and deep blue waters, but this wasn't as she imagined. They were escorted to the Terminal VIP Lounge while their luggage was loaded onto their next aircraft, a C-17.

The lounge had a huge window. Kaitlyn wondered what was beyond the cement and fence outside. She drew closer and could make out several palm trees beyond the wires. Looking around she found the restroom. *I should probably use it.* She figured there would be no facilities on the plane.

After the bathroom, she found Karpinski. He was talking to another military officer. When he noticed she was near him, he turned toward her.

"It shouldn't be too much longer. How are you holding up?"

She wasn't okay, but what else could she say. I'm falling apart because my husband is dying? "I'm okay." *Thank you for asking.*

Several minutes later, at the direction of Karpinski, they boarded. Kaitlyn took a middle seat and buckled her belt. The ceiling stretched several feet above them, giving a hanger bay feel. Large, silver circular vents ran across the ceiling. Silver dominated, except for a few orange and purple pipes.

The aircraft reminded her of a large warehouse. As the plane prepared, Kaitlyn's thoughts went back several years. Mark took her to a warehouse when he had to pick up equipment. He had been preparing for a mission and would be absent for a week. Not wanting to be apart from him, Kaitlyn, pregnant with Carina, spent the day with her husband getting supplies. The plane engines revved up. Kaitlyn sunk deeper into her seat, warmed by thoughts of Mark, then darkened. *I love you so much, please don't die.*

Camouflaged men and women talked to each other. As Kaitlyn scanned the now crowded aircraft, she tried to picture Mark among the group. If he were here, Mark would talk to several guys, while she'd listen. Kaitlyn glanced at Karpinski. "It's so loud."

"The troops are revved up and with the open space—sound travels." Karpinski raised his voice slightly. "They could have added insulation to make it quieter, but that would reduce the amount of weight they could transport, so creature comforts take a back seat to cargo capacity on these birds."

More military personnel entered the aircraft and took the remaining seats. Two windows, one on each side, were the only outside views. A Navy sailor sat by one of the windows, and by the other window, Kaitlyn wasn't sure if the female was Air Force or Army. *Probably Air Force.*

When a loud roaring sounded, Karpinski buckled his seat belt.

The craft rolled along for a few minutes then lifted off. Kaitlyn gripped the edge of her arm rests until the plane leveled off. She did the same several hours later when they landed at Kadena AFB, Japan. They transferred to a four prop C-130, took off and landed at Andersen Air Force Base in Guam. A car transported them to the hospital. Karpinski accompanied her to the front desk, received Steele's room information and led Kaitlyn to the Intensive Care then his room.

She stopped at the door, tears already in her eyes.

A nurse approached. "My name is Sue." She was African American, slightly taller than Kaitlyn, and had a motherly face. Kaitlyn instantly liked her.

"Is he still, uh, in..."

"Your husband is on a ventilator. You can go in." The nurse looked at her watch. "The doctor makes his rounds in about an hour. He can tell you more."

"Thank you."

Something about her accent brought comfort to Kaitlyn. It sounded southern, and it reminded her of childhood years in Texas.

"If you need anything, please ask."

Kaitlyn glanced back at Karpinski. He stood straight with his hat under his arm. "Thank you, I couldn't imagine traveling this distance without your help."

"You're welcome ma'am."

Kaitlyn didn't know whether to hug or salute him. Instead, she squeezed his hand. She went into the room and froze. Mark laid still, ten paces in front of her. Several tubes were hooked to him. Her hand went to her mouth; tears flowed down her cheeks. Her legs stiffened only to be released at the gentle touch of the nurse.

"Let me slip by you so I can check on him," the nurse said.

Kaitlyn stepped aside, her eyes focused on Mark. She remembered to breathe.

Sue looked at the equipment, made notations on the computer, and picked up a cord. "If you need anything, press this button." She placed it back in the holder. Kaitlyn took a few steps. She was now seven paces in front of Mark. Mouth open, she felt weak. *He's not moving.*

You should sit." The nurse pushed a chair toward her.

Hands trembling, Kaitlyn stepped a few more steps. Even though she knew he was in critical condition, she wasn't prepared for this.

Kaitlyn sat mechanically, her eyes still glued on Mark. Big ugly bruises on the right side of his cheek. After Sue walked out of the room, Kaitlyn touched the uninjured part of his face. She took his hand, mindful of the IV. Nothing she did brought a response; not even a twitch. She couldn't help picturing him motionless, like this, in a coffin. The thought deadened her soul. With her head resting on Mark's arm, she gave in to exhaustion and with that image she fell asleep.

An hour later, the door opened. Kaitlyn, lifted, rubbed her eyes, knitted her brows, and attempted to focus on the blue tie man who stood in front of her. He spoke just as she tried to make out the name on his white lab coat.

"I'm Doctor Chamorro. Are you the Commander's wife?"

"Yes." Kaitlyn stood.

"He has suffered internal injuries, and we're attempting to stabilize him. I would like to examine the Commander. Would you mind stepping out, please?"

By how careful and slow the Doctor spoke, Kaitlyn figured English wasn't his native language. She moved into the hallway and leaned against the wall. Two nurses talked at their station; another nurse stared at a computer screen. Down the hall, a curtain opened, and two hospital attendants rolled a patient toward her. They went past her and around the corner at a fast pace. A woman sat alone amidst the still open curtain. Kaitlyn wondered about her story, then dismissed the thought. She needed nothing else to consider. Mark, being worse than she expected, was all she could handle. A few minutes later, the doctor exited Mark's room. "The Commander is still in critical condition. When we stabilize him, we'll send him stateside. You may go back in the room."

Kaitlyn took a deep breath, about to speak when the doctor walked away. She started toward the door but stopped.

"Excuse the doctors around here. They're military all the way and very busy." Kaitlyn followed Sue the nurse into the room. "Let me explain. The tube down his throat helps him breathe. Don't let it scare you." She softened her voice, her eyes imitated her words. "The injuries he sustained require his body to rest. That's why he's sedated."

Kaitlyn saw the nurse's mouth move, her gentle eyes, but the words didn't penetrate. Kaitlyn nodded.

"Questions?"

Kaitlyn heard that and squeezed Mark's hand. She refocused and choked out, "Will he be okay?"

"The Commander is in top physical condition and strong." Kaitlyn took a Kleenex. "Will he be able to walk again?"

"That's our hope," the nurse said. "We'll bring a cot in here so you can sleep."

"Thank you." For the most part, Kaitlyn spent the rest of the day staring at Mark. Occasionally she viewed the scene outside the window, a colorful water fountain, surrounded by a few palm trees. The cadence of the hospital equipment's noises kept her connected to the present. *Had it only been a few hours? Had she held*

Carina, not less than 24 hours ago? Was this Mark in front of her? The one she loved with her entire heart? After the sunset, Kaitlyn moved to the cot and fell asleep but awakened every time a nurse entered. Sunlight announced a new day. Kaitlyn rubbed her eyes and looked at Mark, remembering last night's nightmare—her husband's funeral.

Chapter 4

K aitlyn had fallen into a routine over the past few days. Get up, take a shower, sit next to Mark, and wait. When stabilized, he would be transported stateside to Navy Medical Center, San Diego, more commonly known as Balboa Hospital. And according to the doctor, that could happen after Mark had one more procedure.

Where is the doctor? Kaitlyn paced the floor.

A young nurse entered and bumped Mark's IV pole, moving it a few inches.

"What are you doing?" Kaitlyn launched at the nurse, stopping short of her. "You hurt him." The nurse, wide-eyed, moved the pole back to Mark and looked at Kaitlyn.

"I don't want you around him. Get out, get out now."

"Calm down, please. I didn't hurt him."

"The needle nearly came out of his arm." Kaitlyn turned red.

"Look, everything is okay."

"It's not okay. Nothing is okay." Kaitlyn pushed the nurse's station button and within a minute, another nurse entered. "I want her out of here."

The second nurse stepped between them. "Please calm yourself."

Kaitlyn stared at the nurse. "Tell her to leave."

"It's okay. We'll take care of your husband, but you need to relax." The second nurse motioned with her eyes for the young nurse to leave.

"She could have ripped the needle out of his arm."

The nurse put her hand on Kaitlyn's shoulder. Kaitlyn pushed away and turned toward the window. She hated the "out of control" feeling that raged. People outside were moving. A little boy threw something near the fountain. But her husband didn't move, not one bit. Would he ever?

Several minutes later, the sound of footsteps caused Kaitlyn to turn. Two hospital attendants, dressed in blue, entered the room. "We'll be taking the Commander to surgery," one of them said.

Kaitlyn took a deep breath and composed herself. She wanted it to stop, wanted Mark to be okay, and wanted this to end. "I'd like to go with him."

"Sorry ma'am but we can't allow that."

Kaitlyn stared at the back of the attendant who was getting Mark ready to transport. "How long is surgery?"

"Two hours," the attendant said without turning.

Kaitlyn watched as they took Mark out of the room. She paced, occasionally glancing at the TV. Another bombing. More violence. Kaitlyn didn't care. How could she? Mark filled her every thought. How could she be concerned with the woman down the hall who cried hysterically upon learning her husband had died? *And why did the nurse tell me that?*

Kaitlyn wondered how Carina was doing. She called her mom last night and received a sanitized report of her daughter. Carina could break her leg, and Kaitlyn doubted she'd find out until she got back.

Mid-afternoon, two hospital attendants returned Mark to the room. A doctor followed. "We believe the internal bleeding has stopped. We'll know in a few hours if he is stabilized."

Kaitlyn nodded, sat, and looked at Mark. With her chair near the bed, Kaitlyn rubbed Mark's arm, then kissed his hand.

Her supper arrived, but the aroma of beef, potatoes and gravy did nothing for her appetite. Kaitlyn ate half of it, not because she was hungry, but because Sue would say something if she didn't. From their conversations, Kaitlyn learned the nurse had weekends off, three adult children, one dog at home, and that her husband had died from cancer.

"You need to get fresh air," Sue often reminded Kaitlyn, who would nod and force a smile. Kaitlyn didn't want to see the outside of the hospital until she was leaving with Mark. Period.

She chewed on a celery stick and watched the clock. She tried to think of memories of Mark and her as a couple, but the hospital smells, along with the constant rhythm of the equipment, made that difficult.

Sue entered the room. "How's our patient today?"

"The doctor said he may soon be transferred to San Diego."

"I meant you."

"Oh, I'm okay."

"You're stressed. Are you really okay?"

Kaitlyn nodded.

"You said you live in Coronado?" Another nod.

"Is Balboa close?"

"It's not too far." Kaitlyn watched the nurse check the equipment. "Have you ever flown with patients?"

Sue switched on a computer and typed into it. "I have."

"Can you tell me about it?"

"The Commander—"

"You can call him Mark when you're around me." Kaitlyn smiled.

"I see spunk." Sue laughed. She looked up from the computer. "He'll be transported to the Anderson AFB on the north end of the island, then flown to Japan. The base is called Kadena. They'll put him on a huge plane called a Globemaster."

Kaitlyn looked at Mark. "Can I travel with him?"

"I'll find out for sure, but I don't see why you can't be with your husband."

"I hope so, I don't want to be separated from him."

Sue left the room. Kaitlyn looked around. Time slowed. The clock ticked. The instruments beeped. She looked at the bed. "Mark, you have to get better so we can go home," she whispered. "And I have to go with you." She worried she'd have to make the flight back to the States by herself. It terrified her.

Sue reentered an hour later, and Kaitlyn attempted to read her expression. When Sue smiled, Kaitlyn relaxed.

"You can go with your husband."

Kaitlyn stood and hugged Sue. "Thank you."

"You must put up with me well."

"You're going with us?" Kaitlyn didn't hide her excitement.

"Yes."

"Oh, thank you," Kaitlyn emphasized the words. "Thank the Good Lord."

After Sue had left, Kaitlyn kissed Mark's lips. "We're going home."

***

Early the next morning, Kaitlyn followed Sue, boarded the huge C-130, and walked past an unconscious Mark, who had been wheeled on first. Sue checked the equipment while Kaitlyn took the closest seat to her husband.

Sue sat next to Kaitlyn and exchanged eye-contact. Sensing the warmth, she squeezed the nurse's hand. They buckled and prepared for departure.

After the plane ascended and went above the clouds, Sue undid her seat belt and went to Mark. She looked at each monitor and made notations on her iPad, sat, then smiled.

"I'm sure the hospital staff was glad to get rid of me," Kaitlyn said. "

Actually, you were one of the better ones."

"One nurse would disagree."

"I suppose."

After landing, the crew did a quick transfer. Kaitlyn followed as attendants moved Mark from one aircraft to the other, rolling him into the massive hanger bay of a C-17. Hospital beds lined the sides of the craft. They pushed Mark to his designated spot and secured his bed to the deck. A medical attendee motioned for Kaitlyn to sit in the center aisle across from Mark. The attendants plugged in the equipment then sat; a few exited the aircraft.

After checking the equipment, Sue sat next to Kaitlyn. More hospital beds with patients rolled into the bay and were secured. Kaitlyn wanted to hold Mark's hand. She longed for the day he would reach out and hold her hand.

The large aircraft taxied to the runway, sped up, then lifted into the air. Once they reached the right altitude, the medical staff attended to the patients. Sue checked on Mark, and after a few minutes sat, then squeezed Kaitlyn's hand. "When the Commander arrives in Balboa, they'll reduce the medicine and he'll be responsive."

"Day after day, I've seen him lay there...not moving. You know how hard that is?" Sue softened her eyes and patted Kaitlyn's hand.

"I've missed the simple words, 'I love you.'"

"Tell me how you two met."

"A Navy picnic." Kaitlyn stopped; warmth rushed through her, increasing her pulse. "Someone brought water balloons. One thing led to another, and I was running from this good-looking officer."

"The Commander?"

"Well he was a junior officer then, but yes, and he caught me. You know what he did?"

"He asked you out on a date?"

"After he threatened me with a water balloon."

Sue laughed. "Am I finally seeing the real Kaitlyn Steele?"

"You've been a good friend, Sue."

The aircraft landed in Hawaii, refueled, and loaded on two more hospital beds before flying to North Island.

After landing in California, Sue helped transfer Mark into the ambulance then said goodbye to Kaitlyn. With the lights and sirens off, they drove to the hospital.

Kaitlyn called her mom after arriving at Balboa. "Mom, we're here."

"We'll be right there. Your dad is here so we can bring your car."

"Thank you." Kaitlyn checked the clock every fifteen minutes, each time lifting from her chair. She left Mark's side, entered the hallway and looked both ways—the fourth time, then went back into the room.

Minutes later, Carina's voice sounded from the hall. Kaitlyn jumped out of her chair and rushed to the door.

"I missed you so much, baby." Kaitlyn scooped her daughter into her arms and kissed her.

"I missed you, Mommy." Carina hugged her.

"Were you good for Grandpa and Grandma?" Kaitlyn lowered Carina.

"Yes, Mommy," Carina said. "What's wrong with Daddy?" She pointed.

Tears fell. "He's sleeping."

"Why are you crying, Mommy?"

"I'm so happy to see you." Kaitlyn squeezed her mom and dad's hand.

Chapter 5

Mark attempted to open his eyes, but they wouldn't work. In his mind, he entered a house, weapon drawn. He heard a voice. Scanning his surroundings, he inched forward. With trembling hands, he touched the door knob. A Stench came from under the door, accompanied by screams. He paused.

"Mark, wake up," a female said.

Mark forced open his eyes. A woman and a man in a white coat stood side-by-side staring at him. In heaviness, his eyes drifted shut, unable to keep them open.

"Mark, you need to open your eyes."

At the slightest movement, pain shot through his arms. *Is this real and why are my legs restrained?*

"Talk to him," the white coat said.

"Mark, this is Kate, please wake up."

He reopened his eyes. Was he dragged behind a Hummer? Why? He needed to accomplish his mission. He needed to keep the children safe. Mark closed his eyes and in his mind, he freed himself from the bed's restraints. With military discipline, he pressed on, frantic to enter the next room. Heart pounding and holding his breath, he slowly opened the door. Two boys, duct tape over their mouths, hands, and feet, stood trembling in the middle of the room. An evil presence appeared as a man with a semi-automatic rifle raised it toward the boys. Mark inched forward. Fear slapped him. Gunfire. Two thuds. He locked his gaze on the fallen boys. The assailant fled past Mark. His feet, like cemented blocks, wouldn't move. *I need to go to the boys.* Mark struggled with every ounce of strength. He cried in desperation as screams erupted from deep within him. He inched forward then paused. Two young boys lay at his feet—riddled with bullets. Mark's eyes shot open. *Is this real?* The room and the boys disappeared. He was restrained again. *Or is this real?*

"Mark, honey, wake up, you're at Balboa Hospital." He opened, then shut his eyes. The room reappeared. A woman screamed. Panic entered. Hatred filled Mark. The assailant returned. Boom. Boom. Boom. Bullets to the head. Boys falling backward. Boom. Boom. Boom. Mark could only stare. Evil laughed.

Mark shook the boys. They were sleeping, right? They couldn't be dead. He wouldn't allow it. He turned them over. Execution. "No, no, no!"

Kaitlyn stared at Mark, then the doctor, looking for a reaction. "Doctor, what's happening?"

Mark stirred. "Oh dear God, no!"

Kaitlyn threw her hands to her face and stepped back in horror.

The doctor moved forward. "Commander, you're okay."

Mark opened his eyes. Kaitlyn moved around the bed, looked at him, and held his hand. His eyes closed only to reopen a few seconds later. He licked his lips.

A nurse handed Kaitlyn a glass of ice, and she placed a cube on Mark's tongue. In weakness, he squeezed her hand.

Tension lines formed on Mark's forehead. His eyes shot downward. The monitor registered his blood pressure rising. Kaitlyn took her eyes from the instrument and locked them onto the doctor, waiting for an answer.

The doctor turned toward Kaitlyn. "Please wait out in the hallway."

Not the answer I wanted.

The nurse escorted Kaitlyn from the room. "The doctor will check him."

"Is he okay?"

"We'll let you know when we learn something," The nurse said, then reentered the room and shut the door.

Kaitlyn put her hand to her mouth and tried to breathe. Several minutes passed.

The doctor opened the door and stepped out. "At the present time, he has no movement below his waist. There is swelling on his spine. It prevents the nerve from signaling the lower half of his body. When the swelling goes down the nerves should be free to send signals again," the Doctor said. "He will need rest."

"Will he walk again?" Kaitlyn asked. Tears flowed down her cheeks as she leaned against the wall.

"It's a good possibility this condition is temporary." The doctor motioned for the nurse. "Please stay with the Commander's wife. I'll be back this afternoon. You may go back in, Mrs. Steele."

"Yes, Doctor." The nurse touched Kaitlyn's back, and together they walked into the room.

Mark remained asleep. Kaitlyn touched his feet, skimming over them. *Oh God, please, he has to walk again. We need him.* Tears fell on his blanket as Kaitlyn sat, then lowered her head on his bed.

The nurse must have seen Kaitlyn's tortured expression, for after an uncomfortable minute, she turned on the TV. "Why don't you focus on something different?"

That's easy for you to say, it's not your husband lying in this bed – paralyzed.

The nurse handed her the remote and Kaitlyn waved it away. "Would you like something to eat or drink? There is orange juice and sweet rolls from this morning."

"No, thank you."

Kaitlyn neared the top of her emotional roller coaster, about to go over the ledge. It was becoming more than she could handle. She sat and took Mark's hand. He flinched. In a strange way, she received a little strength. *I'm glad something works.*

The next day Mark opened his eyes for longer periods of time. Mark mumbled a few words, then drifted back to sleep. On the T.V., Kaitlyn saw signs that the world continued to spin, but life inside this room stood still. Kaitlyn's imagination sent her to the bedside often in hopes he would move his feet. She lifted the blanket, squeezed his big toe – nothing. Then tickled his feet, something he hated, but again nothing. In exhaustion, she collapsed into the chair.

A few more days passed, and still no movement in his legs. Her mom, dad, and Carina came up every night for two hours. The five-year-old wanted to know why her daddy slept all the time and why he didn't talk to her.

"Daddy's tired." Kaitlyn bent down to Carina's level. "Yes, daddy will run and play with you again." She forced the words from her lips. Should she prepare Carina for the possibility he may not walk again?

In the morning, a nurse opened the curtain and moved to the bedside. "How's the patient this morning?"

Kaitlyn stretched, about to respond, when something caught her eye. Did the nurse bump Mark's foot?

"Commander, how are you feeling?"

Mark opened his eyes and mumbled. Kaitlyn walked to him. "Has the doctor been in this morning?"

"Not yet," Kaitlyn said. "He should be here soon."

Kaitlyn followed the nurse's eyes. "Why? What's happening? Is something wrong?"

"Nothing is wrong." The nurse left the room. Kaitlyn watched his feet — nothing.

Several minutes later the doctor arrived and by habit, Kaitlyn left the room. The nurse entered with the doctor and shut the door. Seconds seems like hours. Her eyes followed a patient being wheeled down the hallway alongside a mother and a young girl. Kaitlyn thought about last night when Carina spilled juice on Mark. Kaitlyn yelled at her daughter, prompting her parents to take Carina home early. She felt bad about it. *What's taking the doctor so long?* She paced, not going very far from the door.

When the door opened, Kaitlyn braced for the worse. If Mark had to be in a wheelchair, then so be it. At least he would be at home with her, and she would take care of him. He'd never go on another mission, leaving her to wonder if he'd get killed. Kaitlyn took a deep breath and prepared herself for the words: "He'll never walk again."

"Mrs. Steele?" The doctor said, his eyebrows raised.

Kaitlyn realized he had been talking."What? Oh yes."

The doctor looked at her and started over. "Earlier the nurse observed movement in Mark's lower body and called to verify it. Upon examination, I found the Commander has movement in his lower extremities. I'm confident he'll make a full recovery." The doctor said. "His body just needed longer to heal."

Kaitlyn ran into the room. She squealed with delight. She fell into the chair, tears covering her face, relaxing — truly relaxing. Built-up emotions broke, sending more tears down her cheeks. Mark again shut his eyes. Kaitlyn called her Mom. "Mom, Mark's okay. He'll walk again." Kaitlyn talked for several minutes. Elaine had to ask her to slow down several times. After the phone call, Kaitlyn wished she could relay the news to Sue and regretted not getting any contact information from her.

Mark reopened his eyes. "I have to help him."

"Mark, who do you have to help?" She leaned closer. "Who?" Mark closed his eyes.

Kaitlyn kissed Mark, lingering long enough to taste a little salt. She lifted her gaze and saw a tear run down his cheek. "Mark?" She touched the wetness. *Oh Mark.*

Chapter 6

Two weeks later, they returned home. Since Mark had made a quick recovery, the hospital released him earlier than planned. On the drive to Coronado, the once outspoken Mark said little, which bothered Kaitlyn.

At the hospital, he had retreated to hours of silence. He wouldn't be allowed to stay in the Special Forces any longer, and that bothered Mark. He didn't say it, but Kaitlyn knew. She celebrated that knowledge alone, then felt guilty. The important thing was she had Mark, and he'd never go into harm's way again. Ever! Besides, he'd adjust. Right?

At their apartment, Kaitlyn stepped out of the car and retrieved their luggage. It felt as though years had passed since Kaitlyn first learned of Mark's injury. She turned the knob, surprised the door opened. *Why hadn't her parents locked the door? Didn't they know that was unsafe? Had the apartment always been this small?* Cinnamon floated in the air. Her mom's fresh baked bread, with twirls of brown when sliced.

Carina ran to her. "Mommy!"

Kaitlyn dropped the bags, scooped up her five-year-old daughter, then looked at her mom. "Thanks for staying with Carina. I'm glad to be home."

"I would have stayed with Mark, so you could come here."

Carina buried her head into Kaitlyn's shoulder.

"Hi Dad," Kaitlyn said as he exited the bathroom.

"I'll help you with Mark."

"Thanks." She lowered Carina, took her hand, and followed her dad.

"We can stay for a couple more weeks. That's if you want us to," her father said as he continued to walk toward the car.

"Of course, Dad." Kaitlyn smiled.

He retrieved the wheelchair and helped Mark sit, then wheeled him into the apartment. "Mark, I'm sure you're happy to be home."

"I am."

All five of them lived in the small apartment for the time being. Carina happily slept on the living room floor with grandma on the couch. Grandpa slept in Carina's bed. It was smaller than he'd like, and his feet hung off the end of the bed, but he managed.

By the time they left two weeks later, Mark had begun to walk with the help of a walker. Kaitlyn took time off from her job, which increased stress because of finances. But no matter how difficult it was now, it didn't compare to Mark being in Guam. He would be okay, and that kept Kaitlyn going. Her parents supported them financially, and Mark's military checks were still being deposited into their account, at least for now. Everything rested on her as Mark retreated into depression.

As the weeks went by, Mark continued to improve physically, allowing Kaitlyn to return to work part time. She welcomed the break from being cooped up in the small apartment. That gave her hope, but a nagging thought kept resurfacing. She couldn't understand why Mark was so adamant in not allowing her to contact his father. *What is Mark withholding from me?*

"Mark, we should call him and let him know what's happened."

"No."

As usual, he didn't want to discuss it. Many times, Kaitlyn asked Mark to forgive his father for whatever had happened. The funeral of Mark's mother, several years ago, was the last time Kaitlyn had seen Roger Steele. Even in that time, Mark had refused to speak to his father and since had refused to mention his name. Now he was refusing to allow Kaitlyn to contact him.

***

By the time Carina entered kindergarten, Mark had recovered fully. He worked at a local hardware store, and Kaitlyn returned to her full-time job.

At home, Mark stared at a blank computer screen and ran his hand through his hair considering a desk job the military had offered him. He picked up his most recent disability check. Unable to picture himself in that position, he rejected it. Mark folded the check and put it in his pocket.

For Mark, life comprised of work and home. He was an outgoing and take-charge person before his injury. Now he typically retreated to his office, spending hours by himself.

They invited no one over, nor went anywhere other than work. Kaitlyn had given up trying to persuade Mark to get active.

"Mark, telephone," Kaitlyn yelled from the kitchen.

"Who is it?"

"Tracker."

Mark picked up the phone. "Tracker buddy, how are you doing?"

"I'm great. How is the job going?"

"It's a job, nothing exciting," Mark said. "How about you?"

"We did a week of jungle training. But it wasn't the same without you."

"Parachutes?"

"The works," Tracker said.

"I miss it. The most exciting thing I do is talk power tools to old men. I'm bored out of my mind. I'm wired for more."

"That's the reason I'm calling, I know a guy you should contact."

"Why?"

"He has an unusual profession. You may be interested."

"He's not going to sell me anything is he?"

"Hey, I got you out of the Philippines alive. Besides that, you made me best man at your wedding, and I didn't lose the ring. Haven't I always had your back?"

"I can't argue with that." Mark felt he owed his life to his military buddy. The reports showed that Tracker immediately took over the operation after Mark and Bill had gone down. Tracker rushed the enemy, laying down a blanket of bullets, allowing the rest of the team to put Mark and Bill inside the boat and cast them off. After the enemy had retreated into the jungle, Tracker swam to the boat. Later a helicopter picked them up and transported them to safety. Mark owed his life to Tracker because of what happened two years ago. "So who's this guy?"

"Joe lost his wife and nearly committed suicide until he found a new purpose in life."

"I'm not that bad, and I've been to a shrink."

"Nothing like that," Tracker said. "With all the conversations we've had, I've learned one thing from you."

Mark waited for Tracker to continue.

"At heart, you'll always be a Special Forces Commander conducting rescues."

"Go on."

Tracker paused. "I was having a beer and overheard Joe Clark. He told the story of how he rescued an abducted child. I bought him a beer, we talked, and I told him about you."

"You didn't tell him everything, did you?" Mark laughed.

"No, just that you have a thick skull, that you're too focused on yourself," Tracker said. "And according to Kaitlyn you've lost that *loving feeling*." Tracker sang.

"You're a joker and a horrible singer."

"Remember, nothing is funny unless there's an element of truth to it."

"You got me there. I'll check it out." Mark jotted the information on paper and smiled.

The next day Mark punched Joe's number into his phone. "Hi, is this Joe Clark?"

"Yes."

"Joe, Mark Steele here."

"Mark, Tom told me to expect your call."

"Tracker."

"What?"

"I call him Tracker."

"How can I help you?"

"I was hoping you could answer that. Tracker said you have a unique story and profession. I'd like to hear it."

"Well, here's my story. See if it helps you." Joe cleared his throat. "When I lost my first wife and daughter in a car accident several years ago, I felt my life ended. That was until I developed a new perspective...getting my eyes off myself and onto others. I joined a group that researched abducted children and spent a year with them. Time came when I realized I could find the children and bring them home. I've been doing it ever since." Mark listened for the next half-hour as Joe explained the car accident, his personal story, and his current profession.

"I'm interested in hearing more," Mark replied.

"Let me know when and we'll plan an entire day."

Mark made the arrangements and ended the call. He opened the bottom drawer and pulled out a picture of himself, Tracker, Gunner, and Bill in uniform, ready for battle. Mark set the picture on his desk.

Chapter 7

Mark turned left obeying the GPS lady's command. After fifteen minutes she said, "You've reached your destination. Now get out of the car." A chuckle escaped him, at the thought of Carina's selection of the GPS voice. He pulled into the driveway, parked and went to the front door.

A beautiful, long-haired lady answered the door and welcomed him. Mark guessed she was at least ten years younger than the bald guy approaching the door. The man looked like a white Dwayne Johnson. He had a strong jaw and a powerful handshake. Mark imagined him on the set of Fast and Furious.

"Come in," said Joe.

"I'm Mark Steele."

"I'm Joe, and my wife—Jolene. Welcome. We'll go to my den." Joe shut the door and motioned for Mark to follow. "Would you like anything to drink?"

"Coffee would be great." Mark followed Joe as Jolene went to the kitchen. They walked through a huge living room with a high ceiling. The office was straight ahead. Joe pulled a chair from behind the desk, sat, and motioned for Mark to sit on the couch.

A mounted deer with huge antlers and an antelope dominated the wall. A cougar, ready to pounce, stood in the corner of the office. This room, unlike the white walls of the living room, had wood paneling and looked expensive. After a few minutes of looking around, Mark smelled the aroma of coffee, announcing Jolene's entrance.

Mark took the coffee and whispered thank you then turned his gaze back to the wall. "You shoot these yourself?"

Jolene handed Joe his coffee, left and shut the door. He pointed at a gazelle. "That one took us several hours to track. We bagged it in the foothills of the Rockies."

Mark looked at the bear skin rug. "Did you kill this, too?"

Joe laughed. "I'd like to say I did, but no. But I shot everything you see on the walls."

"You must have many stories."

"I do, but you didn't come to hear hunting stories."

"You're right, maybe another day."

Joe took a sip of coffee. "Tell me about yourself."

"I use to be a Special Forces Commander."

"Tom, or I mean Tracker, told me you were severely injured."

"Yes, and after I had recovered, they wanted me to operate a desk. I turned it down and took an early discharge." Mark paused. "Tracker told me about you. I was interested. So here I am."

Joe took another sip of his coffee. "Why this line of work?"

"I'm wired to rescue. It's something that burns in me. Early in my military career, we attempted a rescue for a group of kidnapped children. I was a member of a Special Forces team that conducted the raid. We lost a child." Mark lowered his gaze and stared into the dark liquid. "And the last mission I was on, two kids—murdered. I see those kids in my mind." Mark attempted to control his emotions, then lowered his voice, "It haunts me."

"I didn't see it in the news."

"Military kept it secret."

"That's tough."

Mark felt his face tense. He gripped his coffee with both hands. "When I had to retire from Special Forces, I lost something—purpose for living." Pausing for several seconds, and taking a breath, Mark continued. "Working at a hardware store is only a paycheck, and I have to force myself to get up every morning. I don't want to live like that anymore. When Tracker told me about your profession, I felt a spark. Does that make sense?"

"Yes, it does. I felt lost after my wife had died. And I lived without direction, or as you would say purpose. I felt that 'spark' when I began searching for abducted children. In a way we've both suffered a death. You with the Special Forces and me with my wife. They're two different things, but it ends with the same result—no real motivation. I get that."

Silence filled the air. *He understands.* Mark finally put words to his feelings. Then to interrupt his revelation, a memory flashed.

Missionary's scream. Two dead boys shot execution style. Mark sat up straight. "Enough about me, tell me what you do."

Joe pushed his chair back and perched on the edge of the desk. "I find abducted children and rescue them."

Mark pointed to the pictures on the wall. "Are those the kids you rescued?"

"A few. They are adults now and that one right there..." Joe pointed to a picture on the bottom left. "He's the one that started it all."

Mark waited for the story.

"A father hired me to find his five-year-old son, and I tracked the kid to Mexico. The father didn't tell me, but he was involved in drug trafficking. To ensure payment, they took the boy. I stumbled into a drug operation." Joe stopped and took a deep breath. "They shot the kid in the foot, then shot me in the arm. They let me go so I would deliver a message to the boy's father." Joe paused. "Leaving that child there and delivering that message nearly killed me." Joe looked into the dark liquid. "I determined that would never happen again."

"Was the kid ever returned to his father?"

Joe let out a long sigh. "We'll need to wrap this up around three."

"Okay."

"We'll order pizza at noon, so we won't need to stop. After today, you should have a good understanding of this operation."

"That's why I'm here." Mark took the last drink of his coffee, set the cup on the small table and wondered about the five-year-old boy.

Joe walked to the door, opened it, and asked Jolene if she would bring more coffee. He walked behind his desk and pulled out a folder of papers. "Before I begin, I have to tell you this work is very strenuous."

Mark could see where this was heading. "Physically, I'm good. Of course, I'm not in the shape I use to be, but I'm getting there."

"But they won't let you back into the Special Forces?"

"Difference of opinion on whether I've recovered."

Jolene came in and filled the cups as the men continued to talk. "I don't mean to eavesdrop on your conversation. But Mark are you considering this?"

"Yes."

"Is your wife okay with this?"

Mark stirred in his seat and directed his gaze at Jolene. "I haven't told her anything."

"Joe kept it secret from me, but he left a file on his desk one day. I read it then questioned him about it. He explained it." She looked at her husband, then back at Mark. "I was deeply hurt."

Joe handed Mark the folder, then stood next to his wife. "She was angry with me for a long time."

Mark directed his gaze to the couple. "It was hard on Kate when I was in the Special Forces. She had grown up on a farm. When I first met her, she had an innocence about her, a carefree spirit. That's what drew me. It was something I didn't have. I watched her change over the years." Mark looked at the ceiling, inhaled, and continued. "It's like Kate lost something. In between missions, when I was home, she'd be restless at night and frequently had nightmares. Don't get me wrong, Kate is not weak, just the opposite. I don't want to put her through that again. Maybe I'm selfish. I'm not sure, but I'm certain the best thing is to keep her in the dark about this."

"It's your choice, but trust me, she'll know something is going on." Jolene stepped out of the office and stopped. "What she doesn't know she'll make up... in her mind that is." She closed the door.

Mark realized he had been holding his breath. *Kaitlyn must not find out.*

Joe took a seat on the rolling chair and looked at the file in Mark's hand. "Those papers are years of research."

Mark scanned the files and stopped at the titles: "Operations," "Think Like an Abductor," What Not to Do and Why".

"Those are a good place to start." Joe talked, and Mark listened. When the pizza arrived, they stopped briefly to eat, then went back to the training session.

"Look for weakness or a mistake. The faster you move, the greater the odds of rescuing a child. The perps have a unique language. It's all in the folder. Study everything," Joe said. "I assume your base of operation will be here in California."

"Well, maybe not. My wife's parents made us an offer. They'd like us to move to Austin Texas. I'm considering it."

Joe went to his filing cabinet and pulled out a folder, opened it, and spilled the contents on the desk. "I just received a report..." He fumbled through the papers and retrieved one. "The interstate near Austin, I-35 has seen an increase number of abductions. You can have this if you're interested."

Mark took the paper and scanned it.

"Austin is central Texas, so that would be a great place to work out of. Assuming you're going to move there, I could pass along any cases from that area."

"That would be great."

After a couple more hours of talking, Joe looked at the clock and stood.

Mark took the cue, stood and shook hands with Joe. "Thank you. I have something I haven't had in a long time—purpose and direction."

Joe didn't need to say anything, his face showed he understood.

As Mark returned to his car, he thought about Joe's final words: "Everyone deserves freedom." He shifted the car into gear with an excitement he hadn't had in two years.

***

Back in his office, Mark typed "Austin Texas + abducted children" into a Google search. For several minutes, he examined the sites, then lowered his head and drummed his fingers on the desk. The information was overwhelming. Mark thought about the murdered missionary children. *I have to do this for them.* After another half-hour of scanning websites, Mark whispered to himself, "I can do this."

Mark turned and looked at his daughter. "Carina, you have money for your birthday. Let's get a present."

She dropped her iPad and stood.

"See if Mom wants to go," he said. "Put your iPad away." Carina picked up the device and ran out of the room.

A few minutes later, Carina ran back into the room. "Mom doesn't want to go."

"Are you sure you asked her?"

She smiled and shook her head no.

"You go ask her." Mark chuckled as she ran out the door and returned with Kaitlyn.

"You're going to the store?" Kaitlyn looked over his shoulder at the computer screen.

Carina moved next to Mark. "Want to come with us?"

"I'll stay here. It'll be a special time for you and Carina." Kaitlyn looked at the screen. "Are you checking out Austin?"

"I'm considering it."

"You mean we can move there? My parents will be excited. I'm ready to get out of this apartment and California. Can I tell them we'll take them up on their offer?"

Kaitlyn's parents had a second home and would let Kaitlyn and him live in it.

Mark put his hand around her waist. "Yes."

"What changed your mind?"

"I'm ready for a new start." *Should I tell her about my plans for Austin?* Just as Mark was to reveal his future desires, a dark thought entered him. *She'd hate it because it's dangerous.* He kept the thoughts to himself.

"I'll call them right now. Being closer to my parents...I can't wait!" Kaitlyn turned and walked away.

At first, Mark had resisted moving to Texas. Kaitlyn's parents helped them too much already. Mark knew they had money from oil discovered on their farm several years ago. Until now, Mark fought the urge to accept more help, but now, he had a reason to go forward.

Mark logged off the computer and stood. Looking at Carina, he said, "You ready to go?" She ran to the door.

Chapter 8

Mark turned on the light and hoped he wouldn't wake Kaitlyn and Carina. They were asleep in sleeping bags in the living room because their beds were already in the U-Haul. They'd loaded the truck the previous day, and since the property owner didn't want to get up this early, he'd agreed to inspect the apartment the previous night. He had returned a portion of their deposit and agreed to mail the rest to their new address in Texas.

Mark had already showered and gotten dressed. He sat down in the one remaining chair and thought about how their lives had changed since moving into this apartment almost five years ago. Back then, he'd been a Navy officer in the Special Forces. He hoped the move to Austin would give him a new purpose. He looked at his watch and noted he had a few more minutes before waking Kaitlyn and Carina.

Mark retrieved a Bible he had found the night before while packing. He opened it to the second chapter of Luke and read the story of Joseph and Mary searching for their child, Jesus. Mark lowered the book, put his hands behind his head, and looked up. He imagined Mary and Joseph searching for their lost child. After the sun went down, did they continue to search for him? Did they stop eating during those three agonizing days? Did they sleep at night? How many people did they question as they went through the city? What horrible images passed through the parent's minds? Kidnapped? Beaten? Killed? Did they go to a place of worship as last resort?

Carina stirred. What if she disappeared? He closed the Bible and placed it back in the moving box. Did Joseph and Mary keep their twelve-year-old son within eyesight as they traveled back home to Nazareth? *I would have.*

He knelt beside Kaitlyn. "Kate, time to wake up." He kissed her.

She opened her eyes, rubbed them, then nudged Carina. "It's time to get up." Kaitlyn sat up and stretched. "Mark, it's still dark out."

"I want to beat the early morning traffic. You and Carina can get ready and go to the truck. I'll finish loading."

Mark carried the last items to the car, which was on a tow dolly behind the truck. He went back into the apartment for one last look around. After inspecting each room, he placed the key on the counter and shut the apartment door. It had been five weeks since they agreed to move. It took that long for Kate's replacement to be hired and trained. And it gave Mark more time with Joe.

Mark walked to the truck, turned around, and looked at the building one last time. It was one of those moments that time seemed to stand still. His whole life had been the military, but the injury had changed that. Leaving Coronado was moving away from all he loved. He shook off the feeling and went to the truck. *Texas, here we come.*

Carina was sandwiched between Mark and Kaitlyn, who was in the passenger seat. Both girls were asleep. The seat wasn't as comfortable as their car, and the truck was a little higher off the ground. He adjusted the large mirror outside his window, fastened his seat belt, then shifted into gear.

After several blocks, Mark saw the curvature of the Coronado Bridge. When Mark had first arrived for training, he marveled at the two-mile bridge. He could see the San Diego skyline to his left. Memories of downtown flashed in his mind. On his right he could see Thirty-second street and lights from the Navy ships. More memories. He had been on a few ships and made a lot of Navy friends. He'd miss them. Mark considered the length of the truck and his towed car, then moved into the right lane before merging onto I-5.

His initial training had been difficult, but Mark thrived on difficult situations. The harder the challenge, the more he liked it. He attributed his success to his ability to see beyond the present, a skill he now planned to use when rescuing a child. When he'd get a case, he'd imagine the kid being returned to the parent and work toward that goal.

It seemed appropriate to leave in darkness because he felt a darkness inside of his self. Mark rarely shed a tear, but as the distance from Coronado lengthened, he cried.

Even though he had just met Joe Clark, a little over a month ago, Mark knew they had formed a permanent friendship. The man had lost his first wife and daughter in a car accident, and had nearly taken his own life until he found a new direction, rescuing abducted children. The one child Joe refused to talk about took center stage in Mark's mind. Joe's first rescue attempt. Mark assumed the young child never returned home.

The traffic was light at three in the morning, so after thirty minutes, he merged onto I-8 and proceeded out of Southern California. The same route during the day would probably take at least two hours.

Mark planned and executed each decision with detail. That's why he quickly rose to the rank of Commander. He took risks, causing him to stand out. Faced dangerous situations, making him better. He loved the adrenalin rush and the sheer excitement of the chase.

Texans were risk takers, right? Remember the Alamo? Mark admired James Bowie and Davy Crockett. The Alamo was five hours away from Austin and near the Mexican border. Maybe one of his missions would take him that direction. If that happened, he'd have to stand on the ground of his heroes.

There was no moon, only the light from oncoming headlights as he traveled down the interstate. The truck made a constant, soothing hum that made for good sleeping. Maybe that's why Kate and Carina slept so well. He reached for his thermos of coffee and took a small drink. It was several degrees above warm, and just the way he liked it. The caffeine would give him two alert hours, something Mark needed right now. And then he'd need a bathroom break, exactly as he had planned.

Nature called, right on time, two hours later. Mountains appeared in the distance. Mark lowered his sun visor and noticed Kate opening her eyes.

"Good morning."

Kate squinted at the bright sun and lowered her visor. "Good Morning. Where are we?"

"Yuma, Arizona."

The traffic increased, along with the size of the mountains. Mark took an exit and found a gas station. After the pit stop, Carina saw the golden arches. So, they went there and ordered breakfast under the golden arches of the McDonald's drive-thru. Mark munched on a sausage, egg, and cheese biscuit as he maneuvered the heavy traffic. He moved into the far left lane, which helped him eat his sandwich. Several miles outside of the city, Kate and Carina once again fell asleep.

Although he didn't say it enough, Mark felt grateful for Kate. During his injury, she put up with him. She put up with his bad moods, along with his episodes of depression. But no more. He'd be the best husband and the greatest father. Parenting Carina wasn't too hard since his little girl adored him. He hoped she would stay that way. Mark would joke around with her saying, "You can't have a birthday."

Carina would respond, "Why not Daddy?"

"I don't want you to grow up."

Carina would laugh and say, "You're silly, Daddy."

The sun rose, revealing the desert. A few trees sprinkled the landscape, but mostly barren land dominated the scene. Sometimes reddish brown dirt became visible, noting bulldozers had carved out the interstate. As the miles rolled on, any green gave way to stones and clay. A song came to his mind: "I went through the desert on a horse with no name." He hummed, then he thought of his parents.

As a child, at one of their many homes, they'd lived near a base in the Middle of Nowhere Desert. At least that's what Mark called it. He hated it. There weren't many trees to climb or many kids his age. But there were many rocks to throw. And Mark found himself in constant trouble with his dad because of the many windows he busted.

Mark's mother was quiet. He figured she had to be to survive in the Steele home. She was the opposite of Mark, who wouldn't let anyone silence him, not even his strict, drill sergeant father. Mark tried to shut off the memory of the man. He hated thinking about his dad. Maybe, the radio would help. He scanned the stations. Nothing but static. He hummed the America song again.

Lunch stop, then a gas station, followed by more hours of driving. The truck didn't go the speed limit, especially when they climbed the long hills. Many times, he settled behind a semi. It made for a smooth ride, unless another semi passed on the left side. It gave Mark the "boxed in" feeling he hated.

In the late afternoon, they passed through Las Cruces, Arizona. The interstate turned south and led them toward the Mexican border. For awhile it ran parallel with the southern country. Huge rocks dominated the sides of the road, and more red clay from where the interstate was cut through the large hills. To his right was Mexico. He wondered how many children were taken across the border—kidnapped. He knew of one child that died there, Ramos Gonzales, a ten-year-old.

A special forces team went into Tijuana. The children were rescued except one. Mark hated thinking about Ramos. Probably the same way Joe wouldn't mention his failed rescue.

Mark glanced at Kate, who was now reading a romance novel. Carina was drawing two stick people. He thought about the missionary children. Mark had his child, but the missionaries didn't have their kids. He had to make it right. He couldn't bring the terrorists to justice for executing the boys, but he could do something about future kidnapped children. As they approached El Paso, Mark imagined the children he'd bring back home to their parents. He wanted to erase the image of the mother, Mrs. Gonzales, grieving the loss of her son. Her expression was etched into Mark's mind.

He had remembered his Commander knocking on her door, and the look on her face, seeing two uniformed personnel. Terror, then a blood-curdling scream, followed by her nearly fainting.

Mark shifted his thoughts to the present. He wanted to get as close to Austin before retiring for the night. According to the map, there wasn't much on the other side of El Paso. Tomorrow they'd drive for a few hours hugging the southern border, then turn east again.

"Dad, I'm hungry. How much longer?"

"We'll stop soon." Even with an hour lost through the time change and all the stops, Mark figured they'd made good time today. He wanted to get this far. So, mission accomplished.

The traffic increased as they neared the city. He passed several hotel signs. It wasn't rush hour, so Mark wanted to get through as much of El Paso as possible. It seemed to go on and on.

Nearly three quarters the way through, he spotted a Holiday Inn sign and took the exit. They checked in then had supper.

Since they were only a mile from Mexico, Mark hungered for authentic Mexican food. He knew Kate would agree. Leo's sounded like just the place. The sign said they'd been in business since 1946. The bricks along the wall and high ceiling gave it an old Mexico look. There was no doubt it had been here since the 40's.

Mark held up three fingers to the hostess. On their way to their table, he told Kate they had over five hundred miles to go. If they left early tomorrow morning, they'd arrive in Austin shortly after lunch.

Over dinner, Kate did most of the talking. Mark tried to listen but instead, thought about his plans. A few days prior, Mark had checked out jobs. He found the perfect one—recover repossessed cars. It included travel time, with flexible hours. He needed both so he could use the job as a front while searching for abducted children.

"Mark? Did you hear me?"

"I'm sorry. What did you say?"

"Are you going to find a job at a hardware store?"

"I hadn't planned on it."

Carina knocked her cup of milk over, causing the conversation to stop. Mark breathed a sigh of relief. Since the accident, Kate had become protective. He didn't want her to become suspicious before he could even secure a job. If she suspected a hint of danger, she'd be upset. He didn't want that.

After finishing their meals, they went to their hotel. Mark received the room key, and they went toward their room.

"It'll be nice being close to my parents," Kate said.

Mark wasn't so sure. The two weeks he had spent with the Kramer's hadn't been the best of times. Kate's dad frequently tried to talk to Mark, but just being out of the hospital and still angry about being discharged from the Special Forces, he wasn't in any talking mood. Elaine and Ray Kramer were nice people, but Mark didn't really get to know them. He'd have to change that.

"Your parents will love having their daughter with them, but me—"

"Stop. My parents love you."

"I hope so, because I wasn't so nice to them."

"They understood. It was a rough time for all of us."

Carina ran down the hallway. With an over-night bag in one hand, Mark sprinted after her, scooped her up, and waited for Kate.

"She's happy to be out of the car," she said while trying to catch her breath. "What room are we in?"

"A-56." Mark pointed to the room and handed her a key card.

Mark fell asleep the instant his head hit his pillow and slept longer than he would have liked. As a result, they hit the morning traffic. He started out driving, then turned the wheel over to Kate after lunch. Throughout the afternoon, Carina kept squirming and asking, "Are we there yet?" By late afternoon, Mark was happy to inform her they were close Austin.

The city skyline became visible. It didn't compare with the San Diego high rises, mostly because there was bay. But this would be home. This would be a new start. A place to forget the past.

They found their new home with the help of their GPS. Mark parked the truck, with their towed car, on the street. After looking around in the house, he'd unhook the car and maybe bring things inside the house.

Kate opened the door with the key her mom had mailed to her. She walked in and went to the dining room. The walls were white, the carpet, blue. "I can't believe we're here. It's been a long time since I've lived here."

"I thought you grew up on a farm?"

"I did. But when I was in high school, we moved here."

"Yes, I remember you telling me that. Was that the time your parents struck oil on the farm?"

"Yes." Kaitlyn looked around as Carina ran upstairs, giggling as she went. "She's happy to be here."

"I know I am. After we eat, I'll unhook the car and bring in a few things, then I'm ready for a hot shower and a relaxing night." He followed Kate into the kitchen. In the middle—a counter with four bar stools. The appliances were all stainless steel. Mark hit the ice maker, causing a few cubes to fall. "Hey, this is nice."

Kate turned around and nodded, then she opened the cupboards. It was full of dishes. "And look at this." She took three plates and handed them to Mark.

He took them. "They look brand new."

Kate smiled, then opened the refrigerator. "Mom left us a note." Kate read it. "It looks like we have supper." She put the note on the counter then took the glass dish from the refrigerator and placed it in the oven.

"It looks good." Mark set the plates on the counter. Kaitlyn picked up the note. "Tator Tot casserole."

"Our first home-cooked meal." Mark pulled Kaitlyn into a hug. They kissed.

Kaitlyn gazed into Mark's eyes and touched his cheek. "Thank you."

"For what?"

"This house. I know it was difficult leaving California." Kaitlyn set the oven temperature. "And —"

"How about a tour?" Mark stopped her from speaking. He knew where this conversation was going because they'd been down this road a lot. Kate would tell him how bad she felt bad about his discharge from the military. He'd reassure her he'd gotten over that. But he hadn't, and deep down he knew Kate was only being nice and relieved.

"Sure."

Mark followed as Kate showed him each room, giving him a brief story. "Dad would sit over there," she said and pointed at an over-stuffed recliner. "And Mom would sit..." She looked around. "They must have gotten rid of Mom's chair." A red leather sectional sat in the corner.

"I didn't realize they would give us this much furniture."

"Isn't it great?"

Mark nodded. *Especially the huge television mounted on the wall.* He thought of all the football games he'd watch on it.

"Dad wanted to finish this. He never got around to it," she said in the basement.

Mark scanned the long room, cement floors, and unpainted sheet rock walls. "A weight machine and a treadmill would fit in here." But he was only thinking of training for missions. According to Joe, Mark would have to be in top physical condition. He'd have to work-out for several months to obtain that level again.

Kaitlyn nodded then went upstairs. Mark followed. They heard Carina on the top floor and went to her. Kaitlyn led Mark into the first room at the top of the steps. "I shared this room with my sister." Kaitlyn opened the curtains and looked outside. "Laura and I would watch for dad to come home. We'd race downstairs to see who could open the door for him first."

Mark walked behind Kaitlyn and put his arms around her waist. "Who'd win?"

"Laura was always faster."

"You miss her?"

"I do. We use to talk all the time when she was in the states, but since she moved to Germany, not so much."

"Why don't you message her on Facebook?"

"She's not on social media."

"A teddy bear." Carina lifted the stuffed animal from the bed.

They turned, smiled and returned to gaze out the window.

"Oh, Mark, I'm so happy we moved here."

He squeezed her. He was happy also, but not for the same reasons as Kaitlyn. After a few minutes, they moved from the window. "Why did your parents move out of this home?" Mark picked up Carina.

"Daddy wanted to live in a smaller community."

"I'm surprised they weren't here to meet us."

"Daddy isn't feeling the best." Kaitlyn walked to the door. "I have one more room to show you."

Mark put Carina down and followed Kate downstairs to a room near the living room. "Daddy's office."

Mark looked around as Carina jumped on the chair behind the desk and rolled a few feet. A sliding glass door allowed an ample amount of sunshine in the room. Several shelves stood on the wall across from the desk. He could picture himself behind the desk, working to free children. *I'll need a locked filing cabinet.*

PART 2

Chapter 9

Nine Years Later

G ood morning Austin Texas," the radio announcer for Spirit 105.9 said. "Here's Jamie Grace, It's a Beautiful Day."

Kaitlyn poured two cups of coffee and handed one to Mark. "Any plans for today?"

Mark tossed the paper on the counter. "Light day. I only have one repo." Soon after arriving in Austin, Mark secured a job at the Ford Dealership—returning repossessed cars. His boss, Bob Hanson, gave him flexible hours. Mark picked up vehicles of owners who didn't make their monthly payments. It was a part-time job. He spent most of his time training and planning for his real job, executing rescues of missing children. Mark blew into his steaming coffee. "How about you?"

"After lunch, I'll work a few hours." Kaitlyn worked part-time at as a secretary.

"We interrupt this program for an important announcement," the radio announcer said. "An Amber Alert has been issued for this area. A fifteen-year-old girl was abducted from her home."

Mark's phone sounded. He retrieved it from his pocket and clicked on the automatic Amber Alert. A picture of a blond-haired, brown-eyed girl appeared on his screen.

"She's the same age as Carina," Kaitlyn said.

Mark continued to stare at the picture of the girl—Carley Jones. "Did you say something?" Kaitlyn looked over Mark's shoulder. "Is that her picture?"

Mark nodded, stood and walked away. "Do you want your coffee?"

He turned, retrieved his cup, then went to his office. The picture of the young girl stayed in his mind, not that he wanted it to leave. He tried to find more information on the Amber Alert website.

Kaitlyn knocked on the office door and entered. "Will you be eating lunch here?" He raised his head from the computer. "I'm not hungry. I'll grab something later."

After Kaitlyn had left, Mark took a deep breath and slammed his hand on his desk. He wanted to do something, anything to help find this girl. If her name weren't so generic, he'd locate her address. But so far, he couldn't even locate the parents.

With the TV on, the reports of the missing girl played. *If the reporters interviewed the parent at home and if I recognized the neighborhood...* Mark searched the computer to see if the police had an alleged kidnapper. No picture. Mark stood and paced. Every issued Alert caused a growing desire to do something.

Over the years, Mark kept in touch with Joe Clarke. With each of their conversations, Mark wanted to do more. Joe kept Mark supplied with opportunities, several were empty leads, but three resulted in children being reunited with their parents. But that wasn't enough for Mark. Those conversations with Joe ended six months ago, and Mark didn't know why. One day Mark called, and Joe didn't answer. Followed by a week, then a month of not answering.

At his desk again, he turned his attention to the television. On the screen—a vehicle. "If you see this car, call the officials."

With keys in his hands, Mark yelled, "I'll be back later," and left the house.

On the Interstate, he thought of the abducted girl. Even though he scanned the cars, Mark knew the chances of seeing the abductor's vehicle was near zero. Driving gave him time to think. He switched radio channels until he found the news. After listening for a few minutes, the Amber Alert repeated.

He continued down the interstate. On the outskirts of Austin, he took an exit and re-entered I-35, going the opposite direction. A few miles and thirty minutes after leaving his house, Mark saw an advertisement billboard—a beach. A thought entered his mind.

"If I can't get Joe on the phone, I'll go see him in person."

Chapter 10

C arina bounced into the kitchen and screamed. "We're going to celebrate my birthday at Disneyland."

"You're turning twelve, right?" Mark poured himself a cup of coffee.

"Dad, you know I'm going to be fifteen."

Mark chuckled. "We leave tomorrow, but Mom says you're already packed?"

"Yup and a whole week at Disneyland," she said.

Mark corrected her and told her it was one day at Disneyland.

"Oh Daddy, you're the best." Carina kissed him, turned and ran upstairs.

"She's excited." Kaitlyn entered the kitchen, yawned and tightened her robe. "I didn't think we'd ever go back to California."

Mark squinted his eyes. "We've been here ten years?"

"Nine, but who's counting?" Kaitlyn chuckled.

Mark took a drink of coffee. "It doesn't seem that long," he said. "When we're there, I have a little business I have to do. I can drop you and Carina off at the mall if you'd like."

"Don't tell Carina. It'll ruin her vacation." Kaitlyn half smiled. "At the base?"

"No."

"Are Tracker and Gunner still in California?"

"Both were transferred to the east coast."

"Then what's so important that it interrupts a family vacation?"

"Bob wants me to stop at a few dealerships." Mark hated lying to her, but he couldn't tell her his real intention and the reason he wanted their vacation in the Golden State.

Kaitlyn was about to speak when Mark took her in his arms. "I have the best family and the prettiest wife in Texas."

"You're saying that because you're hungry."

"You read my stomach."

Kaitlyn removed eggs from the refrigerator, a pan from the cupboard then turned on the stove. "Scrambled okay?"

"That would be great." He sat and opened his newspaper.

***

They pulled into the parking lot of Disneyland. "Carina, stay close and no wandering off." Mark shut his car door.

"Dad, I'll be in high school in two months, I can take care of myself." Carina skipped ahead.

"Stay close."

"Yes Dad," drawing out the words. She stopped.

Kaitlyn narrowed her eyes and looked at Mark. "She's a teenager now. We can give her a little freedom."

Mark lowered his gaze. "Stay close, Carina, and I mean it." He felt his pulse race, his face turn red.

"I hope you're able to have fun," Kaitlyn said.

Mark half-smiled as they entered under the sign: "Here you leave today and enter the world of yesterday, tomorrow and fantasy."

Great Moments with Mr. Lincoln was to their right. Mark led the way as Kaitlyn and Carina followed. They watched the show and flowed with the crowd as they left the building.

"That was incredible. What's next Dad?"

Mark took out the Disneyland map. "I made an agenda. We'll start here." He pointed at the map. "Then we'll go here."

Kaitlyn put her sunglasses on. "Yes sir, Commander Steele. As long as we stop at the shops on the way out."

The family walked with hundreds of people. Shops lined each side, people going in and out. A group of teenage girls took pictures with Mickey Mouse. The aroma of cotton candy and caramel popcorn filled the air. Carnation Café was on their left, sounds of games came from the Penny Arcade on their right. People stepped aside at the sound of bells, allowing a horse-drawn passenger car to pass.

Carina's eyes widened. "Dad, could we go on that?"

"Sure, we'll walk now, and when we get tired, we'll take the horse buggy."

Kaitlyn looked at the flowers and took a deep breath. "They smell so good."

A statue of Walt Disney and Mickey Mouse sparkled in the bright sun as carousel music filled the air. People lined against the railing while others took pictures. Parents pushed strollers as young and old moved in different directions.

Carina ran ahead. Mark cringed, quickened his pace and caught up with her, then waited for Kaitlyn. Together they entered the Indiana Jones attraction and snaked around a curvy concrete hallway, then descended into the darkness. An enormous head with glowing eyes appeared above them. The air-cooled. A cave appeared. They followed the crowd as eeriness echoed off the walls. They passed a sign that said: "Take Heed." Mark kept his eye on Carina as they walked.

A black and white film of Indiana Jones traveling through the jungle in a jeep played on a big screen. The film used history lessons to reveal a map and treasure. The line moved forward.

Girls in front of them giggled as they got in the jungle car. The next car pulled up; Kaitlyn entered, followed by Carina. Mark took the end seat, sank into the cushion, and put his arm around his daughter. The attendant checked their seat belts, and the car lunged forward. A massive door opened in front of them. An ugly face appeared from high above as the car proceeded and began to ascend. "Look into my eyes," the closed-eyed face said. Screams! Flashes of light illuminated portions of the dark walls.

"Click, Click, Click" The car went up.

Indiana Jones appeared on the left, disappeared, leaving the entire area dark, only to come to light as a massive fire appeared in front of them. They went forward, what looked like into a fire, but turned left. The cave darkened again; then a tiny light appeared in front of them. More screams. The music became dangerous and eerie. The car moved forward, revealing cobwebs on a cave ceiling. It became dark again. A spotlight hit Indiana Jones as he climbed a rope. "Careful down there, I have a bad feeling about this," he said.

Darkness gave way to the last scene of Indiana Jones. "Goodbye, tourist."

"Dad, it was awesome," Carina said as they left the adventure. A sign read: "Real Rewards Await Those Who Choose Wisely."

They went on a few more rides, then ate lunch. Outside the restaurant, Carina saw a sign.

"Dad, can we go on Splash Mountain?" She ran, not waiting for an answer.

Mark ran to catch her and passed a sign that said, "Attention! Fifty Foot Plunge Ahead."

Mark stopped, his shoulders tightened. "Carina, no."

She disappeared into the crowd.

"She'll be okay," Kaitlyn said as she caught up to Mark.

Mark looked at Kaitlyn and attempted to control his anger. He scanned the area until he spotted Carina. He lost sight of her again as she made her way onto the ride.

The sounds of rushing water and music filled the air. Kaitlyn took out sun tan lotion, applied it to her face, arms, then handed it to Mark. He waved it off, proceeded to the end of the ride, and looked at Carina. "I told you no."

"Sorry Dad, I didn't hear you," Carina said, then looked toward the sound of the park train's whistle.

They boarded and rode the rails for several miles. After disembarking, Mark squeezed Carina's hand and looked up. "Why don't we have a caricature drawn of us?" His real intention was to slow her down so he could have a breather.

"That sounds like a great idea." Carina ran to the booth.

Mark blew out a hot breath. After Mark had paid, they sat. The artist looked up and then back at his easel. When finished he them the picture and handed Mark a cylinder containing the drawing.

Kaitlyn took the caricature. "My sunglasses are huge." She smiled.

"It's too girly." Carina looked over Kaitlyn's shoulder.

"And I look like a cartoon squid," Mark said. They laughed, and he placed the drawing in the tube.

Now late afternoon, they went to the "It's a Small World" attraction. Music filled the air.

Mark looked around. "Where's Carina?"

Kaitlyn stopped walking.

"Where is she?" Tension lines appeared on Mark's forehead.

Kaitlyn pulled her cell phone out and called Carina. "She's not answering."

"What if someone took her?"

"She probably went over there." Kaitlyn, with stress on her face, pointed to the restrooms. "I'll check on her."

Mark paced back and forth, dark images pressed his thoughts. On his mind, Carley Jones, the abducted girl on the Amber Alert—still missing.

Mark's raising pulse slowed when he saw Kaitlyn and Carina coming toward him. "Carina, where were you?"

"Dad, I had to pee."

Mark looked at Kaitlyn. He saw concern washed over her face and lowered his voice.

"You need to let me know where you're going."

In line for the ride, they moved with the crowd, then into a boat. The family traveled through the sounds of children singing, "It's a small world after all."

Mark's thoughts switched to the reason he wanted to come to California—to see Joe. *I hope he's still at the same address.* Since they moved to Austin, Mark had studied Joe's files, read countless cases of abducted children, and sat on a board that helped children. Yet a passion burned in him. *I have to do more.* Over the years, Joe had given him references, leading to cases, but that ended six months ago. Mark hoped to continue his work with Joe tomorrow.

The ride was full of animated characters dancing, spinning, and singing, but Mark saw something different. Black kids, Chinese kids, African kids, kids from every country all danced in front of him and needed to be protected. Mark saw himself, alone in a dark basement. A flash of Mark's Dad went through his mind, followed by hatred. He shut off the thoughts of his childhood as the ride was about to end.

The family went on several more rides, ate supper on Disney grounds, visited the shops, and experienced the fireworks. After returning to the hotel, they had birthday cake and Carina opened her gifts.

"Dad, what are we doing tomorrow?" On her bed, Carina sat up, holding her new blanket. "Tomorrow we're traveling to San Diego. You and Mom can spend time at the mall."

"You'll be there also, right Dad?"

"I have something I have to do, but I'll meet you and Mom after that."

"Oh Dad, I want you to be with us." Carina looked at him, her shoulders dropped.

"It'll only be a few hours."

"Can I go with you?"

"No, you go with Mom."

Kaitlyn patted Carina's pillow. "Go to sleep. It's been a long day."

Carina crossed her arms and plastered a frown on her face. "Sweet dreams." Mark kissed her pouting cheek.

Chapter 11

After programming Joe Clark's address into his GPS, Mark wiped the sweat from his forehead and put his Ford Focus in gear. Mark wondered if planning a vacation for the sake of meeting Joe had been a good idea. He may not want to be found. That was unlikely since they had formed a friendship. Maybe he had a new phone number. He had sent a couple postcards and one letter asking Joe to respond. The unanswered letters haunted Mark. *If he's not there, I hope to find his new address.* After making a right turn, he recognized Joe's neighborhood. A strange sensation came over Mark as he parked in front of his mentor's house.

Mark walked to the door and pressed the doorbell. A woman answered the door. Was this Joe's wife, Jolene? She wore a black dress and looked haggard, nothing like the lady he had met several years ago. He extended his hand. "Jolene? I'm Mark." When she didn't shake his hand, he withdrew his hand.

"Mark?"

"Mark Steele."

"Oh, yes." She drew out the words, stood and looked at him for a few seconds. "Come in." She walked to the couch. Mark followed. They sat. "How do I tell you this?"

"Tell me what?" He leaned forward, his pulse quickened.

"He's, he's..." Lowering her head, she cried. Mark looked at her. Jolene tried to speak, but the words were unrecognizable.

Separated or worse, divorced? Mark waited several minutes for her to regain her composure. When she did, Jolene stared at the floor.

She lifted her head and wiped the tears from her eyes. "He's gone."

"Gone? Where?"

Jolene stood and turned away. "You don't understand, he's..." She cried again.

Realization hit Mark. He put his hands over his face and took a deep breath. "I'm so sorry."

She turned back toward Mark, her mouth tightened. "It was a small funeral, just family."

"I would've been here had I known."

She turned away. "I wanted no one here that..." She took a few steps and stopped. "They killed him." Lowering her voice, still looking away she said, "They murdered him—human traffickers."

A muscle twitched in his jaw, then tightened. Mark wanted to ask questions but realized Jolene didn't want to talk about Joe's death, didn't want Mark at the funeral and didn't want him here now.

She turned to him. "Go into Joe's office and take all the paperwork. I can't stand it being in there. Just leave everything else." Jolene walked away, then stopped. "There are empty boxes in there. My oldest son is coming next week to clean out the office and burn the files." She left the room.

Mark hesitated, nodded and entered the room. The office was how Mark remembered it nine years ago. Joe's passion for children burned in this room and rekindled in Mark's own heart. He could picture Joe behind the desk. He placed an empty box on the desk, opened the cabinet and put the files in it. Mark made several trips back and forth from the office to his car. He wondered what he would tell Kaitlyn about the material. It would ruin her vacation, and she would go into stress mode. Shake factor ten as Mark liked to put it. If she knew about the material and what he planned, she would plead with him not to put himself in danger again. Mark put the last box in the trunk and hoped their luggage would fit in the back seat. He found Jolene and said goodbye. When she didn't reply, he left and drove to a small park.

Joe is dead? Mark felt guilty about the files in the trunk, specifically the folders that contained contact and personal information on each victim. Information that would catapult him into the next phase of his plan. He quieted the guilt, retrieved a few files, reentered his car and read. His passion increased as he reviewed stories of children taken from their parents and notes from Joe's attempts to find them. Mark's determination to find lost children burned greater as he read. From the information, the failed attempts outnumbered the successful rescues.

After closing the files, he returned them to the trunk. The other boxes had general information on how to find and rescue abducted children. One file had lawyer's numbers and addresses, along with other contact information. *This is great.* Mark shut the trunk and leaned against the side of his car.

He returned to his car and imagined children parading before him. Then he saw himself in a dark cellar. Fresh hatred for his father flamed.

After an hour, he shifted the Ford into gear. He had two objectives. One, he would get more active in finding abducted children and two, he would protect Kaitlyn by not revealing his plans to her. She couldn't know about Joe and his death. On an earlier occasion, Mark had tested the air. "What would you say if I became a police officer?" It was a career he wasn't contemplating but needed to know her feelings. She pleaded with him saying, "No Mark, please don't do it." Kaitlyn stated, "I hated it when you were in the Special Forces. You could have died."

He remembered the two missionary's children, a picture that continued to play in his mind. He saw them on the floor — dead. *I have to do this for the parents.*

Mark sent Kaitlyn a text. "I'm on my way." He drove to the mall, stopped at the entrance and waited.

A few minutes later, Carina, carrying bags, ran to the car and got in the back seat. "Dad, look at my new clothes." She rummaged through her sacks, showing him items.

Kaitlyn opened the passenger door and entered. "How did it go?"

"What?"

"Mark, what's wrong? Are you okay?"

"Sorry, what did you ask?"

"Dealership?"

"Oh, yeah. I talked to them." He hoped the lie was convincing.

Kaitlyn told Mark about the clothes she purchased while Mark thought about Joe. When she stopped talking, he said, "I have boxes in the trunk. Will the luggage fit in the back seat?"

"It'll be tight, but it should fit." Her eyebrows knitted together. "What type of boxes?"

"From the dealership." After a few minutes of silence, Mark relaxed, relieved she didn't press the issue.

As they drove, Kaitlyn discussed plans for the evening as Mark tried to listen. She wanted Chinese for supper. "I'll do laundry and get packed. You and Carina could go swimming." Mark nodded.

***

Kaitlyn rolled over expecting Mark to be on his side of the bed. It was empty. *Mark's been withdrawn since yesterday afternoon. Why? And why cut the vacation short and most importantly, what's in the trunk?* She convinced him to take at least one more day and spend it at the beach, to which he reluctantly agreed.

Mark entered the room with two coffees, setting one next to Kaitlyn. "When we're ready, we'll go to the beach."

Kaitlyn sat up, sipped her coffee and looked at Mark, now sitting at the desk, his back to her.

After dressing and packing, they went to the continental breakfast area, had sweet rolls, scrambled eggs, bacon and a variety of fruit. The instant their plates were empty Mark said, "Let's go."

While Kaitlyn checked out, Mark took the luggage to the car.

On the way to Coronado Beach, Carina saw a roadside billboard with a picture of an aircraft carrier. "Dad, were you on one of those?"

"I landed on a carrier once."

Carina leaned forward. "You did?"

"First, they strapped me in, and we took off. High above the ocean, I saw a small ship."

"The ship on the billboard looked huge."

"A carrier is over a thousand feet long." Mark did the math in his head. "Six football fields. But from the sky, it looked like a matchbox car. As we descended, it became larger. The plane came in full speed, touched down on the flight deck and caught the cable to help us stop. My face stretched, and I couldn't move a finger. In fact, I couldn't move anything until we stopped."

"Why so fast?"

"If we missed the cable, we'd have to go right back into the air."

"It must have been scary."

"Imagine going on a high roller coaster. You go full speed toward the bottom and stop. It was something like that." Mark paused. "When we landed, it sounded like the plane would fall apart."

Kaitlyn looked at Carina. "When your dad was in the Special Forces, he lived in danger. I'd stay awake at nights, worried your dad wouldn't come home or afraid he'd be killed. He almost died." Kaitlyn said. "I was the wife of a Special Force's Commander, and I didn't like it."

"Should you be telling Carina this?" Mark glanced at Kaitlyn.

She frowned then directed her attention to the back seat. "Do you have enough room back there?"

"It's okay."

***

At Coronado Beach, Carina once again became agitated by Mark's over-protectiveness. When she approached a group of boys, he embarrassed her by running the boys away. Kaitlyn wondered how long it would be before Carina would rebel. Mark admitted being a little too controlling but wanted to keep his daughter safe. *When will D-Day arrive? He treats her like a child.*

Kaitlyn remembered a line in a parenting book. *The common problem of parents of teens is not transitioning from parenting a child to parenting a teen.* "Reach her heart and develop a relationship with her," Kaitlyn said as she and Mark walked down the beach.

"Carina needs to toughen up. I was raised that way and turned out okay."

I'm not getting through to him. Kaitlyn dropped the subject as she had on many occasions. Concerning Mark, "heart talks," with Carina took an empty seat to: "Do what I tell you." *Discipline without relationship equals rebellion*, she remembered reading. "Mark, are you okay?"

"I'm fine."

Kaitlyn attempted to relax and take in the rays of the sun.

After a few hours on the beach, Mark wanted to leave.

On the way back to the car, Mark led them to the famous Hotel del Coronado hotel at the request of Kaitlyn. He gave a quick history lesson about del Coronado, telling them Marilyn Monroe had visited the hotel. "It has hosted presidents and royalty throughout the years. FDR, JFK, and all the way to President Obama has been here."

"Why couldn't we stay here?" Carina asked.

"Chances are, no available rooms. Besides, it's expensive."

The opulent lobby looked like a movie set. A huge chandelier towered over the room. The ceiling was high, and the walls featured designed wood. An open circular staircase was off to their right.

Carina pointed at the stairs. "Can I go up there?"

Before Mark could speak, she had run to the top of the stairs and looked down at them. "Dad, Mom up here." Carina waved. They looked up, and Kaitlyn returned the gesture.

Kaitlyn looked at Mark and remembered the many times, as an engaged couple, they'd visited the hotel. Warm feelings entered her as the memories returned. "Remember when we first visited this place?"

"How can I forget? I nearly had to drag you here."

Kaitlyn laughed. "I forgot about that part."

"You played hard to get, reminding me of trying to catch a marlin."

"Come to think of it, you never caught a marlin."

Mark chuckled. "Maybe I should use a different illustration."

"Mark, did you enjoy this vacation?"

"I did. Why do you ask?"

"You seem so tense."

Before Mark could answer, Carina ran up to them. "Dad, where are we going next?"

"Home."

Carina put on a pout face as Mark led them to the car.

Near the vehicle, Kaitlyn took her keys and pressed the ignition button and noticed something was missing. "Mark, do you have my trunk key?"

"I didn't want Carina getting into the files in the trunk."

Kaitlyn wondered, if that was so, why take her key? *What was in the trunk and why was he also keeping it from me?*

Chapter 12

T he Austin Texas Courthouse, a concrete building projecting law and justice, nearly dominated an entire city block. Jackie Lane Kulp climbed the marble stairs with her five-year-old son. She dreaded every step. "Robert James you stay with Mommy." She only used his formal name when she wanted his attention. Usually, she called him Bobby. Her voice echoed off the high ceiling. She turned, took his hand and marched him up the stairs. He pulled against her attempting to race his metal car along the wooden railing. Jackie, still fuming about the metal detector, held onto her son's hand. *It's not like the toy was a weapon.* He wanted to keep his car instead of putting it into the basket.

Stepping onto a high polished floor brought her closer to judgment. Concerned at slipping in her high-heeled shoes, she slowed her gait, walked to the courtroom entrance, and stopped. She looked at the court paper on the bulletin board and ran her finger down the list until she found "8:30 a.m. Kulp Verses Kulp, Child Custody." She scanned the waiting area while holding onto Bobby, who looked like his father, Robert Kulp. He was seeking a change in Bobby's primary home, wanting it to be on Grove Avenue in Imperial Beach, California — Robert's condominium.

Jackie located Maria, her nanny for several years, walked over to her, and sat. She'd watch Bobby when Jackie went into the courtroom. She looked for her ex-husband in the crowd of suit and ties, spiked hair, and t-shirts. With a deep breath, Jackie willed herself to relax. She stood, then sat. "Bobby sit by Mommy." When the boy didn't return, Maria retrieved him.

The morning had been stressful. Her curling iron didn't work. She'd changed into three different blouses and went to the mirror several times. She'd chose the white one because it made her look more like a mom. *Right?*

A realization hit her. She'd forgotten to eat breakfast, and more important, she'd forgotten to feed Bobby. Her eyebrows fell as she searched her purse for food. She glanced at her watch and wondered if she had time to get him a snack. As she looked around for a vending machine, the thought evaporated when she saw her attorney. He walked to her, placed his briefcase on a small table and sat.

"How are you doing?" Jerry opened the briefcase and looked through files.

How do you think I'm doing? I might lose my son today. She shrugged. He was the same attorney who represented her in the divorce hearings; a divorce Jackie didn't want. She resisted her husband until he'd threatened the restaurant, a business Jackie had inherited from her father. Robert said that if Jackie didn't sign the divorce papers, he'd demand half the business. She couldn't allow that, so she reluctantly signed them.

Now this. The first custody hearing was two weeks ago. Each attorney had presented their case. They had joint legal custody, with Bobby's primary residence with Jackie during the school year, and several weeks with his father during the summer. Robert's lawyer stated that Bobby would have more school opportunities with his father. Jerry argued against every allegation. Today the judge would render his decision.

Jackie went through her mental to-do list. She texted the restaurant manager and reminded him that a delivery truck would be there at 10:00 a.m. She hoped to be back by then, but if she wasn't, he needed to sign for the order. Jackie finished the text by telling him to inspect the produce for freshness, then silenced her phone and put it in her purse. Robert and his lawyer entered the waiting room. Jackie attempted to restrain her feelings. She believed he'd come to his senses and return to her. Robert walked with his head held high. "He's going to win," Jackie told herself. She took in Robert's features, wavy brown hair all in line, shiny white teeth and a dimple she'd always loved. She smiled when he looked at her, a gesture he didn't return. At least "the witch" wasn't with him, one of many names Jackie had given the woman who took Robert away from her.

Robert waved at Bobby. Taking a cue from her lawyer, she allowed her son to run to his daddy. Robert scooped him up and tossed him in the air. Jackie watched. *He'll do anything to win.* Robert wanted Bobby to live with him permanently. It was difficult for Jackie, during the summer, when Bobby went with his father for several weeks.

A court official motioned for the two lawyers, and they went into the courtroom. After several minutes, her lawyer stepped out of the swinging doors and motioned Jackie. She made eye contact with Maria, giving her a non-verbal instruction to take care of Bobby. Jackie followed her lawyer into the room. A long narrow railing separated the judge's seat from the rest of the court. Robert and his lawyer entered and sat. She swallowed hard and rehearsed the accusations. Yes, mistakes were made because it was difficult raising a five-year-old while managing a restaurant. She was guilty of getting a speeding ticket, but that didn't make her a bad mom. But the one about leaving Bobby alone while she attended the restaurant was false. *I hope "His Honor" doesn't believe that.* Mocking the judge helped her relax until she realized she really needed to use the bathroom.

A few days prior, she had called her lawyer and "spazzed out" as she called it. "I can't go on if the judge gives primary residence to Robert. Bobby is my entire life." Her lawyer had unsuccessfully tried to calm her.

Robert had a stable family. She was just as stable, no matter what he said. He had a spouse that could stay home and take care of Bobby. She had a good nanny. Well, not in Robert's eyes. He had vetted her and found questionable things in her past employment. Okay, the lady smoked marijuana as a young adult, but who didn't? Her lawyer had told her not to worry because it was rare that a judge would take a child from his mother and give primary residence to a father.

"It has happened, right?" Jackie asked. Her lawyer conceded on a rare occasion a judge reversed his original decision, but that was in an extreme case of an unfit parent.

"Jackie, you're a good mother," she remembered him telling her. If that was the case then why did she forget to feed her son? And why didn't she ask Maria to get something for him? She concluded, "I am a bad mom."

"All rise."

Jackie stood. Judge Matthews entered and sat.

"Have a seat." The Judge looked at his papers as the sound of moving chairs reverberated in the room. The Judge went through the preliminaries, stating the past court cases and court numbers. Jackie heard it all before. Judge Matthews looked at Robert, then Jackie. "I've reviewed this case and have given it much consideration. Divorce is always a tragedy. It's not about someone winning and someone losing. I've made my decision based on what is best for the child, but there are areas of concern."

Jackie held her breath as everything went in slow motion. The word, "concern" replayed in her mind. The judge ran down a list of considerations he used to make his decision, employment status, safe home environment, criminal records, and the emotional bond with a child. Her mind strayed for a few minutes until the judge began talking about Maria. *Oh no.* She turned toward her lawyer and whispered, "You told me not to worry about that." He motioned to look at the judge.

"The concerns are minor, not enough to affect my decision. According to the court study, a strong bond between mother and son exists. Based on that and the fact the father lives in a different state, my ruling is primary residence will continue with Jackie Lane Kulp," he said. "And summer visits with Robert Kulp."

Jackie looked at her lawyer, hoped she heard the judge correctly. Her tension disappeared when Jerry smiled. Jackie directed her attention to Roberts's Lawyer, who spoke.

"Your Honor, my client would like an unsupervised visit."

"I will approve a two-hour unsupervised visit. I trust the attorneys can make the arrangements." The judge stood. Then everyone rose as he left the courtroom.

"No," Jackie whispered. She didn't have a good reason not to trust him, after all, he had Bobby for several weeks in the summer. A "bad feeling" wormed its way through her. "I'm afraid."

Jerry scratched his head, walked to Robert's attorney then returned. "Robert will return Bobby to your house in two hours."

Outside the courtroom, Jackie found Bobby and held him. Tension reappeared on her face. With wild eyes, her son in her arms, she again whispered to her lawyer she didn't like this. With a downcast expression, he shrugged. She held on to Bobby for several seconds then handed him to her lawyer. The boy squirmed, holding out his hands to Jackie as Jerry reentered the courtroom. She hoped to see her son in two hours as she ran to the bathroom.

Chapter 13

Mark kissed Kaitlyn in mid-tune, touching her curly brown hair. "I'm not sure who sounds better." Mark poured himself a cup of coffee. "Come, sit with me."

"I have a lot to do before Tracker and Gunner get here."

Mark poured Corn Flakes then milk into his bowl as Kaitlyn hummed along with "The Good Morning Song," now playing on the radio.

He sat at the counter. "Thanks for taking the day off."

"It's slow on Fridays."

He patted the chair next to him. "Last night was wo wa wa."

Kaitlyn sat, looked him in the eyes and touched his cheek. "It was. "

"Ewww." Carina bolted into the kitchen and opened the cupboard.

Mark turned. "Good morning, Carina."

"Mom, do we have any Lucky Charms?"

"Your dad said good morning."

"Oh, hi," she said. "Well, is there any?"

"No, I didn't get to the store yet," Kaitlyn said.

"Why?" She slammed the cupboard door.

"Carina, you will be respectful. " Mark stood.

"Yes, Dad." After emphasizing each word, she left the kitchen.

"She's getting worse. I'll set her straight."

Kaitlyn looked at Mark. "Please, not before school. It'll turn into a battle."

Mark spooned another mouthful of cereal, then took the last drink of his coffee. "Okay, besides I need to get to the airport."

Kaitlyn turned. "I thought their flight didn't arrive for another four hours."

"Tracker caught an earlier flight, but Gunner's flight is on time."

"Aren't they stationed together?"

"No, different bases." Mark stretched his shoulder back.

"Is that giving you problems again?"

"I'm okay."

"Will they have to remove the bullet fragment?" Mark carried around evidence of a battle that nearly cost him his life. The piece posed no threat, but a few months ago, an irritation appeared.

Mark finished his Corn Flakes. "Don't worry, it'll be okay." He left the house.

With the dishes in the dishwasher, Kaitlyn went to the living room. After lunch, Mark would return with Tracker and Gunner.

"Mom, where's my blue t-shirt?" Carina yelled, then pounded down the stairs. "Mom, where are you?"

"I'm in the living room."

Carina, fifteen-years-old, had a long face, small lips, and muscles, giving her a tomboy look. "My blue shirt?"

"Check the bottom of your clothes basket." The teen ran back upstairs.

Kaitlyn yelled, "School in twenty minutes."

"Yes, Mom."

***

The school newspaper fell on the floor as Carina moved past her dresser. She picked it up, turned to page two and read, "Why does everyone hate me?" Carina had submitted the question to Atty's Advice. Atty, a senior, with the supervision of Mrs. Simms, English teacher, answered questions in the paper.

This would be the third time she read it. "Dear Down Cast," Carina read, then stopped and looked around her room. Softball, basketball, and soccer trophies adorned her shelves. But that didn't matter because she didn't play sports anymore since no one cared.

Carina continued reading. "You feel everyone is against you. In expectation, you want your friends to help you feel good about yourselves, your clothes to make you feel beautiful. When those expectations are unmet, you feel worthless. Did you see how many times I used the word feel? Following your feelings is like flying a plane in the fog with no instruments. Don't allow your feelings to run your life. Your heart, who you are, is most important. See yourself as beautiful."

Carina reread the last sentence, then picked up a picture of her dad and her standing together, she holding a fish they had just caught. After looking at it, she remembered how much they used to do together. Warmth flowed through her. Then just as fast, in anger, she shut off the emotions and flipped the picture over. She continued to read.

"First, know who you are, then write positive things about yourself."

Pulling a paper with her name on top, numbers on the side, she again tried to think of something positive about herself. She stared at it.

"Carina, school."

"Yes, Mom." She crumpled the paper and threw it in the trash. *Why am I such a freak?* No "best friend" and no "boyfriend." The teachers were on her case, and her dad seemed like he didn't know she was alive unless she did something wrong.

Carina opened her history book, pulled out a paper and read her poem. "I feel so alone inside my head, I wish I were dead. I feel so empty, I am alone, Why am I like this? Why am I unknown?"

Carina placed the poem back into her history book, picked up a princess crown and put it on her head. "Mirror, mirror on the wall." She took the crown off and tossed it on her dresser. "That was stupid."

A noise brought her to the present. Carina stepped into the hallway — the vacuum cleaner. She dug through the basket of clothes, took off her pajama top and replaced it with a blue shirt. In her room, she strapped on her backpack, shot down the stairs, and out of the house.

Chapter 14

The car doors slammed outside. Kaitlyn went to the front door, opened it, and recognized Gunner, who was in the middle of a story. The men followed Mark into the house as Gunner continued to talk. He stopped to greet Kaitlyn.

"We have a spare room upstairs where you'll be staying." Mark pointed. "For now, set your bags over there."

They dropped their luggage and entered the living room at Mark's direction.

"Would anyone like something to drink?" Kaitlyn asked.

"Kate, sodas, please." Mark sat and looked at Gunner, who was talking again.

Kaitlyn prepared and served the drinks to the men then sat. The men talked for three hours. Kaitlyn listened to the men some of the time. Other times, she went to the kitchen. Close to four, Kaitlyn heard the front door open and shut. She assumed Carina was home from school.

Gunner leaned forward. "I cut through the forest like it was butter. I had to throw the monkey off my back." The men laughed. "What, it actually happened."

"And I suppose it left bite marks on your shoulder," Tracker said.

"As a matter of fact, it did." Gunner rolled up his sleeve. "Kaitlyn can verify it."

Mark winked at Tracker. Gunner waited until Kaitlyn was close. He yelled causing her to jump and scream. The men laughed.

Kaitlyn hit Gunner's arm and grinned. "You men are awful."

Carina ran down the stairs. "Who screamed?"

"They played a trick on me."

Kaitlyn turned to Mark. "Everything is in the outside refrigerator, maybe if you men can break away from your war stories you could go to the patio."

With their sodas, they followed Mark outside. Carina tagged along. Once seated, Gunner talked as Mark fired up the grill.

"Dad, want to see my roundhouse move?" Carina lifted her leg in a circular arc. Kaitlyn motioned for her to stop. Carina brought her foot down and went up with the other one.

Gunner paused, looked at the teen, then continued. "We entered the boat and covered the Missionaries." He stopped and looked at Mark. "But when I saw you and Bill laying there..." Silence hung in the air for several seconds, until Carina spoke.

"Dad, watch this." She kicked her foot straight out. "If someone tries to attack me I can kick them right in the throat."

"Yes, that's nice Carina." Mark stared straight ahead. "I called Bill last week, but he didn't want to come. Makes me wonder if he's ashamed of being in a wheelchair."

Kaitlyn lowered her head and wondered what Mark would be like had he been in a wheelchair. She watched him put the steaks and vegetables on the grill. *At least, he's not doing anything dangerous now.*

Carina went into the house. Kaitlyn followed her into the kitchen. "Honey, the guys are talking about something serious."

"Mom, I've heard it all before."

"Yes, but it helps your dad to talk about it."

"Bill and Dad get shot, and Bill is in a wheelchair, and Dad can't go back in the Special Forces. And the missionaries are rescued. La De Da." Carina stomped off.

Kaitlyn watched her walk away. After going back outside, she stood and attempted to compose herself. *This is hard enough to relive. I don't need Carina's attitude on top of it.*

A smoky, barbecue aroma drifted through the air. Gunner took an onion off the grill and popped it into his mouth. "I have a seal buddy that told me that he was near Iraq when the frogs faked the amphibious landing. Hussein had taken the bait and moved his troops over to the west."

"If I remember correctly, General Schwarzkopf faked out the news media. I remember newscasters waiting for an attack and no U.S. forces came ashore." Mark paused and smiled. "I love what he'd said, let me see if I can remember it." Mark looked at the ground, then back up. "Oh yes. Yesterday at the beginning of the war, Iraq had the fourth largest army in the world. Today they have the second largest army in Iraq." They laughed.

"That had been a brilliant move by Schwarzkopf," Tracker said.

"How would you know, you were still in diapers?" Gunner laughed.

Mark chuckled and turned the meat. He put the onions and green peppers on a higher rack. An occasional flame flared up from the grill. He closed the lid and turned to listen.

"That smells good." Tracker took another soda from the outside refrigerator.

After opening the lid, Mark cut into one steak. "A little longer."

Kaitlyn put salads on the table, along with the condiments, plates, and silverware. After several minutes, Mark announced the steaks were ready.

The men attacked the T-Bones. Kaitlyn looked at them as she nibbled on her food. Feeling like an outsider in their conversation, she tried to contain her jealousy. Kaitlyn had frequently attempted to talk to Mark concerning him being shot, but he stopped her, citing it was too painful. Now he was reliving the incident like it was a movie. It was clear he could talk with his buddies but not with her and that bothered Kaitlyn. Once finished, she stood, put on a smile, and asked, "Would anyone like dessert?"

"We're going to watch the game I taped. We'll take it in there. Thanks, Kate." Mark went to the living room, the guys followed.

Kaitlyn dished up the cakes and took it to the men. She tensed up when she heard their topic of conversation and asked, "Why would you jump out of a plane?"

"Who said anything about jumping out of a plane?" Mark picked up the remote and muted the sound.

The wrinkles in her forehead lessened. "You're talking about skydiving, right?"

"We're going to that indoor skydiving place. I hear it's an incredible experience."

"Go along with us, Kaitlyn." Gunner forked his cake.

"I'll tag along, but I'll leave the flying to you guys. Carina may enjoy it."

Except for a fork hitting a plate, the room was silent as the men finished their cake.

"That was good." Tracker handed his empty plate to Kaitlyn.

"Would you like more?"

"I'm not turning down that chocolate sensation."

"Anyone else?" The guys nodded and handed her the plates. Before going to the kitchen, she stopped at the stairs. "Carina, do you want any chocolate cake?" The sound of pounding feet gave Kaitlyn the answer.

Kaitlyn went to the kitchen, Carina followed. "We're going to the indoor skydiving place tomorrow. Would you like to go with us?"

"No, I don't want to go," Carina said.

Kaitlyn rolled her eyes. "You'll like it. You and your dad are so much alike when it comes to adventure."

"I'm nothing like him and stop saying that."

Mark entered the kitchen, looked at Carina, and whispered. "Why are you yelling? I heard you from the other room." Mark moved when Carina pushed past him.

Kaitlyn put the knife down. "Here's the cake for everyone. I'll talk to her."

***

Mark gave each man a plate.

Tracker waited for Kaitlyn to walk upstairs then spoke. "Mark, what's new on the rescue front?"

"Did you hear about Joe Clark?"

"What about him?"

"Killed by human traffickers."

"Really?"

Gunner forked a piece of chocolate cake. "What's this about?"

"Not so loud. I don't want Kaitlyn to know." Mark looked toward the stairs. "Tracker introduced me to Joe. The guy rescues children. I've been doing the same for the past several years."

"Any success?"

"A few cases, but nothing like Joe has accomplished. I hope to change all that shortly."

Gunner wiped chocolate from his face. "Let's hear the story."

"A teenage girl ran away from home and got caught up with a gang. I managed to find her and... Tell you later." Mark lowered his eyes.

Kaitlyn returned and picked up the plates. "Mark, we're out of sodas. I'm going to the store. Did you need anything else?"

"Some chips would be great."

After Kaitlyn had left the house, Gunner looked at Mark.

"I convinced the girl to return home, and it was as simple as that."

Tracker leaned toward Mark. "I can understand now why you couldn't get a hold of Joe. That's horrible. Did you talk to his wife?"

"Actually, we took a vacation to California during the summer. I went to Joe's house and found out he'd been killed."

"And you're filling his shoes?" Gunner asked.

"I guess I am."

Gunner leaned forward. "So, you're a private investigator that finds abducted children?"

Mark shook his head yes.

"How do you know where to look?"

"Joe's wife gave me all his files—lots of contacts. I called each one and put my name out there. Lawyers, PI's, group leaders, that sort of thing. I've been getting calls, mostly small cases."

"Why?" Gunner asked.

"What do you mean why?"

"Why do you do it?"

Mark's eyes narrowed. "You remember those boys in the Philippine jungle?"

"Missionary kids who were killed?"

"Yes. We should have saved them."

"You can't blame yourself for that."

"I know," Mark said. "But I can't get their images out of my mind."

"So this is a way you're dealing with your past ghosts?"

"I never thought of it that way."

"I think all of us have that deep desire to rescue," Tracker said.

Gunner nodded. "Why don't you want Kaitlyn to know?"

"She hated it when I was in the Special Forces and worried all the time. I don't want to put her through that again," Mark said then pressed play. "Let's watch the game."

They turned their attention to the screen.

Chapter 15

Five minutes late. Jackie looked at her uneaten ham sandwich and wondered if Robert had fed Bobby. *This wouldn't be happening if it wasn't for that witch. He was happy with me until she came along.*

Ten minutes had passed since the scheduled time. While looking out the window, she became conscious of a new disturbance. A sharp, metallic sound, like the stroke of a hammer hitting a frying pan struck through her thoughts. It rang in her ears. Its re-occurrence was regular but slow. She awaited each stroke with impatience. The intervals of silence grew longer; the delay became maddening. Turning from the window, she looked at the clock on the wall. Another stroke of the hammer.

Thirty minutes late. Jackie determined to call her lawyer. "Bobby is not back." She listened, then cut him off. "You told me it would be okay. I trusted you." She pulled the phone from her ear and shouted. "It's not okay, find him!" She clicked it off and tossed it on a chair. The clock sounded louder. She called her mom.

"Mom, Robert took Bobby." She gasped. "I lost Robert, I can't lose Bobby."... "What do you mean forget about Robert? Did you hear me, he took Bobby."... "Okay, Mom, I have to go, someone is trying to call me."... "Yes, I'll keep you updated. Goodbye."

"Hello?" After discovering it was the restaurant, her face turned red. "Just take care of it! Can't you do anything when I'm gone?"... "What?"... "Send it back. And don't call me unless the place is burning down."... "Yes, I'm okay."

Jackie rechecked her phone to make sure she had hung up the call and waited. More agonizing minutes passed. It was now an hour after the scheduled return.

She jumped when her lawyer's name lit up her phone. "Yes?"

"I talked to Robert's lawyer." A pause and a sigh came over the phone. "He tried to contact Robert—no luck."

"He stole Bobby!"

"Let's not to jump to conclusions. He may have had a flat or something. If he shows up with Bobby, stay calm and call me. Okay?"

"And you want me to sit here and do nothing?"

"He won't hurt Bobby."

"No, he's going to keep him from me. I can't live without my son."

"Let me see what I can do." He hung up.

Jackie picked up her sandwich, took a bite and threw it back on the plate. Tears flowed down her cheeks.

***

Mark parked in front of iFly. The building stood four stories high, featured red and white stripes, and had plenty of glass.

On the iFly website, Kaitlyn viewed videos of ascending and descending adventurers in a weightless glass tube.

They entered the building, paid, and went to the stairway as instructed.

"I'll stay out here and watch the other fliers," Kaitlyn said.

"We'll be right back. They're giving us instructions," Mark climbed the stairs with Trapper and Gunner.

Kaitlyn sat by the two story glass air chamber.

Loud, rushing wind rattled the windows near Kaitlyn, as a young man and woman entered the large circular structure. They held hands and hovered horizontally near the bottom of the tunnel. A dozen young people crowded around the glassed-in area. Smiles lit their faces as they chatted. Kaitlyn extended her ear toward them while looking at the couple who rose into the air. A voice spoke from the group. "He is proposing." *No Way!* Kaitlyn's face brightened. The couple twirled and ascended. The crowd whispered and watched.

After several minutes, the couple descended and stood. The wind decreased, and the crowd silenced. The guy pulled an object from his pocket. Kaitlyn leaned closer to see what it was. He opened a small box, removed a ring, and put the box back in his pocket. The girl's face radiated, and Kaitlyn's eyes softened. "Aww!" A large sign pressed against the glass. Kaitlyn assumed it said, "Will you marry me?" The girl nodded, and he placed the ring on her finger. They kissed, held hands, and ascended together in the power of the wind. The couple spun, descended, and ascended.

Kaitlyn wiped tears from her cheeks and went back in time. She recalled her wedding proposal. At an Italian restaurant, after dessert, Mark lowered to one knee as violinists played: "Love is in the Air." With several eyes upon them, he asked the question.

For several minutes, Kaitlyn thought about the genesis of her marriage as the couple twirled, ascended and descended.

Mark put his hand on Kaitlyn's shoulder. She glanced up, then stood and gave him a hug.

"What was that for?"

"Can't I hug you in public?"

"And those tears?"

"It was so beautiful. He proposed." Kaitlyn pointed to the couple who was exiting the tunnel. The couple blended into the group.

An iFly employee entered the wind tunnel. He leaned forward, and in a flash went to the top. He performed several somersaults and descended faster, stopping before reaching the bottom then ascending as quickly as the first.

"That's impressive." Mark put on his helmet.

Gunner stepped forward, and from the outside, looked up into the air tunnel. "Oh, I can do that in a coma."

"Hey! that's not funny," Mark said.

Gunner grinned. "You're a little touchy."

"I'll show you touchy."

The door opened. They stepped forward and entered.

***

"Did it hurt when you hit the glass " Kaitlyn turned toward Gunner. The guys laughed. Mark started the car and left the parking lot.

"It's easier when you're jumping out of an actual plane." The laughter deepened. "There's not a glass tube to run into."

"No, you collide into a person." Mark was referring to a training mission. The men had been parachuting, and Gunner jumped too soon. It was a minor incident, and no one got hurt. Mark turned on his signals and stopped at the red light.

"Hey, that wasn't my fault. He said jump, and I jumped. How was I to know you were that close?"

The light turned green, and Mark drove through the intersection. "We'll watch the iFly video when we get back. I love a comedy show." The laughter shot up again.

Gunner wasn't laughing. "Funny. We doing any rock climbing?"

"Maybe later this afternoon when your concussion is healed," Mark said.

"I will beat you this time," Gunner said. "That reminds me, do I need to go soft on you? I mean you won't hurt yourself, will you, old man?"

"I'll show you old man. Give it your best shot." Mark checked the traffic and merged onto the interstate.

Kaitlyn considered Gunner. Several people had jumped when he hit the glass. He'd taken off his helmet before exiting the wind tunnel, but did one last somersault and misjudged the closeness of the glass. The red mark on his face accentuated his scar. She remembered Mark relating how Gunner had received the scar—a fight with a British sailor. Gunner had insulted the Queen. Kaitlyn wondered what story the Special Forces guy would come up with for a black eye.

Kaitlyn noticed Mark's phone on the seat. "Your phone is blinking. Want me to get it?"

Mark picked it up, looked at it and put it in his pocket. "That's okay, I'll check it later."

Why is Mark all of a sudden nervous?

Chapter 16

B illy West wore black pants and a black shirt. His hair was black. The only thing that wasn't black was a silver chain he used as a belt and sometimes as a weapon. He had a small nose ring, along with an ear ring. No one messed with "The Kid," a nickname given to him by his dad.

Billy shot up in his bed, his heart raced at the voice from downstairs. With his earplugs in, I-pod on, he clicked until he reached Disturbed—"Land of Confusion," his favorite song. Volume on high, he sang, "a million screams and marching feet."

On his wall hung a large poster with crooked words spelled out, "Disturbed." A skull lay on its side in the corner, clothes scattered throughout the room.

He opened his bedroom window and jumped onto the garage. He climbed down the makeshift ladder and stopped outside his home.

His old man yelled again, wanting him to take out the garbage. "Take out your own trash," he thought but dared not say out loud. One night his dad had beat him, teaching Billy a valuable lesson: "Don't be home when he's drunk." The next day his father had remembered nothing and accused Billy of fighting. Since he didn't want to go to school with a black eye, Billy skipped classes until it healed.

He jogged away from his home.

The alley was vacant as he opened the dumpster behind the Chinese restaurant. A cat leaped out. Billy jumped. He searched for a styrofoam container with sweetened chicken, his favorite. He found scraps of burnt meat, but nothing edible.

"Get outta dere," the Chinese man yelled. Billy took his time and gestured with his middle finger. The Chinese man came closer with a broom and raised it in the air. Billy laughed, then left.

"Someday I'll take the broom away from you," he yelled as he went down the street.

The air smelt stale behind the bar. Billy moved toward a drunk. The guy stumbled. *This is going to be great.* Billy moved closer to the staggering man, got behind him, and felt for a billfold.

"Hey! What are you doing?" The drunk stumbled forward and turned, his eyes opened as he attempted to look at Billy.

"I'm taking you home. Give me your keys."

"I can drive." The drunk took his keys from his pocket and flipped them into the air.

Billy grabbed the keys and pressed a button. He found the car, opened the door and rummaged through the glove compartment. After finding cigarettes, he shoved them into his pocket. The drunk fell into the car, on top of Billy. The kid gave him a kick, sending him into a trash can. A dog barked. Billy snatched the guy's billfold, took the money, and tossed the wallet back at him. He threw the keys on the roof and left.

Several alleys down, Billy spotted Sam. "Hey, you got a light?" Sam lit his cigarette. Billy blew out a puff of smoke. He stuck out his chest and told his taller friend about the drunk. "He tried to jump me, so I beat him." They both laughed.

"That's nothing. I scared a group of chicks." The long-haired kid opened a bag and revealed a pack of fireworks.

"Where did you get 'em?"

"In my brother's garage. Let's scare somebody."

"I'm hungry. You have any food?"

"We can go over to my house. No one is home." A half hour later, they arrived at Sam's house.

"Don't touch anything." Sam opened the refrigerator, took out a leftover chicken and placed it on the table. It didn't take long for the boys to eat. They licked their fingers, left and walked down the street.

Billy removed the money from his pocket, counted it, twenty and two ones, then returned it.

"Where did you get that?"

"From the drunk."

They laughed, then after several blocks, arrived at Walmart.

Billy pointed. "Two old ladies."

84

Sam pulled out his phone and handed the package to Billy. "You put the firecrackers behind their car, and I'll videotape it."

After frightening the women, the boys ran to another section of the parking lot. Sam replayed the video. "That took the ugly right off her."

They laughed.

"And put it on the other one." Billy laughed. They watched the video several more times. "What time is it?"

Sam checked his phone. "Eight." He returned the phone to his back pocket. "Isn't that the girl you have the hots for?"

"Carina Steele, oh yes. Hey, why don't you get lost, I'll catch you later."

"Sure, dump me for a girl. I see how you are." Billy stepped into Sam's personal space and stared at him. Sam left.

***

Trapper and Gunner walked to the car. Mark pressed the trunk button; it opened.

"I was faster, and you know it." Gunner threw his bag in the trunk.

Tracker put his gear next to Gunners. "Stop whining. Admit it, you're slow at wall climbing."

Mark closed the trunk. "It was a great weekend. I wish we lived closer."

The men hugged, promising to do it again soon.

Mark's phone rang. He answered it, then looked at his watch. "I'll be right back."

The female caller talked as Mark entered the house. After a few minutes, he asked her to hold, put his hand over the phone, and yelled, "Kate, would you take the guys to the airport?"

Kaitlyn came from the kitchen. "Why can't you take them?"

He gestured by lifting the phone. "Kate, please, I'll make it up to you."

She extended her hand, and he tossed her his keys. "Thanks, Kate, you're the best. Tell the guys something came up, and I'll call them later."

She went to the car.

Mark continued. "Sorry about that. I've had company, and I didn't get to my messages." He listened a few more seconds. "Please calm down and talk slower."

Jackie Lane Kulp continued to talk as he went to his office. Sunshine filled the room via a large window. An exercise bike and a stomach cruncher machine lined the wall. Mark closed the door, walked to his desk, and pulled out a pad of paper. With the phone on speaker, he perched on his desk and penned notes.

"Okay Jackie, I think I have all I need. Robert Kulp age 41, last known address is Grove Avenue in Imperial Beach, California. I have his birthday and social security number right here." Mark discussed his fee, set up a time to meet and ended the call. He then booked his flight to San Diego, along with a rent-a-car. For the next hour, he searched the web looking for information on Kulp and tried to contain his excitement. This case had the potential for success. Dangerous, but he was ready for an adventure.

When the front door opened over an hour later, Mark shut off his computer screen.

Moments later, Kaitlyn stepped into his office. "That sounded serious."

Mark stood. "Bob at the dealership. I have an assignment."

"It couldn't wait?"

"No, and he wants me to fly out to Southern California." Mark hated the secrecy and the lies. In his mind, he was doing what was best for his family. When he was a Special Operations Specialist, he had kept information from Kaitlyn. This was no different. Right?

"When do you have to go?" Her eyes were downcast.

"Tomorrow," Mark said. "The guys okay?"

"If you mean, did they get on their flight? They did."

Mark noted her sarcasm. "I need to get supplies. I'll be right back."

She placed his keys on the desk and left.

In his car, Mark programmed Jackie Lane's address into his GPS. Turning on the street as directed, he found her house and parked his Ford Focus, then went to the front door. A tall, skinny lady greeted him. Mascara smeared across her face. This wasn't the lady he pictured from their conversation. On the phone, she sounded strong, in person not so much.

"Have a seat. Can I get you something to drink?"

"No, thanks."

"I need something. I'll be right back."

Upon return, her face was clean, in her hand a glass of brown liquid. Mark assumed it contained alcohol.

With a notepad and pen in hand, he spoke, "I have a question. You could've reported your husband for kidnapping. Why didn't you?"

She handed him a check and looked him in the eye. "I contacted the police."

Mark raised his eyebrows and leaned forward. "Go on."

"They're not taking me seriously. Every time I call, I get the run-around. They tell me they're working on it, and the police department in Imperial Beach is working on it. I'm tired of their definition of 'working on it.' Besides, when Robert lived here, he was friends with several of the police officers. I have no proof, but I think they're dragging their feet to help Robert."

"No Amber Alert?"

"I requested an alert, but they said no. Robert had a judge appointed visit and Bobby wasn't in any imminent danger. They would've sounded an Amber Alert if Robert had taken Bobby from my home without my consent."

"That makes sense. Shouldn't you wait a few more days?"

"Do you want the case?"

Mark played with the check in his hand. "I'll take it under one condition. I do this myself, and we don't involve the police." Mark saw her knitted brow. "Most police departments don't like private investigators. And from what you've said, they may restrict me from getting Bobby."

"We'll do it on your terms."

"Does your ex-husband own a gun?"

"Yes."

"All right." Mark crossed his arms.

His pulse raced.

Chapter 17

A Taylor Swift song played in Carina's ears as she lingered at the crosswalk. A yellow Corvette passed through the intersection. She imagined herself in the car, a boyfriend in the passenger seat. Carina didn't want to be in the sophomore class without a boyfriend any longer.

The "walkman" lit up, and Carina jogged across the street. Her heart raced. A long-haired boy stood in front of Highland Mall. She shut off her I-pod and removed her earplugs. The night before, at Walmart, Billy West showed interest in her. He was exciting, fun, and her boyfriend as of the previous night. Carina approached him.

Billy took out his earplugs. "Sup?" Through his black hair, he scanned Carina. "You have any money?" Several people walked past them.

Carina drew her eyebrows together. "No."

With her hand in his, they entered the mall. Billy stopped in front of the water fountain and let go of her hand. In the water, he retrieved several coins. She put distance between them. "I do this every time I come." Billy smiled as he put the coins in his pocket.

"Hey punk, what's up?" a Chinese guy asked. His slit-like eyes were clouded hazel, his eyebrows hidden in thick, black hair.

Billy turned. "Hey Chang, just here with my girlfriend." Chang rubbed his fingers together.

"I'll get something better than money." Billy moved down the hallway, Chang followed.

Carina walked fast to keep up with them. "What was that all about?"

"Forget it." Billy went into Spencer Gifts.

Carina stopped and in her mind, heard her dad's voice. "Don't go in Spencers. It's not a place for a young girl." She hesitated, entered the store and went to Billy. *Dad's being over-*

protective – again. Billy picked up a game, chuckled and showed it to Carina.

"That's disgusting." She put it on the shelf. Billy moved to the posters, bumping into a few people. A girl shot a look at him when he brushed up against her. The guy with her squared off with Billy, who slightly pulled up his shirt displaying a knife. The guy and girl left.

Carina moved up the aisle toward the front of the store away from Billy. She considered leaving. At the T-shirt rack, she observed Chang standing near the entrance, outside Spencers.

Billy brushed past her, then left the store. A buzzer sounded. She stopped. Billy handed something to Chang.

The manager ran out of Spencers. "Stop, what do you have?" He grabbed Billy.

"Search me." Billy extended his arms as Chang walked away.

The manager drew in a breath and let it out as he checked Billy's pockets, finding nothing. Billy stepped toward the manager. "Get out of my face."

The manager went back into the store. In the hallway, several people stared.

Carina buried her face in the T-shirt rack. The crowd's eyes followed Billy as he walked back into the store and stood next to her. Embarrassment crept into Carina. The manager glared at them. She wished for a superpower – invisibility. Hopes of having a boyfriend vanished.

Chapter 18

Early morning, after passing security, Mark stuck his non-stop ticket to San Diego in his pocket and went to the boarding area. Removing the file of Robert "Bobby" Kulp from his briefcase, Mark reviewed his findings. Kulp was a computer geek who probably had a home security system. The guy was a contractor who sold computers to the military. Eight to Five job. After reviewing the information, Mark spent the next half-hour going over his plan. The announcement to board came over the speakers.

After entering the aircraft, Mark found his seat in the first-class section. He placed his carry-on bag in the overhead compartment, sat, then took out the floor plan of Kulp's condo. After scanning it a few minutes, he put it away when the stewardess gave her safety lecture.

He buckled his seat belt. The winding of the jet engines fueled memories. Mark missed the military days, the camaraderie he had with his buddies, and the military community. The helicopter rides, the high-speed boat chases, and the times he traveled by ship played in his mind.

Once the plane reached a safe altitude, Mark reclined his seat, closed his eyes, and prayed a quick prayer. Soon, he drifted to sleep until the plane shook, waking him.

"We are experiencing a little turbulence, the captain has turned on the seat belts light. For your safety, please fasten your seat belts."

Mark looked at his watch. He had slept over an hour. For the rest of the flight, he watched the clouds and reviewed his mission. The plane began its descent, then landed.

He went to baggage claim to receive his luggage, then found a rent-a-car. While sitting in the car, he called Jackie and asked her for her flight information. He noted she would arrive late tomorrow afternoon. "If all goes as planned you'll have Bobby soon. Questions?" Mark explained again why they were traveling to the Phoenix Airport instead of San Diego. "In case the authorities look for you and your son. Too much downtime at the Lindbergh Field Airport. After we get your son, we'll be a family headed to Phoenix. It'll be less chance of getting caught."

After consideration, Mark concluded Kulp wouldn't alert the authorities. After all, he illegally took the boy. But to take no chances, Mark decided driving to Phoenix would be the best choice. He ended the call by saying, "Contact me when you land in San Diego." Mark tossed his phone on the passenger's seat and considered what could go wrong. A screaming kid and police patrolling the neighborhood, for example. Robert Kulp having a gun. But what made him also nervous was an irrational, emotionally unstable mother named Jackie.

***

"Carina, time to get up for school."

"Okay, Mom." Carina thought about the incident at the mall. *I should've told the manager that Billy passed something to Chang.* She dismissed the thought and readied herself for school.

Carina went to the kitchen and grabbed a banana.

"I could drop you off at school before I go to work."

"I'm good. I'll walk."

"Okay, have a good day."

Carina left. On her way, she considered avoiding Billy. He wasn't what she expected, but he was exciting and her life was boring, even though she felt danger. She didn't see him in the crowded hallways at school. But on her way home after school, Billy caught up with her. "Want to hang at my place?"

"I don't know."

"Come on." Billy took her hand.

Her emotions overtook her brain, and she nodded yes. Carina texted her mom telling her she'd be at a friend's house. Without waiting for a response, Carina walked with Billy. A voice inside her screamed no, but she silenced it.

After a half-hour, the neighborhood turned trashy as they turned on 9th street. They passed a car with two flat tires, then turned toward what she thought was Billy's house.

"Is that your dad's car?"

"No." Billy kicked a beer can off the sidewalk, then entered the house. Carina followed.

Billy looked around the room. "Want to go upstairs? My old man is at the bar and won't be back for hours."

Carina stepped over clothes and crinkled her nose at the locker room smell. She wanted to say no, but instead gave in, figuring she could handle Billy. "Hey, I could show you my karate moves."

He laughed, started up the steps and turned. "I'd love to see your moves."

His eyes scanned her. Carina lowered her head and reluctantly followed him upstairs. Her phone sounded. She stopped.

"Come on." He took a few more steps. "Up here."

She took another step and her phone sounded again. She looked at it: a text from her mom.

"I have to go. Mom wants me home."

"And do you always listen to your mom?"

"Uh, well no, not all the time."

"Stay, we'll have fun."

She looked at her phone and shook her head no.

"Go home to mommy, little girl. I wouldn't want you to get in trouble." He descended a few steps.

Go or stay? She looked at Billy. Excitement and fear battled within her. She hadn't felt a rush like this in a long time. Thoughts of her dad popped into her head. His words of warning, like flashing lights, echoed in her mind. Carina descended the stairs.

"Where are you going?" Billy unbuckled and removed his belt.

"What are you doing?"

He put the belt on her hands and pulled it.

"Stop." She pushed him, causing him to fall against the steps. She removed the belt, then ran out of the house.

Fear gave way to loneliness as she ran. She convinced herself that no one loved her. Billy wanted something she didn't want to give him. His yelling and name calling stuck in her thoughts as she headed out of the rough-looking neighborhood. "I'm not a slut," she screamed. Carina wondered what possessed her to go to Billy's house to begin with.

While walking home, Carina reminisced of a particular family vacation, one where she had caught a largemouth bass in Onion Creek. Her dad cooked the fish on an open fire as her mom prepared the rest of the meal. Then, the three of them hiked the nature trail and stopped at "Old Baldy," a tree estimated to be more than 500 years old. By the time she arrived at her home, a thought had developed in her mind.

She opened the door and yelled, "Mom, where's Dad?"

Kaitlyn came out of the kitchen. "He left early this morning to California. Supper in ten minutes. Wash up."

Carina's face dropped. "I'm not hungry." She ran upstairs and slammed her bedroom door. The question she wanted to ask her dad now tortured her. The memory of McKinney Falls State Park, a camping possibility now became a prison for an unasked question.

Chapter 19

J ackie arrived Wednesday, 8:15 p.m. at the San Diego airport. Mark met her at baggage claim, received her luggage, and went to the car. Her son was the main topic of conversation as they traveled to the motel. She mentioned Robert and the other woman, shifting the conversation poisonous. Interstate traffic came to a stand-still.

"You don't talk much, do you?" said Jackie.

"Sorry, I'm going over the plan in my mind."

I wonder if he's married? Jackie glanced at his hand and noticed his wedding ring. *Darn!*

They inched forward two miles until the traffic picked up again. "Was there an accident?"

"Probably."

Jackie was still talking when they drove into the parking lot.

After parking, Mark exited, opened the trunk, and took her luggage to the motel. Inside the room, she took her bag, tossed it on the bed, unzipped it and pulled out a negligee. Married or not she didn't care.

Mark opened his briefcase. "Please sit. We need to review a few things." He took out a picture and handed it to her. "Yesterday I posed as a cable repairman and told the woman answering the door I was looking for an address. A little boy was there. I snapped his picture. It's blurry, but is this Bobby?"

She began to cry "Oh, my precious..."

"I assume it's your son?"

She nodded. "How did you get a picture of Bobby without her seeing you?"

"I have a clipboard that has a camera embedded in it."

Jackie raised her eyebrows and lowered the photo. "Clever." Her eyes settled upon a half- eaten pizza.

"Go ahead."

"The plane food was blah." She took a few slices, put them in the microwave, waited and retrieved the hot pizza. Mark handed her a cola from the small fridge. Jackie ate as Mark talked, then looked at the bed.

"After we're finished, rest. I want to be at the condo at 2:00 a.m."

Her mind wandered. Jackie stopped Mark several times, asking him to repeat his instructions. *I'm frustrating him.* She had that effect on almost everyone in her life, even irritating her mom. The only person who didn't view her as an irritation was a little boy a few miles away. Her mind switched to Robert. *One day he'll grow tired of her and come back. I know he loves me.*

"Please pay attention," Mark said.

"Sorry." Her phone rang, and she answered it. "Hello?"

Mark continued to talk. "We're a married couple on our way to Phoenix."

Sounds fun. "Hello?" She looked at the number, the same area code as Austin Texas. Mark continued to talk.

After several seconds, she repeated it again. "Hello?"

Mark stopped. "Do you need to take this?"

"No, probably a wrong number." Click. "What if something goes wrong?"

"Nothing will go wrong if we stick to the plan." Mark walked to the door

"You're leaving?" *Please don't.*

"I need fresh air."

I don't want to be alone.

"I'll be back around 1:30 and we'll go over the plan one last time."

The door closed. Jackie went to the bathroom, showered, dressed, then went to the bed and fell asleep. In her dreams, Robert held her. The other woman entered the room. Jackie picked up a knife and went after her. The witch laughed when the knife missed her. Jackie swung again, missing her another time. More evil laughter.

***

Kaitlyn ended the call and tossed her phone on the table like it was on fire. She picked up Mark's handwritten note he had crumbled and left next to the trash can: *Call Jackie 512-388-4992.*

He's with another woman, pretending to be married. And why is he in Phoenix? He told me he'd be in San Diego. No — I have to trust him. There has to be a logical explanation. I'll call him.

She waited several minutes, then punched in his number. Her hand shook. "Mark?"

"Kate? Is something wrong?"

"No, nothing is wrong."

"You're usually asleep by now. Isn't it around midnight your time?"

Oh, it is late. She found the note earlier in the evening and put off calling. The irritation didn't go away. "Sorry, I couldn't sleep." Kaitlyn allowed silence to fill the airway, while pressing her ear on the phone, trying to hear any sounds. "Where are you?"

"I'm in my car. Are you sure everything is okay? Carina?"

"Yes, we're okay. How was your day?"

"It was good."

"Are you in California?"

"I told you that before I left."

"I'm trying to talk to you. Is that okay?"

"No, but you seem upset."

Kaitlyn paced. "When are you coming home?"

"I'll be home tomorrow." More silence.

Kaitlyn let out a sigh.

"Kate, are you still there?"

"I'm here." She wiped a tear from her eye and kept her voice from cracking. *If I stay on this phone...*

"Kate?"

"I can see you're busy. Bye."

"I'm not busy right now if you want to.." Click.

Why did I do that? She walked to the bathroom mirror, placed her phone near the sink and looked at herself. *I almost lost him once in death; now I'm losing him again.* Her phone rang — Mark. Kaitlyn took a deep breath and contemplated answering it. It rang three more times. "Hello?"

"I think my phone cut-out."

"Yes."

"How was Carina today?"

"Okay."

"Did she get into any trouble?"

"No."

There was silence.

Kaitlyn calmed herself. "Mark, I'm tired. I'll see you tomorrow."

"Well okay. Good night."

Click.

Oh Mark, what are you doing?

***

Strange call. Mark walked to the beach, parked and got out of his car. A cool breeze came off the water, and street poles lit up the beach. *Why is Kate upset?* The cadence of the tide didn't calm his nerves. He walked under the sign, "Imperial Beach." Off to his left was Mexico. *Steel, get your mind in the game.* He willed himself to concentrate on the present, but distractions were mounting. First, there was the unpredictability of Jackie. Now, there was Kaitlyn. *Maybe she had a difficult time with Carina. That's it. Carina irritated her.* Why didn't she say that? His thoughts switched to dangerous things he'd done in his life. How he'd put a choke hold on an escaping assailant. Once he knifed a kid who tried to kill him. Back then, he had an entire team of professionals. Now, with a mother robbed of her child, fears surfaced.

He strolled across the sand attempting to clear his mind. Close to 1:00 a.m. he returned to the Imperial Beach sign and stopped under a light. He tried to keep his mind focused, but as the time drew closer, it became exceedingly difficult. He pulled the list from his pocket. Rental filled with gas — *check.* Paid for the room — *check.* Equipment in the car — *check.* He checked everything off his list. He was physically ready, but mentally? Not so much.

After several minutes of watching the ocean, he went to his car and drove back to the motel.

Chapter 20

M ark knocked on the motel door several times. With eyes half-open, Jackie released the chain, then opened the door.

"Is your luggage ready?" Mark asked.

"Almost." Jackie left the door open, put her items in the bag and zipped it. "It's ready."

He placed a bag in the trunk and waited. A few minutes later Jackie exited the motel.

Mark went over the plan as they drove down Palm Avenue, concluding with, "And if we're confronted?"

"I'll let you handle it."

"And?"

Jackie rolled her eyes. "I'll stay in the car."

His smile didn't reach the top part of his face. *I'd rather be in the middle of a jungle.*

He found Robert's condo and parked half a block away. After exiting the car, Mark lowered his hat and headed down the street. His cell phone vibrated. He answered it—Jackie. "You forgot Bobby's stuffed animal."

"Sorry, I'll have to do without it," Mark said and proceeded. A few more steps and his phone vibrated again. "Yes?" He tried to hide his frustration.

"Bobby is being tested for seizures."

"Seizures?" It came out louder than he intended. Mark lowered his voice. "Could he have one if he's frightened?"

"I don't know."

"Describe an episode."

"He stares into space for several seconds." Mark paused. "So it may not be a seizure?"

"The doctor thought so, but ordered more tests."

Mark took a deep breath. "Let's keep with our plan." He looked at his watch. "Be ready." In Mark's pocket was a baggie with a chloroform soaked cloth, something he didn't want to do and reserved only as last resort. He'd heard a person having a seizure had the possibility of swallowing their tongue. Not knowing if this was true, Mark would use the sleeping chemical on Bobby. *If he's sleeping, he can't have a seizure, right?*

He approached the condo, found the utility room, picked the lock and entered. With a flashlight, he found the electrical box. He took his mini bolt cutter and cut the small lock on the box, then shut off the electricity. *Good – no backup for the security system.* Outside the utility room, he put his flashlight and bolt cutters into his pocket.

With a clear sky and a full moon, Mark could see the balcony. But that also meant someone could see him. He tossed a rope to the railing, hooked it, then climbed over the ledge. He crouched behind a two-foot potted green bush.

In the distance, a horn sounded, along with the faint sound of waves. Across the street, a light shown from a window. Being patient made the difference between success and failure. Three minutes later the light went off. A car drove by. Two more minutes passed, and Mark crept to the window.

He scanned the room through a small crack in the curtain and saw an empty bed. *Where was the kid?* Mark unhooked his rope, stepped outside the metal fence, and tossed the rope to the next balcony. It hit metal. Not good. He knelt down to take cover. No movement. No lights. The only sound – waves.

He tested the strength of the metal structure – secure. With the rope in hand, he climbed on the ledge, swung and bounced off the concrete siding. When he stopped swinging, he climbed up, then pulled himself over the railing. Mark hid behind another potted bush. He became still. No one suspects anything if it doesn't move. Two blocks away a car went through an intersection. A dog barked, Mark estimated at four blocks away from him.

Crawling to the glass door, Mark scanned the room through a two-inch opening in the curtain. A couple slept, Robert, on the left side and Cindy on the right. No Bobby. That could be good. For now, it only meant he wasn't in bed with them and was probably on the floor. Mark tried the door – locked. With his knife, he cut the screen. After opening the unlocked glass door, he slid into the bedroom. Someone stirred. Mark froze. A few seconds later, Cindy snored.

On his stomach, Mark inched his way to the end of the bed. The carpet smelled of body odor, urine and something else he couldn't identify. The bed moved slightly. He pushed under it and froze. A blanket and little boy laid on the floor, three feet from Mark. A foot, followed by another foot appeared. *If he tries turning on the light, he'll have two options. First, check the breaker. Or. Two, go back to sleep and check it tomorrow.* Not everyone turns on a light when using the bathroom at night. They leave the door open. Would the moonlight be enough? The guy left the room. Thirteen steps. No door sound. Mark laid still. No one can see you if you don't move.

One minute. Mark held his breath and listened. Two minutes, but no footsteps. The toilet flushed. The man returned and covered the boy. The bed pressed down on Mark. Two minutes later — snoring. This time the man.

Mark inched out from under the bed. No movement. One minute, two minutes, three. Patience brings success. Crawling on all four, Mark moved toward Bobby, removed the chloroform soaked rag from his pocket and palmed it. He laid down, then inched closer until he was parallel with the boy. Robert's arm fell over the side of the bed. One minute passed. Mark hated this part. With the rag, he placed it over the boy's mouth for several seconds. Knowing the chemical would knock Bobby out momentarily, Mark backward crawled to the door, dragging the boy.

He positioned him as close to the exit as possible, then moved onto the balcony. The guy rolled over. Mark stopped. He waited one minute, then heard snoring. This time a symphony. Mark scooped up Bobby and placed him on the balcony, then shut the sliding door, stopped and waited several seconds. No movement on the streets. No sounds except the distant waves.

With the rope still hooked on the ledge, he tossed the rope over the side and tested to make sure it was secure. Mark stopped and listened for sounds from the bedroom. The symphony of snoring continued.

Bobby moved, and his eyes widened. Mark again put the cloth over the boy's mouth. He held it there while counting to one hundred and twenty. Just the right time for a boy his age. It wouldn't hurt him. The boy appeared so peaceful. Unlike the stories, Jackie told him. With the harness straps, he tethered the boy to himself and climbed outside the railing. Movement in the room. Nothing on the streets.

Mark slid down the rope while holding onto the boy's motionless body. After retrieving his gear, he quickened his pace, moving away from the condo. Upon hearing footsteps, Mark sent up a prayer. He crossed the street, opened the back car door, placed the boy in Jackie's arms and shut it. After tossing his gear into the trunk, Mark turned. A shiny object flashed in the darkness.

***

Kaitlyn shifted in bed, trying to sleep, but couldn't. Mark's voice, "We're a married couple in Phoenix," looped. The other woman's seductive voice sounded in her thoughts.

Kaitlyn left the bed and searched to see if Mark left his wedding ring. She turned on the light, then opened each drawer. Tension built until she shut the drawers, not finding the ring.

After twenty minutes of searching the rest of the room, Kaitlyn decided to call someone. First thinking of her sister, but took her off the list. *She wouldn't understand.* Her friends wasn't a choice because each had husbands, who were friends with Mark and she couldn't think of anyone at work she could trust. It came down to her mom.

"Mom? I'm sorry to wake you, but I need to talk."

After a few seconds of hearing movement from her phone speaker, her mom spoke. "I'm going into the next room, so I don't wake your dad." A few seconds later: "Kaitlyn is everything okay?

"No, Mom."

"What's happening? Who's hurt?"

Kaitlyn propped herself up in bed and told her story. She started with finding Jackie's phone number. She talked for five minutes. "Mom, I don't know what to do."

"Oh my, that's horrible. It looks bad, and I can see you're very upset. Do you mind if I pray?"

"Sure."

Kaitlyn's mom prayed a simple thirty-second prayer. As usual, Kaitlyn felt better. "Honey, when I'm unsure of what to do, I become quiet before God and wait."

"But how can I do that?"

"Remember when you were little, and a girl at school was picking on you?"

"Yes—Tammy. "

"Do you remember what we did?" Kaitlyn paused. "We prayed?"

"What happened after that?"

"We sat there?"

"Exactly. We prayed and waited for God's whisper. " Elaine paused. "You remember what that was like?"

Kaitlyn tried to think. "Peaceful?"

"Yes."

"After that, when she picked on me, it didn't bother me. She eventually quit."

"I could have protected you, but instead, we listened to God," her mom said. "What I'm saying is first calm your heart." Silence filled the airway for a few seconds. "Then, you must talk to Mark."

Kaitlyn took a deep breath. "That's so hard for me."

"I know. You've always had a sensitive heart."

"Mom, you're right."

"God can drop a thought into your mind. When He does that, you'll know," her mom said. "Above all—in the right frame of mind—talk to Mark."

"Thanks, Mom, I feel better. I'll let you get back to sleep. Bye."

After shutting off the lights, Kaitlyn went under the covers and attempted to stop the thoughts. An hour later, she fell asleep.

***

Robert Kulp, out of breath, stepped in front of the car. Mark faced him.

"That's my boy you took out of my home. I'm calling the police." Robert lifted a gun. Jackie left the car and shut the door.

Robert's facial expression dropped. Mark looked at Jackie, then held his hand in the stop position.

Mark stepped closer to Robert "You'll be charged with kidnapping."

Robert stared at Jackie. "Is this your boyfriend?"

When Mark opened the back door, the interior lights came on. He pleaded with his eyes for her to enter. Jackie went toward the door, then spun around.

"What if he was?" She moved next to Mark.

"I don't care, I want my son back," Robert said as he walked to the car.

She placed her hand on Robert's chest. "You jealous?" Jackie's eyes softened. Over Robert's shoulder, she glared. "What's she doing here?"

Mark stepped between the vehicle and Robert. "Jackie, please get in the car." At Robert, Mark said, "You back off. Now!"

Jackie pushed past Robert and faced Cindy.

"We're all going to jail," Mark thought.

Robert turned. "Cindy, go back to the apartment." He put the gun in his pants.

Cindy stared at Jackie. "You don't deserve to have your son."

Jackie took Cindy's long blond hair and yanked her to the ground, then jumped on her and tried to slap her. Cindy put her hands on her face and took a fetal position.

Mark rushed to Jackie and pulled her off the woman. Robert gripped Jackie's arm and let go after Mark moved her back a few feet. Robert helped Cindy stand.

Jackie struggled to kick her. "You witch! You stole my husband!" Across the street, lights lit up windows. Jackie slipped away from Mark and slapped Cindy. As Robert tried to restrain Jackie's hands, the gun fell to the ground.

Mark kicked the gun under the vehicle. "We're leaving, Jackie please get in the car."

"I loved you, and you left me for this pile of crap." Jackie pulled at Robert's grip.

"Let me go."

Robert relaxed his hand. "You can't leave with my son."

"Your son? He's our son."

"Get it through your head, I'm not coming back. I'm never coming back. "

Jackie moved toward Cindy.

Robert shielded his wife then looked at Jackie.

"You need to be locked up, " Cindy said.

Mark watched Cindy, her phone now in her hand. "You'll be locked up if either of you calls 911."

Robert turned. "Cindy — don't."

"She assaulted me. I want her behind bars."

"Oh, yeah? You think that was an assault? How about this?" Jackie swung again and connected with the woman's jaw.

Cindy flew back into the street, like a rag doll. Her cell phone broke into pieces as it hit the cement. Another light came from a house near the scene.

Mark opened the car door before Robert could react, then stood between him and Jackie. "Get in — now."

"I'm not finished with her. She has to pay for what she stole from me."

Still facing Robert, Mark said, "We need to go, or we're all going to jail."

Jackie smoothed her hair.

"Mommy?" A little boy's voice sounded from the vehicle.

Jackie ran to the car and entered. Mark shut the door. Robert followed. Cindy stood.

Mark positioned himself between Robert and the car. "Don't be stupid. You'd be arrested for kidnapping," Mark said. "She hired me to get her son back."

Headlights appeared from down the street. Mark lowered his head as the car passed. Mark then made eye contact with Robert. "We're driving away. I suggest you leave Jackie and Bobby alone. The next time I see you, I won't charge her a cent. Am I clear?"

"You talk tough, but my lawyer will call you."

"Go ahead, We'll discuss your stupidity."

Robert moved toward the back window. Mark blocked his way. "I want to say goodbye to my son."

"No."

With blood dripping from her nose, clothes torn, hair in a mess, Cindy stood behind Robert. She wiped the blood from her face and brushed it onto her robe. "Put her in jail."

Robert lowered his head.

In the distance, sirens sounded. Mark jumped in the car and sped off, leaving Robert and Cindy.

Jackie took a deep breath. "Sorry, I hate that woman so much."

"I can tell."

A block over, a police car, lights blaring, sirens sounding, raced in the opposite direction.

"Do you have the court paper and his birth certificate, in case we get pulled over?"

"Yes."

"Keep watching." Mark thought about Jackie's out-of-controlled behavior. *I hope Bobby didn't see it.* Periodically looking in his rear-view mirror, Mark hoped he'd be able to drive out of Southern California. With each mile, he became less tense, then relaxed when the landscape along the interstate became the desert. With a full moon, they traveled throughout the night to Phoenix.

Chapter 21

The rays of a new day burst in front of Mark as he drove down the interstate. A few hours from Phoenix, he became drowsy. After stopping at Love's Travel Stop, he woke Jackie asking her if she wanted anything. She didn't, so after locking the doors, Mark pumped gas, then went inside to pay and get coffee, as the mother and son slept. Stretching his legs and splashing water on his face, Mark felt refreshed.

Back in the car, with his coffee in the cup holder, Mark finished the rest of the drive and pulled into Phoenix during the rush hour. They reached the airport several hours before their flight.

Mark found the designated spot for the Hertz rental car and woke Jackie. "We're here." She stretched then lifted Bobby, who opened his eyes.

Mark removed the luggage as a shuttle arrived. The driver loaded their luggage. They entered and sat behind the driver. After telling him their flight information, the shuttle pulled away from the curb.

"The flight leaves in three hours. We'll get checked in then have breakfast," Mark said.

An airport security officer passed them. Jackie turned to Mark. "Will the police find us?"

"I don't think they're looking for us." Mark hoped that was true.

"Maybe we should have involved them," Jackie said.

"You told me the police weren't helping you. And your ex-husband knew a few of the officers."

"Yea—that," Jackie said. "Could Robert get the police's help?"

"I doubt it. Typically, the police stay out of civil matters."

The shuttle stopped at the entrance. After checking in and going through security, they had breakfast at Chelsea's Kitchen.

Mark ordered the classic French omelet with smoked ham, Jackie a cheese omelet with bacon. She shared her meal with Bobby. A half-hour passed. Mark took a drink of his coffee then finished his meal. After the waitress had placed the bill on the table, Jackie put her credit card on it. Noticing a newsstand across the hallway, Mark excused himself and bought a newspaper.

Before opening the paper, Mark sent a text to Kaitlyn. "I'll be home mid-afternoon. Love you."

Kaitlyn replied, "okay."

A small boy, the front page of the newspaper, triggered a memory: Two boys, tied up, in fetal positions lying on the floor — dead. The image and terror on the missionary's faces haunted Mark. Screams of the mother and the helpless look of the father played in his mind. The rescue of Bobby lessened that heaviness, at least for now.

Jackie spoke, bringing him out of his thoughts. "How long before the flight?"

It took a few seconds to register her words. Mark looked at his watch. "Two more hours before we board." Bobby became restless. "Let's go to the terminal." Mark stood, folded the newspaper, and put it in his briefcase.

Jackie held Bobby's hand. "First time he's flown."

Mark lowered himself to Bobby's level. "You ready to get on the airplane?" The boy shook his head and hid behind Jackie.

They walked at the small boy's pace to the waiting area for the sky train. A few minutes later, it arrived, releasing a gush of air, when the door opened. They entered, gripped the metal pole and held on as the vessel quickly shot down the rail. The computer generated voice announced their gate. They exited and walked down a crowded passageway to the boarding area. After waiting an hour, they entered the plane.

Bobby sat next to the window which overlooked the jet's wing. Jackie buckled her son then took her seat in the middle. Mark put his briefcase in the overhead compartment and took the aisle seat. Fifteen minutes later, the plane taxied, then jetted down the runway, and lifted.

Once in the air, Jackie talked. Mark listened to stories of Bobby. *She seems like a good mother.* Mark raised his eyebrows as she told story after story of Bobby's childhood. Jackie stopped to receive soda from the stewardess for her and Bobby. After nearly a half-hour of non-stop talk on Jackie's part, Mark's eyes grew heavy. "I'm sorry, but after driving through the night, I'm tired. I can't stay awake. "

"That's okay. You sleep." Jackie turned to Bobby and talked to him.

Before falling asleep, Mark thought of Kaitlyn. Her phone call earlier puzzled him. He tried to convince himself it concerned Carina but couldn't quite believe it.

Mark awoke to the stewardess asking him to raise his seat. After landing, they exited and went to baggage claim.

After retrieving their luggage, they went to Jackie's car. "You be good for your mommy," Mark said to Bobby.

The boy buried his head into Jackie's shoulder.

"Thank you." Jackie gave Mark a hug with Bobby in the middle.

He said goodbye and went to his vehicle. On the way home, he stopped at a flower store and picked up a dozen roses.

***

After waking Carina for school, Kaitlyn went to the kitchen. The phone calls from the prior evening still weighed on her mind. The words of her mom seemed distant now.

Several minutes later, Carina entered the kitchen, books in hand. "Good morning Mom." Carina put her books on the counter, then bread in the toaster.

"Good morning. You're chipper today. "

Kaitlyn's phone sounded. She palmed it and read the text from Mark. "Your dad will be home this afternoon."

"That's nice." The toast popped up, and Carina retrieved it, buttered it and took a bite.

"It's been a while since you've had friends here."

"I know."

"Can I ask why?"

"Dad."

"He doesn't have a problem with your friends."

"I have to go... Bye." Carina shot out of the kitchen.

"You forgot your books."

Carina ran back, retrieved them and left the house.

Why did I have to bring that up? Kaitlyn missed the girl talks she had with Carina. They'd talk about make-up, clothes and sometimes boys, but not lately.

Since she didn't feel like eating breakfast, Kaitlyn put a lid on her coffee and left for work. She'd only have to work until noon and would be home by the time Mark arrived.

In the car, then behind her desk at work, Kaitlyn tried to stay positive. That proved to be difficult, especially since her boss displayed a foul mood. Most days Kaitlyn enjoyed her job, today she endured it.

Back home, Kaitlyn had gone to the door several times thinking Mark was there. She cleaned when she was nervous. Since returning home from work, she had vacuumed the floors, dusted the furniture, and Windexed many of the windows. When the door finally opened, Kaitlyn took a deep breath, determined to confront Mark.

"Kaitlyn, I'm home," Mark said.

At the kitchen sink, she splashed water on her face and hoped he wouldn't notice she had been crying. Kaitlyn pushed herself into the living room then stopped. The sight of the flowers melted her heart. She needed to talk to Mark but lost her willpower at the site of the roses. She hated confrontation. *Did the flowers prove he was guilty?* She told herself no. With a fake smile, Kaitlyn took the roses. "Thank you."

Mark embraced her as Kaitlyn tried to relax. She didn't know if he felt her coldness. He stepped back and kissed her. She again willed herself to accept it from him. Her lips didn't part in tenderness as they had on other occasions.

"Tonight—Japanese with the Hibachi grill?" Mark asked.

"Sounds good."

Mark turned toward upstairs. "I'm tired; I need a nap. It's nice being home."

I'm sure you're tired. "Mark?"

He stopped at the foot of the stairs. "Yes."

Kaitlyn paused, struggling for the courage to confront. His wedding ring was on his finger. "Have a nice sleep."

"Thanks."

Kaitlyn watched him ascend the stairs, heard the door close and stared at an empty stairwell. She could lay in bed with him, but dismissed the thought. Disappointed with herself for not confronting Mark, Kaitlyn turned on the television, a rare occurrence during the day. She flipped through the channels, past the news, past the talk shows, stopping at Lifetime. She watched several minutes of a love story, then let her mind wander.

Two years before meeting Mark, Kaitlyn's fiancée, Joe, died in a tugboat accident. So instead of planning a wedding, Kaitlyn planned a funeral.

When she first met Mark, she avoided him. She was afraid of being hurt again, even though it was two years after the tugboat accident. Mark, an ensign in the Navy, pursued Kaitlyn. Dreams of Gondola boat rides, romantic sunsets, and walks on the sand danced in her mind and collided with thoughts of today. She fell asleep, thinking her marriage was over.

Yet, when she dreamed, Mark held Kaitlyn. The two walked on the beach, he in a white uniform, her in a sun dress. The setting sun, the rhythm of the waves, made for a perfect evening. They sat and talked. Then another woman approached and took Mark's hand away from her.

Mark stood and left with her.

She felt a touch on her shoulder. A voice called her name. Kaitlyn opened her eyes and saw Mark standing over her. The image of Mark walking away with another woman seemed so real.

"Are you okay?"

Kaitlyn stood, picked up the remote and shut off the TV. "I'm fine."

"Would you join me for lemonade on the patio?"

"Sure."

***

Mark glanced at Kaitlyn as she sipped her drink. He almost didn't disturb her, but wanted her company, and wanted to know if everything was okay with them. He was about to ask when Carina yelled.

"Mom, Dad? Where are you?"

110

"We're on the patio," Mark said.

Carina opened the screen door. "Dad, can we go camping this weekend?"

"Camping? Oh, Carina, I don't think so. I've had enough traveling."

"How about bowling?"

"Not tonight, we're…"

Carina slammed the screen door and left before he could finish. Kaitlyn stood before Mark could react. "I'll check on her."

"Please let her know we're dining out tonight."

Kaitlyn nodded.

***

About to go upstairs, Carina's phone beeped. "sup," Billy texted.

"nothing."

"park come over,"

"brt" Carina put her phone in her pocket. Helping Billy made her feel important. Right now she needed that feeling.

"Headed to the park." Carina opened the door and ran. She donned her earplugs and thought she heard her mom. She turned the music louder.

At the park, she scrunched her nose as she approached Billy and a few boys. A strong sweet smell filled the air. Billy, hazed over eyes, put his arm around Carina. She pushed it off her shoulder.

"You want in?" Billy lifted the marijuana to her lips. She shook her head. "What daddy might get mad?"

She looked at the boys. Her phone chimed. A text from her dad: "Where are you?" She could almost hear the old lectures screaming in her mind.

A boy bounced the basketball at Billy. "Let's shoot hoops." He dribbled, shot and missed by several feet. The boys laughed, each one shooting, also missing the hoop. After several minutes, they stopped to smoke.

"You sure?" Billy lifted the smoke toward her. Again, Carina shook her head no.

A police car drove by, and several boys moved from the area. Billy lowered his joint and stood there.

Carina text'd her dad, "at the park"

The boys came back a few minutes later and continued shooting hoops. She watched them for several minutes until she heard her dad's voice.

"Carina, come here," Mark yelled.

She ran to the car, on her mom's side.

"We're going to the Japanese Restaurant." When she didn't respond, Mark politely asked her to get in the car.

She waved at Billy, jumped in the back seat, and put her earplugs in. Before she could play her music, Mom tapped her leg. She took out an earplug. "What?"

Mark turned toward the back seat. "Why did you leave the house without asking?"

"I told you where I was going."

"That isn't what I asked."

Earplugs back in, she turned her music on high.

"You will…"

Chapter 22

B renda Houston clicked on Skype. Chris, "Show Biz" Cahill, filled the screen.

Her bedroom had everything in place, and not a speck of dirt on the floor, just the way Brenda liked it. Pink pillows laid perfectly on the flowered bedspread. Strawberry scent filled the air since Brenda had sprayed the air freshener upon entering her room.

"I love your long brown hair and your brown eyes," Chris said.

"Thank you."

"Are you blushing?"

Brenda, hands covering her face, giggled in her 17-year-old way. Chris, 26, told Brenda his age was 18. He had started the Internet connection with the high-school senior beginning with Facebook, Instagram, and now Skype.

"You have a pretty smile and a beautiful voice. Sing again, please," he said.

Brenda sang. Her skin tingled as she hit every note like her choir director taught her.

Chris ran his hands through his unruly hair. "That was great." He backed away from the screen, stood and clapped.

Her heart beat fast, a smile radiated her face. "Really?"

"I know so." Chris sat. "My agent will sign you up if you want to be a star."

"Oh, yes. I'm sure my dad will be excited."

"Hold it. No telling anyone. Girls, like you, have lost contracts because of over-cautious parents."

"Okay. What do you want me to do?"

"Send a video of yourself to the email I gave you and I'll show it to my agent."

Before Brenda could say a word, Chris's image disappeared. She took her phone and propped it against her computer. In video mode, she sang, watched it, erased it, sang again and repeated the process until she had the perfect recording. Brenda sent it to Chris, who responded an hour later.

Chris reappeared on her screen. "Hi, beautiful."

"Did you listen to it? Do you like it?"

"I loved it, and my producer loved it."

"He did?"

"Yes. I sent it to him right away," Chris said. "You're not afraid to sing in front of the camera. That impressed him."

Brenda daydreamed of stardom ever since she met Chris online. He talked to her twice a week, sometimes three, over the last two months. That changed last week to everyday. Chris removed her loneliness, and Brenda felt loved.

"Listen, I have something else to tell you." Chris's picture froze on the screen then returned to real time a few seconds later. "I want to offer you an opportunity."

Brenda, her hands holding her face, with dreamy eyes stared at the boy in front of her.

"Don't cut that beautiful hair of yours."

"Okay, I won't."

"I like the way your smile lights up your face."

Brenda's face reddened.

"Your dimples accent your face."

Her pulse raced. She lowered her eyes and waited for Chris to speak, waited for him to tell her what the opportunity was.

"I'll come to get you."

"Get me? What?"

"Yes, silly. You must meet my producer, in person."

"I haven't been away from home...by myself."

"You wouldn't be by yourself. You'd be with me. Wouldn't you like that?"

"Yes."

"It's settled. It's our secret, okay?"

"Okay. My dad is home. I gotta go."

Brenda shut off the screen and opened a school book. A few minutes later, her dad, Tony Houston, knocked on her bedroom door. "Come in."

He opened the door, loosened his tie and walked behind her. "How was your day?"

"It was okay."

"I see you're doing your homework," Tony said. "Do you have a lot to do?"

"Not much."

"It's pizza night. I came home early to pick you up."

"Dad, I'll find something here, you go."

"Are you sure? Your Uncle will be there."

"I have a report due tomorrow."

"Can you do it when we return?"

Brenda intensified her gaze upon her book. *Please Dad, just leave.*

"Okay. But, I wish you'd go."

She listened for the front door to close, ran to her window and watched the car leave. Back at her computer, she steadied her hand and emailed Chris.

***

Billy felt his pocket, in it was the reason he wanted to find Carina. He sent her a text asking her location and received an answer. He was failing history, and the teacher told him if he didn't hand this worksheet in, he'd have to call his dad.

Billy called for a taxi. While waiting, he googled the restaurant's address. The taxi pulled up to the curb. Billy entered and gave the location to the driver. He shot Carina another text, asking her to help him with his worksheet. After several minutes, the taxi pulled in front of Fujiyama Japanese Steak House.

He entered the restaurant, waved off a short Japanese lady, and looked for Carina. He spotted her, made eye contact and motioned her toward the back. Carina met Billy outside the bathrooms.

"Please do this for me." He handed her his homework. "or my old man will kill me." Her eyes widened as she looked at the paper. "Put it away before someone sees you." She put the sheet in her pocket and before she could say a word, Billy left.

He slipped out of the place and found his taxi. After directing the driver to go through McDonald's Drive Thru, he ordered a quarter pounder, fries, and drink. The taxi drove forward; Billy paid and received his food.

"Don't spill."

"Shut up and drive."

"Listen kid. I don't get paid enough for your smart mouth."

Billy put his earplugs in then tore into his sandwich. With money left over from selling drugs, he thought he'd appease his dad and give him thirty dollars.

At his house Billy paid the driver and hid the extra cash under a rock by the garage, then walked into his home, causing his dad to stir. Billy held out three tens. "Here."

James opened his eyes and took the cash. "Kid, that's all you have? It doesn't look like much. Are you holding out on me?" He stood and checked Billy's pockets, finding nothing; James backhanded him. "Come here."

Billy wiped the blood from the corner of his mouth and moved closer to his dad, not wanting the consequence if he didn't.

"Clean up and take the trash out."

Billy gathered the trash, bagged it and took it to the curb. He tried to sneak past his dad upon reentering the house.

"I don't care where you got it, but you better get more. Understand?"

"Yes." Billy continued to walk.

"Get over here."

Billy inched his way to his dad, stopped and directed his attention to the picture on the wall, one of an outlaw wearing a black derby hat. The young man in the photo had a cloth tied around his neck, a dirty handkerchief. He wore a leather vest over top a torn long sleeve shirt. One eye was bigger than the other and had crooked teeth.

"You're living up to your name boy — Billy-the-Kid." James pointed at the picture and laughed. "You get more money."

"Yes, Dad." Billy shot up the stairs.

Chapter 23

K aitlyn opened the kitchen curtains. The sun had gone down. The moon and stars were shining, casting a peaceful ambiance. Yet, Kaitlyn felt no peace.

Mark sat on the patio while pain rose in her heart. She wanted to scream at the man outside the window. At the restaurant and during the drive home, Kaitlyn almost vomited out her troubled thoughts. With a deep breath, she went to Mark and sat beside him.

Before Kaitlyn could speak, Mark put his hand over hers. "Remember the day we brought Carina home from the hospital."

"What made you think of that?"

"I spent a lot of time looking into the nighttime sky during that time, wondering what our daughter would become." Mark paused and made eye contact with Kaitlyn. "I didn't envision it to be like this."

"Like what?"

"We're not close."

Kaitlyn raised her eyebrows, sadness etched across her face. "Really?" *Is he going to tell me our marriage is over?*

"Oh, not us." He squeezed her hand. "I'm talking about Carina. She's become distant, like a stranger." Mark paused. "I miss my little girl."

Kaitlyn let out a breath that she'd been holding. "If you weren't so strict." *Just tell him.*

"I grew up disciplined, and I turned out okay."

"Mark, you're a guy, she's a teenage girl. Who are her friends? What are her dreams? How is she doing in school?" Kaitlyn's eyes widened. "Well?"

"Why are you getting upset?"

"Because you're gone all the time." *Tell him the real reason.*

"We talked about this when I accepted this position. When a car is repoed, I go."

"To California?"

He shrugged his shoulders.

After several seconds, she turned her gaze away from him. "Mark, would I be able to go with you?"

He lowered his eyes. "That's not a good idea."

"Why?"

"Sometimes it's dangerous."

"You promised me it would be safe."

"Let me think about it. Okay?" He stood, encouraged her to stand then hugged her. "I don't want to fight."

A breeze moved the branches. Kaitlyn wanted to confront him but found herself confused.

What if I'm wrong, what if it was a misunderstanding?

Mark stepped back and looked at her, breaking the silence. "I'm sorry, I know Carina is being difficult. But we'll get through it."

That's not it. Kaitlyn glanced at the kitchen window and felt herself getting angry. *He doesn't want me to go with him.* "I should do the dishes."

Mark looked at his watch. "I'll talk to Carina."

She watched him enter the house. *Carina isn't the only one.* After wiping her tears, she headed to a sink of dirty dishes. After glancing around the room, she whispered, "Will Mark will leave me?" More tears flowed. *In his heart, has he already left me?*

***

Carina tossed her history book on the bed and stretched across the mattress. She opened the book and pulled out Billy's worksheet, his name on top. Carina didn't like the idea of doing someone else's homework but wanted to help him. He had a way of making her feel guilty if she said no.

She heard a noise and turned. Her dad stood alongside her bed. "Dad, you scared me." *Did he see Billy's name on the paper?*

"Sorry, I should have knocked."

"Yea!" She drew out the word. *Why is he looking at my bed?* She closed the book, tossed a pillow on it and stood.

"Can we talk?"

"I have a report to finish."

"Can I read it?"

"No." She said it too quickly, then glanced at the pillow. Billy's name was still visible.

"I could help you."

"I just need to get it done."

"Why are you getting mad?"

"I'm not, Dad, It's just this report. Thanks for wanting to help but it would take too long to explain it to you." Her eyes went back to the pillow.

"You always shut me out Carina, and I don't like it. I came in here to talk, and you're doing it again." His face reddened.

"Well, I'm sorry that I can't live up to your expectations."

"Don't raise your voice at me."

"Can I just do my homework?" She whispered.

Mark forced a smile, nodded and left the room.

Carina moved the paper inside her pillow and fell on her bed. She wanted to talk, just not now.

Her phone rang — Billy, "sup"

"going to sleep"

She read the next text: "homework done?"

She considered crumbling the paper, but instead, agreed to complete it and give it to him at school. Carina tossed her phone on her nightstand and closed her eyes. She tried to sleep, but thoughts of her dad kept her awake.

Chapter 24

B renda Houston opened a suitcase and set it on her bed. She removed pants and blouses from hangers and tossed them into the case. The 17-year-old glanced at the clock on the wall—8:30 p.m. Brenda had thirty minutes before her dad came home. Her heart raced. After a quick inventory, she zipped the bag.

With luggage in hand, she stopped at the mirror and giggled. Brenda ran her hands through her long brown hair. The blouse that Chris loved sparkled and accentuated her curves. *I love it.*

8:45 p.m.

With the lights off, she shot out of the house. On the corner, she saw Chris's car and ran to it. He gave her attention, unlike her dad who had to work late almost every night, except on pizza night. Chris promised her a future in modeling, an opportunity she couldn't resist.

Chris bolted out of the car and ran to the passenger's side. "Glad to see you can make it. Let me get your luggage." He opened her door, then put her bags in the trunk.

Brenda giggled, entered the vehicle and rolled down the window. Outside her door, Chris removed several bills from his pocket and handed it through the window to her.

Brenda looked at the money. "That's a lot."

"It's only the start. You'll be making bundles more."

"Then my dad will be proud of me."

"You can call this on-the-job training."

Brenda smiled, bursting with excitement.

"That's that cute face I like."

Brenda blushed. She liked the compliments he continually gave her. "Where are we going? How long to get there? When will I see your producer?"

"Slow down. Nashville. About twelve hours. And Tomorrow."

With excitement, her eyes followed him as he rounded the car to the driver's side. He sported a wild look, hair below his ears, uncombed, with slight dark shadows under his eyes. Brenda imagined him without a shirt, his muscles flexing. *He came for me — me, I can't believe it.*

Chris entered the car, reached over and kissed her cheek causing sparks to travel through her. One other guy had kissed her, an awkward gesture at the end of a movie. That boy was shy, much like herself. But Chris wasn't shy and his kiss wasn't awkward. Brenda looked forward to more of the electricity.

A car's headlights, in the driveway, told her that her dad was home.

Brenda opened the door. "I should talk to my dad."

They had this conversation yesterday via Skype. Chris convinced Brenda to keep this a secret.

"I should, at least, tell him where I'm going."

"That's a good idea. He'll insist you go to college, and you should. Many girls want an opportunity like this. If you're not ready, go back to your daddy. I turned down another girl, she'll be excited when I call her." Chris opened a notebook.

"You won't wait for me while I can talk to my dad?"

Chris held his phone in front of him, ignoring her question. "Jill will be excited when I contact her. I need to go, please get your suitcase. I'll need the money back." He held out his hand.

Brenda bit her lower lip and shut the door. "I changed my mind, I'm going. Let's go before he sees me."

Chapter 25

Mark left his house a half-hour after sunrise. Dogs barked as he ran down the alley, toward the park. After reaching the path, he increased his speed, moving past two people out for an early morning walk. The thick trees briefly blocked the sun as he jogged underneath. The light reappeared when he reached the other side of the canopy.

Mark stopped, caught his breath and sat on a park bench. Austin skyscrapers in the distance and flowers made this his favorite spot.

The valley of death.

Where did that come from? Mark tried to recall the next sentence, something about not fearing evil. He had his share of fear, especially from what just transpired with the rescue of Bobby. As he sat, he couldn't shake the feeling that something was wrong. His family?

An unsettling feeling wormed its way into his thoughts. Kaitlyn became upset at him last night. Carina! That must be the reason. If he could get her on the right path, everything would be okay, and Kaitlyn wouldn't be stressed. "I'll plan a family outing, that'll fix it." A squirrel scurried away at Mark's voice.

***

Carina, on her way to Billy's after supper, thought about the incident earlier in the day at the miniature golf course. She had told her dad she didn't want to go, but he insisted. Because Billy hadn't gone to school, she needed that time to get his homework to him.

"Dad, do you see any other teens here?" She remembered refusing to acknowledge the two people he pointed out. "That doesn't count. They're on the chess team."

Forced to listen to her dad's lecture instead of her music, she became irritated. On purpose, she missed every shot, sometimes sending the ball beyond the greens. They left before finishing the game.

As she walked, her music drowned out the irritation. She quickened her pace and marched up to Billy's house. Something told her not to go, but she decided it was fear, and she had to conqueror it, right? Besides, she had to give him his homework.

She knocked on the door's window. Billy opened it and stepped outside the house. "Sorry, I couldn't come…"

Billy put his finger to his mouth and partially shut the door. "I don't want my dad to find you here."

Carina drew her eyebrows together. "I couldn't come right after school because my dad made me go to miniature golf."

"You have my paper?"

Carina extended the paper towards Billy. "Why weren't you in…"

"Kid, you out there?" A voice came from within the house.

Billy opened the door. "Yes."

"Who's at the door?"

"Carina."

"Get me a beer and tell her to come here," James said. "Hey, that rhythms. What do you think about that, boy?"

Carina stayed outside as Billy went to the kitchen.

"Come in." James West stood. "So you're Billy's friend?" She nodded and entered.

"Shut it."

Carina closed the door.

Billy handed the beer to James West. "This one doesn't talk?"

"We're going to the mall to hang out."

"No, I'll order a pizza, and we'll have family time." He laughed. "Carina, you like family time?"

She squirmed.

"I'm not hungry." Carina looked at the door.

"You too good for us, girl? Come closer."

Carina took one step. Smelling alcohol, she paused, looked at Billy and with her eyes said: "Help." Billy didn't move.

"I'll go with you. Where are my car keys?" James West fell forward. Billy grabbed him and helped him sit.

Carina, eyes wide open, took another step toward the door.

James backhanded Billy, causing him to fall. "Get your hands off me boy."

Carina bolted for the door, Billy behind her.

"Get back in here now. You're dead if you..."

Once outside, Billy slammed the door, somewhat drowning out the drunk's voice. "Tell no one about this. You hear me?"

She nodded her head and followed Billy. He walked faster.

Carina caught up to Billy. "Where are we going?"

"Arcade."

Under a bright sun, they walked down the street. A half-hour later, they entered a dim lit game room. Carina squinted.

"Get off punk—now." Billy pushed a boy aside and took over his game. The young boy lowered his head and left the arcade. Billy tore into the game and for the next thirty minutes fed the machine his money.

Carina watched him take out another dollar bill. "I'm bored."

"Let's get out of here, I'm not winning." He shoved the dollar back into his pocket.

They left the arcade and entered the mall hallway.

"Billy, is your dad like that always?"

"He's great when he's sleeping." Billy half-smiled and lowered his head. "Your parents good to you?"

"My dad doesn't know I'm alive unless I do something wrong."

"I wish my dad ignored me."

"When we talk, he's always lecturing me and doesn't let me live my life the way I want."

Billy slowed. "Does he hit you?"

"No." They walked past a movie theater and a long line of people.

"Are you scared of him?"

"No, I'm not scared of him."

"Then why do you let him push you around if he doesn't hit you?" Billy stopped at the water fountain.

Carina looked in the water and shrugged her shoulders. "Why do you stay with him?"

"My old man's not so bad when he's sober." Billy touched the water. "Maybe I will—move out that is." A group of goth kids walked past them.

"You'd look good in black clothes."

"You think so? My dad wouldn't let me wear all black. He barely lets me put on make-up."

"How would you know if you didn't try it?"

"I don't have any money."

Billy pulled out a hundred-dollar bill. "Take this."

"I can't repay you."

"Oh, I think you can." He rubbed her back, but she moved away. "Okay then, take it as a down payment for helping me with my homework."

"Billy, I shouldn't be doing your homework."

"You want me to flunk out of school?"

She reluctantly took the money. A voice screamed inside her not to do it, but it was too tempting.

Chapter 26

Seventy-two miles to Nashville.

"Can I change the radio station?" Brenda asked.

Serious-faced, eyes on the road, Chris said no. His first word in two hours.

Brenda had become suspicious last night when they stayed at Super-8. Chris paid for one room.

"I can't stay in a motel room with you," Brenda said.

"I won't spend the extra money so you can have a room to yourself."

"Can I sleep in the car?"

"No."

In bed, with her clothes and shoes on, she spent a sleepless night watching the door and Chris, afraid he would come to her bed. But he didn't.

Today, they had been on the road for several hours and Chris, unlike yesterday, was silent. In the seat between them, an uneaten cinnamon roll and her cell phone. Chris insisted her phone stay there — shut off, refusing to give her an explanation. Brenda's impulse to check her iPhone grew stronger.

The quarrels with her dad didn't seem so important now. When he was home, they fought over the clothes she wore and the makeup she put on. Brenda looked at the phone, wanting to text him, to tell him she was okay. Out of fear, she decided to leave it there.

Instead, she thought of her mom. When Brenda had turned thirteen, her mom left. She didn't even say goodbye. One day Brenda overheard her dad talking to the neighbor, "She ran off with a guy."

Then it hit her; I'm doing exactly what she did. More than ever, she wanted to reach her father.

***

Tony entered Brenda's bedroom after calling the police department for the second time. The first time was last night. Each call—the same answer: "Mr. Houston, we consider your daughter a runaway."

Which meant: "We're not doing anything about it."

He went through her closet and found empty hangers. Tony refused to accept that his daughter would leave home on her own.

With Brenda's computer on, Tony clicked on Facebook—no new entries. After explaining to the officer that Brenda's phone had an app that allowed him to track her location, he added, "She shut off her phone. Brenda never does that." He checked his iPhone to see if Brenda's location appeared—nothing.

Tony considered the question posed by the police officer, "Does your daughter want to be found?" then dismissed it because Brenda, in his mind, couldn't have run away. She was too innocent and shy to leave home. She hadn't stayed away from home without family—ever.

Perched on her bed, Tony lowered his head and put his hands to his face. No matter how many times he told himself he would find Brenda, he struggled to believe it. His wife, Sharon had left over a year ago and, for several months, he didn't know where she went. Tony lost the two women most important to him. For what? A job he wouldn't have in ten years? Working long hours was his idea. It helped him get through the day so he wouldn't miss Sharon as much. Look what it cost him. He stood up, determined to fight until he found his daughter.

***

Yesterday, before stopping for the night, Chris told Brenda she'd have voice lessons in Nashville and live in an apartment. "It'll be two bedrooms, a large patio, and a huge dining area. You can have many friends over."

"Will you be close by?"

"I'll be down the street."

Brenda dreamed of singing in front of large audiences. Her teachers at school told her she had a beautiful voice. When her mom was still home, they'd sing together while doing dishes.

When I hit it big I can find mom, and we'll sing together again, she thought.

But unlike yesterday, she now sat completely still, afraid to speak, lest Chris would tell her to shut up again. She was afraid of what she'd done, afraid of the person who was driving, and afraid she may never see her dad again. The Nashville skyline loomed ahead. Brenda missed her daddy.

She looked at Chris, then to her phone. Brenda inched her fingers toward it, then moved it to her side. Glancing at Chris, seeing him focused on the road, she palmed the phone and moved it to her view. After turning it on she pressed her dad's name and typed: "hi dad i love you" She hit send. After a few seconds, her phone sounded.

Chris's face turned red. "What are you doing?"

"Nothing."

Chris held out his hand. "What?"

"Give me your phone."

"I won't use it again."

"You used it?"

Brenda reluctantly looked at it. "I checked my texts." He grabbed the phone, shut it off, lowered his window, pulled into the far left lane, and threw it out the window.

Brenda's face dropped. "I want out."

Chapter 27

Mark entered the kitchen, sat and unfolded his newspaper.

Kaitlyn yawned and walked to the counter. "Would you like coffee?" Mark lowered his paper and lifted his cup. "Thank you."

"Mark, would you consider church?"

"How long has it been?"

"A long time — before Carina was born."

"I suppose it wouldn't hurt. Any place in mind?"

"I've been looking at a few."

Mark's phone rang. He held up his hand and mouthed, "Sorry." He listened, took a pad of paper and pen from the drawer and wrote notes. Kaitlyn looked over his shoulder.

Mark heard feet pounding down the stairs, followed by the opening and closing of the front door. Mark ended the call and placed his phone on the counter. "I assume Carina's going to school?"

"She's probably fuming from last night." Kaitlyn handed Mark a cup of coffee.

"I tried talking to her, but she shut me out." Mark took a sip. "Do you work today?"

"No, why?"

"Would you like to go with me?"

"Where?"

"There's an abandoned car on the west side of Austin. I need to deliver it to the dealership."

"Can I make it another time, I promised a few friends I'd have lunch with them."

"No problem."

"Tell me again, how does that work?" Kaitlyn poured coffee into her cup.

"When I get to the location, I call the dealership, and they throw a special switch that allows the vehicle to be started. I drive the car on the trailer and return it." Kaitlyn's sudden interest in what he did puzzled Mark. He'd tried to talk about it in the past, but she wasn't interested.

"That's amazing how the dealership can remote-shutoff a car then turn it back on."

"A couple months ago I went to pick up a Ford Mustang. The owner told me she drove to work, but after getting off, it wouldn't start. She had it towed to a mechanic, but he couldn't figure it out. She insisted I wouldn't be able to start the car. You should have seen her face when I put the key in the ignition, and the car fired up. I thought she..."

Kaitlyn interrupted Mark. "Tell me about the car in California."

***

Billy felt the bottom part of Carina's black leather vest. "Someone has good taste in clothes."

"Thanks" She blushed then handed him his math worksheet. Billy walked.

"That's not the way to school."

"I know a shortcut."

Billy walked several blocks, turned into a wooded area, slowed, then jumped over fallen branches. Carina followed. In the open again, she heard a train whistle in the distance. They moved across a railroad track and went deeper into the woods. After several minutes, Billy stopped. "How do you like it?"

They were standing in an open area surrounded by trees. The empty, crushed beer cans and burnt tree logs made it an obvious teen partying place. Billy kicked the cans into the trees and picked up a blanket, shook it, and sent dust into the air. He sat and signaled Carina to sit.

"We need to get to school."

"Relax, we have a lot of time." Carina turned.

"What, are you afraid you'll get in trouble?"

"Maybe."

"You'll never grow up if you play it safe." Billy stood and glanced at the blanket. "Okay, have it your way, but you don't know what you're missing."

Carina walked toward the school, Billy followed.

***

Mark entered the Ford Dealership. "Bob, what's the scoop on the car I'm picking up?"

"A lady purchased it several months ago and only made a couple payments. We shut it down last week. Here's the address." Bob handed him the paper. "Thanks for taking this one."

"No problem."

"Mark, something else. You still doing the PI thing?"

"If you mean locating abducted children—yes. Why, did you get something?"

"Yes, sir. After all, you asked me to keep my ears open." Bob handed Mark a name and telephone number.

"Tell me about it."

"A seventeen-year-old girl disappeared."

Mark looked at the paper. "Why aren't the police involved?"

"They're calling it a runaway."

Mark had asked Bob to keep his ears open because people talked about all sorts of things at the dealership. "Go on."

"A few days ago this guy talked about how his neighbor's wife ran off, then his daughter disappeared. I asked for details and the same afternoon I got the guy's number."

"I'll get the car." Mark looked at the paper. "Then check into this. Thanks."

"If I keep giving you tips, I'll need to charge a finder's fee." Bob smiled.

Mark laughed. "Hey, the wife wants to go along sometimes. Any problem with that?"

"No problem."

"I didn't think so. Bob, another thing…" Mark asked Bob to confirm his story in California, should Kaitlyn ask. Bob slapped him on the shoulder and said he'd do it. The man didn't ask for details, only winked at Mark.

Chapter 28

Mark phoned Tony Houston after returning the repossessed car to the dealership. "How did you get my number?" Tony asked.

Mark explained how Bob Hanson overheard Tony's story.

"If Bob vouches for you, I'll hire you," Tony said. "Your number is on my caller ID, I'll call you right back after I call Bob."

A few minutes later Mark's phone rang. "Can you find my daughter?"

"I'll do my best."

"Find her, no matter how much it costs," Tony said. "Can we meet now?"

Mark agreed and programmed Tony's address into his GPS and went there.

After pulling into Tony's driveway, Mark called Kaitlyn. "Something came up, I won't be home for supper." He asked about her lunch with her friends and about her day. They talked for a few minutes, then Mark ended the call.

With a pad and pen in his pocket, Mark walked to the front door. He noted the size of the house—huge, the well-manicured lawn and a Porsche in the driveway. After going inside and shaking hands he asked, "Have you had any contact with your daughter?"

"One text, the day after Brenda left."

"Any clue where she's at?"

"No, I sent her several texts—no response. There's an app on my phone that gives me her location."

"Did it work?"

"No, and that's the strange part."

"Could she have disabled the program?"

"It ran in the background of her phone. Brenda didn't know that."

Mark took out his pad. "Let's check her room. There may be something there to help find her."

In Brenda's bedroom, Mark glanced around and observed pink curtains, white dressers, and flowery bed covers. "Brenda always keep her room this neat?"

"Yes, she's like her mother—organized."

Mark removed the pen from his pocket. "When your wife left, did your daughter take it hard?"

"Yes. Brenda stayed close to home. That's why..."

"I'm sorry, but I have to dig."

"That's okay."

Mark wrote notes. "Okay, let's start with her computer."

Tony sat at her desk and hit keys, unlocking the computer.

Mark raised his eyebrows. "Any more passwords?"

"It was all under her keyboard." Tony stood, picked up the paper and handed it to Mark.

After sitting, Mark explored the computer.

Tony placed a stack of papers next to Mark. "These school papers may help."

Mark thumbed through the papers then returned to the computer, maneuvering through the programs. "Where are you, Brenda?"

After several minutes, Mark motioned for Tony to sit. "Tell me more about your daughter."

"Brenda's always been a good girl, one I trusted. She didn't give me much trouble. I couldn't even raise my voice without her getting her feelings hurt. Brenda and her mother were close. They did a lot together. After Sharon left Brenda became withdrawn, stayed in her room most of the time, except for school activities. I knew that because of the tracking app on my iPhone." Tony paused for several seconds, his eyebrows drew together. "You know, she changed about a month ago. I received notices from the school that her grades were dropping. I also found out she wasn't eating. The bill for her school meals was less than ten dollars for the month. I questioned it and the school told me she wasn't eating lunch there."

"Did Brenda go somewhere else to eat?"

"No. I checked my iPhone. Brenda remained at school." Tony lowered his eyes. "And began wearing more revealing clothes." He took a deep breath. "That led to more arguments."

After writing more notes, Mark made eye contact with Tony, waiting to hear more.

"I tried talking to her." Tony paced. "Then backed off thinking she needed a little space. In hindsight, I was wrong." Tony stopped in front of Mark. "Brenda's grades improved a little, and she promised to eat at school so I figured everything was okay."

Mark waited a few minutes to see if Tony would speak again then turned toward the computer. "We may find clues in here." Mark spent the next several minutes reading emails, incoming and outgoing. "Your daughter doesn't email too much."

"I wouldn't know."

Mark went to an outgoing email. He clicked it, then stopped. "I found something." Tony looked over Mark's shoulder.

Mark read the email: "Here is me singing. Hope you like it."

Tony's face dropped. "Brenda?"

Mark nodded, then silently continued to read. Glancing at Tony, who looked terrified, Mark said, "It's from Brenda to a guy by the name of Chris Cahill. Do you know of anyone by that name?"

"I don't. Will you be able to find her?"

"I'm hoping I can find something. I'm a little thirsty. Could I get something to drink?"

"Sure. I'm going to make myself a sandwich, want one?"

"Sounds good."

Mark actually wanted a little time without Tony looking over his shoulder.

Several minutes later Tony returned with ham sandwiches and sodas. Mark took a bite, then continued to investigate.

After an hour of searching the computer, Mark shook Tony's hand, then walked to the front door. "I'll do my best to bring your daughter home. But I have to tell you up front, we'll need a miracle."

"I'll pay whatever it takes to get her back."

Mark opened the door. "I'll be in touch."

Chapter 29

From the basement window, Brenda viewed an empty lot and imagined herself beyond the locked gate outside of her room. She grabbed the pillow on her bed, propped it in the corner of the room, sat, and thought about when she had first arrived in Nashville. Was it a month ago? Soon after Chris had thrown her phone out of the car window, he stopped at a motel to meet the man he called his agent.

Brenda took one look at the guy and said, "I want to go home." The guy looked rough, a few rotten teeth, a tattooed tear near the corner of his eye and a scar on his cheek.

"We're here. I didn't bring you all this way to turn around and take you back home." Chris left, never to be seen again.

"Get in the car," Scar Face said. When Brenda didn't move, he yelled, "now," and showed her a knife.

She entered the car. In terror, Brenda looked out her window as they traveled through Nashville. They stopped outside the city at a fenced in area. The guy got out, ran around the car and opened her door. "Scream and I'll cut you."

He took her by the hand, unlocked the gate and pulled her past it. After re-locking it, he escorted her to a concrete building. After unlocking the door, they went downstairs to a ten-by- ten room. He pushed her inside and slammed the door. Brenda pounded on the door for hours. When it opened, the hope of being released vanished, and the nightmare began. A different man of average build entered.

The Man, the name Brenda had given her new captor, entered. He told her he'd never hurt or touch her, and would give her what she needed if she obeyed.

"I want to go home."

"Sorry, you can't."

Brenda asked why, but instead, he gave instructions. Handing her a grape, coated with oil, he instructed her to swallow it. "You will practice until you can do it without gagging."

She was about to ask why when the realization hit her by his gesture. "No, that's disgusting. I won't do it."

"Have it your way." The Man left several bottles of water and walked out. Two days later, he gave the same instructions, more grapes coated in oil, and again she said no. Leaving more water, he left for a couple more days.

After several days with only water, she was hungry and nodded yes. That's when she received her first meal. Then after the sun went down, the first pair of shoes walked past her window. Her first rapist whispered words of love, words stolen from a poet. On his tongue, however, it was leprous. That was weeks ago.

The window was a reminder of life beyond this room. She stood and tossed her pillow on the bed. Her stomach reminded her she hadn't eaten for several hours. The night before, Brenda cried uncontrollably. When told to stop, she couldn't. Now, "The Man" was punishing her by withholding her meals. She had to learn to control her emotions, or she'd starve.

In the long hours of monotony, the fear came almost as a relief, for it meant human interaction, a reminder of her humanity. But the relief was short-lived. When shoes appeared in the window, she thought, what now? For Brenda, the room was a prison of boredom and fear in equal portions.

She struggled to keep her hopes alive by thinking of home. "Daddy, I'm so sorry." She feared she'd never see him again or worse he'd be killed.

Thoughts of "The Man" and the other men overpowered her memories of what use to be. "If you don't cooperate, we'll hurt your dad." He showed her pictures of Tony Houston entering his house. "This is your dad, right?"

Tears had flowed down her cheeks as she nodded.

She perched on her bed. The door opened. *No, No, it's too early.* Brenda squeezed her legs together, closed her eyes and waited.

"Get up and take a shower." A female voice filled the room. Brenda opened her eyes and smiled. A heavy-set black woman with facial hair resembling a man towered over her. The deep voice boomed again. "Get in there and shower. I'm here to clean up this hog pen." Brenda's smile disappeared.

"If you don't get in there now, I will rip your clothes off and throw you in. I don't have all day. Now, move." The woman yanked the sheets off the bed, causing Brenda to fall to the floor.

In her innocent world, Brenda had experienced no abuse, especially sexual. Her daddy, as she now thought of him, protected her. He never raised his voice. She rubbed her elbow and stood. The woman pushed Brenda while degrading her with obscenities.

With an open door, she made a dash for it. Brenda ran upstairs and tried the doorknob—locked. The large woman screamed. Brenda ran down the hallway and found another door. After opening it, she stopped. A tall man put his hand on the door and slammed it shut. "Get back to your room."

In fear, she ran back as he followed. The woman, out of breath, grabbed Brenda and dragged her back into the room.

"You stupid idiot, why did you leave the door open?" the tall man said.

Brenda ran to the corner and took a fetal position. She heard a slap, a thud, and feared she would be next.

The door closed, and the woman, blood dripping from her nose, stood in front of Brenda. The woman lifted her and threw her toward the bathroom. "I'd kill you, but you're worth too much."

Brenda wished she were dead.

"Shower now and throw your clothes out here."

Brenda complied. She didn't care if the water was cold. The pain inside hurt worse than the bruises on her arms and legs. The woman watched while holding a towel. Brenda covered herself as she showered.

The woman threw her a bar of soap. "Here, use this and get all that grime off you. The boss wants you smelling good." She put clothes on the towel rack. "Put this on, then help me clean this place. You try anything, and you'd be eating that soap."

After showering, Brenda dressed then walked into the room.

On her way to the bathroom, the woman pushed a mop toward Brenda. "Mop."

After several minutes of cleaning the floor, Brenda said, "I want out of here."

The woman turned and laughed. "Child, you never gett'n out of here."

Brenda attempted to restrain her emotions, but she began to cry. "Why are you doing this?"

The woman came closer. "Because I needs the money. And you're making me a lot of money."

"My dad has money. He'll give you some if you let me go."

The woman laughed again and reached into her bag. "Here take this. If you gots any diseases, it'll cure you."

Brenda leaned the mop against the wall, took the pills and bottled water from the woman, and swallowed the pills. "Open your mouth." The woman stuck her pine sol smelling fingers in Brenda's mouth, causing her to gag. "Just checking, other girls like to cheek the medicine and throw it away. We can't have that, now can we?"

Other girls? That explained the noise from the vents. *What kind of torture place is this? Why doesn't my daddy come and get me? Why doesn't anyone get me?*

"There's a high paying guy coming tonight. You treat him well. You hear?"

Brenda wished the goose bumps would go away but had no control over that either.

Items from her bag in hand, the woman motioned for Brenda to come closer. "We need to make you look pretty. Use this to cover the bruises."

Brenda took the camouflage cream and brushed it on her arms. "Get your legs."

Her pants rolled up, Brenda applied the cream over her bruises.

"Can I talk to my daddy?"

"Daddy? Girl, you best grow up. You's a woman now."

If this was being a woman, Brenda wanted none of it. The medicine, on an empty stomach, nauseated her.

The woman brushed foundation on Brenda's face then scanned her. "You best not throw up on my clean floor." The woman handed Brenda a bag. "Here eat this and get food in you's."

Brenda tore it open and shoved the sandwich in her mouth. What, they don't feed you, child?"

Brenda glanced at the woman. "No."

"I'ma change that. You're too skinny. Men don't like skinny." The woman finished cleaning the room then gathered her items. "You better sleep. You'll be up all night." She laughed.

Brenda devoured the food. A minute later, the woman's shoes passed by the window.

Perched on her bed, she dreaded the thought of the setting sun. After several minutes the door opened. She shut her eyes as every muscle tightened. "You tried to run away," The Man said.

Brenda opened her eyes and put her head down. "Sorry."

"I see you feel bad. Maybe I can get the bad people to stop from hurting your dad."

"I won't do it again, I promise" Brenda lowered her gaze. He raised her face with his fingers.

"I believe you and I'll tell them not to harm your dad. They should listen, but I can't guarantee anything next time."

Brenda kept her eyes glued on him since his fingers were still under her chin.

"We can move you to a nicer place and you can have a roommate. If you're a good girl. Will you be a good girl?"

She motioned she'd be good.

"Great. Let's go over what you'll do if someone tries to remove you from here." He stared at her. "Tell me."

"I'll scream until you get here."

"You didn't do that last week."

"I'm sorry."

"What happened because you failed the test?"

Brenda put her head down wishing she could forget.

"You don't want that to happen again, do you?" She shook her head no. "Okay, I think you'll be good. Someone special will be here tonight. I want you on your best behavior. Can you do that?" She motioned yes. "If he wants you to talk then you talk. And no crying."

"Okay."

The Man left and she watched his shoes walk past the window. She went back to the fetal position in the corner and thought about the electric shock for failing "The Man's" test.

That terrible night, her door had opened. A good smelling man entered, and at first Brenda thought he was there for sex, but he whispered, "Follow me."

She put her shoes on and followed him outside. It was her first breath of fresh air in a long time. Her heart raced as she took a glimpse at freedom. But it was a cruel entrapment.

The Man stepped up. "What are you doing?"

Brenda's facial expression fell.

"Take her back to her room." The guy who tricked Brenda dragged her to her room, then wired her with an electoral device. She couldn't remember ever screaming as much as she did that night. Sharp currents of shock rolled through her body. Nightmares woke her out of sleep many nights after that. On that night Brenda concluded she'd never escape and to trust no one.

Chapter 30

The school bell rang, filling the halls with students and faculty. Carina, books in hand went to her locker. She found Billy leaning against it.

"Please move so I can put my books away," she said.

Billy inched over to the next locker. "I'll walk you home."

"Don't you have someone you need to throw off an arcade game?" Carina grinned and walked out of the school. The past few weeks Carina had tried to stay away from Billy, but the more she pushed him away, the greater he pursued her.

Billy followed, then ran in front of her and walked backward. "Hey, I'm thinking of throwing a pharm party. Raid your parent's medicine cabinet."

Carina stopped. "What? No, I won't do that." Carina knew a pharm party meant the kids mixed medication together and took whatever pill they drew out of a bowl.

"We'll pay." Billy found a tree and sat, motioning for her to sit.

"What are you doing?"

"The cheerleaders have practice, and I watch them. Sit down."

"That's sick." Carina narrowed her eyes when she saw Sally. "I don't like her. She thinks she's better than everyone else."

Billy stood. "You want me and the guys to take care of her?"

"What do you mean?"

"Oh, I don't know, we'd come up with something." He laughed. "Here have some of this."

"Hey watch it. You spilled it on me."

"Sorry."

Carina left and hoped the alcohol odor disappeared before she got home. She thought of how Sally flirted with the boys. *At least, I'm not like her.*

At home, she opened the front door and was about to go upstairs when she heard the name—Billy. She stopped, turned, and came as close to the kitchen as she dared so she could listen to her dad speak.

"James West is on disability, something about being wounded in the Gulf War. He's not a good person. There have been several arrests for drunken disorder and he lost his driver's license." Mark stopped to clear his voice. "Nothing was done when the Social Services investigated. Billy West has a record, but it's sealed since he's a juvenile. I learned something about the boy."

"What was that?" Kaitlyn asked.

"An officer couldn't give specifics but said Billy is trouble and should stay away from young kids."

"Are you saying he molested children?"

"The officer wouldn't say," Mark said. "Makes me wonder if the boy is involved with drugs."

Carina turned and started toward the stairs.

"Carina?" Mark asked.

"Yes."

"Come here please, we need to talk."

Carina entered the kitchen.

"We want you to stay away from Billy West."

"Dad, I'm old enough to take care of myself."

"What's that smell? Alcohol?" Mark stood. "Carina?"

"No. Billy..."

Mark stopped her. "You're drinking. What's gotten into you?" His face turned red.

"I'm not perfect like you!"

Before Mark could react, Kaitlyn stepped forward and looked at Carina. "Honey, we're concerned."

"I did nothing wrong and Dad's yelling at me."

Kaitlyn shifted her stand. "What about college? You don't want to throw it all away."

"I don't care about college."

Mark stepped closer to Carina. "You should care. If you get in trouble, it'll jeopardize..." Mark stopped when Kaitlyn touched his arm. He lowered his voice. "Your chances of getting a scholarship."

Kaitlyn sat and patted the seat next to her. "Your Guidance Counselor called and has concerns. Please have a seat."

"Why should I care? You don't care." Carina stared at Mark.

He locked his gaze on her. "We care about what happens to you."

"What, so I don't embarrass you?" Carina turned, ran upstairs, slammed the door, and threw herself on her bed.

The longer she stayed on her bed, the angrier she became. *They don't understand me. I didn't do anything wrong.* After a few minutes, in anger, she lifted off her bed and went to the bathroom. "If they think I'm doing something wrong I may as well do it."

Carina opened the medicine cabinet, took a few pills out of each bottle and palmed them. She had no intention of taking part in Billy's "pharm party," but could use the extra money and punish her parents for not believing her. Carina counted the blue, red and orange pills—twenty. Since she took only a few from each bottle, her parents shouldn't miss the pills. She knew one to be pain medicine, the others she didn't know. With the pills in her pocket, she texts'd Billy, then headed back to her room, stopping when she saw her parents.

***

Mark waited until Carina came out of the bathroom and ambushed her. That's the word that came to Kaitlyn's mind.

She had convinced him to wait a little while before confronting Carina. They waited ten minutes.

"That girl needs discipline. She's been getting more defiant," Mark said.

Kaitlyn looked at Mark with concern. "Please, calm yourself before you talk to her. What she needs is to feel loved."

Mark took a deep breath, then sat. "I suppose you're right. Nothing good happens if we're both worked up. I'll give her a little space then I'll show her a little tough love."

Kaitlyn turned and sighed, then filled Mark's cup

The scene in the hallway ended as fast as it started, with Carina slamming her bedroom door and they walking down stairs.

"That girl clicks my buttons."

Kaitlyn nodded. "Carina will be okay, just love her. Besides, she can't stay a teenager all her life."

Mark half chuckled. "Three more years."

A month had passed since Mark had been in California, but in Kaitlyn's mind, it was like yesterday. *I should talk to Mark.* She tried to dismiss it, telling herself she misunderstood the situation. As each day passed, Kaitlyn vowed to talk to Mark about it, but couldn't.

"Mark, I need..."

Before she could finish, Mark's phone rang from downstairs. He mouthed sorry and headed to his office.

Kaitlyn wanted to cry. Instead, she shut down her emotions, went to the kitchen, and wondered who was calling Mark.

***

Inside his office, phone to his ear, Mark listened. "Mark, this is Tony. I received a call from a Boy Scout Leader. His troop was cleaning the highway outside Nashville and found Brenda's phone."

"Great! That's the break we've needed. How long since Brenda's...?"

"Thirty-four days."

"Can you get the phone?"

"Yes, they'll send it."

"I need to see it."

"I'll get it to you." Tony paused. "Again—money is not an object."

"Okay. I'll wait to hear from you." Mark ended the call, then googled, "sex trafficking+Nashville." A recent report showed in a three month period, over 2000 ads advertised sex for sale in the Nashville area, many assumed to be under-aged girls. Darkness came over Mark, and a fight rose in him.

He googled sex trafficking in the Austin area and discovered a picture of a middle-aged black woman by the name of Tanasha Striker. She was at the top of the search results, and her advertisement read: "Tanasha Striker, a survivor of the sex trade industry will speak at Austin First Baptist." After clicking on the web page, he discovered her topic would be: The Dangers of the

Internet. After escaping the sex trade, Tanasha traveled around to share her story. He determined his family would go to church this Sunday.

Chapter 31

Mark put his tie around his neck.

"Let me help you." Kaitlyn took the tie, straighten it, and tied it.

"Thanks" Mark slipped on his suit jacket, left the bedroom, and in the hallway said, "Carina you need to hurry."

Mark and Kaitlyn went downstairs.

In the kitchen, he picked up a sweet roll and took a bite.

Kaitlyn placed bread and a Pop-Tart in the toaster and pushed the lever. "Would you like coffee?"

Mark looked at his watch. "I don't think we have time since it's on the other side of Austin."

The toast popped up, and she buttered it. "Why not a church around here?"

"It's a topic I thought would be of interest." Mark tossed the last piece in his mouth. "The dangers of the Internet."

Carina stretched as she entered the kitchen. "Good morning Mom."

Mark cleared his voice.

"Hey, Dad," Carina said. "Why are we going to church?"

"It'll be good for us." Mark went to the front door as Kaitlyn handed Carina a Pop-Tart. "Hurry, let's go."

They drove to the church in silence. Kaitlyn applied her make-up as Carina ate her Pop-Tart.

Mark found a parking spot and led his family into the church. Several people were milling around the large foyer. After shaking several hands and receiving a bulletin, Mark, Kaitlyn, and Carina went to the main auditorium and sat.

When the music started, Mark motioned Carina to stand with everyone else. She rolled her eyes and stood. For several minutes, they sang four songs as the words appeared on a screen on stage.

After the music, the congregation sat. The music director, along with the guitar and drum players, left the stage. A suited man walked to the platform. Mark assumed he was the pastor of the church.

"Today we have the privilege of listening to a gifted speaker. I have known Tanasha Striker for several years. Her husband Roger and I have been on many mission trips. Our mission was to catch as many perch as possible."

Everyone laughed.

"Tanasha Stricker is a true servant of God — Tanasha." The Pastor handed Tanasha the microphone as she entered the stage, then stood behind the podium.

She used the screen behind her to show a presentation. A picture of a young black girl on a swing appeared on the screen. "This is a picture before I was abducted." A different picture came on the screen, one showing a much older girl with scars on her face and a weathered look. "And this is me after I escaped. I don't want to glorify this business so I'll talk briefly about what happened between the first picture and the second one," she said. "Then we'll go on a journey of how you can change the lives of children forced into this industry."

Tanasha's abductors took her to an abandoned house. "Left alone for days with only water, I became famished to the point I'd do anything for food." Tanasha paused and allowed the words to hang in the air. "While I was there, another girl introduced me to Jesus and told me that God cried. I didn't understand then, what I know now. God had a plan to free not only me but many girls from the bonds of slavery through the ministry that my husband, Robert, and I have founded, Freedom Now."

For twenty minutes, Tanasha explained the ministry and how people could help. Pictures of several girls appeared on the screen. "These are the girls that our ministry has helped... The video coming up is about a girl by the name of Teresa."

Tanasha stepped aside as a video projected on the screen. Teresa, a black-haired, young woman spoke of how the ministry helped her. Mark guessed her age to be in the lower twenties. After the two-minute clip, Tanasha referred to books in the foyer for sale. "It has personal stories of some of the girls we've helped, including Teresa, the girl in the video."

The music played softly. Mark stood with the rest of the congregation.

Tanasha continued, "I made it because of Jesus. He was there in my darkest moments. Want light in your life? Come forward. Are you lonely? Come forward."

Several people walked to the front of the church as Tanasha continued to encourage them. After a few minutes, the pastor walked next to Tanasha and stood in front of the congregation and the several people now standing in front. He led them in the salvation prayer.

"Repeat after me," the pastor said. "I'm a sinner... Jesus take my sins away... thank you for saving me..." The people repeated the words, then went to a side entrance at the direction of the pastor. He explained they would receive information to live the Christian life.

Ushers came forward to collect an offering after a prayer of blessing. Mark threw a ten into the collection basket when it passed by him. The pastor said a final prayer, then dismissed the congregation.

As the people filed out of their seats Mark turned to Kaitlyn, "Honey, I need to use the restroom, I'll meet you and Carina in the car. Here are the keys." Kaitlyn took the keys and left.

With his eyes, Mark followed Tanasha and Robert to a side door, then caught up with them. "Excuse me."

Tanasha turned. "Yes?"

Mark introduced himself and his line of work. He turned to Robert. "Can I take you and your wife to lunch tomorrow?"

Robert looked at Tanasha who nodded. "We have another speaking engagement on Wednesday, so we're still in the area. Yes, that'll work."

"Great. I'd like your advice on a case. It's similar to what you shared in your talk." Mark shook Robert's hand then Tanasha's. They agreed on a restaurant near the couple's motel. "I'll meet you there at noon."

After going to the restroom, Mark ran to the car and entered. "Did you like the service?"

Kaitlyn didn't turn towards Mark and didn't answer.

After starting the car, Mark backed out of the parking space and proceeded out of the lot. "You didn't like it?"

"Why did you have to talk to the speaker without Carina and me?"

Mark stirred in his seat as he stopped at the traffic light. "I said hi on my way to the restroom."

"The restroom was on the other side. You knew that because the usher told us. You went straight to her, then after talking to them, you went in the opposite direction."

"They told me where the restrooms were located."

Kaitlyn rolled her eyes. "I don't know why we traveled across Austin when we have a church close by."

"We can go to that church next week."

Silence filled the vehicle for many miles until Kaitlyn spoke. "Why are you interested in sex trafficking?"

Again Mark stirred in his seat. He looked in the rear-view mirror and noticed the earplugs in Carina's ears. "For Carina's sake." *Kate's not buying it. Maybe it was a bad idea.*

For the next ten minutes, silence dominated the vehicle again. Mark glanced at Kaitlyn. "Want to stop somewhere for lunch?"

"No."

Yes, it was a bad idea.

Chapter 32

Monday at noon, Mark went to Denny's restaurant and asked for a place in the back. At the table, he opened his briefcase, took out a notepad, and sat. A few minutes later Robert and Tanasha joined him. Mark stood and shook Robert's hand.

"Thank you for meeting with me." They sat. The waitress placed menus in front of them and took their drink order. They ordered water.

"We're happy to do it," Tanasha said. "I didn't put it in my presentation yesterday, but we work with private investigators. I'd like to get your name and number for the parents who look for help," Tanasha said. "Of course, we'd have to do a background check."

Mark pulled out a business card and handed it to her. "I would appreciate that." The waitress placed drinks in front of them.

"Before we get started I'd like to ask you, why?" Tanasha said. "Why do you do this?"

Mark lowered his menu and asked the waitress for more time. "It goes back to when I was a kid. I had a strict military Dad, who had his own way of discipline. But what sparked in me was something else. I was a young Ensign and a rescue operation went bad. We lost children, and I volunteered to go with my Commander to talk to the mother of one of the dead children. I wanted to impress my Commander, but the experience shook me to my core." Mark continued to tell his story, advancing several years when his team attempted to rescue the missionary family in the Philippines but lost the boys. "I'll never forget the look of the missionary's faces when I told them their boys were dead "

Both Robert and Tanasha sat in silence after Mark finished.

"That's horrible, " Tanasha said.

"Yes." Mark picked up his menu, prompting Robert and Tanasha to do the same.

The waitress returned and took their orders.

They talked about their families until their meals arrived. Robert and Tanasha had grown children and two grandchildren, who they hadn't seen in a two weeks.

Mark, eager to direct the conversation toward the main reason he came, began after Tanasha ate the last bite of her chicken sandwich. "I need advice on the case I'm working on."

Tanasha took her napkin, wiped her mouth and looked at Mark. "Tell me the entire story."

Mark spent the next ten minutes going over the case, including his assumptions.

Her eyebrows gathered. "From what you've told us, it sounds like an abduction. Interstate 35 is a route used for the sex trade. If that's the case, Brenda's in trouble."

Mark took a drink of his soda.

"An organization uses young men, like Chris to lure girls into the trade. He probably has another job and blends into his surroundings. You may get something on him, but you won't get much. More than likely he doesn't even know where they've taken her. He's expendable in the eyes of the organization, and he could be dead already. But if he's alive, it's doubtful you'll get much information from him. Be careful if you approach him."

"Why?"

"It could put Brenda's life in danger."

"They'd kill her?"

Tanasha lowered her eyes and nodded.

"Can the police do something?"

"Even if Chris is arrested, with no evidence, the girls and the captors are seldom found."

"So how do I find Brenda?"

"You must dig. Check out construction sites, abandoned houses and buildings that don't have public access. Girls are taken there for indoctrination."

"Indoctrination?"

The girls are trained and brainwashed so they won't run away." Tanasha took a drink. "Food becomes a reward for doing what the abductors want. They use threats against the family to control the girls."

Mark took notes, then looked at Tanasha. "Anything else?"

"Go to Adult Book Stores. With the right amount of money, they'll open their books and let you see pictures of the girls."

"Books?"

"Photo album of available girls." Tanasha looked down, then back to Mark. "How long has this girl been missing?"

"Over a month."

"They break the girl, sometimes after a week. When broken, the abductors advertise the girls. Brenda's picture may be in one of those books."

"Sick."

"These people are demented. They seek innocent children." Tanasha took another drink. "They took me when I was fifteen. Like I said in my presentation, for over a week I was in a room by myself, given only water. I hated being hungry and alone. They broke me down. They gave me food because I obeyed. When I quit fighting, I joined other girls. My abductors made it clear I could be taken away any minute and put in solitary. They showed me pictures of my family and told me if I cooperated they wouldn't be hurt. I believed them." Robert took Tanasha's hand. "I learned to detach my heart from my body."

"Thank you for telling me this."

"If we can help one girl, it'd be worth it." Tanasha continued, relating how her captors played good cop, bad cop. "One person was the protector. He becomes a father figure who protects the girl. It's a game of deception."

"That must have been torture."

"It was. You forget what's real and what's imaginary. I became afraid of thoughts of home, fearing it could get my family killed. I hated the moving."

"Moving?"

"Yes, they would put me in a van and we'd spend many hours, sometimes days on the road."

Over the next hour, Mark listened and gained much insight into the sex trade industry. "Thank you, very much. I'd like to stay in touch with you and your wife," Mark said as he shook Robert's hand.

"We would like that," Robert said.

Mark paid for the meals and left.

On the way home, Mark plotted a strategy to get Brenda back to her father.

Chapter 33

T he next day, Mark had Brenda's phone. Tony had paid for overnight delivery. After Mark read the texts between Chris and Brenda, he was convinced Brenda was lured into sex trafficking.

Via the Internet, Mark vetted Chris Cahill and found a Nashville land line. Mark pulled out his smart phone. After selecting the white pages, he did a reverse phone option, keyed in the number and came up with an address. *Why does he have a land line? This kid doesn't have a clue.* Mark penned the information and called Tony.

Early Wednesday morning, Mark woke his wife, kissed her goodbye and left for the airport. He went through security, to the waiting area, then boarded his plane. During the two-hour flight, Mark reviewed his strategy.

After exiting the plane and getting his luggage, he secured a rental van and drove to his motel. Once there, he changed into a plumber's uniform. After placing magnetic signs for a fake business on the sides of the van, Mark went to Chris's address.

Mark arrived at an apartment building. He entered the building and proceeded to apartment number fourteen. Since the building was old, Mark figured there would be no security system. He rang the doorbell and received no answer. Mark picked the lock and entered the home. After a few minutes of scanning the room, he discovered a laptop. Mark copied the files on Chris's computer to a jump drive. As it was downloading Mark went through the desk and drawers. The files took several minutes to download. Once complete, he removed the jump drive, left the apartment, and went back to his motel.

***

The sun beamed through Carina's window. Once dressed, she headed downstairs.

In the basement, she expected to hear the clanking of the weights being lifted. It was silent, and no lights. "Dad?"

With no response, she went to the kitchen. "Mom, where's Dad?"

"He caught an early flight."

Carina turned away.

"You can call him. His flight may not have taken off yet."

"Forget it."

"Honey, if you need something..."

"Forget it." Carina stomped away.

In her room, she lifted her mattress and, with new resolve, retrieved the pills from last Friday. Billy had bugged her for them, but she told him no. But now, in anger, she put them in her back pocket then shot out the house.

Carina texts'd Billy. "hey"

"sup"

"I have it"

"Meet me at the spl" She knew that to be the code for the school parking lot.

After walking to school, she spotted Billy. Matthew Jones, the quarterback, nicknamed, "Jonzy," stood next to Billy. Carina walked to them.

Jonzy smiled and nodded, "Carina." He never acknowledged her before, and now he was calling her by name. She pushed out her chest and smiled. That's when she saw it—a scratch on Sally's car.

"A present for you," Billy said as he waved his hand the length of the car.

Carina stared at the vehicle.

"You like it?"

She stared at the scratch then back at Billy. She didn't like Sally, but she didn't want this.

"Come over here." Billy glanced up at the camera on top of the light pole. He positioned himself with his back to the device.

"Here take this." Billy handed her a small bag. "Don't stare at it, you need to hide it. Give it to Jonzy after school, right here."

"Why don't you give it to him yourself, he's standing right there?"

"He doesn't want to get kicked off the football team. He has the hots for you, but I told him you are my gf. I think he will make a pass at you."

Carina put it in her book bag and stood there, her face tightened. She couldn't believe she agreed to this, but not wanting to say no to Jonzy, she did.

"Pass — football — get it?" Billy laughed.

"Oh yea football," Carina said.

***

The secretary motioned for the principal after he entered the room. She had been watching the parking lot video feed. "Mr. Wimmington, look at this."

Robert Wimmington, the High School Principal, stood 6' 3. Since it was football season, he wore a Wild Cat t-shirt. He walked to Alice's computer screen. "Rewind it please." She hit a button, reversed the video, then played it.

Wimmington pointed at the screen. "Stop. Who's standing next to Jones?"

"Billy West."

"Wasn't he busted with drugs last year?"

"Yes."

"And the girl?"

"I didn't get a clear look at her."

"Have the boy's lockers searched and find the girl. I'll be walking the hallways. Page me if you need me. And good job."

***

Carina's eyes darted both ways before putting Jonzy's baggie in her locker. Her heart beat fast as she raced to her class and entered.

"You're late Miss Steele."

A few students snickered as she walked to her seat.

"Bad girl," Sally whispered.

Carina stopped. "Scratches need itching."

156

Sally's eyebrows drew together.

Carina smiled, surprised it slipped out her mouth. She was about to tell Sally about Jonzy and the attention she received from the star quarterback when a voice came from the front of the class.

"Miss Steele, you're late, and you're talking in my class. Something you want to share with the class?"

I sure do. Carina shook her head no and sat.

"Open to page 54 and take out your assignment."

For the next half hour, Carina thought about Jonzy. The jock only dated girls like Sally. *Did he see Billy scratch the car?* Carina smiled at the thought. Maybe Jonzy would ask her to sit at the "jock's" table during lunch. *Wouldn't that be great?* Her popularity would skyrocket.

The voice of her teacher snapped Carina out of her thoughts. "Miss Steele, go to the Principal's office." Fear appeared on Carina's face as she stood.

She picked up her books, then went into the hallway. Her pulse raced, and her face fell as she walked past her locker, now wide open. Sickness came over her as she looked down the row of opened lockers. A police officer and a dog were in the hallway. Carina's eyes darted toward the exit.

Wimmington and a female police officer met Carina at the office door. "Carina Steele you are under arrest. Please turn around."

She remembered the pills in her pockets as the female officer frisked her. The officer removed the pills from Carina and placed it on the desk, next to the bag of weed.

When she figured things couldn't get any worse, Sally's angry voice filled the office with words like car scratched and Carina Steele admitted she did it.

Carina, handcuffed, felt stupid and used, but stood silent.

Chapter 34

B ack in the motel, Mark inserted the jump drive into the USB port of his lab top. Several files appeared. He opened the file labeled girlfriend and viewed several photos of Chris and a young woman. Closing it, Mark opened the family file and viewed pictures of babies, children, and adults. Chris was in many of the photos. Mark spent the next hour looking through images and reading documents.

He picked up his spiral research notebook. Next to Chris's name, Mark wrote: college student, studying horticulture, lured Brenda to Nashville for money. Mark scratched Chris's name off his list. Mark had written several addresses of adult bookstores from his notebook. He ripped out the page and went to his vehicle. One after another he drove to each store, inquired about young teen girls and left his card. The rest of the day he spent visiting stores hoping to flush out useful information.

Mark noticed his iPhone was dead. He fished his tracker phone from his other pocket and noted a full charge. *Good, at least, I have one charged phone.* Tossing his iPhone on the passenger's seat he went to the fifth store on his list. Mark parked in front of Adult Books and Movie Arcade, went into the store, and walked past a few customers.

Behind the counter, a fat guy, looking like he had just climbed out of bed, barely looked up from the magazine he was thumbing through. Not wanting to talk in front of customers, Mark went to the back of the store and pretended to look at the material.

Several minutes later the guy from the counter stepped into the aisle. "Are you looking for anything special?"

"I'm looking for some young action, any of that around here?"

"Not in the flesh, just magazines." The guy played with his beard, appearing to get food out of it. Mark noted his body language. *Doesn't stand still. Eyes wanting something.*

"I'd be willing to pay good money." Mark took out a wad of cash. The guy stared at it.

"I wish I could help you, Mr. Grant."

With the hint, Mark handed the guy a fifty.

"You know Ben I want to help you."

Mark pulled out a hundred-dollar bill and showed the guy the picture of Benjamin Franklin. "Do you know where I could find an eighteen-year-old girl or younger for hire?"

"It's possible. I'll have to check on it."

"If you find something, here's my number." Mark handed him a card with his tracker phone number and fake name, then took the fifty from him.

The man took the card. "Mike Green?"

"That's my name."

"Mike, I'm a fan of the Dead President's Club."

"Give me something and I'll give you an autographed Ben, maybe throw in a couple Jacksons and a Grant." Mark put the cash back in his pocket.

"Here's an excellent magazine." The guy pointed.

Mark waved it off. "Call me if you find something." He exited the store, went to his rental and went to another store. Mark hoped a lead would produce something because if it didn't happen soon, he'd be flying back to Austin by himself.

***

Kaitlyn sat at Mark's desk, computer on, viewing his Internet history. She discovered he had googled sex trafficking. Further down the list, she found he searched construction sites and adult bookstores. "Mark, what are you doing?" Confused, she continued to view. On-line dating sites? She felt sick but continued. On the United Airlines site, she found where Mark had booked his flight. Something caught her eye. He booked a round trip for himself but an extra ticket for the way back. What's going on? She closed that link then opened, "Freedom Now Ministry," and saw a picture of the woman who spoke on Sunday. She then brought up Robert Kulp's Facebook. Kulp? That sounded familiar. "Was Kulp the last name of the woman on the phone? The woman Mark pretended to be married to?" Her pulse rose; fear gripped her. She was about to go to another website her phone rang. "Carina you're where?... Why?... Drugs? I'll be right there."

As Kaitlyn raced to the police station, she wondered what Carina had gotten herself into and wished Mark were here. What's he going to say? How's he going to react?

At the police station, Kaitlyn found a parking spot and quickly exited the vehicle. Kaitlyn entered the station and walked across the waiting room to a tinted glass window. She took a deep breath and stabilized her emotions. She prepared to speak, hoping her voice couldn't crack. "I'm here to get Carina Steele." After showing her ID, she was told to have a seat.

Kaitlyn scanned the crowded waiting room, then sat next to a woman who was filing her nail.

"Your daughter in trouble?" she said while smacking her gum.

Kaitlyn briefly took her eyes off the tinted window and answered, "Yes."

"I have to get my boy out once a month. I'm waitressing, and he's lucky it's slow right now." She continued to file her nails.

Kaitlyn smiled.

"It sounds like they had a big drug bust at the high school—dogs and everything. Too many drugs. It's not the kids fault. It's like telling them not to eat any candy when they're in a candy store."

Kaitlyn turned toward her and suppressed the urge to ask her to keep her opinions to herself. "Excuse me, I have to use the restroom." In the bathroom, Kaitlyn splashed water on her face and stared in the mirror. She never dreamed she'd have to get her daughter out of jail, or sit next to a tattooed woman who wanted to justify her son's drug usage. After several minutes, Kaitlyn returned, grateful someone had taken the seat next to the tattooed lady. *Mark, you should be here right now.* A tear fell down her cheek as she looked around the waiting room, attempting to find another chair. There weren't any. She wiped her face and stood against the wall.

For the next fifteen minutes, Kaitlyn observed several people approach the window, some scared, some angry, but none smiling. The tattooed woman received her son. Kaitlyn overheard their loud conversation.

"I lose money every time I have to leave work, to get your sorry self out of jail."

The long-haired, underwear-showing, teenager said, "Mom, just sign the paper and get me out of here."

The tattooed woman looked at Kaitlyn. "What are you staring at?"

She dropped eye contact with the woman and glanced at the exit, wishing to be anywhere but here.

Ten minutes later, a door opened. Carina walked out behind a female Police Officer.

"Who's here for Carina Steel?"

Kaitlyn's stomach rolled. "I am." She stepped toward the officer.

"Are you her parent?"

Feeling all eyes on her, Kaitlyn said, "Yes."

The officer handed Kaitlyn a clipboard. "Please fill out the contact information section on top and sign at the bottom. Your ID please."

Kaitlyn handed her driver's license to the officer. She looked at it and gave it back.

"We're releasing Carina into your custody. You'll receive a notice in the mail for her court date."

"What's she charged with?"

Carina's lowered her eyebrows, pressed her lips together, and crossed her arms.

"Possession of drugs on school property and pills on her person. We'll send those to the state lab to determine if they're narcotics. We also did a urinalysis on her. We'll notify you of the results in a few days. And the destruction of personal property."

"What property?"

"A vehicle in the school parking lot."

Carina unfolded her arms. "I didn't do it."

"Enough." Kaitlyn completed the form, signed it, and handed it back to the officer.

"You are free to go. And young lady, you need to stay out of trouble and away from drugs."

Carina rolled her eyes.

After exiting the police station, Carina came alongside Kaitlyn. "Mom, I didn't damage any car, and I didn't take any drugs."

"Why did they arrest you? Drugs? Carina, you used to be a straight-A student and played sports. What's happened to you?" Kaitlyn walked faster, then entered the car.

Carina entered. "Mom, I didn't key that car, and those drugs weren't mine."

"Don't raise your voice."

"Nobody believes me."

"That will not work on me." Kaitlyn drove in silence for several miles. "I'm taking you back to school, if they let you attend."

Chapter 35

B renda didn't want to be in this room. The Man had told her she'd be moving soon, maybe out of state. That part scared her. Brenda wanted another girl to talk to but not if it meant being further away. What did it matter? Home seemed a distance of a million miles.

Yesterday, The Man had taken her to a McDonald's drive-thru. He said it was a test, one she passed. She received a microwave and refrigerator as rewards for her obedience. Brenda opened the small refrigerator and took out a soda, her third within the past hour.

She tried to remember her old life and pictured herself in school, in history class. Her teacher, a young man, with black hair, topped her list of favorite teachers. Brenda's thoughts went back and forth between scenes of school and home.

Her mom took center stage in her thoughts. They would go to the mall on Saturday afternoons and browse through the stores. One particular Saturday, her mom had her try on a blue sundress. "Brenda, you're beautiful," she remembered her mom saying. But now, she felt ugly and stupid. Tears flowed down her cheeks as she wished her mom was with her. "Mom, tell me I'm beautiful."

Her memories shut off when she opened her eyes. The bruises on her arms had disappeared, but the emotional pain didn't. Dread rose inside her as it did every night when the sun set.

***

In her pajamas, Kaitlyn tried Mark's number again. "Why aren't you answering?" She wondered what Mark was doing and fought the ugly thoughts: dating sites, sex trafficking, two tickets on the return flight, Jackie Lane Kulp and now Robert Kulp. She had found the note that had Jackie's name on it and confirmed her suspicions—Jackie and Robert were connected. The information confused Kaitlyn.

She thought about the words from last Sunday at church. "Darkness can't exist in the light, the two can't co-exist. It's one or the other. You think you can see, but you're looking through a dark glass."

"Help me."

Kaitlyn thought of her mom and called her.

"Hi, Mom."

"It's late Kaitlyn, is everything okay?"

"Carina was arrested for drugs and Mark is away on business."

"Oh no, drugs?"

"That and she damaged a car at school."

"Will she have to go to jail?"

"I don't know. We'll find out when she goes to court." Kaitlyn paused.

"Last year, Carina was doing good in school," Elaine said.

"She claims she didn't do it, and I haven't known her to lie."

"Carina is a good kid. I think she's going through a bad time."

"Mark is hard on her." Kaitlyn paused. "I have good news. We went to church last Sunday. It was Mark's idea."

"God works in mysterious ways," Elaine said. "Is everything okay with you and Mark?"

"I haven't talked to him about the phone call if that's what you mean."

"That happened over a month ago, right?"

"Yes."

"And you haven't talked to him about it?"

"I wanted to, things got better, until today."

"Carina?"

"It's not completely her. I found suspicious links on Mark's computer, and I haven't heard from him since he left."

"What made you check his computer?"

"The topic at the church was sex trafficking. I thought it strange."

"You can't let this fester."

"I know Mom. I'm not good at this kind of thing."

"You never were, but you must do it."

"You're right. I should try calling Mark again." In a lower voice, she said, "I've been trying all day."

Kaitlyn ended the call and phoned Mark. It went to voice mail—again. After leaving a message, she placed the phone on the nightstand and shut off the light. Kaitlyn climbed under the covers and before falling asleep, thought about Carina's insistence she did nothing wrong. Kaitlyn wanted to believe Carina, but the evidence against her seemed solid. She was glad the school allowed Carina to resume her classes with in-school suspension. Kaitlyn's thoughts went to Mark and prevented her from sleeping.

***

Early in the morning The Man, entered Brenda's room and placed a box near her bed. "I have good news. How would you like a roommate?"

Brenda nodded and squeezed out a yes.

"I've been getting good reports and you've earned another reward."

Brenda wanted to be happy, but guilt overruled.

"Aren't you excited?"

"Yes."

"You'll be moving soon. Do you like the refrigerator and microwave?"

"I like them, thank you." Brenda lowered her gaze.

The Man lifted her chin. "Keep that face-up and put on confidence." He opened the box and pulled out a skimpy dress. "Put it on, I'm taking pictures and videotaping you in it."

Brenda started toward the bathroom.

"No, stay. I'll take pictures here."

Brenda froze. This was something different. So far he hadn't touched her or even seen her without clothes.

"Go on."

She took a deep breath, began, and heard camera clicking sounds. Brenda feared the changes.

***

Mark woke early, checked his notes and made plans to visit several construction sites around Nashville. He opened the safe and pulled out his plane tickets. His return flight would be tomorrow. Tony insisted he purchase the second ticket. Mark wanted to believe Brenda would use it. "God, help me find her today." After placing the tickets back in the safe, Mark grabbed his tracker phone and list. He was about to take his iPhone when he remembered Joe's words of caution. "When dealing with these people they'll check everything, even your vehicle." Leaving it plugged in, Mark left the motel.

Mark went from site to site, stopping only for lunch. After visiting all the places on his list, on a hunch, Mark returned to a site called West Construction. The fence and the locked gate made it a perfect spot for an illegal operation.

Mark parked a safe distance from the gate. In the late afternoon, with his binoculars, he searched for anything unusual. The last truck drove past the gate and stopped while the driver exited and locked it. He returned to the truck, then drove away. In the bushes, Mark waited a few more hours. As the sun set, he noticed light emanating from a small window at ground level. Just as he was about to investigate, his tracker phone vibrated.

"Is this Mike Green?"

Mark paused and remembered his fake name.

"Yes, this is Mike."

"Jim from the Adult Book Store on 5th street. I have something for you."

"I'll be right there."

***

Soon after Brenda had put the dress on, The Man's phone went off, stopping the photo session. Now sitting on her bed, she viewed a squirrel outside her window, its tail swishing back and forth. It appeared every day over the past several days. The wide-eyed brown creature gave her a momentary reprieve from her imprisonment.

The squirrel, dashed away, then returned holding something to eat between its front paws. *How cute.* Brenda had named the squirrel Seesaw. For several minutes, the animal gnawed on its food. She loved its big eyes and jerky movements.

Its ears perked up, the food now gone. Seesaw turned toward the window, investigating who was inside. Its head turned one way, then the other. With a quick movement and tail in the air, the little animal scurried away.

In Brenda's mind, she left with her new friend, Seesaw. They scurried together across the lot and onto a grassy field. Seesaw waved for her to follow. Like Alice in Wonderland, Brenda went down a large hole, and stood when she found the bottom.

The squirrel, now in front of her, also stood. "Follow me," said Seesaw. Brenda went through a maze of tunnels that led into a large room.

Brenda looked around and noticed several animals. She pointed to a rabbit, "You look like a Nadia." Then a gopher, "I'm naming you Charley."

Unlike Alice, Brenda didn't want to be an adult; she wished to be a child. In her imagination, Brenda picked up a bunny and squeezed her. They danced. Seesaw jumped on her shoulder as music filled the air.

"Hey," The Man's voice cut into her fantasy. Brenda hated that no one used her name. She wondered if The Man even knew her name. He was at the door, receiving a box from someone. Phone still in his hand, he tossed the box to her. "Inside are jeans and a shirt. Put on the clothes." He continued to talk on the phone.

Brenda wondered what the change of plans meant. She removed the clothes from the box, went to the bathroom and changed. He was on the phone when Brenda returned. Clothed in a plaid cowboy shirt and blue jeans, she sat and went back into her imagination, where she felt loved.

Several minutes later, The Man said, "Here's what I want you to do."

Brenda tried to suppress her fear as, The Man, told her the new plan. He returned to his phone.

***

Mark ran to his rental and drove to the Adult Book Store. Upon entering, he approached Jim. "You called and said you have something for me."

Jim walked to the front door, turned the open/close sign around and locked the door. "Follow me."

Mark followed Jim to a back room. He switched the light on exposing an overflowing garbage can, uneaten food on a table, and shelves of unorganized magazines.

Jim pushed the trash off the table and motioned for Mark to sit. "We had to make sure you wasn't a cop."

Mark felt relieved his preparation and fake websites worked.

A tall man entered and placed a briefcase on the table. "Turn around and spread eagle."

Mark stood, placed his hands on the wall, leaned against it and spread his feet.

"Jim, frisk him."

Jim did a thorough pat search. "No wires and he's not armed."

The tall man motioned Mark toward a chair. "Name is Jack. Sit." He had slicked back hair, suit, no tie, and shiny shoes. "Jim, tells me you want to be a customer."

"I'm looking for something young."

"We can supply a young girl." Jack moved his suit jacket to the side, revealing a gun. "This speaks for me. If you turn out to be a cop or one of those do-gooders, I'll kill you. Do you understand?"

As Mark was about to respond, a guy in a muscle shirt came in and handed Jack a billfold and phone. "Boss, I found this in his van." Jack opened the billfold, took out the driver's license and compared the photo to Mark. Satisfied, he went through the phone's contacts. Muscles whispered something into Jack's ear. "Why do you have night goggles in your van?"

"Comes in handy for bird watching. If you know what I mean." Mark winked and pushed out a laugh.

Jack handed Mark his phone and billfold. "You pass." Jack turned to Jim, "Show him the girls. Everyone is over eighteen." Jack laughed.

Mark viewed several pictures before seeing Brenda's photo, an image he had burned into his memory. He looked at more pictures, found two older girls, then returned to Brenda's. He placed all three photos in front of himself. "It's among these three. Which one is the youngest?"

Jack examined each picture and pointed to Brenda's photo. "She is, and she's new."

"That's the one I want."

Jack opened his briefcase, pulled out a calendar book and handed him a card. "Tomorrow night is open. Show up at this address at ten."

Mark looked at the card and concealed his emotions. It was West Construction. He had been so close to her. "I was hoping for something tonight." Mark was fishing for more information.

"I have a blond that's available tonight."

"That's okay, I'm partial to young brunettes. I'll be there tomorrow night."

Jack closed his briefcase. "Go to the front gate, someone will let you in. You'll have thirty minutes with the girl."

Mark took a hundred out of his pocket and handed it to Jack. The guy held out his hand. "I have to pay my employees."

Mark gave him a fifty.

"When you get to the gate, you'll be expected to pay another hundred and fifty."

Mark left, thinking, "that's what you think." After getting into his rental, he thought about Joe and his words of advice: "When dealing with these people they'll check everything, even your vehicle." He tossed his billfold with the fake driver's license onto the passenger's seat and breathed a sigh of relief that he left his iPhone in the motel. If he had brought it, he might have blown his cover.

After returning to the motel to pick up his equipment and now a charged iPhone, Mark punched in the address of West Construction and followed the GPS directions. If everything went as planned, Brenda's days of captivity were close to ending.

The construction site came into view. He parked and watched as truck after truck left the area. The last trucker locked the gate. Donning his night vision equipment and carrying a bag, Mark ran to the entrance and hid behind a tree.

Several minutes later a large woman, carrying a box, opened the gate, entered, and re-locked it. Thirty minutes later she exited through the same gate.

Soon after that, a man in western gear, cowboy boots, with a hat to match approached the gate. He unlocked the gate, entered and re-locked it, then went to the same building as the woman.

The sun had set and there was no moon in the sky. Mark walked around the perimeter. He studied the layout as he proceeded around the large fence. With the help of his night vision goggles, he kept watch on the front of the gates. One building within the compound had lights on. Behind that building, Mark cut a section of the fence with wire cutters, then replaced it making it appear unbreached.

Chapter 36

Brenda's imaginary world disappeared when The Man said, "Hey," again.

"My name's not hey," she thought but dared not say aloud.

"Someone's coming to redecorate this room. When she gets here, help her."

"Okay."

"I'll be right back." The Man left, leaving Brenda to her imaginary world and friends.

Fifteen minutes later a woman entered the room. "You're not getting away from me this time." The black woman tossed a box to Brenda, then locked the door. "Remove the bedding."

"What for? It's clean." Brenda stood.

"Shut up and do it."

Brenda followed every direction without speaking. They changed the bedding into a western theme and hung pictures on the wall. Brenda cringed at the whip on the table.

"You get pink cowboy boots and what do I get—nothing." The woman took the box, shoved all the old bedding in it and closed it. "I hope they use that whip on you." She laughed as she left the room.

A few minutes later, The Man reentered and set up video equipment in the corner. "Everything must be just right." He picked the rope off the floor and put it on a small table and adjusted the pictures on the wall.

He left and returned with a sawhorse and saddle. "Ever ride a horse?"

"No."

"Well, you will ride a horse tonight." He laughed and went behind the camera. "Move around. I need to check the focus." She walked in front of the camera as he adjusted the lens.

After a few minutes, Brenda sat on the edge of her bed, this time, her imagination wouldn't work. Fear canceled the Alice in Wonderland show. As hard as she tried, Brenda couldn't keep her thoughts away from the horrible night she knew was coming. The man turned on some country music, and she hated it. Her heart beat faster when cowboy boots showed up in her window.

***

If everything went as planned, Mark would have Brenda within the next few hours, and tomorrow they'd be on a plane to Austin. He imagined the reunion Tony would have with his daughter. But first, Mark needed to find Brenda's room.

Dressed in black with black paste smeared on his face, he slipped through the section of the fence he had cut, then replaced it. He ran to the front of the building and looked in each window.

He saw a girl sitting on a bed. A man was buttoning his pants. Mark pushed away the hatred and the disgust. The girl stood and tossed a shirt to the guy. *It's not Brenda.* Mark turned from the window, looked into the next one—a blond headed girl. He moved to the next window.

The main door opened as two men exited. Mark plastered himself against the building. When the men were close to the gate, Mark scurried to the left side of the building and waited. He peeked around the corner and observed them on the outside of the compound. Mark went to the next window.

After checking the third window on the ground level, he noticed a cowboy hat next to the bed. He listened: "Do it again, this time, get it right."

Mark looked through the window. A girl, clothed, sat on a saddle, simulating riding a bucking horse and doing a bad job of it. Mark was sure this was Brenda. He controlled his emotions and went to the next phase of his plan.

He would use surveillance cameras to get evidence. With the proof, Mark would contact the local authorities and together they would rescue Brenda. In theory, that's what Mark hoped to happen. He knew the police wouldn't work with him unless the evidence were clear for a search warrant.

Mark placed a small camera near the window and another one under the door. He ran back to the fence, climbed through it, replaced the wire, and went to his van. With his iPad, he brought up the images from the cameras. Brenda, still on the saddle, had her back to the camera. Her shirt hung loose. *Come on, Brenda turn so the camera can see you.* Mark had the tracker phone in his hand, ready to contact the police once he had Brenda's face on video.

The screen went blank. "Darn." He rewound the video, hoping to get a clear shot of Brenda's face. No clear picture of Brenda, only the bare back of a girl. He considered his options. Mark could call the police and give them his suspicions, but without proof, they wouldn't act. *Why didn't I get the better camera?*

As he contemplated his plan, he noticed the cowboy nearing the gate, then lingering with a couple other guys. Mark couldn't return to the window without being seen, so he waited until cowboy and the two men left.

Around 2:00 a.m. Mark exited his van, ran to the cut section of the fence, donned his night goggles, and entered. He would do this without the police, something he hadn't planned. Mark would get Brenda and take her to the police station.

After making sure there was no movement, he ran to the front of the brick building. All was dark, except for a tiny amount of light coming from the light pole in the middle of the compound. He checked the main door—locked. Mark crawled along the building and went to Brenda's three foot by two foot window. With his night goggles, Mark saw someone on the bed. She was in fetal position, her back to him. Mark took a deep breath and formulated a new plan. The unknown, inside the building, concerned him.

Mark restrained his emotions and proceeded to the locked door. He picked the lock, opened the door, and placed a rock in the corner, so he had a way of escape. In silence, he went down the stairs into a hallway. He stopped and listened in front of a door—silence. He manipulated the lock and opened the door. The girl didn't move. With a small flashlight, he scanned the room and noticed her tennis shoes in the corner. With the shoes in his hands, he went to her.

***

Brenda, still wearing the western clothes, felt a touch in the darkness. Her eyes tightened, hoping it wasn't real. She opened her eyes and tried to see. Brenda felt humiliated from being videotaped. The whip the man used on her, stung and left burns on her arms and legs. Brenda looked up as her eyes adjusted. A shape stood at her side. She suppressed the urge to cry out.

The shape changed, and she felt hot breath on her neck, a hand over her mouth.

A male voice whispered in her ear. "I'm here to help you."

Brenda nodded. *Am I dreaming?*

He reached for her hand and drew her out of bed. She stumbled, but he caught her and kept her from falling.

"Put your shoes on."

Brenda complied. He led her out of the room. *Is this another test? If she failed…*

Her thoughts went back to the time she thought she'd die from the electric shocks. With the ordeal fresh in her memory, she asked herself again, "Is this a test?" She wanted to be free, but she also didn't want to experience the electricity. The Man promised it would be worse next time. How could it be worse than that night? The thought terrified Brenda.

The hallway was dark, except for the guy's flashlight. He looked like someone that could give her freedom—but so did Brian. Everything seemed to stop. Brenda watched him climb the stairs. Would she be free soon? Or another shock treatment? Her heart beat fast as she struggled to make a decision that would change the course of her life.

Chapter 37

Brenda stopped and let out a blood-curdling scream. Mark attempted to place his hand over her mouth, but she had moved down the stairs. A door opened, a man exited, and a light shined.

The Man pulled out a gun. "Stop."

Mark froze, then jumped over Brenda, knocking her and The Man to the floor. The gun fell out of his hand. Mark wrestled the guy, turning him on his stomach and punching him several times in the face. That should do it.

The Man squeezed out, "Shoot."

Apparently not. Mark punched the guy, silencing him.

Brenda pointed the weapon in his direction.

Mark held out his hand. "Give me the gun."

Brenda's hands shook, and terror filled her face. Close to giving Mark the gun, another door opened, causing her to turn.

Mark stretched further. "Hand me the gun, now."

A crack of a gunshot echoed in the air. Mark jumped toward Brenda, knocking her to the floor. Mark reached for the gun, palmed it, and fired at two men. They ducked behind the door.

Mark had limited bullets, so he planned his escape. Firing the last two bullets into the ceiling lights, causing the hallway to become dark, he took Brenda's hand and climbed the stairs. He stayed low, pulling her with him. His shoulder jerked forward, and he lost his grip causing Brenda to fall. In terror, he descended a few steps. She lay motionless at the bottom of the stairs. *Was she dead?* Time stopped. Mark yelled her name. She didn't move. *I have to get her.* Before another step, a hand pulled Brenda out of the hallway. Gone. More bullets hit the wall. He stopped.

Mark, with no choice, ran up the stairs, and out of the building. Zig-zagging and moving fast, Mark made it around the building. Bullets hit the ground near him, sending his adrenaline higher. He heard no gunfire and figured they were using silencers. Barely able to see the fence, Mark ran. Relief came when he found the cut section. He pushed the section out and climbed through it. On the other side, he felt a pain in his shoulder that sent a tingling sensation down his arm. Mark ran again. For the first time since the shooting began, he turned and looked — darkness. He stopped and removed the night goggles from his bag, donned them, and saw a guy near the building. After a few minutes, the guy left. Mark assumed he went back into the building. Mark proceeded to his vehicle.

After tossing the bag of equipment onto the passenger seat, Mark started the van, then spun out. He touched his shoulder then looked at his hand — blood. With one hand he steered, with the other he applied pressure to his wound.

A few miles from the construction site, Mark pulled over to the curb. He took off his jacket and t-shirt, tore the shirt in sections and wound it around his shoulder to stop the flow of blood.

Mark felt for and found both the entry and exit holes. The bullet went through the muscle part of his arm, which was bleeding. He thought no artery had been severed and no bone hit. At least, he hoped. His heart pounded all the way to his temples.

Mark's shirt, soaked in blood, caused him concern. He was afraid that he may lose consciousness, so Mark tried to come up with a plan. One thing was crystal clear: the hospital was not an option. The hospital would notify the police of a bullet wound, and he would be questioned and lose valuable time. Mark needed to assess the situation and try to get Brenda. He hoped she was still alive. So he called the police, anonymously, and reported the address of a gun being fired, then sped back to the construction site. Mark shut off his headlights as he approached.

With his good arm, he took out the iPad and viewed the one remaining surveillance camera that still worked. Mark noted the lights were off with no movement. Mind focused on what he had to do, he quelled his dizziness.

He slipped his night vision goggles on and examined the front of the building. *Why aren't the police here?* Mark searched for the vehicles, then rummaged through his bag to get GPS tracking devices he could place on the bumpers.

His now charged i-phone caught his attention. It was blinking, signaling several messages from Kaitlyn. Mark noted the last message was an hour ago. *She wouldn't call in the middle of the night unless it were an emergency.*

He pressed play and listened.

"Mark, Carina is gone."

Mark dialed Kaitlyn. "Kate?"

"Mark? Is that you?"

"Yes. What's going on?"

"The police arrested Carina for drugs yesterday. I couldn't sleep, so I checked on her. She's gone, Mark. She's gone. Carina is gone."

"What? How? Slow down."

"I've been trying to get a hold of you."

"Sorry, I forgot to charge my phone."

"They arrested her at school, and I had to get her from jail."

"Carina, drugs?"

"Yes. I wanted to talk to you but I kept on getting your stupid voicemail."

"And Carina's gone?" His headache worsened.

"I couldn't sleep. I worried about Carina." She paused, then whispered, "and you."

Mark hung his head, opened his window attempting to get fresh air in his lungs. His stomach revolted and, thinking he'd throw up, he opened his door, leaned over, phone still by his ear.

"Mark, are you still there?"

"I'm here."

"You don't sound good. Are you in a car?"

Mark sat up and attempted to calm his breathing. "I'm okay. Go on, please."

"I checked on Carina around midnight and she was gone. I didn't know what to do, so I called the police. They came here, took a statement and said they'd check into it."

"I'll catch the earliest flight and be home as soon as possible," Mark said. "I love you."

"Okay, I'll see you when you get here. Bye."

Mark lowered his phone. Gone was his resolve to get Brenda, replaced with thoughts of Carina. As he drove to the motel, Mark passed a police car.

After entering the motel lobby, with his jacket on and his bag over his good shoulder, Mark walked to the elevator as normal as possible. The front desk attendant never looked up at him. Every movement made Mark's shoulder hurt. After fishing his motel card out of his pocket with his left hand, he put it in the slot. He knew from experience that once the adrenaline subsided, the pain would increase. His pain level was a six.

Back in his room, he examined his wound, cleaned it and re-bandaged it. Mark cleaned the blood on his jacket, then took a shower. The sun was rising as he packed his bags.

If it didn't get worse, Mark figured he could get himself back home. He'd taken bullets before and learned how to survive, this would be no different. His next challenge was to get through airport security without being frisked. He hoped he would see businessman he could follow. They typically packed light and moved through the security much faster with less suspicion.

***

Relieved the security check was uneventful, Mark boarded the plane, then sat next to a dark-complexioned man of Eastern descent. The plane taxied down the runway and lifted. After several minutes, a stewardess offered a drink and snack. Waving it off, Mark closed his eyes and saw Brenda's face—her terrified look and the gun pointed at him. He opened his eyes and imagined Carina. He hoped she wasn't in the same situation. Mark didn't want his imagination to go there, but his analytical mind went that direction, so he reached for the barf bag.

Unable to get comfortable, Mark repositioned himself for the tenth time. The passenger next to Mark displayed an irritated look—again. "Sorry."

He told himself that Carina was okay, that she was at a friend's place, but he didn't believe it. His mind refused to release the thought she was in a basement somewhere being abused like Brenda.

He shifted in his seat again and drew another look from his dark faced passenger. This time, Mark looked out the window.

Sleep came, along with nightmares as he relived the moments with Brenda. In Mark's dreams, Brenda's face morphed into Carina's. Then, his mind took him to the beach and the firefight with the Abu Sayyaf group. An image of the lifeless bodies of two young boys, the missionaries' children, froze in his mind.

The plane hit an air pocket, startling Mark awake. Were bullets flying? Who was shooting? He turned and woke up in fright, his hands above his head, sweat on his forehead. His dark faced passenger gave him "the look" again, causing Mark to realize his location. He sighed, lowered his hands and looked out the window. The clouds were angry and dark.

"Why Brenda, why?" he whispered to the clouds. *I hope she's not dead.*

Mark dreaded the idea of talking to Tony.

He wanted to be with Kaitlyn. *She needed me, and I wasn't there for her. Carina, where are you? Are you in trouble? Kidnapped?*

After a few hours, an announcement came: "This is your Captain speaking. We are ahead of schedule and will land in Austin shortly. We hope you enjoyed your flight with us today."

The clouds gave way to clear sky, the landscape became clearer, and buildings took shape as the plane descended. Pain shot through Mark's shoulder after the wheels hit the ground. The craft slowed, and the airport terminal came into view. This wasn't the victorious return he had planned.

The plane came to a stop. Mark waited for everyone to leave the aircraft, then removed his bag from the overhead compartment and followed the group out and into the airport. A few people bumped into him, sending more pain through his shoulder and arm.

Mark struggled to get his luggage off the rotating baggage handling belt. Every step brought pain as he rolled his luggage out of the airport. He considered calling Kaitlyn for a ride but dismissed the thought after exiting the building. A new sense of, "I'm okay to drive home," came over him. *She could be at work.* He was a Special Forces Commander, and he could do this. With his luggage, he walked to his car.

After his luggage was in the trunk, Mark tapped his i-phone, drew up favorites and hit Tony's number.

"Tony, this is Mark Steele. I wish I had better news for you." Mark could hear the fear in Tony's voice.

"Go on."

"I had her, and we were exiting the building," Mark said. "I'll shorten the story — they got the jump on me and took Brenda." He couldn't bring himself to tell Tony, the reason he didn't have Brenda, was because of her actions.

"What happened to her?"

"I'm sorry, but they have her. I called the police. You see, I was..." Mark stopped, felt his shoulder, and reconsidered his words. *I should have told him in person.* After several seconds of silence, Mark took a deep breath. "I'm sorry." He paused.

"You'll try again? Right?"

Several seconds passed. "I'm not. I can't."

"Please find Brenda."

Finally, Mark said he'd consider it and ended the call. He maneuvered himself into the car, put the vehicle in gear with his good arm, and traveled home. The journey felt like it wouldn't end. Exhaustion, jet lag, pain, Carina, and Brenda were colliding at one intersection. He felt himself losing control. *I'm trained. Right? Then act like it.*

Relieved that he missed the rush hour, he pulled into his driveway after thirty minutes. Mark knew the signs of shock, clammy skin, fast pulse, and nausea. He had all three. After opening his car door, he stopped, realizing how stupid it was to drive home. Three minutes later, he stepped out of the car and went to the front door.

Inside the house, Kaitlyn met him and gave him a hug, causing pain to shoot down his shoulder into his arm. The hug was the tipping point.

"Mark, what happened to you?" She saw the hole in his jacket and pulled it back. "Your shoulder, it's bleeding."

Mark felt himself getting weaker. "I need to sit."

Everything spun. In his training, he knew he could endure an injury, provided he had a goal to finish. But also knew without a mission his pain threshold would be unrestrained. His pain level was quickly reaching ten, and if he didn't sit soon, he'd fall.

Kaitlyn helped him to the couch. "Mark, I should take you to..."

PART 3

Chapter 38

I n the hospital, Mark reached for Kaitlyn's hand. She pulled away. "Kate, are you okay?" An occasional beep sounded from the equipment near Mark's bed.

He's asking me if I'm okay? He collapsed. I should be the one asking him that question. Or do I want to know? Kaitlyn backed away and leaned against the wall, refusing to look at Mark.

A minute later, the doctor entered. "I see you're awake." He placed his stethoscope on Mark, who flinched.

Kaitlyn stared at the doctor.

After removing the stethoscope, the doctor placed it in his pocket. "The bullet went through muscle tissue, missing anything that would cause permanent damage. It'll heal."

Kaitlyn moved to the end of the bed. Her facial muscles tightened. *Did he say bullet? Was he shot?*

Mark slightly raised his hand.

No way Mark. Kaitlyn shook her head. Mark lowered his hand.

"There's a slight infection. Antibiotics will take care of that. We'll get you bandaged and send you on your way." The doctor shifted his eyes between Kaitlyn then Mark. "I'm curious. How did this happen?"

Mark lowered his head, embarrassed, a rare occurrence for him.

Kaitlyn cleared her throat. *Go ahead Mark, tell us how this happened.*

The doctor turned his attention to Kaitlyn.

After a deep sigh, she said, "I don't know."

The doctor checked Mark's pulse. "Your pulse is normal." He stepped back, crossed his arms. "So tell me, how..."

A police officer entered the room. The doctor left.

Mark's eyes widened. "Where's Carina?"

The police officer's radio sounded. He lowered the volume.

Why did Mark get shot? Why is there a police officer here? And why did the doctor leave the room?

The officer removed a notepad and pen from his pocket. "What's your relationship to the patient?"

Kaitlyn glanced at Mark. His eyes drew together, lines on his forehead became more pronounced. *At least, he's worried about his daughter.*

"I'm his wife."

"Your name, please."

Kaitlyn gave her name. He asked if she knew the cause of the gunshot wound.

"I don't."

As Mark's wife, why didn't she know what happened to her husband? How many people will ask that question? Her stomach churned.

The officer checked his notes then directed his attention back to Kaitlyn. "Didn't you call the ambulance?"

Her muscles constricted as her eyes fell upon his badge. She lowered them like a grade school child being scolded. "My husband came home and collapsed, so I called 911."

"Where was your husband?"

Everything felt like it was spinning out of control. *Please, I want to sit. Stop asking me questions.* "You'll need to ask him."

"I will ma'am, but please answer my questions."

Did she just disrespect a police officer? *Get it together Kaitlyn.* "He said he was in Tennessee."

"You say it like you don't believe it."

"No, I mean he was in Tennessee."

"Do you have any guns in your home?"

Does he think she shot him? Her heart beat faster. "No." *Did I say that convincingly?*

"Okay, ma'am. Please step into the hallway so I can speak with your husband. Alone."

Finally.

The interrogation probably only lasted a minute but felt like it would never end. As she left, her muscles relaxed. Any more questions and she wasn't sure she'd be able to control her emotions. She had dealt with enough with police stations and the police for a lifetime. In the hallway, she called Bob Hanson at the Ford Dealership. "Bob, this is Kaitlyn Steele. Did you send Mark on an assignment in Tennessee?"

She waited for an answer. *You're taking too long Bob.* "Are you there?"

"Kaitlyn, hello. Um, Yes, I sent him."

"Well, he got shot. What did you assign him?"

"Shot?"

"Yes, shot."

"Is Mark okay? Is he in the hospital?"

"Yes. It's only a minor wound. He'll be released soon."

"Tell Mark I'm thinking about him."

"I'll do that, but you still haven't answered my question. What did you assign him?" Kaitlyn looked to the floor and tapped her finger on her phone.

"Uh. Well." Bob coughed. "Excuse me. I hate to cut this short, but a customer just came in. Can I call you back?"

"No, that's okay." Her eyebrows knit together and her pulse raced as she ended the call. She punched in her mom's number. *Was he covering for Mark?* Kaitlyn tried to calm herself.

"Mom, do you have time to talk?"

"Sure. You sound upset. Are you okay?"

Kaitlyn cleared her throat, attempting to steady her voice. "I'm in the hospital with Mark."

"What happened?"

Kaitlyn paused. She didn't want to say the words. *Why was the hallway suddenly full? And why were they looking at her?* She turned toward the wall. "Gunshot wound."

"What? Shot? Is he going to be okay?"

Mom, please stay calm and help me through this. "Doctor says he'll be fine," Kaitlyn said. "And be released soon."

"How did it happen?"

"I don't know." Kaitlyn lowered her head and rested it on the wall. "A police officer is talking to Mark right now. He came home and collapsed, so I called the ambulance."

"I don't understand. How did he get home?"

"He drove from the airport to the house." Kaitlyn turned and leaned against the wall.

"Oh, my. Why did he do that?"

"Mark considers himself Superman."

"How are you and Carina?"

"Carina is in school."

"And you?"

Kaitlyn's hand shook. "I'm so angry with Mark, I can't stand to look at him. He called me at two this morning, from his car in Nashville. At two, Mom, at two."

A nurse looked up from the station, causing Kaitlyn to pause.

"Go on, take your time."

Kaitlyn lowered her voice. "Mark was acting strange on the phone which makes me wonder if he'd already been shot... I called Bob at the Ford Dealership. He's the one who assigns Mark to get repossessed cars. I asked Bob if he had sent Mark out on an assignment."

"And?"

"He avoided my question." Kaitlyn pushed the words from her mouth. Bob had been to their house several times when they barbecued. She trusted him, even recommended his dealership to her friends. Not anymore. "He's covering for Mark. There's only one reason."

"And you think Mark's cheating on you?"

"What other reason would there be?" Kaitlyn paused. "Sorry Mom, I'm upset. I didn't mean to yell."

"That's okay. Could he be involved in something illegal?"

"I suppose. I just don't know."

A minute passed. "The last time we talked, Carina had been arrested."

Relieved that her mom changed the subject, Kaitlyn continued, "Carina's been getting into trouble. She left the house in the middle of the night, but was in her room this morning."

"At least, she's home. Where did she go?"

"I don't know that either." Kaitlyn stared down the hall. A young girl entered a room. "There's good news. Carina's urinalysis came back negative. She didn't have drugs in her system."

"Oh, good. I was worried about that."

Kaitlyn wiped tears from her eyes then cleared her throat. "Mom, I can't handle it any longer. Can Carina and I stay with you and Dad?"

"When you were young, I left your father for a week."

Kaitlyn lowered herself to a sitting position against the wall.

"Yes, and I regret that choice. Please don't make the same mistake. Let me—"

"I can't take it anymore." Kaitlyn wiped the sweat from her forehead.

"Give Mark a chance to explain, but if you feel you need to leave, you're welcome to come here until you work things out."

Glancing at her watch, Kaitlyn realized the officer had been talking to Mark for over ten minutes. "Even if he explains it, I'm not sure I'll believe it."

"Kaitlyn?"

"Yes, Mom?"

"Please give yourself a few days. Let Mark explain his side of the story. Can you do that? It may be as bad as you think it is, but there may be something else going on you haven't thought about."

Kaitlyn remained silent for several seconds then stood when the officer exited the room. "I..." She waited for her mom to talk again.

"At least, wait until tomorrow and if you still want to leave, you're welcome to stay here. But I hope you work this out with Mark."

"Okay, Mom. I'll consider it. I love you. Bye."

***

Mark's shoulder hurt. The doctor's report didn't match the level of pain he felt. The police officer had asked many questions, causing the events of yesterday to become fresh in Mark's mind. He almost had Brenda, was shot, then lost her. He flew to Austin, then drove home. From the officer's expression, Mark wondered if his story was believable. He found it hard to believe himself.

Mark called for Kaitlyn—nothing. Twenty minutes later, she entered and turned away from him.

"I'm sorry," Mark said.

Kaitlyn spun toward Mark. "You're sorry!"

Mark's eyes widened.

"You come home and collapse. Why? Because of a gunshot!" Her cheeks reddened.

Pain shot through Mark as he adjusted. "I can explain."

"I hope so, and I hope you can explain what you were doing in Tennessee because Bob sure couldn't."

"Bob?"

"I called him."

"It's not his fault."

"Who's fault is it, Mark?"

"I haven't been truthful with you."

"You think?"

Mark pulled himself into a sitting position, more pain shot through his upper body. "Please sit down." He motioned toward the end of the bed.

Kaitlyn backed away. Turning away from Mark, she lowered her voice. "I called my mom and asked if Carina and I could stay with them for a while."

Mark tried to process her words. *Did she just say she's leaving?*

Kaitlyn cleared her throat.

"Carina? You told me —"

"She's at school."

"School? I caught an earlier flight and rushed home... And you didn't tell me?"

"You passed out, remember."

Silence.

"Where did she go?"

"Did you hear me? I'm leaving."

He softened his voice. "Why?"

She crossed her arms.

Mark took a deep breath. "Please... I can explain."

"Okay. Talk. But know this, the only reason I'm not packing our bags right now is because Mom asked me to give you a few days. I'm doing this for her, not you."

Mark rubbed the back of his neck. "I went to Tennessee, to do a rescue mission, to bring a young girl back home. I want you to believe that."

"You lied about it, and you're involved in something... maybe illegal. For all I know, a jealous husband shot you." Kaitlyn walked to her purse, pulled out a paper and handed it to him. "Explain this!"

Mark studied the credit card bill. "Where did you get this?"

"It was in your trash."

"I stayed there when I was in California."

"The hotel registered you as Mr. and Mrs. Steele. I wasn't with you Mark, remember?"

"It's a mistake." Why did he say it that way? "I mean—"

"No, Mark it's not! I called this number, and they said, and I quote, 'the room is registered to Mr. And Mrs. Steele.'" She handed Mark a second crumbled piece of paper.

A nurse walked in the room. By the look on her face, she had heard Kaitlyn yelling. "The doctor has cleared you. I'll get a wheelchair for you."

"I'd rather walk, thanks."

"The hospital prefers—"

"He said he'll walk." Kaitlyn's eyes narrowed.

"I'm sorry, but he can't be released unless he's wheeled out." The nurse handed Mark his clothes, then closed the curtain. "If you need anything press the red button." She left the room and returned with a wheelchair.

As Mark dressed, Kaitlyn's anger concerned him. In fact, it scared him. His gentle wife changed into a person Mark didn't know. The glare she shot at the nurse sent daggers into his heart. He shoved the discharge papers into his pocket and wondered if she would even talk to him.

***

Kaitlyn wheeled Mark to the car. When he talked, she remained silent, not wanting to spill her emotions in the hospital, at least any more than she had already. She added up in her head the number of people she'd recently snapped at. *The doctor, police officer, her mom, and then the nurse. It wasn't their fault she had a husband who was living a secret life.*

In the car she let loose. Tears flowing and red faced, she raised her voice. "Mark, you were shot. Shot! And you drove home. What were you thinking?"

"It wasn't that bad."

187

"Wasn't that bad! You collapsed, and I had to call an ambulance." Kaitlyn wiped her eyes and stared at the steering wheel. "I'll take you home. Then, I'll get Carina from school."

"Kate, I'm sorry. Please listen to me."

Kaitlyn turned. "Before you continue. I called that number, and you know who was on the phone?"

"Jackie?"

"You admit it. Are you having an affair?"

"What? No, nothing like that."

"You were with a woman in a motel room at night." Kaitlyn's pulse raced. What other answer was there?

"I wasn't with a woman."

"I heard you, Mark. You were pretending to be married."

"It was part of the plan. I was there to get her son."

Kaitlyn rolled her eyes. "Right."

"I swear, that's the truth. Listen, you can speak to Jackie yourself. She owns a restaurant downtown. If you talk to her, she will verify my story."

Silence.

"Here's what happened." In the hospital parking lot, Mark spent the next several minutes explaining the story of Jackie's son. "She'll tell you the same thing."

"You want me to see her? A woman you were with. At a motel." *Is he really suggesting this?*

"I wasn't... I mean I was there to get her son."

"So let me get this straight. You pretended to be married only to get her child from her ex-husband?" Kaitlyn's voice cracked.

"I still have the check she wrote." Mark removed his billfold, took it out and handed it to Kaitlyn.

Jackie Lane Kulp signed the check. Was this the truth? She hoped so, desperately. But it still didn't explain his gunshot wound. "This is crazy." She handed it back to him.

"It may be crazy, but it's true."

"And I suppose you were rescuing a child in Tennessee also?"

"Yes."

Kaitlyn started the car. If she didn't see this woman, she would continue to wonder. But if she visited her, would she know if the woman was lying? Covering up her part in the affair?

"I'm telling the truth."

"Please, let me think." *Why was he making life so complicated? First, Carina and now this.*

She wished her mom would have told her to come over now. But she didn't. She said to let Mark explain. Kaitlyn lowered her voice. "Where's the restaurant?"

She drove in silence, her eyes straight ahead. Irritated at the car in front of her, she honked her horn and dared Mark to say a word. Except for directions, he remained silent. If Jackie was covering for Mark, Kaitlyn hoped she'd be able to see through her story. God help her if she was messing around with her husband. Then she felt stupid. Like she would really do anything to this woman.

At the restaurant, Kaitlyn parked in front. "Stay in the car."

"Are you sure?"

Kaitlyn shot him a look, exited the car and walked into the restaurant. She rehearsed her first line. *Are you having an affair with my husband?* No, that wouldn't be good. She tried the second line, *How do you know Mark Steele?* Not good either.

At the cash register, Kaitlyn hit the bell. *What if Jackie's a psycho?* Kaitlyn dismissed the thought when a well-dressed woman walked her direction.

"May I help you?"

"I'm Kaitlyn Steele. Are you Jackie Lane Kulp?"

"Yes."

"I'd like to talk to you."

"Steele? Are you Mark's wife?"

She knows he's married? "Yes."

"You have a wonderful husband. Let's go to my office."

Kaitlyn followed Jackie through the kitchen to a small room. From the back of Jackie's head and the way she walked, Kaitlyn saw a self-assured woman. They entered, and Jackie shut the door. Kaitlyn glanced around, her gaze landing on a torn photo of a woman holding a small child.

Jackie sat behind the desk. "Please sit. How may I help you?"

Kaitlyn sat. Maybe Mark should be here. She rubbed her hands together and made eye contact with Jackie. "That picture, is he your son?"

Jackie picked up the photo. "Yes...I ripped my ex-husband's picture out of it."

"How long have you had this restaurant?"

Jackie's eyebrows knitted together. "Over ten years."

"Do you have any other children?"

"I have one son."

"What's his name?"

"Mark knows all those details. I don't understand."

"My husband hasn't told me anything about you or your situation," Kaitlyn said. "Until twenty minutes ago."

Jackie's eyes widened. "You don't think—"

"I don't know what to think."

"Your husband is a great man, a trained professional."

Kaitlyn shifted in her seat. What was that look in Jackie's eye? Was it admiration? Or something else? "I heard you talking to Mark—on the phone."

"When?"

"Late one night, I called your number, and you answered. Mark was with you. Something about being married on your way to Phoenix."

Jackie looked confused.

"I found a crumbled piece of paper near Mark's desk, had your name and number on it."

Jackie stood and pulled a chair closer to Kaitlyn and sat. "That's all true. It was part of the plan should we get caught. He left me in the motel room. Alone."

Kaitlyn took a deep breath and attempted to steady her hands.

"Trust me, he didn't touch me. The only thing your husband did for me was to find my child."

"That's what Mark told me." Kaitlyn wiped perspiration from her forehead. "You have a good man."

"Did he ever mention me?"

"Yes, more than I wanted to hear, if I'm being honest. You have a teen daughter. Her name starts with a C or a K."

"Carina."

"Yes, Carina. And you have a part-time job as a secretary. Trust me, he loves you and your daughter."

Kaitlyn repositioned herself.

"I wish my ex-husband were half the man as Mark Steele."

Kaitlyn listened as Jackie complained about her ex-husband. After a few minutes, Kaitlyn interrupted. "Excuse me, how did you find my husband, anyway?"

"I'm sorry. You came to talk about Mark, and here I am, talking all about my ex-husband. My lawyer, he gave me Mark's contact information."

"When did you first call Mark?"

With the date and time, Kaitlyn made the calculations. Jackie had called before Tracker and Gunner left for the airport. So far everything was adding up.

"Mark's an incredible guy. He backed Robert—that's my ex-husband—down when he flashed a gun."

Gun? Kaitlyn had heard enough and wanted to leave, but Jackie kept talking. Not wanting to be rude, Kaitlyn sat for several more minutes. When she realized this woman wouldn't stop, Kaitlyn stood. "Thank you."

Jackie stood and embraced Kaitlyn. The hug lasted too long. It felt awkward.

Jackie walked to the door and opened it. "You and your husband are welcome here anytime. The meals are on me."

Kaitlyn nodded and walked out of the restaurant. She could never eat in this place. It seemed as if a thousand ants were crawling over Kaitlyn's skin. She wondered, did Jackie ever hug Mark? Had she ever tried to turn their relationship into something more? No, don't go there. The point that mattered was...Mark hadn't been unfaithful to her. That's what mattered. Hold on to that. But then...why did Mark lie to her? Not just once or twice, but a lot. How could she ever trust a man who lied so often, and with such ease?

Chapter 39

Kaitlyn and Mark drove for several miles in silence. Had Mark uttered a sound, she'd be upset. After ten minutes, Kaitlyn saw a restaurant they'd been to a few weeks ago. It was one of her favorite places. "I believe you."

"Thank you. I would never do that to you."

"Jackie said you left her at the motel room—alone."

"I went to the beach. That's where I called you."

"Why, Mark? Why couldn't you tell me the truth?" Kaitlyn brushed away a tear, occasionally glancing at him.

"I didn't intend to hurt you. I was trying to protect you."

"Well, it felt nothing like protection" She was glad there was no mistress but, still, Mark had a secret life, and it didn't include her. She stopped at a red light. From the corner of her eye, she watched a couple walking on the sidewalk. Would she and Mark ever walk hand in hand like that? A horn sounded. She went through the intersection.

"I have more to explain."

Kaitlyn rolled her eyes. "I don't want to hear it unless it's the truth. I can't take any more of your *protection* or secrecy."

Mark spent the rest of the travel time telling Kaitlyn a drawn out and convoluted tale that began with Joe in California and ended with Brenda in Nashville.

Kaitlyn parked in their driveway. "I'll pick up your prescription then get Carina from school. And I guess I better stop and get something for supper." She faced forward as she spoke. Mark touched her hand. She moved it higher on the steering wheel, away from him.

***

Mark paced in his office. The weight of her words, "I'm leaving," burdened him like a backpack full of rocks. After explaining everything to her, he had tried to get a visceral reading, but Kaitlyn's face remained blank. He needed to do something and quick. He couldn't face life without his wife and daughter. For the next hour, Mark reviewed his options. Thoughts about Carina and her rebellion added to the tension. Get that situation under control and he'd improve his relationship with Kaitlyn. Right? Maybe he could paint the living room like he and Kaitlyn had discussed. No, to do that he'd have to wait until his arm healed. He needed a solution he could put into action right now.

Pacing between his desk and window, Mark rehearsed how he would deal with Carina. He watched the clock. *What's taking Kate so long?* He wanted to talk to Carina in the car together, but Kaitlyn made it clear she didn't want him there. As he was about to sit, he heard the car pull in. *Kaitlyn and Carina must be home now.*

Mark walked to the office entrance. "Carina come here please." He took a deep breath. This could work.

"I have a lot of homework."

"Come here." It was louder than he intended. He softened his voice. "Please."

Carina, dressed in black, stopped near the office door. Kaitlyn stood behind Carina.

His nose flared. "Sit down." He motioned toward the couch.

Carina glared. "I'd rather stand."

Mark glanced at Kaitlyn, then back to Carina. "Okay, stand."

She sat, looked at the ceiling and crossed her legs.

Mark looked at the empty spot next to Carina in attempts to calm himself. He rubbed his mouth. "What's going on with you?" He perched on his desk.

Carina's mouth tightened. She crossed her arms.

Mark stared at her. "I have a daughter who doesn't care if she scares her mother."

"I'm not the one who doesn't care, Dad." Carina drew out the title and stood up.

"Sit down."

"No, not with you screaming at me. I hate you! I hate this house! I hate my life!"

Mark wanted to drag his daughter back to the chair and let her have it. But that's the kind of thing his Dad would have done to him. Instead, Mark looked at Kaitlyn, then Carina, and softened his voice. "Please sit."

Carina's pupils narrowed as she leaned forward.

It's not working. If Carina exploded again, this room would be a toxic mess. The look of pure anger on Kaitlyn's face weakened him even more. And it was aimed at him, not Carina.

But Carina didn't say a word. She got up, left the room and stomped upstairs.

Mark took a deep breath and released it. "We'll work everything out." He wasn't sure any longer.

"Right." Kaitlyn turned to leave then stopped. Facing away from him, she said, "I'll put the food on the table for you and Carina. I need time to think. I'll see you later."

A minute later, the front door opened, then slammed. Never in their seventeen years of marriage had Kaitlyn left the house in anger. They'd always worked out their disagreements. Mark wondered if that was even possible anymore.

Loud music started playing upstairs. It increased Mark's headache. He wanted to give Carina time to cool down. Who was he kidding? He needed time to control himself.

In the dining room, he removed the Chinese boxes from the sack. Lemon chicken, garlic pork, fried rice, and egg rolls. If Kaitlyn had been here, the food would be in bowls. But she wasn't here. Mark sat and stared at the Chinese lettering. Everything went wrong. *How?*

Brenda was now a distant memory. It seemed like months since the gunshot wound, yet it was only a few days.

He walked to the bottom of the stairs and yelled above the music. "Carina, supper time."

Back at the table, he scooped food from each box onto his plate. After dipping an egg roll into the spicy mustard sauce, he took a bite and hoped Kaitlyn wouldn't be gone too long. He needed to talk to her. And needed to know if he still had a marriage.

With his food half eaten, Mark thought of something. What if Carina tries to leave her room? She could get out her window, onto the roof, and sneak away. He ran to the garage, opened a drawer and took out a latch and padlock. He had planned on attaching it to the outside shed, now it would be for her window.

On his mental shopping list, Mark added a door buzzer, so if she left her room, it would sound.

***

Kaitlyn had determined to talk, possibly work it out, with Carina. But Mark confronted Carina first. *He always has to fix things. Our daughter isn't an object that needed to be fixed.* She needed to be loved, and Kaitlyn needed love too.

Was it anger? Fear? Or something else? Whatever the emotion, she was at her breaking point. What felt like twenty different feelings were congregating at one intersection, and none yielded. But there was one unanswered question that bothered her the most. *Why didn't Mark trust me?* Was she the problem? No, she knew that wasn't it. It was Mark.

The radio station played a love song. Kaitlyn shut it off.

Even if he wasn't having an affair, he hadn't been honest. Isn't that like an affair? Mark hid a part of his life and disguised it as protecting her. He wasn't protecting her. At least it didn't feel like protection. She gripped the steering wheel tighter, then slowed because of the car in front of her.

Getting through the weekend became Kaitlyn's goal. *Monday would be better.* She wasn't sure how long she and Carina would stay at her parent's home, maybe a long time. Maybe forever. At least the drive to work would be shorter. But Carina would need a ride to school. Could her mom help with that? The traffic stopped. After Mark's discharge from the military, Kaitlyn figured she wouldn't have to worry about his safety any longer. That all changed when the doctor said, "gunshot wound."

She lowered her windows and eased up on the brake, inching forward. An officer directed traffic. It appeared two cars had a head on collision. An ambulance was at the scene, along with several police cars and a fire truck.

The nightmares of the days she'd spent in Guam and Balboa hospital with Mark had dimmed over the years. But with Mark's gunshot wound and this accident, the images returned in vivid color.

The officer directed her to turn left, but not before Kaitlyn saw someone being loaded into an ambulance. At least the cover wasn't over the person's head. Kaitlyn pulled far left, not wanting to run over any glass. In a small way, she understood soldiers having flashbacks of combat. Her imagination put Mark on the stretcher being placed into the ambulance.

Stress and lack of food worked together to make her anxiety worse. She was tired and hungry. A mile away from the accident, she spotted a McDonalds. Maybe a chicken sandwich would settle her stomach. The Chinese food sounded good, but not with Mark.

Ten minutes later, the sandwich had done its job. But the hot fudge sundae didn't improve her emotions like she'd hoped. After a couple more hours of driving, she noticed the gas gauge nearing a quarter and turned toward home.

Chapter 40

B illy prepared to make a peanut butter and jelly sandwich. He wanted to disappear before his old man arrived. The front door opened and closed. *Darn.*

Billy smelled the alcohol once his dad stepped into the kitchen.

"What are you doing?"

"Uh…uh…"

"Spit it out. You getting stupid on me?"

Billy lowered his eyes. "No." He finished spreading peanut butter on his bread.

"Give me that. I'm hungry."

Billy gave him the sandwich and pulled out more bread.

Staggering away, the drunk turned and spoke, food shooting from his mouth. "This tastes like crap." Reaching out to the counter, his hand slid in a glob of peanut butter. "Why can't you keep this place clean?" He kicked a beer can across the floor.

"I will." Billy dropped the bread and reached for the broom. He drew a deep breath and prepared for a slap in the face.

"Give me that." He dropped his sandwich and took hold of the broom handle. "What are you going to do, boy?"

Billy backed up. His dad came at him, jabbing him with the broom.

"Come on, boy. You're not a man, you're a scared kid." He dropped the broom and knocked Billy to the floor.

He scrambled back on all fours until he pushed against the wall. Blood flowed from his nose. "You're a coward. I can't stand to look at you." Billy shot up and grabbed a butter knife.

His dad laughed. "What, are you going to spread peanut butter on me?"

Billy tossed the utensil, opened the drawer, and picked up a sharper one. Back against the wall, knife extended, Billy scooted around the kitchen until he reached the door. His dad tried to take the knife and cut his finger. Vulgar words filled the air. Billy dropped the knife, shot out the door and stopped behind a tree.

"You okay?" A neighbor boy, younger than Billy, stepped closer.

Billy lifted his head and wiped the tears from his eyes. He grabbed the boy's shirt. "You best not tell anyone about this. Or you'll be sorry." He pushed him backward.

The boy fell to the ground. "No...I won't tell anyone." He jumped to his feet and ran down the sidewalk.

Billy, red-faced, raised his fist. "I hate that man. I should kill him."

He rubbed blood from his nose onto his shirt. A new determination rose within him.

***

At the voice of her dad, Carina turned up the music. She was hungry, but more than that, she was angry. No one believed her. It wasn't her fault. Falling on the bed, she pushed her face into the pillow.

After several minutes, her phone chimed—a text from Billy. He was asking her to run away with him. Before she could reply, "no," the door opened.

Her dad entered. He looked mad. "Carina, didn't you hear me? Supper is ready."

She sat up and tossed the phone onto her bed. "You didn't knock. This is my room."

"I want to talk to you without this becoming a shouting match. Please turn down that music."

"You always think the worst of me. I did nothing wrong."

Mark lowered the volume. "You left the house in the middle of the night, you skip school, get caught with drugs and vandalize. And you're arrested. Help me understand how you didn't do anything wrong."

Carina stood. "Hey, why are you putting a lock on my window?"

Mark continued to install the latch. "You're not going to leave in the middle of the night, worrying your mother. You're grounded until further notice. After school, you come straight home. I'm also putting a buzzer on your door."

"You can't do that."

"Yes, I can." With the latch secured, lock in place, Mark slipped the key in his pocket. "Come downstairs for supper." He left.

Carina screamed and threw herself on the bed. After several minutes, she saw a suitcase in the closet, retrieved it, and placed it on her dresser. *I'll show him.*

After filling the suitcase with clothes and putting it back in the closet, Carina sent Billy a text. "Okay. I'll do it."

***

Mark went to the dining room. That didn't go so well, but at least Carina couldn't sneak out of her room. He returned to his food, sat and wondered how to get his house under control. The clock seemed to tick louder and move slower. Mark pushed around the fried rice, lined up the chicken, and stared at it for a long time. With his appetite gone, he shoved his food toward the center of the table. After an hour of sitting, he stood and went to the window. Squirrels played in the trees. Mark imagined Carina on the swing set.

For an hour, he revisited the good times they had as a family—vacations, camping, and Disneyland. Yet he couldn't recall any good recent family memories. He sighed deeply. A setting sun told him at least two hours had passed since he last spoke to Carina, and she still hadn't come down. At this point, he might as well leave her alone.

Mark heard a car door slam, then the side door open. He called for Kate. She didn't answer.

He put his dishes in the sink, wiped the table, and went to their bedroom. He would give her an update on Carina.

Kate was in the bathroom, so he perched on the bed. After an hour of waiting, he undressed, got under the covers, and stared at the ceiling. A few minutes later Kate came into the room and entered the bed—in her clothes. His countenance dropped. He glanced at her. She always faced him while sleeping, but not tonight. *Should he talk to her?* No. He didn't want to suffer rejection again. His mind did not release him to sleep until after midnight.

Nightmares woke him several times throughout the night. The gun, the defiance, Abu Sayyaf, blended together in his dreams. Brenda, Carina, and now Kate continued to play in his mind.

In one of the dreams, a voice from his past haunted him. A door opened, and a tall uniformed man entered. Mark found his feet locked and couldn't move them. He struggled to get free, attempted to stand up to the powerful authority but couldn't.

"Help me!" Mark shot up, soaked in sweat and shifted his feet to the floor.

Kaitlyn opened her eyes. "What's the matter?"

"Horrible nightmare."

"You scared me."

"I'm going to go check on Carina." Mark left the bed and returned a minute later. Kaitlyn, back in the same position, faced away from him. As he drifted to sleep, Mark attempted to take her hand, but she pulled away.

***

Under the covers, anger continued to boil in Kaitlyn. She thought about sleeping on the couch but rejected the idea. This was her bed. She hated sleeping in her clothes, something she'd never done before, but she wanted Mark to know how deeply he'd hurt her. It felt so unnatural to sleep on her right side, but she would not face Mark. Sleep finally arrived, but only after thoughts of betrayal darkened her mood further.

In the morning, she woke to Mark knocking on Carina's door. Kaitlyn stood behind him. He entered the room.

"Wake up. I'm taking you to school," Mark said.

Carina rolled over and rubbed her eyes. "Why?"

Mark waited for Carina to sit up then left the room. He nearly ran into Kaitlyn. "I didn't see you standing there. Good morning."

"Hi." Kaitlyn stepped back when he tried to kiss her. She walked to the bathroom.

Several minutes later, Carina knocked on the bathroom door. "Why is Dad taking me to school?"

"Ask him, he's downstairs."

Kaitlyn opened the door. "Do you want something for breakfast?"

"I'll eat at school, and I'll walk."

"Talk to Dad."

Carina stomped to her bedroom and slammed the door. "I wanna walk."

Kaitlyn went to the kitchen. "Carina's determined to walk. Just so you know, she's wearing all black."

***

Mark waited at the front door. Taking charge brought him a little relief. He hoped it was enough to win his wife back. A few minutes later Carina appeared.

"Dad, I'm walking." She moved past him.

Mark restrained himself. "I'll drive you to school."

Carina spun around and put her hands on her hips.

"Get in the car."

Carina stomped to the vehicle and entered.

Mark glanced at his daughter as they traveled to school. *Why is she so rebellious? Was she on drugs?* He and Carina use to be close. "Carina, I'd like you to think about your future. Drugs can mess you up and put you in jail." For several blocks, Mark tried to help his daughter.

A block away from the school, Carina interrupted him. "Drop me off here."

"I'll stop in front of the school."

Carina rolled her eyes.

He stopped at the entrance. "Have a good day." Not a word nor a look from Carina. He didn't expect it, but it still stung. His eyes followed her as she walked into the school.

Maybe Mark had read too many cases of abducted children, but as he drove away, he feared Carina doing something stupid, something that would jeopardize her freedom. Then Mark would be like Tony — with a missing daughter.

Chapter 41

After returning home, Mark searched for Kaitlyn. He looked in the kitchen for a note—nothing; in the garage for her car—not there.

Back in the kitchen, with his iPhone in hand, Mark texted her. Kaitlyn's cell phone chirped nearby. He rolled his eyes, then poured himself a cup of coffee.

Half way through the dark liquid, Kaitlyn's phone played music. Mark answered it, knowing it was Elaine, Kaitlyn's mother.

"Hello."

There was a pause. "Mark is that you?"

"Good morning, Elaine."

"Good morning. I was expecting Kaitlyn."

"She's not here. As usual, she forgot her phone," Mark said. "Do you want to leave a message?"

Elaine cleared her throat. "Mark, do you mind if I'm blunt with you?"

"I... I guess."

"Kaitlyn is heartbroken."

"I know. Carina is going through—"

"Mark, it's not Carina. Your daughter has little to do with Kaitlyn's unhappiness."

He locked his eyes on the counter.

"Mark, you're the reason for Kaitlyn's sadness."

"I don't see how—"

"Let me finish. Kaitlyn feels betrayed." Elaine paused. "She believes you're having an affair. Are you?"

Mark took a deep breath. Is she really asking me this? "We cleared that up already. It was a misunderstanding. I rescue abducted children."

"That's commendable, but why didn't you trust Kaitlyn by telling her?"

"She may not trust me, but I trust her. I didn't tell her because I wanted to protect her." He clenched his fists.

"Or did you want to protect yourself?"

"What do you mean?"

"Maybe it was easier to manipulate the situation, so you didn't have to consider Kaitlyn's feelings. Or maybe you didn't involve her because you didn't want her to interfere, or try to stop you."

"Manipulate is a strong word."

"It is, but could it be true?"

Mark relaxed his hands. Is that what he was doing? Manipulating the situation? "You have me questioning my motives."

"Good! And in honesty, doing something this big all on your own… well… "

Mark pressed the phone closer.

"…You robbed me of an opportunity to pray for the people you're helping. Not just me, but Kaitlyn, too. You don't think she might care about children in danger as much as you?"

"I never thought of it that way."

"That's the problem with secrets, we don't consider the feelings of others. But that still doesn't answer my question."

Mark tried to remember her question. "Which is?"

"Why don't you trust each other? You said you trust her, but if that were really true, you would have involved her in something this big and this important to you."

"I guess… I don't know why." Irritation crept into his voice.

"Did you keep secrets from your wife when you were in the Special Forces?"

"Yes, but what has that to do with this?"

"Was Kaitlyn okay with those secrets?"

His eyebrows drew together. "Yes."

"You were away for days, sometimes weeks, and you didn't tell her where you were at. And yet she trusted you?"

"Yes."

"So why doesn't she trust you now?"

Mark fixed his eyes on the counter for several seconds. "We're not as close now as were then?" He waited for her to continue.

"Another person doesn't have to be involved for it to feel like an affair."

He shook his head. "I'm confused."

"Kaitlyn has felt distant from you for a long time."

"Why didn't she tell me?"

Elaine again cleared her throat. "She didn't tell me either, but I know my daughter. My guess is you started this secret life when you first moved to Austin."

"Yes, how did you know?"

"Like I said, I know my daughter. That's when I saw a change in her. I asked Kaitlyn about it, but she's always been a private person, not wanting to share her emotions, even with me. But I knew."

"Knew what exactly?"

"That she didn't feel loved anymore."

Mark sighed. This was making sense. He had hurt his wife.

"So, when she discovered you were living a double life, well, she thought the worst. And since, in your words, you weren't that close, it had to be another woman. In her mind, that is."

"But I'm not having an affair. Kaitlyn believes me now. She even checked the situation out. Yet she's still angry."

"Like I said it doesn't take another person for it to feel like an affair."

"I'm not following you."

"You put something else above your marriage, and it took Kaitlyn's place."

Mark stayed silent, attempting to sort out what he heard. Realization hit him. He had built his own world and put Kate on the outside. If his mind had been a stadium, every light just turned on. He sighed deeply.

"Mark are you still there?"

"I'm here."

"Did she tell you she wants to leave?"

"Yes, and I'm trying to make everything right to keep that from happening." A wave of weakness hit Mark. He pulled out the stool and sat.

"The only reason she hasn't left already is because I asked her to give you a little more time."

Mark swallowed hard.

"If you don't do something soon, though, you'll lose your family." She hesitated. "I can tell you a solution if you'd like to hear it."

Nothing I'm doing is working. "Sure."

"Return to your first love, God, and with Kaitlyn."

"I'm just not getting it. Would you explain what you mean?"

"Remember the first days with your relationship with the Lord?"

"It was a long time ago, but yes. I loved reading the Bible and prayer."

"And the first days when you met Kaitlyn?"

Mark paused and smiled. "That sounds so simple."

"Kaitlyn loves you very much. It's hidden beneath a skin of hurt. You must show her and Carina they are both the most important people in your life."

I hurt her. The words played like a dirge.

"Mark, I'll pray for you and Kaitlyn. And Mark?"

"Yes?"

"If Kaitlyn insists on coming here, please let her. She may need a little space."

"I'm not sure I could do that."

"Remember, love never controls."

Mark's muscles tensed. "I'll do my best."

"That's all I'm asking. Goodbye, Mark."

"Goodbye." After placing the phone on the counter, Mark went to his office and sat behind his desk. He had excluded his wife from his life, causing her to feel totally unloved. He put his hands to his face. "I've been selfish and self-serving."

And how had he treated his daughter? Like a soldier? No wonder Carina had become rebellious. He remembered several occasions when Kate had tried to warn him. The realization thundered down on Mark. Why did it take Kate threatening to leave for him to understand?

He had to show Kate he loved her. And he needed to become a father to Carina, not a drill sergeant. Finally, the source of his problems had become apparent. The solution would be difficult and he would only have a few days, because Kate planned to leave on Monday.

Mark made some calls, then showered, and dressed in a suit and tie. He returned to his office and waited to implement phase one of his plan.

An hour later, the side door opened. He quickly left the office. "Kate?"

She closed the door. "Yes?"

"Carina's at school. You're sure she can't ditch class?"

"She has in-school suspension until the end of the week."

"Listen… I don't like you being angry at me." He waited for an answer. Not happening. "I'd like to show you that I love you."

"That's nice."

"I've been thinking about when we were dating."

She turned.

"Can I take you out for lunch?"

"Mark, I'm tired."

"And probably hungry. Please."

"I really don't want to go out."

"I don't blame you. I wouldn't want to be around me either."

Kaitlyn lowered her eyes and walked to the steps.

"Please say something, I'm taking the advice of your mother." His voice cracked, and he attempted to steady it.

Kaitlyn stopped and turned. "My mom?"

"You left your phone, and I answered it."

"She called?"

"Yes. She said things I didn't want to hear, words like *manipulating and controlling*." Mark paused.

"*Manipulating* describes my feelings."

Mark felt the urge to defend himself but heard the words "stand down" shouting inside his head. He needed to listen.

"When you came home and collapsed, I figured you had a heart attack. Then I found out about the gunshot wound, well I didn't… Yes, I did. I believed you had an affair. It's something I've been wondering about for a long time and tried to convince myself you'd never cheat on me." Kaitlyn pulled a Kleenex from her pocket and wiped her nose. "I'm hurt, angry and confused. After talking to Jackie, I felt foolish. She told me how lucky I am to have you. That you're dedicated, and she wished she could have a loyal man like you. But, I don't feel lucky. I wish I did. Instead, I feel rejected, lied to and betrayed."

Mark lowered his head. "I'm sorry."

"Saying sorry, won't fix it. I'm going to need a little more than words."

"I didn't want to tell you what I was doing because of the danger involved." Mark's face softened as he took her hand. She withdrew it and lowered her face. "I was wrong. I should have included you."

Kaitlyn looked at him. "You don't trust me… and that hurts. I'm starting to wonder… Do we have enough to keep our marriage going? I'm not sure you even love me."

Mark flinched, a rare tear ran down his cheek. "I do love you."

"You have a strange way of showing it."

"I'll prove it to you."

"I'm not sure you can."

"No more secrets, Kaitlyn. I thought rescuing kids was my mission in life, but no longer. Not if it means losing my family." Silence hung in the air.

Kaitlyn stirred. "You'll stop?"

"Yes."

Kaitlyn sat on the step.

"Would you, at least, give me a chance?"

With a raised eyebrow, Kaitlyn crossed her arms. "You can't give a command and make everything okay. You lied to me. Maybe not about another woman. But still, everything you've been doing, everything you've been telling me about your work. It's all lies." In a lower voice, she continued. "I don't know whats the truth is anymore. I'm giving you a few days because Mom asked me to. I'll give you till Monday."

"Then I have a few days. Would you wear your purple dress and the necklace you wore at the wedding? I'd love to take you on a date."

"You remember the necklace?"

Mark nodded. "I want to relive the early days of our relationship and earn your trust again."

Kaitlyn stood. "Where are we going?"

"Italian restaurant."

Kaitlyn nodded.

"Great! As soon as you're ready, we'll go back to the beginning."

"You're not making any sense." She turned and kept walking up the stairs.

Looking in the mirror, Kaitlyn positioned the small heart-shaped diamond necklace. Dainty and silver, it had been a gift along with an engagement ring when Mark had proposed. Did he still love her? He insisted that he did, but was it true?

Rescuing children, on the whole, was a good thing. But why did it bother her? He said he'd give it up. Could he, really? Or would he just hide it better?

She had heard of a pastor's wife who'd left her husband because he neglected her and cared more about the church. Back then, Kaitlyn didn't understand how a minister's wife would get jealous of a ministry. Today, Kaitlyn understood.

She pulled the purple dress from the closet and removed the plastic cover still on it from the dry cleaners. The last time she'd worn it, they had celebrated their wedding anniversary, nearly six months ago.

After dressing and styling her hair, she put on makeup, then perfume. A little on her neck, a dab on her wrists. She sat perched on the edge of the bed.

Did she want her marriage to work? Of course. Did she believe it could be saved? She wasn't certain. Was she being cold-hearted? Uncaring about abducted children? She shouldn't feel that way, but she did. *What's wrong with me?*

After fifteen minutes of trying to calm her conflicting emotions, Kaitlyn walked downstairs. "You're beautiful," Mark said.

She felt nothing. "Thanks."

He put his hand on the necklace. "This has many memories."

"Yes."

"I'm glad I asked you to marry me." Mark gazed into her eyes. She lowered them. He gently lifted her chin. "I know I hurt you. I was wrong, and this weekend I'm going to make it right."

It won't change anything. Kaitlyn moved his hand and stepped toward the door.

While driving to the restaurant, Mark struggled for the right thing to say. "Do you remember when I first called you Kate?"

"At the picnic, right after you threatened me with a water balloon." She remained face forward. A few seconds later she turned toward him. "Are you sure you're okay to drive? I mean does your arm hurt?"

"I'm good. There's a little pain, but I'm clear-minded." A mile down the road, Mark said, "When I first met you, I knew you were the one. I constantly thought about you and when you played impossible to get... well, I wanted you even more."

Kaitlyn suppressed a smile. *If only he would love me like he use to.*

"Why did you agree to marry me?"

For a few minutes, Kaitlyn relived those early days. "You wouldn't give up, and I fell in love with you."

"I'll prove I love you — again."

Could he? Ten minutes into the drive, silence filled the vehicle.

Chapter 42

An Italian woman, dressed in a white blouse and black pants set menus in front of them, then took their drink order. They sat at an outside table near a railing, enjoying the shade of a large umbrella. Close by, water flowed naturally over rocks. Birds chirped and sang little tunes.

Mark pushed his menu to the side. "Do you remember a place like this?"

She shook her head no.

"Doesn't this look like the restaurant I proposed to you in?"

"I suppose it does." Kaitlyn spoke softly.

A few seagulls landed near the water and moved on the sand. They watched the birds for a few minutes. The waitress brought their water.

Mark stirred in his chair. "I've caused you to doubt."

Kaitlyn took a drink and glanced at him.

"I didn't give up then, and I won't give up now."

She slightly smiled.

"Remember the walkie-talkie at work?"

"How could I forget? You embarrassed me."

When he first met her, Mark had wanted to get her attention. With the permission of her boss, Mark sent a walkie-talkie to her work site. He asked her to lunch and in front of all her co-workers, she said yes.

Mark took her hand. "Admit it, you liked it."

She didn't withdraw. "A little."

The waitress approached and placed a basket of breadsticks on the table. "Would you like to order?"

Mark moved his hand. "We'd like the lover's special." The waitress nodded and left.

"That's not on the menu."

"I called ahead and asked if it could be specially made."

"Just like that day." Kaitlyn's expression softened. "When I knew you loved me."

Mark waited. He was careful not to make things worse.

"You pursued me and made me feel special." Kaitlyn slightly uncomfortable dropped her gaze, and took a breadstick.

"And you don't feel special any longer?" Mark picked up a breadstick.

"No, I don't. And it also feels like…I don't know you anymore."

"If you allow me, I'll show you and Carina I can change."

"You can't be so strong with Carina. You need to learn how to win her heart. If you do that, it might turn your relationship with her around."

"Are you speaking for just Carina or yourself?"

"Both."

Mark motioned for two violinists. They played light music. He got down on one knee. "Kate, would you marry me, again?"

After several seconds, she slightly turned up the corners of her mouth. "You're making it hard for me to be mad at you."

Mark moved back to his chair and smiled.

Love songs floated in the air. After several minutes, when the food came, the violinists left. So did the seagulls.

"I have a weekend planned. You, me and Carina, then on Monday…"

The waitress interrupted. "Excuse me, would you like anything else?"

"No, thank you," Mark said.

"Weekend?"

As they ate their spaghetti and heart shaped meatballs from the same plate, Mark told Kaitlyn his plan. "I made reservations at a resort near Lake Austin Canal."

"Really?"

"Yes."

In sarcasm, she said, "We would have gone there last summer, but you changed it to California." Looking away she whispered, "Now I understand why."

To Mark, the air suddenly seemed heavier. He thought Kaitlyn would be excited about spending a weekend away. Instead, she had discovered their vacation to Disneyland had been a deception, a plan to meet Joe. "The resort has a spa, a swimming pool, and great food."

Kaitlyn pushed the plate toward Mark. "You can have the rest."

"You barely ate anything."

"I lost my appetite."

"Would you like something different?"

"No thanks." Another seagull landed. "California wasn't a family vacation. And that stuff you put in the car and took away my key…was that business?"

Mark nodded.

"Then you became depressed and cut your business trip short. Was that when you learned of Joe's death?"

Eyes downcast, Mark nodded again. As he finished his meal, he occasionally glanced at Kaitlyn. *I really hurt her.* Was this even fixable? Would he lose her? Each time he spoke, Kaitlyn nodded, but her eyes told Mark she wasn't interested.

Several minutes later, the waitress returned with the bill. Mark handed her his credit card.

On the way to the car, Mark asked, "Should I cancel the reservations?"

"Mark, this has been nice, but it's not —"

"Please, Kate… I'm sorry. I have a bad habit of interrupting you. Go on."

"A weekend away can't fix months or years of lying."

"I'll do whatever you say. If that means driving you to your parent's home, I'll do that. You don't have to wait for Monday."

Mark opened Kaitlyn door. She got in.

For awhile, Mark kept silent. He wondered whether she would end up packing for the resort or her mother's?

Ten minutes into the drive, Kaitlyn broke the silence. "Okay, I'll go along with this. But it doesn't mean I have to be happy."

"Deal… call it a second honeymoon." He kept quiet the remainder of the time fearful she may change her mind.

After the twenty minute drive, Kaitlyn exited the car. "I'll pack."

Mark followed her into the house. After she'd gone upstairs, he went to his office and called his mother-in-law.

"Thank you." After giving her the details, she gave him more advice.

"Mark, come here," Kaitlyn shouted from upstairs.

"Excuse me, Kate's calling." Mark ended the call and shot up the stairs. He found Kaitlyn in Carina's room.

"You need to see this." Kaitlyn stood beside Carina's bed with a suitcase in hand. "I found this in her closet, and it's full of her clothes."

Mark was shocked. The nightmare had suddenly become worse. "You think she's…" He swallowed hard. " …planning on running away?"

"You didn't tell her about your plans did you?"

"No." *I'm the reason she's*…Mark didn't want to finish the sentence, even if it was only to himself. "Am I really that bad?" He thought so considering both his wife and daughter didn't want to be with him any longer.

Mark sat on the edge of Carina's bed. When she was young, she would jump on his back, and he'd race through the hallway bucking like a horse. She'd squeal in delight. After several minutes, he'd drop her onto the bed.

Kaitlyn's voice broke into his memory. "Mark?"

"I'm sorry. You said something?"

"Never mind. I'll finish packing." Kaitlyn left the room.

As a young boy, Mark wanted his dad's approval but never received it. Instead, he got the back of his hand.

He recited Elaine's words. "Mark, I believe you care about your family, but it's like you're speaking French when they only understand English."

"What do you mean?"

"Speak the language of love in actions not in words. Show Kaitlyn and Carina you love them. Cause them to feel important again."

War broke out inside him. One part him wanted to take charge and command the situation with words. The other side took Elaine's words to heart and desired to show love. He couldn't ignore that Carina could runaway. No matter how much he tried to watch her, if she was determined to leave, she would. He needed to demonstrate both to his daughter and his wife he loved them and wanted them close to him. Hopefully, the weekend would show Kaitlyn. but how could he show Carina? After much thought, an idea came to him. Mark hoped it would be enough.

Chapter 43

A fter entering the school, Carina locked her gaze on the man in front of her, the Principal, Mr. Wimmington.
"Please come with me," he said.
"Again?"

In the hallway, students whispered to each other as Carina passed. Was there a huge zit on her forehead that everyone had to stare at it? They entered a classroom, two boys, one on each end of the room and a teacher in front.

"I thought yesterday was my last day of prison."

"It's called in-school suspension." The Principal directed his attention to Miss Kent. "Contact the office if you have any problems with any of these students."

"Yes, Mr. Wimmington."

After the principal had left, Carina dropped her books on a desk next to a boy with long black hair and a faded green shirt.

Miss Kent stood and pointed to a desk in the middle of the room. "Carina, sit over here, please."

She slowly picked up her books and went to the desk. Even though Miss Kent looked young, Carina knew this teacher wouldn't hesitate to call the principal. There were other teachers, mostly assistants, who were in their mid-twenties and were push-overs, but not Miss Kent. In the short time she'd been at the school, she already developed a reputation for being tough.

"I expect you to work on your assignments. You know the drill, you've been here before," Miss Kent said.

Yeah — too many days.

The kid with long black hair raised his hand.

"James?"

"I don't have a calculator. Can I go to my locker?"

"I have one right here." Miss Kent sat, removed a calculator from her drawer, and placed it on the end of her desk.

Carina opened a book and put the others under her desk. She intended to check in, sneak out, get her luggage, then meet Billy.

Those plans were postponed. She thought about leaving at lunch when the teacher was not looking, but she didn't think that would work. The school would call her parents, and they'd be waiting for her.

Instead of doing her assignment, she propped her head on her hands and closed her eyes. After all, she wasn't planning on attending school anymore after today.

Startled awake by hearing her name, she sat up and pretended to look at her history book. She glanced at the clock. Only thirty minutes had passed. "Excuse me, but are we going to get any food? I didn't eat breakfast."

The teacher looked up from her papers. "First, raise your hand and I'll call on you. Second, you've been here before, and you already know the answer."

If she had super powers, her eyes would have shot a laser hole at the teacher and set her desk on fire. Carina chuckled at the thought.

A shorthaired student raised his hand. "Can I go to the restroom?"

"I need to go also," Carina said, this time, her hand raised.

The teacher placed her papers on the desk and stood. "Everyone, to the bathroom."

"I don't have to go," the longhaired boy said.

Miss Kent sighed. "Go... Everyone."

Carina stayed in the restroom for five minutes. When she exited, the boys were already with the teacher. The hallways were vacant except for the janitor and a few students.

Back at her desk, her dad snaked his way into her thoughts. She wouldn't have to put up with him much longer. She pushed him from her mind and sketched a drawing of Billy. It wasn't that she liked Billy, but instead, viewed him as a way of escape. She hoped he wouldn't pressure her to "go further." She had made a vow to stay pure until marriage. That seemed like a long time ago and very old-fashioned. She'd have to re-think that. She erased Billy's nose and drew it again.

At noon, in the cafeteria, Carina nibbled at her lunch. While in school prison, she didn't get the choice of which line to go through. Miss Kent chose the main line, hamburger casserole. Yuck. Carina wanted the other line, cheeseburgers, and fries.

Part of her wanted to sneak away with Billy, the other part wanted to go home. The warring thoughts remained as she placed her tray of nearly uneaten food in the window, then followed Miss Kent and the two boys through the crowded hallways.

In the classroom, Carina pretended to work on her assignments, periodically checking the clock. When the final bell rang at 3:30, she rushed to her locker and put her books inside. *How can I get my suitcase out of the house?*

Carina walked down the hallway then slowed to a stop. A crowd of students stood near the front entrance. Something was going on outside. They stepped back when a man in a tuxedo, white gloves, and shiny black shoes entered the school. "I'm here for Carina Steele."

Was he saying her name? More trouble? The students looked around, some toward Carina. Standing next to tuxedo guy was the Principal. *Why is he smiling?*

"That's me." A recent movie scene flashed in her mind. A woman stood on a dark stage unknown until huge spotlights turned on. Carina realized many students were now staring at her.

Like Moses parting the Red Sea, the students stepped back, allowing her to pass through the crowd. She should slip amongst them and act like she hadn't heard her name. The Principal motioned her to the front door. She couldn't ignore him any longer. Carina moved through the on- lookers, toward the entrance.

Tuxedo guy hooked his arm. Stopping and standing like a statue, she took a deep breath.

"It's okay." Principal Wimmington placed his hand on her shoulder.

Realizing she had been holding her breath, she breathed.

Carina put her arm in Tuxedo's arm. Her skin tingled as they walked out of the building and stopped. The students poured out of the school and around the red carpet that ran from the entrance to the curb.

Her pulse raced. *What could this mean?*

"Your Father."

Her dad, wearing a suit and tie, walked toward her. A hush fell over the crowd. Even the birds weren't chirping, at least, Carina heard nothing. The sun seemed brighter. Like a movie camera zooming in, her dad's smile took center stage. She consciously closed her mouth, realizing it had been open. At each of his steps, her heart raced faster. He extended his hand, and she took it. Then like a speaker system being turned on, the sounds became clear again. Some shouts, but mostly whispers. Electricity soared through her.

"Carina, I've not been the father you deserve." He looked over to the Principal. "Mr. Wimmington has been kind enough to allow me to make a formal apology to you in front of your school."

Carina shifted her stand, not wanting to look up, not wanting to see all the eyes on her.

Mark lifted her chin. "This is embarrassing, I'm sorry. But this is something I need to do, in front of your school. I'm responsible for the path you've taken. I've been strong with you and pushed you away, not taking your feelings into consideration. This is the start of me changing. I was wrong, and I'm sorry."

What's happening? Dad's apologizing? He's never done that before. Is someone dying? Is he dying? He continued to speak, but the words turned fuzzy. She snapped out of her daze when he looped his uninjured arm though Carina's arm.

"Are you ready?"

Carina nodded. For what, she didn't know.

They walked arm and arm toward a large black vehicle. If Carina's feet were on the carpet, she couldn't tell. She could only feel a smile as large as the sky on her face.

He stopped at the limousine and turned toward her. "One day, I'll walk you down an aisle and give you to the man you'll spend your life with... But today you're my little girl."

He opened the door, and Carina looked back at the crowd who now moved closer. Without a thought, she waved her hand.

A loud cheer erupted out of the crowd. Carina spotted Sally. Was that a tear in her eyes? She felt horrible about the scratches on Sally's car, even though she didn't put them there. Clapping and whistling continued to flow from the students, who now moved closer to the limo.

As the celebration subsided, Mark directed Carina into the car. She lowered her head and entered. "Mom?"

Kaitlyn hugged Carina. "That was beautiful and entirely your dad's idea."

***

Kaitlyn soaked in the event. Many years ago, a young ensign went to extraordinary efforts to win her reluctant heart. That man walked her daughter down the red carpet. *It's Carina's moment, but it's my moment as well.* Kaitlyn smiled and allowed a few tears to fall.

Carina beamed, like a fireplace on a cold, dark evening. Even though she was conflicted between letting go of Mark's deception and accepting this, Kaitlyn controlled her emotions. She had to for Carina's sake. *Mark Steele may get a lot of things wrong, but he sure knows how to apologize well.* As Kaitlyn sat in the back seat with Carina and Mark, a thought formed. Maybe she wouldn't leave on Monday.

Chapter 44

Inside the limo, Carina sat wide-eyed. *Was this really happening? Did her dad actually apologize, in front of the school? The whole school?* When he lowered the window, the cheering spilled into the vehicle.

Carina moved to the side as the limousine slowly pulled away from the curb.

A block down the street they turned a corner. Now that the school had disappeared from view, Carina checked out the vehicle's interior. The black leather seats formed a square. The ceiling was also black except for tiny lights that spread throughout randomly reminding her of a starry night. On the side of the car, there was a basket of goodies on a small counter.

Her dad pointed at the basket. "If you're hungry, you can get something. Or thirsty."

Carina thought about it. Below the counter was a refrigerator. She opened it and viewed an assortment of drinks. "Mom, want one?"

"Is there a Pepsi?"

"If there is, I'll take one also," her dad said.

Carina handed the sodas to them and took one for herself. The music drowned out the opening of the soda cans. "That sounds familiar. Is it Star Wars?"

"Yes."

"Dad, really?"

"Hey, we're on an adventure that's out of this world."

Kaitlyn rolled her eyes.

The limo stopped at a red light. Carina smiled at her dad. Being hungry, she picked up a Danish, took a big bite, then wiped raspberry from the corner of her mouth.

"Let's have some fun." He pushed a button, and the sunroof opened.

Carina was the first to put her head out of the ceiling, followed by her mom, then her dad. The sky was blue with a few clouds. They could see trees on one side, houses on the other, the Austin high-rises in the distance.

The light turned green, and the limo proceeded, curving around windy roads. Cars passed them. Carina waved, occasionally moving hair out of her eyes. She was familiar with the sites since she grew up in Austin, but today everything seemed brand new.

Several minutes later, they merged onto an interstate, then lowered back into their seats. The music reminded her one Saturday when she was a little girl. They had all watched Star Wars the entire day. Carina loved that day.

The limo turned on Lake Austin Blvd.

"Dad, where are we going?" She had a guess and hoped she was right. Carina peeled a banana.

"A resort near Lake Austin Canal." Mark popped a few peanuts in his mouth.

A huge smile broke out on her face as she went for another sweet roll. She was right. "You're sure hungry," her mom said.

"The food today was yuck." Her face turned sour.

Carina switched seats again, this time near the front. Grassy fields and trees replaced the concrete. Forgotten were the plans she had for today, replaced by the adventure in front of her. Her dad moved closer to Mom and put his arm around her shoulder. She was unusually quiet.

"Mom, are you having fun?"

"Yes." She got up and moved next to Carina. "The real question is, are you enjoying this?"

"I love it."

"There's a sign." Her mom pointed.

"Ten miles to the resort." Carina tossed her banana peel into the trash and finished her soda.

A few minutes later, they pulled into the resort. She saw the family car in the parking lot.

Carina's door opened. Tuxedo man held out his hand, and she took it, then exited the car.

She met her parents behind the vehicle. "Everything is so green." She slowly spun in a circle.

When she stopped, Mark put his arm around Carina. She didn't resist.

"This will be fun," he said.

Tuxedo guy shut the door, re-entered the limo, then drove off the resort.

"Are you ready?" her dad asked.

Carina reflected on the way she had treated her father the past several weeks. Really, both of them. "Mom, Dad, I'm sorry. I've been horrible to you guys lately."

"I appreciate you saying that, Carina," her dad said. "I want us to enjoy this and forget about the past. Well, the bad parts anyway. You good with that?"

She nodded her head. *You good with that?* Strange. He didn't talk like that, but she wasn't complaining. Her mom had a slight smile.

Carina followed as they walked to the main entrance. Inside the lobby, a huge chandelier hung from the ceiling. Her dad picked up three pamphlets, handing them each one, then walked to the counter.

Carina took the colorful brochure and looked through it. "Dad, there's miniature golf."

He turned, smiled, then continued to check in. After, he handed them each a key card.

Opening his pamphlet, he showed them a picture of the spa. "What about this?"

"Mom, what do you want to do?"

"The spa sounds nice."

Carina found the picture. "It does to me, too."

"When you're at the spa, I'll visit the fitness center." He put the brochure in his pocket. "Let's get our luggage and go to our room."

At the car, he pressed the trunk button, and it sprung open.

Carina stopped. The same suitcase filled with clothes she had planned to run away with, lay right in front of her. She lowered her eyes. "I'm sorry about that."

He lifted her chin. "We'll have none of that. This weekend, I'd like us to live forward. It's something I hope we can do." Mark glanced at Kate then lifted Carina's suitcase. "Besides, in a way

I'm partly responsible for the way you've been acting. I've been way harder on you than I should have been. I really mean that."

Her mom had a strange look on her face, an expression Carina couldn't interpret. She wondered if her parents had been fighting too. "Thanks, Dad." Carina took her suitcase.

Pain etched on his face as he lifted the other luggage.

Mom stepped forward. "Do you need help with that?"

"Dad, does your arm hurt?"

"He won't admit he's in pain." Mom took a bag.

"We have a room on the first floor. Follow me." With one piece of luggage, he walked back to the entrance. They followed.

Several men in tuxedos and women in beautiful blue dresses milled around the opulent lobby. A large painting of a castle dominated a wall behind them. The group laughed, each with a drink in their hand.

Carina assumed it to be a wedding party. As the family passed through, she looked for the bride and groom, but didn't see them. At room 12A, Mark opened the door and allowed them to go in first.

"Carina, your room is back there." Mark pointed.

She ran and tossed her suitcase on the bed. After returning, she sat on the window ledge. Mark opened his bag and hung his clothes in the closet while Kaitlyn put items in the dresser.

Carina turned and opened the curtains. There was a lush green golf course on one side and on the other, a swimming pool.

"What do you want to do first?" Dad looked at Mom, then Carina.

She turned. "I'm hungry."

"Kate, is that okay with you?"

"I'm hungry also."

"Supper it is."

Carina looked at her black pants and shirt. Suddenly she felt stupid. "I'd like to change, but all I have are these goth clothes."

"There's a shop somewhere. I think my ladies should have some new clothes."

Mom took Carina's hand. "We better take him up on his offer. He's usually not this generous." She laughed, and Carina giggled.

"Hey, are you calling me cheap?"

Kaitlyn winked at Carina. "If the shoe fits, buy it."

***

Mark waited as Carina and Kaitlyn tried on several articles of clothes. This was going better than expected. At first, the Principal had sounded like he wouldn't allow the red carpet and limo, but when Mark explained he wanted to apologize, Mr. Wimmington agreed. In fact, the man insisted on being a part of the event, along with all the high school students. "Carina's always been a good student," he said. "It's only lately we've had any trouble with her. This is unusual but, okay, I'll permit it."

Mark looked at the closed dressing room door. How was Kate processing this? Her lack of words in the limo concerned him, but he stayed determined not to read anything into her silence. *I need to give her time.*

Carina came back in a western shirt and pants.

Suddenly, an image of Brenda in captivity flashed through his mind. He looked at Carina and worked to suppress his feelings.

Carina viewed herself in the mirror—pink cowboy boots with light red jeans and a western shirt. Mark stood behind her.

Carina turned toward him. "You don't like it?"

Mark couldn't get the image of Brenda in western clothes out of his mind. He shook his head. "Sorry, no."

"I'll get something different."

"Would you?"

"Sure Dad, I had another outfit in mind."

"Maybe just not western?"

"Sure, Dad." Carina went back to the changing room and emerged wearing a white shirt with a short dress. Mark would have liked it to be longer, but he didn't want to reject another one of her selections. He smiled.

"I'm not an expert, so let's ask someone who knows style." Mark directed his attention to the store keeper, hoping she'd say it was too short.

"Yes, you're a pretty young woman," the manager said.

Carina smiled, then went to Kaitlyn's dressing room and knocked on the door. After the door had opened, Carina said, "Mom, you like it?"

"You're beautiful."

"I'll take it."

Several minutes later Kaitlyn left the dressing room wearing a blouse and holding two others. "Help me decide." She held up the blouses. "Which one looks the best?"

Mark looked at the clothes. "I like the one you're wearing."

"Mom, you look great in blue."

"You think so?" Kaitlyn said.

"It matches your eyes." Carina said.

Kaitlyn handed the blouses she was holding to the attendant, then changed back into her shirt.

After paying, they went back to the hotel room, then to the restaurant.

At the Hill County dining room, Mark requested outside seating. After a brief wait, a man in a white jacket escorted them to a table near a railing. The shiny wood floor matched the high polished wooden tables. A few trimmed ash trees brushed up against the deck. The sky had a bluish- yellow haze. In the distance, a silhouetted building, hinting at the life beyond the resort.

They each picked up a menu.

"Glass of wine?" Mark and Kaitlyn shook their heads no. The waiter removed the bottle. "Can I get you something else to drink?" They gave their order and with it, Mark requested toasted lobster ravioli as an appetizer. A minute later their drinks arrived.

"Dad, what you did at the school and the limo… thank you."

"I meant every word." From Carina's expression, Mark felt she believed him. But Kate was still a mystery. He momentarily squeezed her hand.

Kaitlyn lowered her menu. "Carina, what are you having?"

She pointed to the crab pasta, then lowered her menu.

Minutes later, the waiter placed the lobster ravioli in the middle of the table, then took out a pad and pen. "Are you ready to order?"

After ordering, Mark divided the ravioli.

Kaitlyn leaned forward. "That smells good." She took a bite.

Mark watched her. How could he have excluded her from his life? This weekend had to be perfect. He took a bite of the ravioli and glanced above Kate. "Look, at the moon between those two trees." Mark pointed.

Kaitlyn took another bite and turned. "It's beautiful."

"Remember all the moonlit walks we had on the beach?"

She nodded her head. Together they gazed at the sky and ate their appetizer. Kate had been reluctant in those early days to date anyone. Two years before Mark had met her, she lost a fiancée to a tugboat accident. That was another reason he felt he needed to keep his dangerous job a secret. But now, he realized the foolishness of that decision. Carina finished her last bite of ravioli when their house salads came.

"Farmed local field greens, red radish, sorghum pecan granola with apple cider verjus vinaigrette." The waiter placed the three salads in front of them. "Madam, your lobster and crab pasta will be right out." Then looking at Mark and Kaitlyn he continued. "Your boudin-stuffed Texas quail, with Carolina gold rice and smoked sweet onion jus will be here shortly."

"Thanks, Mom and Dad, I love this." Carina dug into her salad.

"I haven't been the father…" Mark turned toward Kate. "…or husband I should have been. That will change." Being here with both of them made him realize…he had something great and took it for granted. But no more.

When they finished, the waiter removed their salad plates while another person placed their meals in front of them.

"Dad, that limo ride was so much fun."

Kaitlyn lowered her fork. "That wasn't the first time he used a limo for… let me say it this way, to get attention."

"Dad?"

"It was nothing."

"Nothing? You call sending Sir Lance-a-Lot nothing?"

Mark chuckled as Carina had a look of anticipation.

"While we were dating, your dad sent a limo driver to my door, requesting my presence so he could take me on a gondola boat ride."

"That's because you were ignoring me."

"Mom, did you go?"

"Yes."

Mark took a drink of water. "After she made me wait a long time." He forked a part of the quail and took a bite.

"That wasn't all he did. He sent a walkie-talkie to my office to ask me out to lunch."

"Again, because you wouldn't return my calls."

Carina's mouth was slightly open, her eyes went back and forth from Kaitlyn to Mark.

"That was embarrassing, but *again* I went with him."

Over supper, they continued their conversation. Carina asked questions about their past as they ate, Mark spoke first, followed by Kaitlyn.

Thirty minutes later, with their plates already removed from the table, the waiter approached them. "Would you like dessert?" He stepped aside to show them a cart loaded with cakes and pies. Kaitlyn shook her head no.

"I'm full," Mark said. "Would you like something Carina?" She shook her head. "I guess not," he told the waiter.

The waiter pushed away his cart.

Mark stood. "Anyone for a swim in the pool?"

"If it's okay, I'd like to go to our room. It's been a long day," Kaitlyn said. "You and Carina can go."

"Carina?"

Her face brightened. "Can we watch a movie?"

"Sure, if you'd rather do that."

Mark paid the bill, and they went back to their room. Once there, Carina ran and flew on to her bed. "This is so much fun." She bounced off, opened her suitcase, then glanced up.

Mark saw the look on her face. "Don't worry. We'll get you another change of clothes tomorrow."

She closed it and smiled.

Mark tossed the remote to her. "Find a movie, please." It seemed like he might get his daughter back.

She scanned the channels, then stopped. "Is this okay?"

"It's okay with me if it's all right with your mom."

Kaitlyn nodded.

The movie, Stand Near Me, was about a cheerleader being mean to a nerdy guy until he saved her from drowning when her car went into a lake.

Kate had dozed off, but Carina's eyes stayed glued to the screen.

***

After the movie was over, around midnight, Carina went to her room. Kaitlyn was now awake.

Mark stood. "Would you like a cup of coffee and sit outside?"

"That sounds nice, but make it decaf please." Kaitlyn opened the balcony doors and stepped out into the warm night. She sat.

Mark placed two decaffeinated coffees, each with creamer, on a small table next to her and sat. He took a deep breath. "This air smells so clean."

Kaitlyn nodded. "What you did for Carina… that was nice. That, and the things you said to her. I don't think she'll run way anymore. Are you planning to talk to her about it?"

"Words may hurt the message I've already sent her."

"You may be right." Kaitlyn lifted her cup.

"How about us? Is everything okay with me and you?"

Kaitlyn wanted to believe Mark had changed. More time would have to pass for her to know for certain. "It's a start."

"You know I love my family when I agree to a cheesy high school love story instead of an action thriller — right?"

Kaitlyn put her hand on his shoulder and he flinched. "Does it still hurt?"

"My heart will hurt until I know you're back in there."

"Mark, talk about cheesy. I meant your arm."

He smiled.

They drank their coffee as the moon rose in the sky, going under clouds, then reappearing. Some of the same feelings she had for Mark when they were dating were returning. It had been a long time since she sensed warmth and love from him. She hoped it was real and would stay.

Around mid-night, she stood and stretched. "I'm going to get ready for bed. Are you staying out here?"

"Maybe for a little bit."

Kaitlyn went to the dresser and retrieved her night clothes, an old t-shirt, and wooly pants. She went to the bathroom and locked the door. Perched on the tub's edge, she contemplated her relationship with her husband. The pain of deception had faded a little. He was definitely trying. But was it enough?

Removing her clothes, she turned on the shower. For a long time, she stayed under the warm water. Her marriage was better, but not completely there. Mark had shocked her with the apology in front of the school. She knew that must have killed him because humbling himself was difficult for Commander Mark Steele. She had married a naval officer, one who had to be strong at all times. It was nice seeing this side of him. To Kaitlyn, this didn't make him weak but strengthened him. A half-hour later, she dressed.

Back in the room, Mark was already in bed. On her side, he threw back the covers. "I love you."

"I love you, as well." She tried to sound genuine. Kaitlyn entered the bed and turned toward him.

Mark took her hand. "You remember when we were first married, and we'd fall asleep holding hands?"

Kaitlyn remembered those days. Then, she had felt loved, cared for and the object of his love. With his fingers interlocked with hers, she wondered if he still felt the same. "I do."

Kaitlyn wanted to trace the lines of Mark's smile with her finger but restrained herself. Restoring what they had would take time. "Good night, Mark."

"Good night."

Kaitlyn closed her eyes. She was glad Mark hadn't tried to be intimate. It saved her from having to say no.

Chapter 45

A t home, late Monday afternoon, Kaitlyn opened the oven. The pizza wasn't golden brown like she wanted it. She closed the door.

"Kate?"

"I'm in the kitchen, Mark."

Kaitlyn placed dishes in the dishwasher. For Carina's sake, she'd stay. She was in such a great mood this morning; Kaitlyn didn't want to ruin it for her.

Mark stepped into the kitchen. "I wasn't sure I'd find you home."

"I'm still here."

Mark removed a bottled water from the refrigerator and took a drink. "I talked to Bob, and he gave me an office job."

"Will you also get repos?"

"Yes, but that's no more than once a week."

"Really?" Mark went to the dealership nearly every day. "So, that was part of the deception?"

"Sorry."

She put more dishes in the machine. "Mark, you don't even like paperwork."

"I know, but it's the only way I can keep my income up and not have to travel so much. I thought you'd be happy about it."

Carina, backpack on her shoulders, shot into the kitchen. "School was killing it today. All the kids were talking about what happened on Friday. My history teacher even had me come up front and talk about it." Her voice increased. "Hashtag embarrassing." She opened a bag and removed a cookie. "Oh, and a few cheerleaders want me to practice with them."

Kaitlyn smiled.

"They wanted to know everything. I must have told them a million times. And get this, I've added hundreds on my Facebook."

Mark set his bottle on the counter. "Hundreds?"

"Okay, not hundreds, but a lot." Carina turned toward Kaitlyn. "Mom, I'll need a new dress. Prom is coming up, and I want to look pretty."

"Isn't that next month?"

Carina took a bite of her cookie. "Yes."

"That shouldn't be a problem." Kaitlyn continued to load the dishes.

"And Dad?"

"Yes."

"Can we play miniature golf this weekend?"

Kaitlyn turned.

Mark in a questioning voice said, "All right."

"Can I bring some friends?"

"Just a couple." Mark leaned against the counter. "Kate?"

"Sounds like fun."

"Can they stay overnight on Friday?"

They both nodded yes.

"I'm calling them right now." Carina ran out of the kitchen.

Kaitlyn yelled, "Carina, supper in ten minutes."

Carina's feet pounded up the stairs. "Okay Mom" put another smile on Kaitlyn's face. *Who took my daughter away and replaced her with this one?*

"Wow, she's like a hurricane. What did I unleash?" Mark took another drink.

"She's just excited. And I love it. Thank you, Mark."

"You're welcome." Mark paused. "I've been considering something."

Kaitlyn took the pizza from the oven and set it on the stove, then directed her attention to Mark.

He pulled out his cell phone and handed it to her.

"What's this?" Kaitlyn looked at it. "I know what it is, but why are you giving it to me?"

"I want you to keep it until... well until you can trust me."

"Mark, that's not necessary."

"Do you trust me?"

"It's too soon for me to answer that."

He closed her hand over the phone. "Then keep it until you do."

"Won't you need a phone?"

"I'll get by without one for a little while."

"If that's what you want." Is he serious? "What if your boss calls you?"

"I'll give him your number. Would that be okay?"

"I suppose."

"I feel like I'm treating you like a little kid."

"It's only for a few months."

"All right." Kaitlyn cut the pizza. "Would you tell Carina it's time for supper?"

**

Mark glanced at Kate a few times during the meal. He hated giving up his phone. But what other option was there? When Tony called, Mark felt like he was doing something behind Kate's back. Mark, returning home from work, Tony pleaded with him. "I'll pay you whatever it takes to get her home." Mark pulled over and listened, then gently told him no. After hanging up, Mark knew he had to inform Kate of the phone call. Not rescuing someone in need went against everything he valued. He wanted to get on the next plane to Nashville. When it came down to it, Mark didn't trust himself.

Kate was right, he hated paperwork. But until he found another job, he'd endure it. His first day in the office was horrible. He filed papers in the wrong place and put signatures in the wrong spot. Mark tried to focus on work, but his mind kept going to Brenda. He had to forget about her and wondered if he could.

Later at dinner, Carina talked the entire meal. Girl talk and mostly to Kate. He couldn't remember the last time Carina had been this happy. Typically, they'd eat in silence, or he'd be lecturing. Why did he do that? Now he realized...that's probably why no one was happy.

"Dad, can I get my driver's license?" Carina asked.

"You think you're ready?"

"I drove a golf cart at the resort."

"That's different than a car, but yes, I can teach you to drive. I'll pick up a book at the DMV tomorrow so you can study."

"Study? I thought all I'd have to do is drive."

"It's more than that. You take a written test, then you'll get a learner's permit."

"Then I'd be able to drive?"

"Only with an adult."

"I can't wait."

Mark squeezed his soda can. "I have something to say." Several seconds passed. "Tony, called me, that's Brenda's dad. He still wants me to get his daughter." Mark watched Kate's expression. He didn't want to put any guilt on her. "I told him I had a new job and couldn't get off work." Part of that was true.

"I thought the police would get her?" Kaitlyn asked.

"A patrol car scanned the area. They saw nothing. There were no vehicles and no evidence of a crime being committed so they couldn't or wouldn't get a search warrant. They'd watch the area, but that was all they would do."

It wasn't all he could've done. He had to rush home because he thought Carina had run away. If he had to do it over again, he'd personally talk to the Nashville police as they instructed him. But obviously because he spoke over the phone, they didn't take him seriously.

***

Kaitlyn stopped eating. "You were shot. Doesn't that matter to the police?"

"I didn't tell the Nashville police I was shot. I reported a girl being held hostage."

"You mean they can't get Brenda? That makes little sense."

"If I had a better video camera, I could have sent proof that Brenda was there. I failed." Mark crushed the soda can.

A teenage girl is missing. The realization hit her. "Can't he find someone else to get his daughter?"

"He's tried."

Kaitlyn glanced at Carina, her eyes wide. Was it okay talking about this in front of her? Brenda wasn't Kaitlyn's responsibility, and Brenda was no longer Mark's responsibility either. Kaitlyn hated the feeling that dropped on her. Picking up the empty plates, she walked to the kitchen. Yet the image of an abducted teenager remained with her. What if her daughter were missing?

She suppressed the feelings. When she returned, Mark was talking to Carina.

"I'd like to hear your side of the story of what happened last week."

Carina avoided eye contact. "Sure."

Kaitlyn sat.

"Billy had a bottle of alcohol. I told him I didn't want any, but he pushed it at me, and splashed some on my shirt."

"Okay, that explains the alcohol. What about the marijuana and pills?"

"Billy asked me to keep a bag of weed and give it to Jonzy after school. I was stupid to put it in my locker. As for the pills, Billy asked me to bring them. I took them to school because I was mad."

"Where did you get the pills?"

Carina hesitated, then whispered, "From the upstairs bathroom." In a hurried voice said, "And I swear I didn't scratch Sally's car."

"Who did it?"

"Billy."

"Sounds like Billy is a bad influence," Mark said.

"Yes, he is. But it's not all his fault. I made bad choices."

"That's being mature," Kaitlyn said.

Carina turned toward her. "Mom, do you believe me?"

"I believe you." Kaitlyn glanced at Mark, who appeared to be deep in thought. Come on Mark, reassure your daughter and don't lecture.

"I believe you, too," Mark said.

Kaitlyn's shoulders relaxed.

"Thanks, Mom, Dad."

"You still have to suffer the consequences by going to court, but we'll face it together," Mark said.

Kaitlyn took a deep breath. May as well test this. "Tell your dad why you were mad."

Carina hesitated.

Kaitlyn stood and put her arm around her. "Carina?"

She looked at Mark. "I was mad because you didn't believe me, and you're always lecturing me, never allowing me to explain."

"Go on," Mark said.

"I feel like I can't be myself around you. It's like you want me to be someone different. Someone I can't be. You're not doing it right now. But every other time..."

Kaitlyn watched Mark's hands. He squeezed them tight. She expected him to raise his voice and defend his actions as he had done on so many other occasions.

"You're right. I've been unreasonable...treating you like a military recruit. Someone suggested I was controlling, only looking out for my own interests." In a lower tone, "She was right."

Kaitlyn sat. "That sounds like something my mom would say."

Mark nodded and looked at Carina. "But I'm still your Dad. That doesn't mean you can do whatever you want."

Kaitlyn shifted in her chair and cleared her throat. *Mark, this is going good, don't ruin it.*

Mark glanced at Kaitlyn. "I've said enough."

"Am I still grounded?" Carina asked.

"Have you learned your lesson?"

Carina nodded her head yes.

"I don't see any reason you should stay grounded. Kate?"

"I agree."

"Thanks, Dad, Mom." Carina finished her soda.

Now's the time. Kaitlyn touched his hand. If he's changed, the next few minutes would tell. "Mark, I know this is tough for you, but there's something I feel you should do."

Mark slightly opened his mouth, his lips tense, as if he'd anticipated her next words.

"Please call your dad."

Mark's countenances fully dropped.

Oh Mark, please don't say no. For the sake of your family clear this with your father. A few minutes passed. The last time Kaitlyn had seen Roger Steele was at the funeral of Mark's mother. And there, Mark refused to talk to him. She tried to discuss it with Mark, but he wouldn't. "Mark?"

He straightened his back then stood. Silence filled the air for another few minutes.

Come on Mark.

He whispered. "I'll need his number."

"I have it right here." She handed him a piece of paper and his phone. Kaitlyn had found the number earlier in the day.

Mark palmed his phone and looked at it, then called. "Hi, Dad. Can we talk?"

Kaitlyn moved closer.

More pain appeared on Mark's face. *Was it wrong asking him to call?* Just as Kaitlyn asked herself that question she watched Mark's face relax slightly. "Dad, I forgive you." Then Mark's eyes narrowed, and tension lines reappeared. For the next several minutes, he pressed the phone to his ear, only saying a few words. Then it was over. Mark set the phone on the counter. When he looked up, a tear slid down his face. He quickly wiped it away.

With her eyes, Kaitlyn attempted to draw an explanation.

Mark sat and folded his hands. "When I was 8 years-old, I had a small dog. It wet on the floor one too many times. Dad got rid of him, so I ran away."

Kaitlyn kept her gaze on Mark.

"We had just moved to Killeen, Texas." He stopped, momentarily squeezed his eyes shut, then continued. "I had to find Rex."

"You had a dog named Rex?" Carina asked.

Kaitlyn placed her hand on Carina's hand hoping to stop her questions. This was a delicate moment, not to be ruined.

"Yes, I had a dog named Rex, and I loved that mutt. My dad found me later that day." Mark tightened his fist.

Kaitlyn touched Mark's hand. He relaxed and laced his fingers with hers.

"Dad dragged me in the cellar. I can't remember what I said, but it angered him, and he told me I needed to toughen up, then he closed the door."

"How long did you stay in the cellar?" Carina asked.

"It felt like days, but it was probably only a few hours. I was terrified. The sky was dark when he let me out, and I was very hungry."

"That's horrible, was that the only time?" Kaitlyn asked.

"No, it happened several other times. Sometimes I didn't even know what I did wrong."

Kaitlyn now understood why he wouldn't have anything to do with his dad, even at his mother's funeral.

"I don't think I've ever forgiven him for it, until a few minutes ago," Mark said.

In a gentle voice, Kaitlyn asked, "What did he say when you told him you forgave him?"

"He told me there was nothing to forgive."

It had been a long time since Kaitlyn saw Mark this vulnerable.

"He said he was protecting me for my own good." Mark looked at Kaitlyn. "Like I was doing to you."

Oh, Mark.

"I was wrong, just like my dad was wrong."

"Don't you understand, you broke the connection?"

He squeezed her hand. "I don't want to live my life without you and Carina, and I don't want my past to define my future."

A few minutes later, Kaitlyn broke the silence. "I know that feeling of not letting go of the past."

Carina, teary eyed, leaned closer.

Kaitlyn felt it was time to confess to Carina. With all eyes on her, she continued. "Before I met your dad, I was engaged to be married to a young man named Joe. He worked on a tugboat." She hesitated. "He was killed in an accident. When your dad came along, I couldn't let go of my past until..."

Carina's eyes widened. "Until what?"

She paused for several seconds. "Until a good deal of time had passed. It took the love of the people who cared about me, who wouldn't give up on me, that brought me out of it." Kaitlyn looked at Mark as he spoke.

"Your mom had a huge part in that."

"Grandma?" Carina asked.

"Yes," Kaitlyn said. "She helped me release my past and get beyond that night. Those were her words, not mine."

Chapter 46

Kaitlyn opened a photo album that contained a rose. Early in their relationship, Mark had given Kaitlyn a red rose to celebrate their one-month engagement. With tenderness, she felt the flattened petals, now darkened from years under the plastic.

Her thoughts went back to that beautiful Southern California afternoon. Mark held something behind his back. Kaitlyn tried to look. After several seconds, he handed her a rose.

"Will you marry me?"

Kaitlyn received the flower. "Mark you asked me already, and I said yes."

"Are you more in love with me now?"

"Hmmm." Kaitlyn tapped her fingers on her chin and looked skyward. "Let me think." She smiled, then hugged Mark. "If that's possible."

She turned the page and threw her hand to her mouth. Why had she put a funeral announcement in this book? After a few minutes, she remembered. It was important to Mark. Terrorist killed Ramos Gonzales, a ten-year-old, during one of Mark's missions. He said nothing about the operation but talked about the boy and his mother. The incident changed his life and defined Mark's personality. During that time, she remembered his passion and his desire to help the innocent. She fell in love with Mark because he opened his soul to her. How could she have forgotten that?

Her phone sounded. Kaitlyn looked at the caller ID. "Hi, Mom."

"Kaitlyn, how are you doing?"

"Good."

"And?"

Kaitlyn pulled the flower vase closer. "Mark got me roses, and I like them. I really do. But he's trying too hard."

"Give it time."

"It's been two weeks since he returned from Tennessee. Why can't I just let it go?"

"He hurt you deeply. Some wounds take longer to heal. But at least you've stayed and worked it out."

"Will the bad feelings ever go away?"

"The memory won't but I pray your feelings turn into love."

"I hope you're right."

"Mom, there's something I want to talk to you about."

"I'm listening."

"When I had first met Mark, he was terribly upset over a death of a child. Then in the Philippines, two missionary kids died." Kaitlyn stopped. She didn't know how to put her feelings into words.

"Was that when Mark nearly died?" her mother said.

"Yes."

"Is that what's bothering you? That he could've died when he was in Nashville?"

"It bothered me, but that's not completely it." Kaitlyn paused. "Today, while going through our picture album, I remembered his passion, his dreams. I fell in love with him, partly because of that side of him. I don't see that anymore. He still thinks about it. I can see it in his eyes, but he doesn't talk about it."

"But he's trying."

"I know, and I appreciate it. Last night he woke me up saying, 'Hold on, I'm coming to get you.' I assumed he was dreaming of the abducted girl, Brenda."

"The police haven't found her yet?"

"I don't think so."

"I'm sorry to hear that."

"Am I being unreasonable? Stopping Mark from what's he's passionate about?"

There was silence for several seconds. "What I'm going to say won't make any sense. But think about it. The meaning will come to you. Just don't react right now. Okay?"

"All right."

"It's something Jesus said. If you seek to save your life, you'll lose it."

Was that it?

"If you seek to save your life?"

"You'll lose it."

"You're right Mom, I don't understand the meaning."

"Over time, you will. I'm sorry, but this is something you must figure out yourself. Remember in the garden, Jesus was in such agony he sweat great drops of blood. He had to do something he didn't want to do."

"Okay Mom, I'll think about it."

"Did you have to work today?"

"I went in for a few hours this morning." Kaitlyn repositioned her wedding ring, bringing the diamond to the center.

"Anything planned for this weekend?"

Kaitlyn stood and went to the kitchen window. "Mark said he had a surprise."

"You don't sound excited."

"The last two weekends have been busy. I wanted a relaxing time at home."

"Did you tell Mark your feelings?"

"I plan on telling him."

On the phone, a door bell sounded. "Kaitlyn, I have someone at the front door."

"Bye Mom."

Why were her emotions conflicting? Mark had changed, right? She pushed the flowers to the center of the table and closed the album. She went to her bedroom and placed the book back into the closet. Perched on her bed, Kaitlyn attempted to understand, "If you seek to save your life, you'll lose it."

***

Bob thumbed through the open filing cabinet in Mark's office. "Where's the Kaiser purchase agreement?"

Mark ran his hand through his hair and released a sigh. "It should be there."

Bob put the file back and withdrew a second one. "Okay, I have the Kaiser folder, but not the agreement."

"I'm sure I put it there." Mark walked to the cabinet.

"It's not here. That's the third one this week that's missing."

"I'll find it and bring it to you."

"Make it quick." Bob left the office.

Mark looked through the files. He hated this job. Getting repossessed cars, now that's where the action happened. But he only had one of those last week.

That repo had taken less than an hour, and there was no resistance from the owner. Not even a, "Hey, what are you doing?"

After a few more minutes of Mark looking through the files, Bob yelled from the other room. "I found it."

"Where?" Mark asked.

When Bob didn't respond, Mark returned to his desk. A few minutes remained before he could leave. It was Thursday, and that meant only one more day until the weekend. Mark watched the second hand. He hoped Kaitlyn liked the flowers and appreciated his sacrifice — this job. He wasn't sure she did.

As Mark traveled home, he thought about past rescue missions like Brenda. He wondered if his passion for this kind of work would ever diminish, whether thoughts of helpless children in captivity would ever leave him alone. But as he tried to think of something different, he passed a billboard of kids splashing and having fun at a water park. His thoughts of kidnapped children intensified for several miles until he reached another billboard that advertised jobs.

Online, he found a few jobs that interested him. A security guard position was available. When he suggested it to Kate, fear registered on her face. He wouldn't press the issue, at least not right now. An ex-specialist commander could only do so many things, and most of them required carrying a gun. In a way, he understood Kate's fears. After all, she went through a traumatic time in her life. Two if he counted his accident.

"It took a long time for me to get over Joe's death," Mark remembered her saying. Two years before meeting Mark, her wedding plans turned to funeral plans. Kaitlyn linked that experience to Mark almost getting killed. "I can't handle any more," she'd said. "I almost lost you in the Philippines. Then in Nashville...I relived the pain of death all over again." After several seconds, she whispered, "I'd feel better if you had a safe job."

Safe job? Those words shot into Mark's spirit. He enjoyed living on the edge. Even as a teenager, he had to find danger. Like once, when he heard a rattlesnake, he tracked it down and killed it. Another time, he antagonized, on purpose, an older and much taller teenager. After Mark got slammed to the ground he got right back up and continued his taunting, causing the kid to walk away saying, "He's crazy." It was pure adrenalin for Mark.

How long could he put up with this office job, or how long before Bob fired him? That probably wouldn't happen since Mark had directed several people to the dealership who then bought cars. But even selling cars would be better than shuffling papers. Unfortunately, there were no sales positions. Bob didn't want to anger any of his current salesmen by creating a new position. It had only been two weeks since Kate had become so upset she wanted to leave. He kept telling himself he could make this sacrifice because he didn't want to lose her.

Another billboard changed his thoughts again—a beach scene. Their honeymoon had been two weeks of Caribbean heaven. That's the way Kate described it. Maybe they could plan a cruise soon. But first, he'd have to save a lot of money. He returned to thinking about jobs.

His current job paid the bills but left no extra for savings. His rescue missions had paid a lot, increasing their standard of living. Since Kate wanted nothing to do with the finances, Mark easily hid the source of the money from her. But now, they had no extra cash. That was another point of contention. It was a reminder of him deceiving Kate, deception Mark now regretted a million times over.

At home, he found Kate in the back yard. She was on her knees by her flowers, a pile of weeds next to her. "Hi, Kate."

She turned and sat on the grass. "Hi."

He leaned down and gave her a kiss. "Did you like the flowers?"

"Thank you. They were nice."

Mark sat next to her. "Did you do anything special today?"

"I talked to my mom."

"Did she have any news?"

"Dad is doing better." She took off her dirty green gloves.

"I'm glad to hear that. Was it the flu?"

"That's what Mom thinks."

Several seconds passed with Kate staring straight ahead. Something in her eyes troubled him. "Are you okay?"

"I feel great."

"No, I mean emotionally."

Kaitlyn turned, and Mark could see tears on her cheek. He put his arm around her. She put her face on his shoulder. He held her for a few minutes, then whispered. "Please say something."

The front door opened. Seconds later Carina yelled, "Mom? Dad?"

Kaitlyn straightened then wiped her cheeks. "Out here, Carina."

Carina flew through the screen door, causing it to slam hard. She held out a paper. "Can you sign this? It's for this weekend."

Kaitlyn scanned the paper.

"This is a travel release form. Where are you going?"

"Crockett High School. We're playing them...a basketball game." In a faster voice, she said, "and I'm a cheerleader."

Kaitlyn signed the paper and handed it back to her. "You made the squad?" A smile filled Carina's face. "Yes." She turned and ran back into the house.

***

After Carina had gone inside, Kaitlyn returned to her flowers. Why did she cry so easily? She should let Mark know what she was feeling. Could she? "Would you mind if we just stayed home this weekend?" Maybe she and Mark could really talk, especially since Carina would be gone.

"Sure we can do that."

"Thanks."

"Something is bothering you. Please tell me."

She stood and walked to a chair. Mark followed, and they sat. "I pulled out our wedding album today. The flowers you put on the table reminded me of the roses you gave me when we were first engaged. I guess I've been thinking a lot about those days, missing what we use to have." That was only part of it, but she didn't want to give Mark the wrong impression. If she told him she missed the passion he had for helping the innocent, he'd take it as an invitation to go back into dangerous situations. She wasn't ready for that. Would she ever be ready? If she embraced Mark's passion, she'd also have to accept the possibility of him getting killed. Her mom would probably call that irrational thinking. But to Kaitlyn it was real.

Mark reached for her hand, pain slightly registered on his face.

"Is your shoulder still hurting?" she said.

"Not much."

Guam hospital flashed in her memory. She could see Mark lying in a hospital bed. She still felt the fear of wondering if he'd live, then wondering if he'd walk again. She concluded, at least for now, that it was better to live without the shadows of death hanging over her.

"We'll get back to the way we were before." Mark squeezed her hand.

How can we Mark when I'm afraid? She nodded.

Chapter 47

Another week had passed, and Kaitlyn was no closer to total reconciliation with Mark. She tried over the weekend, but fear and mistrust kept that from happening. Their conversation stayed on surface issues, like the weather, family, and what their friends were doing. She could see that Mark had changed. He was paying far more attention to her, talking not just to her more often, but also with Carina. What more could she ask for? The issue was clear: trust. She still didn't trust him with her feelings. She was afraid if she let him all the way back in, he'd manipulate her again.

Kaitlyn knew how much Mark disliked his desk job and wanted a different one. Kaitlyn felt bad about shooting down each one of his suggestions. All three positions involved carrying a gun.

She noticed the new next-door neighbor watering her flowers, left the house, and went to the fence. "Do you have everything moved in?" Kaitlyn asked.

Tamie, her neighbor, had brown hair and wore glasses. She reminded Kaitlyn of her own mother, easy to talk to and straightforward..

"Almost... a few more boxes," she said. "Thank you for the banana bread. It was good, and Roger loved it."

"I'm glad you liked it." By Kaitlyn's estimation, Tamie and Roger were around fifty-years-old, several years younger than Kaitlyn's mom and dad. Tamie had a tan, suggesting a lot of outdoor time.

Tamie moved toward the gate. "Why don't you come over? I'll toss a few slices in the microwave. We can sit on the deck and enjoy this nice weather."

"I'd like that. Besides, there's something I'd like to ask you."

"Is it a continuation of yesterday's subject?"

Kaitlyn nodded yes then went to the deck and sat under a large umbrella. Off to the side was a bird feeder. A few birds landed and pecked the seeds. Another bird flew and perched on the edge of a birdbath. This past week, Kaitlyn had really gotten to know Tamie. She and Roger had just moved from San Antonio where Tamie had a counseling position at a woman's clinic.

Tamie placed the dishes of banana bread on the table. "Would you like tea?"

"That would be nice." Kaitlyn sat outside.

From inside the house, Tamie asked, "How was your work this morning?"

"Since my boss is gone, I caught up on some filing."

"How long will he be gone?"

"Not long enough to get everything organized the way I'd like it." Kaitlyn laughed. "He'll be back tomorrow."

Tamie returned with two tall glasses of iced tea, then sat.

Kaitlyn held the cup to her cheek, then took a long drink. "Oh, that's good."

"It's supposed to get up to 90 degrees today."

"It has to be that hot already." Kaitlyn wrapped her hands around the cold glass. "It's a good thing you have all these shade trees in your back yard."

"It was one of the reasons we bought this house." Tamie pulled a plate of banana bread toward her. A cat jumped up on the fence, and the birds flew away. "Oh that cat, I could just take a broom to it." Tamie stood and waved her hand at the animal. "Scoot, scoot." The cat jumped off the fence and ran off. "You had something you wanted to talk about?"

For the next several minutes Kaitlyn explained Mark's accident, and the time he spent in the Guam and San Diego hospital.

"Does that still bother you?" Kaitlyn nodded yes.

"You told me your husband use to investigate missing children. How did you feel about that?"

"I didn't like it." In fact, she hated it.

"Why doesn't he do that any longer?"

Tamie had a way of going straight to the issue. The ice in the tea melted and the breeze seemed to get warmer. Kaitlyn tightened her lips. The conversation had become more personal than she liked.

"You don't have to answer if you don't want to."

Did she want to? Earlier this morning Kaitlyn had determined to talk about Mark and his deception. But now, the spotlight was on her.

"Years ago, when Roger and I first met," Tamie said, "we did something we shouldn't have. Well, I got pregnant, and since I was still in high school, my mom took me to get an abortion. For years, I lived with the pain of knowing I took a life. Every time I saw a baby, I felt death. I eventually talked to a friend who recommended I face that pain."

"How did you face it?"

"Well, God forgave me then I forgave myself, then I volunteered to work in the church nursery. I loved on those little babies. It hurt at first, but I pushed through the pain." A few chirping birds returned. "Eventually, we had our own child."

Kaitlyn could see the pain in Tamie's eyes. "Does it still hurt?"

She nodded yes. "I don't think the pain ever fully goes away. But it turns to love. And as the song goes, love hurts."

The words, *love hurts, ooh love hurts*, by the 70's group, Air Supply, played in Kaitlyn's mind. She agreed with the hurt part. But love? She wasn't there yet.

"Time doesn't heal all wounds." Tamie took a drink of her tea. "But time heals all clean wounds. Many years ago, a young girl came to the clinic I worked at. I can't reveal her real name, so I'll just call her Susan. Well, Susan was distressed, and that's saying it mildly. Her boyfriend had verbally abused her. A simple solution would be for Susan to leave him, but she didn't want to do that. We drilled down to her problem, which took several meetings. Eventually we exposed the real fear."

Kaitlyn took a bite of banana cake.

"When she was around five years old, Susan became separated from her parents at a busy airport. The family was late for their flight, then they couldn't get seats together. In the confusion they boarded the plane without Susan. They didn't figure it out until shortly after takeoff."

"How can parents lose their children at an airport?"

"Their fifteen-year-old watched Susan. Well, you know how teenagers can be sometimes. He wasn't alert and lost her. And they had two other kids as well."

"That must have been horrible for Susan." Kaitlyn remembered Carina at that age.

"For Susan it was terrifying. The dad caught a flight back, but it took several hours to reunite Susan with her parent. But from that point on, she was afraid of being alone. Long story, short, that's why she had to have someone around her all the time."

"All because of a bad childhood experience."

A squirrel ran across the branches, causing Tamie to momentarily pause.

"The healing began in Ci..., I mean Susan because she understood the root of her fear, thus making it a clean wound. It didn't go away completely, but she faced it. The last time I heard from her, Susan was in a good relationship, and in college studying to be a teacher."

"I love happy ending stories." *I wish mine were like that.* "Were all the girls you talked to able to get help?"

"I wish that were the case, but no. Some girls, after revealing their root fear, did just the opposite. They chose to live with the fear, and there was nothing I could do for them. It became their hellish prison cell."

Kaitlyn's eyes widened. *If I seek to save my life, I'll lose him for it.* The right thing was to allow Mark to be himself. Tamie looked at Kaitlyn. *She wants me to talk about my fear.* Her pulse increased as they sat in silence for several seconds. "You have new flowers."

"I hope I can keep them alive. I've never been good with plants." Tamie chuckled.

The awkward moment passed. Kaitlyn's pulse returned to normal. She didn't know what a panic attack felt like, but if she were to guess it would be close to what she just experienced.

For the next half-hour, they talked about the weather and plants. Safe topics. Kaitlyn looked at her watch and stood. "Mark will be home shortly. This has been nice. Thank you."

"When we get completely settled in, Roger and I would like to have your husband and you over for dinner."

"That'd be great."

Tamie stood, and they hugged. "Same time tomorrow?"

Kaitlyn smiled. "Yes, I'd like that." She left her neighbor's back yard. Kaitlyn stopped short of going inside her house. Why did that conversation bother her so much? What did she fear? After a few minutes, it dawned on her. Mark could die and she'd be left alone. Kaitlyn had a dirty wound, by Tamie's definition. A wound that wouldn't heal.

Mark's cell phone rang. Kaitlyn ran inside and picked up his phone. Before saying a word, Tony spoke.

"Mark, this is Tony. I know you've told me you're finished with rescues, but I'm pleading with you as a father. I've tried everything to get Brenda back. The police are still convinced she's a runaway. I've called everyone I know, and no one will help me. You're my only hope. I beg you to try one more time. I miss my daughter so much." He cried.

"Tony?"

"Who is this?"

"Kaitlyn, Mark's wife. I'm sorry, but Mark isn't here right now. Do you want him to call you?"

"Please."

Kaitlyn lowered the phone.

***

Poor Tony. She couldn't imagine having a missing child. *How will Mark respond? Am I stopping him from finding this girl?* Kaitlyn tried to silence the words, the way she had over the past several weeks, but now those words wouldn't stay quiet.

The front door opened and closed. Kaitlyn poured a cup of coffee as Mark took a seat at the counter. "How was your day?"

"Same thing, filing, typing reports, and shuffling papers. I'm shocked Bob hasn't fired me yet." Mark half-smiled. "But it's getting better. Bob isn't yelling as much." Mark chuckled.

She may as well get this over with. "You had two calls." Kaitlyn handed Mark a paper with a number and his cell phone.

"Thank you." He punched in the numbers and put the phone on speaker. "Mark Steele here."

"Sam Tims. I received your number from my lawyer. I'm from West Texas and my son disappeared a few days ago. My wife and I suspect he ran away. Would you take the case?"

"I'm sorry, but I don't do that any longer."

"Do you know of anyone else? We've been basket cases since he left."

"I don't know of anyone. Aren't the police helping you?"

"They're supposed to be. But nothing is happening."

"I'm sorry."

A female's voice came on the line. "Please help find Cody. We only have one child..." She cried making the rest of the words unrecognizable.

Kaitlyn watched the struggle in Mark's facial expressions. *It's killing him, not being able to do this.* Mark placed the phone on the counter and crumbled the paper, then stared into his coffee. "Mark, that really bothers you."

"It doesn't matter." Mark, shoulders slumped, looked at Kaitlyn. "I won't let it bother me." *He's miserable.*

His sadness cut into her soul, along with the grief of Cody's parents.

"You said there were two phone calls?"

"Tony called."

Mark straightened, his eyes locked onto Kaitlyn. Anticipation on his face. "And?"

I wish I had good news. "He still wants you to find Brenda."

Like air rushing out of a balloon, Mark sunk into his chair. "Did you tell him I can't?"

"No. He wants you to call him."

***

With his elbows on the desk and his hands on his face, Mark recalled the phone call he just had. He'd gently told Tony no. Brenda's Dad had pleaded, then fell silent. Several seconds later, Tony thanked him in a whisper and ended the call.

After ten minutes of nursing dark feelings, Mark took out a notebook. The same book he'd used when he began looking for Brenda. After thumbing through it, he stopped at a page marked POI, persons of interest. His energy returned.

He couldn't help it; he had to think of a way to rescue Brenda. On the page, he had written several license plate numbers, along with the car's description. He'd return to the Nashville bookstore, wait, and follow one of those vehicles until he found Brenda. Since a month had passed since he'd been in Tennessee, Mark hoped they hadn't moved Brenda out of the area. If they had, he saw no way he'd be able to get her back. *Unless.* With his key, he opened the bottom drawer and stared at his gun. He hoped it didn't come to that. Of course, he'd have to drive to Nashville if he wanted to bring the weapon. After locking the drawer, Mark mentally went over his rescue plan. But a huge question surfaced. How would he do this without Kate's knowledge? Mark stopped. He'd lose his family. For several seconds he stared at the notebook, then at a family picture on the wall. He closed the book. A few minutes later, the front door opened. "Carina is that you?" he yelled.

Mark returned the notebook to the drawer. He had to forget about Tony, Brenda, and the parents from West Texas. *What was their son's name? Cody?* He needed to forget about Cody as well.

A few seconds later Carina stood in the doorway. "Hi, Dad." Mark stood.

"How was your day?"

"Okay."

"How do you think you did on your history test?"

"The teacher hasn't graded it yet, but I think I passed."

"When we reviewed the material, you knew it." Mark searched his mind for any other points he wanted to bring up with her. "Oh, what about cheerleading?"

"I don't know. I'm not that good."

"Let me be the judge of that."

Kaitlyn entered. "Judge of what?"

"Dad wants to see a cheer."

Mark moved toward the door. "Let's go to the living room."

Carina set her books down on the couch, then moved to the center of the room. They watched as she did a cheer, ending in splits.

They clapped.

"You have to like it, you're my parents."

"Don't sell yourself short." Mark put his hand on her shoulders.

"Okay, Dad." Carina smiled, picked up her books, and went to her room.

Mark watched her leave, then glanced at Kaitlyn. Yes, he needed to forget about the missing children. But more important, he needed to silence the resentful feeling that had sprung up from being forced to choose between two things he deeply cared about.

Chapter 48

Four roses from Mark. One for each week since the resort. The first rose had died. Kaitlyn removed it and tossed it in the trash. "Something has to die before there can be new growth," Kaitlyn remembered Tamie saying.

Kaitlyn opened her window and saw her neighbor. "Good Morning."

"Good Morning. I have coffee brewing," Tamie said.

"I'll be right there."

Even through Kaitlyn had only known Tamie a short time, it seemed like a lifetime. They spent every day talking. Each day the topics went deeper and became more personal. Kaitlyn felt as though she had been on an emotional operating table.

By the time she sat down on Tamie's back porch, coffee was on the table. "Thank you."

"You're welcome." Tamie took a drink. "I'd been thinking about our talk yesterday. You helped me sort out some of my emotions. Thank you."

Kaitlyn laughed. "That's funny because I could say the same thing."

They smiled, and Tamie patted Kaitlyn's hand. "Were you able to have that heart-to-heart talk with Mark?"

Kaitlyn wrapped her hands around her coffee. After leaving her neighbor's house yesterday, Kaitlyn intended on sharing her feelings with Mark. She wanted Mark to know that Tony's call bothered her. That she wanted to see Brenda rescued. And she also wanted to talk about the emotions she'd experienced over the past month. Kaitlyn shook her head no.

"Early in our marriage, Roger became passionate about hunting. I hadn't picked up a gun my entire life and didn't want to. For him, hunting became an obsession. He did it all the time."

Kaitlyn took a drink of her coffee. A tiny bird landed in the feeder.

"My little friend is here today." Tamie broke off a piece of bread and tossed to the ground. The bird left the feeder and flew to the bread.

Kaitlyn directed her attention back to Tamie. "What did you do?"

"I became jealous and treated hunting like it was another woman. I hated it when he went on hunting trips or even when he cleaned his guns." She turned toward the bird. "I wasn't free like that little sparrow." Tamie lowered her head. "My emotions made me a prisoner."

"But your husband has a cabinet full of guns."

"Yes, and it doesn't bother me any longer. We had to go through marriage counseling. Can you imagine that? Me a counselor, going to counseling?"

Kaitlyn chuckled. She enjoyed Tamie's truthfulness.

"In one of our sessions, we had to talk fifteen minutes non-stop concerning what bothered us. I went first. Roger's hunting became the subject. With prompting from the counselor, I went deeper into the root cause. And like I said earlier, I was jealous."

The sparrow flew away. Tamie poured more coffee into their cups. "My husband had no idea I felt that way. After talking it out, he admitted putting hunting above his family." Tamie looked down, then back to Kaitlyn. "That was the start of our healing."

Will my marriage ever heal? Mark's passion to locate missing children was still alive, she could see it in his eyes. And that was the problem. At one time Kaitlyn loved his passion, but it became more important than her. She hated her feelings. After all, his passion was rescuing children. *That was a good thing, right? Yes, a hundred times yes.* Yet, she couldn't get past the negative feelings.

"Kaitlyn, it seems obvious why Mark stopped rescuing children, but you've avoided talking about it. Can I ask why? But before you answer, I need to get something. I'll be right back."

Only a few minutes passed, but Kaitlyn's anxiety made it seem like hours. Could she face this? Images of the past paraded in front of her; Joe in a coffin, Mark near dead in a hospital bed. Kaitlyn took a deep breath when Tamie returned.

"Here's what I wanted to show you." Kaitlyn took the framed certificate.

"It's my award—a shooting award. After Roger and I had worked everything out, I found I wanted to go hunting with him." Tamie folded her hands and made eye-contact with Kaitlyn, then silence.

This time, there was no panic and only a small amount of fear. Kaitlyn pushed it aside. Her desire to face her pain became bigger than the fear. She handed the award back to Tamie. "To answer your question, I asked Mark to stop. No, I demanded it. What he did was dangerous, and I was afraid. Afraid he'd get killed." Kaitlyn paused. "And I was jealous because he made rescuing children more important than me. I know it's horrible to think like that. But I did."

The air seemed clearer and the sun shining brighter. The tension was gone. She verbalized her feelings and felt like shouting it. She broke into tears. It started as a few drops, then burst into a flood.

Tamie handed her a box of tissue. "Here."

Kaitlyn wiped her eyes. Her thoughts went to a young Mark Steele. He stood before her, fearless and happy. Another bird, this one larger and bluish in color, flew to the feeder. She took the last piece of bread and placed it on the railing. "Come and get it." The bird hopped to the railing, took the crumb and flew back to the feeder. "Did you know all along I was jealous of Mark's passion?"

Tamie nodded yes.

Kaitlyn stood and hugged Tamie. "Thank you. I feel alive, like a huge something is gone."

"Because something died… your jealousy and fear."

Kaitlyn mixed crying with laughing. "I'm sorry, I'm getting your shoulder all wet." She stepped back and wiped her face with the tissue, then sat.

"Happy tears on my shoulders are always welcome." Tamie smiled. "Please tell me more," she said as she moved her chair closer to Kaitlyn.

For the next half-hour, Kaitlyn talked about her root fear, being alone. She described the pain she experienced when her fiancée, Joe, died, then Mark's hospital stay. Kaitlyn relaxed. "When we were first married, Mark wasn't afraid of anything. I was this shy girl, and he was fearless. And I loved that about him." She lost track of time, and repeated herself, going over and over about Mark's courage.

"Would you like a refill?" Tamie said.

"No, thanks. I should be going." Kaitlyn stood. "You're a good friend. Have you ever thought about going back into the counseling business?"

A smile filled Tamie's face. "I think I have." She made eye contact, then took Kaitlyn's hand. "You've discovered something about yourself. Now, what are you going to do about it?"

"I'll send Mark over here." Kaitlyn chuckled. "I'm joking. I can talk with Mark, now. Thank you."

"I'm happy to help."

Kaitlyn went back home. She no longer felt the need to clean as a distraction. The glass seemed clearer, and the floors brighter. When Mark returned from work, Kaitlyn met him at the front door. "Mark, I'd like to talk to you. Please."

He set his briefcase down, followed Kaitlyn into the living room, and sat. "It sounds serious."

"Yes. Before I begin would you like a cup of coffee?"

"No thanks. I had one on the way home."

Kaitlyn sat, then looked at her hands. She cleared her throat. "I'm not sure how to begin." Mark leaned forward. With a deep breath, she began. "You've been miserable with the office job."

"It's—"

She held up her hand. "Please let me finish while I have the courage."

"Okay."

"I appreciate you taking this job for our marriage, and I appreciate you stopping *your* rescue missions." Kaitlyn thought she had been ready, but with Mark looking directly at her doubt slipped in. She forced the next words. "*Your* deception hurt me, and I want to tell you why." There she said it.

Mark drew his eyebrows together. A flash of concern raced across his face.

It was the expression she hoped to see. He looked bothered, maybe sorry for his secrets. She continued. "When we were dating, you pulled crazy stunts to get my attention. The walkie-talkie at work, limo driver, boat ride, then all those walks on the beach, yelling to anyone who would listen that you loved me.

And I'm only naming a few. You embarrassed me, but you made me feel like a princess, like I was the only person on the earth. But that wasn't the only thing that drew me to you."

"It wasn't?"

"No. I fell in love with a 'live on the edge' kind of guy who had a deep passion. I first saw it when you told me about the murdered boy."

"Ramos Gonzales?"

"Yes. You were deeply crushed and expressed a desire to help those who couldn't help themselves. I saw a person who was tender and passionate on the inside. I fell in love with *that* person, and I married *that* Mark Steele."

Mark squeezed Kaitlyn's hand.

"I had forgotten about that until Tamie —"

"Tamie?"

"Our next-door neighbor? The one who invited us to supper this Friday night?"

"Yes, I remember."

"Tamie helped me sort things out. That week you were in Tennessee...I thought our marriage...well, was over...it's not," Kaitlyn said. "After your secret life became known, I became more jealous. You made something more important than me." Kaitlyn saw something in Mark's eye. Guilt?

"About that," Mark said. "I love you very much, but I haven't forgotten about...you know."

"I know. The passion for it is still in your voice, and I see it in your eyes. It was there when you talked to Tony."

"But I even plotted how I would rescue Brenda and how I would do it without you knowing about it. Then I talked myself out of it."

This was news to Kaitlyn, but it proved her point. The passion still lived deep within her husband. "Over the past month, you've put me first, and made me feel like a princess all over again. I saw a guy who'd lay his life down for innocent children. And now I know, you'd lay down your life for Carina and me too. The jealousy left, but the fear remained."

"Fear?"

"I was afraid of being alone. Afraid you'd be killed."

"But I'm —"

Kaitlyn put her hand to his lips. "You've changed...and not in a good way. You've become...someone I don't recognize."

"I thought—"

"You've been doing everything I expect." She stopped. "Well, not the plotting part. But it's like you have nothing to live for anymore, just like the time after your accident. You had no passion then either. No drive. I now understand why you changed when we moved to Austin. I thought it was because we had a new life. But that's when you began deceiving me. Right?"

Mark nodded and exhaled a pent-up breath. "That's when I took cases, yes."

"And that's when I started being jealous. I battled thoughts of 'another woman'. It started out as a small feeling, then it grew into something I couldn't control. And it was even more difficult because it didn't have a name. Well, until you got shot and your house of cards fell down, revealing your secrets."

"I know I've said it a lot lately, but I am sorry I deceived you. I didn't know it hurt you that bad."

"Well, it did. Deception kills relationships. And ours was on life-support. It took me to places I'd rather not had visited." Kaitlyn paused and felt like a dam ready to break. She gathered her emotions and pressed forward. "This past month I've beat myself up, not understanding my feelings. After all, you had been rescuing children from a life of misery. Who was I to stop that? But you deceived me. I was justified to hate you for that. Right?" She didn't expect him to answer. "The battle tore me up inside. And when Tony called, it really messed me up. But like I said, Tamie helped me uncover the real culprit and as much as I hate to say it, it wasn't completely you."

"It wasn't?"

Kaitlyn's voice became stern, as if a switch had been turned on, her eyes narrowed. "Trust me, you were definitely wrong for lying to me. That'll never be okay with me, so don't ever think of doing it again."

He looked like he had something to say but kept silent.

Kaitlyn looked into his eyes. "What I'm trying to say is, I faced my fear this morning. I don't want it any longer. I want the real Mark Steele back. The man I married, the man I love...not a man with no passion or direction...and definitely not a secret agent man." She surprised herself, being able to joke about it. It felt good to be in control of her emotions. But she never wanted to hear him joke about it.

The front door opened and closed, and feet pounded up the stairs. Carina was home.

"You faced it?" Mark leaned closer.

Kaitlyn continued. "I faced it. And you know what? It's not this horrible monster, I've made it out to be. I'm not alone, anymore. God is with me."

"Anymore?"

"A little bird reminded me we needed to be free." *Yes, Mark, we need to be free to live our lives as our Creator intended.*

"Huh?"

"Never mind. I actually thought I was mean spirited by not wanting you to rescue children. But that was me trying to save my life. Do you understand?"

"I think so," Mark said the words slow, then talked normally. "You were afraid I'd get myself killed?"

"Something like that."

"But I've told you I won't do that again."

It wasn't as important that Mark fully understood as it was that Kaitlyn finally did. She threw her arms around Mark and hugged him. After a few minutes, she leaned back and removed the hair from her eyes. "Don't you understand? You have to live your passion, we have to live in that passion, and I want to be a part of it."

"What are you saying?"

"I'm saying…go get Brenda, then get that other kid."

Mark's eyes widened. "Are you serious?"

"Yes. Go, before I change my mind," she said. "And Mark?"

"Yes."

"Don't ever do any of this by yourself ever again. Because if you do, I won't be afraid to leave you."

"Yes, Ma'am." Seriousness turned to a smile.

"And Mark."

"Yes."

"Keep your phone."

***

Mark placed the phone on speaker so Kate could listen. "Tony, this is Mark. What's the update on your daughter?"

"Update? What do you mean update? There's nothing," Tony whispered.

Kate put her hand on Mark's shoulder.

"What are the police saying?"

"They're still calling her a run-away, so I don't think they'll do much."

"Well, I've decided to return to Nashville and track down her down." After several seconds of silence, Mark spoke. "Tony, did you hear me?"

"Are you saying you're back on this? You'll try to find Brenda?"

"Provided they haven't moved her out of the area, I think we have a good chance of finding her. I'll fly to Nashville tomorrow and plan on staying there at least one week." For now, Mark postponed the gun idea.

"Oh, thank you so very much. I can't tell you how much this means to me."

"Don't thank me yet. Let's save that for when I return with Brenda." After Mark had ended the phone call, he looked at Kate, then Carina, who entered the office at the end of the call. "As a family, let's pray." Mark formed a circle, paused and looked at Kate. "Would you pray for Brenda?"

Chapter 49

With her hands behind her head, legs crossed and lying on her bed, Carina thought about her dad, who had left three days ago for Tennessee. He seemed so excited about finding Brenda.

Each night during meal times, he called. The first two days he had nothing to report. But last night he seemed hopeful. Mom put the call on speakerphone. "I think I've located Brenda, but don't know for sure. I'm staking out a place she may be at, in fact, I'm there right now. A girl that matches her description went inside a motel room with an older woman. They've been in there for several hours."

"I hope you find her," her mom said.

"I'll keep you informed."

Mom told him to be safe, and that she was proud of him. Carina was very proud of her dad as well. "Dad, I told everyone at school about this."

"I'm not sure that was a good idea. Have you revealed her name?"

"No."

"Good. Let's not do that."

"Okay. But can I tell them you may have found her?"

"I suppose that wouldn't hurt since you've already told them about her." He had to go because someone was coming out of the motel room. He said he loved them, then goodbye.

She had put a second pillow under her head. "Your dad should speak at a school assembly," Carina remembered one of her classmates had said. Several other girls also encouraged Carina to ask him. That was Monday. Today she couldn't walk down the hall or enter a classroom without someone asking her about the abducted girl. Carina was excited to go to school tomorrow and give them the update, especially since her dad may come home tonight.

She had promised she would pray every day for Brenda. So Carina sat up. "God, I hope you can hear me. My mom says you can. Anyway, would you keep my dad safe. And bring Brenda back home. That's all I can think of right now. Goodbye." *Goodbye? Is that how you pray?* She shrugged her shoulders, then went to her desk and opened her history book. Pulling out a paper she looked at the "A" on the top. As a warm feeling shot through her, Carina heard her mom's voice from downstairs.

"Carina, there's someone to see you."

"Okay, Mom." She ran downstairs and stopped. Billy stood by the front door. Carina said hi, then stepped outside. He followed, and she shut the door.

"Where have you been? Is your phone broken?" Billy asked.

"I've texted you."

"Not today."

"I've been busy." That wasn't a complete lie. She had some homework to do after school. Actually, she didn't feel like texting him. She could only take so much of Billy. Carina was attracted to him but not in a relational sense. He was a challenge, similar to a school project. Deleting the texts was easy, but dealing with Billy standing in front of her was difficult.

"Why didn't you answer my texts? I've been texting you all day."

Carina didn't appreciate the tone in his voice. "I don't need to explain anything to you, Billy West." As Carina was about to step inside, Billy flashed a smile. She felt the tension leave.

"Hey, it's all good. Let's hang out. I'm going to the mall."

Carina hesitated for a few seconds. *If Dad puts his life in danger for kids, at least I can try to help Billy.* She opened the door and yelled, "Mom, I'm headed to the mall." Before her mom could respond, Carina shut the door. She instantly felt bad and thought about going back to ask permission, but changed her mind and caught up with Billy. *I'll just text her.* She felt for her phone and remembered she left it in her room.

Two blocks down the street, they walked past a tree full of birds. Billy picked up several rocks and threw them into the tree causing the birds to fly.

"Hey, you'll hurt a bird and besides aren't you afraid you'll hit a window or something?" She thought she should go back home. *But what about Billy?*

"I haven't yet." He dropped the rocks.

For twenty minutes they walked in silence because Billy had popped in his ear buds. Carina thought it rude of him, but she didn't feel like saying anything. Besides, he would probably talk dirty, and she didn't want to hear that.

They crossed the mall parking lot, entered through the main entrance, and walked down the hallway toward Spencer Gifts.

He shut off his music and removed his ear buds, then walked into the store. Carina stopped. "I'll stay out here."

Billy moved the hair from his eyes. "Why?"

"Because I don't want to go in there."

"What? You might get in trouble?" Billy chuckled.

"I said I don't want to go in there." She said it more forceful than she intended. Being with Billy was harder than she had realized.

"Have it your way. Want to play video games?"

"Sure." She knew he meant, want to watch *me* play video games.

They walked to the arcade. Once inside, Billy put his hand on a younger boy's shoulder. The boy stepped aside and Billy started playing the machine.

Carina blew out a hot breath. How could she help a jerk? Maybe if she couldn't help Billy, she'd help the kid. Once she did that, she'd go home and apologize to her mom. She turned to the kid. "I'm sorry, he's just a bully."

"Shut up. What are you doing?" Billy said as he maneuvered the controls of the game.

"You stole his game. That makes you a bully." The kid stood behind Carina. Billy stopped playing and stared at her. He then stepped into her personal space, nearly touching his nose to hers. "You can't bully me, Billy West." Carina glared.

After several seconds, Billy stepped aside. "Okay kid, finish your game." In reluctance, the boy returned to his game.

She decided to stay for a little longer, besides she had a question she wanted to ask him. She'd wait for the right moment. After watching for a few minutes, they walked out of the arcade.

"Billy, are you still living in the park?" Carina ran to keep up with him.

"What's it to you?"

"I was just wondering."

"No, I went back home."

"You should report your dad."

Billy stopped and faced her. "You shut your mouth or else."

"Or else what, you'll do to me what your dad did to you?"

"I might."

"Try, and I'll put you on the ground." Carina couldn't believe the words were coming out of her mouth. Billy's fist tightened, and for a few seconds, Carina wondered if he would hit her.

He continued to walk. "No one would listen, they'd think I'm lying."

"My dad would believe you."

"No one does anything for Billy-the-Kid or even likes me."

"My dad's different, he rescues kids."

"He does?"

"Yes, he's in Tennessee right now trying to rescue a girl. He can help you if you let him." *Please, Billy let him help you.* They stopped at the water fountain, each looking toward the water. Carina had to figure a way to get his attention. "Unless you're afraid of my dad."

Billy turned. "I'm not afraid."

"Sure, right. You don't fool me Billy West."

"Maybe I'll talk to him, but I have to think about it first."

"Thank you."

A grin slowly appeared on his face. "You should come over to my house and help me think about it."

"No. I'm going home. If you want to go to my house, I'll ask my mom. I'm sure you can stay for supper." *And maybe dad's there already.*

"Forget it, I'll just hang here. Go back to your mommy."

"Billy West, you don't know help when you see it. You're too stuck on yourself, and you're too valuable to allow your dad to beat you." Carina surprised herself at her bravado. "The offer stands." As she moved down the hallway, Carina glanced back at Billy. He was sitting by the water fountain, his head tilted down. She felt sorry for him.

Chapter 50

T he announcement came over the speaker for Mark's return flight. He picked up his carry- on luggage and got in line for first class. A Japanese family was in front of him, a teenager behind him, with a man and woman behind her. Mark boarded the aircraft. After several minutes, the plane taxied then took off.

The two-hour flight gave him time to reflect upon the events of the past month. It seemed like years since he'd been shot, which now had healed. He thought more about how close he'd gotten to losing Kate. She was almost ready to leave him. That memory struck terror in him. Thankfully, the resort weekend and the efforts he'd made to win Carina back had saved his marriage.

As the plane leveled out, he compared his life to a roller coaster with extreme highs and lows. He knew from experience either one would cause him problems. He needed to level himself off, and this weekend he planned to do that by doing nothing. On Monday he'd call the next family and find out about Cody.

Initially, it bothered Mark that Kate had confided in a stranger about their personal life. But since it resulted in Kate giving him the green light to return to the rescuing business, Mark decided to overlook it. Hopefully, none of their personal stuff would come up in the conversation. If it did, he would change the subject. He now had a much healthier marriage and a wife who was at least trying to understand him. Each call to Kate revealed how eager she was to stay connected to his world. In return, he was eager to know what was happening in their lives. This development was so much better.

The fasten seat belts light turned off. Mark thought about his job at the dealership. Bob seemed relieved when Mark told him he planned to leave. Mark chuckled at the thought of never having to do paperwork again. But he still looked forward to getting repossessed cars.

Mark bowed his head, closed his eyes, then prayed. "Father God, thank you for the family you've given me. I know You work all things for the good. Please be with Brenda." After Mark ended the prayer, he let his mind drift to his last conversation with Tony.

"When Brenda was eight, we went to the Grand Canyon. Jane, Brenda and I rode mules into the canyon. Brenda was so excited. She talked about it non-stop for the rest of the vacation. She was more excited about the mule ride than the canyon. Jane and I had laughed about that."

"Sir, would you like something to drink?" The stewardess interrupted Mark's thoughts.

He requested a coke and received it. The girl next to him wouldn't acknowledge the stewardess, so she moved to the people across the aisle.

Mark hurt for Tony and suspected he missed his wife as much as his daughter since most of his stories included Jane. "We went to a zoo. A gorilla stared at Brenda and Jane. They got close to the glass and Brenda made a funny face at the ape. Apparently, the animal didn't like it and slammed against the window, causing the girls to scream." Tony half-smiled and briefly paused like he was trying to relive the event.

Mark waited several seconds. "Any other moments?"

"Brenda accidentally cut herself. Jane took her to the ER, and I arrived later." Tony paused. "I've never been good at that kind of stuff. Seeing the cut, I felt queasy and had to go to the waiting room. Jane said that Brenda took the stitches well, without crying. Both girls gave me a hard time for leaving." Tony half smiled.

Several seconds of silence. "Anything else?"

Tony's mood darkened. "After Jane left, Brenda took it hard. She stayed with me, even slept on the floor outside my bedroom. She ran to the phone every time it rang, hoping it was her mother and felt crushed when it wasn't. It nearly killed me. Even at restaurants, Brenda looked for Jane."

Mark didn't want to remember any more. He looked at his watch. Ninety more minutes of flight time. He closed his eyes and drifted to sleep as the plane flew on to Austin, Texas.

***

Carina left the mall. At home, she'd apologize to her mom for leaving without permission. Billy's refusal of help bothered her. She felt like she should just forget about him. After all, she tried.

She waited for the cars to pass so she could cross the road. It took awhile. She noticed the clouds were getting darker and hoped it wouldn't rain. When the street cleared, she jogged to the other side.

Her court date was next month, but she wasn't afraid of it any longer. Her dad said he'd go with her. With good grades and a favorable report from the principal, she was confident it would be okay. That's what her dad had told her, and she believed him.

Before he left for Tennessee, they'd talked about their summer vacation. She hadn't gone jet skiing before, but it sounded exciting. Her dad even said he'd bungee jump with her. Her mom said no way to that. She couldn't wait to see her dad and find out about Brenda. Maybe he'd be at home when she got there. That's why she had wanted Billy to come along with her, so he could talk with her dad.

Carina knew she wanted to help people, possibly be a police officer or a counselor. As she walked, she glanced at her hand. On her ring finger, she wore a purity ring. Her dad had asked her to wear it. "Take this ring off when you put your wedding ring on," she remembered him saying. Carina readjusted it so the heart faced up. *I will, Dad.*

***

The plane hit an air pocket, waking Mark. He glanced at the girl next to him. She had a blank stare of fear. He smiled, but she intentionally turned away. Outside the window, dark, angry clouds signaled a storm.

The plane began its descent, jerking at times. Mark had tried talking to her, even relayed some of her dad's stories, but Brenda other than saying thank you, had said little. Mark figured she was very embarrassed, likely in shock. Or maybe she viewed men differently. In any case, Brenda appeared to be thankful, but very shy. Hopefully that would change when she readjusted to home. Now, she just stared at the dark clouds. Was she reliving the nightmares she had experienced? *They tore so much out of her.*

Mark made a mental note. *Talk to Tony and share with him how much I had messed up, but then recaptured my own daughter's heart.* It wasn't the same situation, but maybe it would offer some hope, since Tony felt like such a failure. Mark knew that feeling well. He completed the rescue, but Brenda's recovery had just started. Mark hoped he could be a part of that process, too.

When Mark took Brenda to the police station, a lady officer spoke with Brenda alone. After the interview, the police officer talked to Mark. "She gave us descriptions and, with your information, I'm sure we'll find those responsible." Mark thanked the police officer.

When the plane landed, Mark called Kate letting her know he was back and he'd tell her all about the rescue once he got home. After they'd arrived at the gate and the pilot had shut down the engines, Mark rose and grabbed his luggage from the overhead. Brenda didn't move. "It's time to meet your father." She unbuckled her belt and stood.

Brenda followed as they exited the plane, went down the hallway, then the escalator to baggage claim. Mark found his luggage on the conveyor belt. As they walked to the exit, Mark saw fear on Brenda's face. "It'll be okay."

"My dad will hate me," Brenda said.

"He won't hate you."

"I feel like I'm going to be sick."

"Do you need to go to the restroom?"

"Not that kind of sick."

The bright sun greeted them, along with Tony. He ran to his daughter and embraced her. She reluctantly hugged him back.

"I'm sorry, Dad," she said.

"It's okay. I'm just glad you're home."

After a minute, Mark motioned for Tony. He stepped a few feet from her. Mark whispered, "It'll take time. She may need counseling."

Tony stared at Mark for several seconds, then with a look asked, "What happened?"

"They abused and raped her, continually. She's been through a horrific ordeal, Tony."

Mouth turned down, eyes closed, Tony put his hand on his face in anguish.

"Here's the police officer's name who talked to Brenda," Mark said as he handed Tony a form. "And the police department's phone number."

Tony whispered, "I have a week off from work."

"If you need someone to talk to, I'm available." Mark extended his hand.

"Thank you." Tony shook Mark's hand then Tony looked across the street and motioned for someone.

A woman exited a car and walked toward them. After she had crossed the street, Brenda yelled, "Mom" and ran into her arms.

Tony looked at Mark. "Jane and I are back together. When I told her Brenda was coming home, Jane returned." Tears welled up in Tony's eyes. "Mark, I have my wife and daughter back."

"Go to your family. I'll talk to you in a few days."

"Thanks, Mark. I'd can't tell you—"

Mark put his hand on Tony's shoulder and whispered, "Go."

Tony went to his family and put his arms around them.

For several seconds, Mark watched the reunion, then walked to his car, tossed his suitcase in the back seat and drove toward home. He hoped Tony, Jane and Brenda would stay together as a family.

He deliberately switched gears and thought about what he and Carina would do tomorrow. Mark promised her they would have a "date night" once he returned. Even though the traffic was heavy, Mark hit almost every green light and made good time on his way home.

Less than a mile from his house, he saw Carina walking down the sidewalk, pulled over, then rolled down his window. "Out for a stroll?"

"Dad! You're back." She ran and got in the car. "Did you find Brenda?"

"I did." Mark eased back onto the street.

"Is she at home now?"

"She's probably at her house, but it'll take time for her to feel home again."

"I get what you mean," Carina said.

Mark smiled. He nodded and put his hand over hers.

A few seconds later, Carina turned. "Dad?"

"Yes?"

"Would you talk to Billy? I know he's not someone you want me to hang out with, and I get why. I've decided we'll not be close friends. But he's abused, Dad. His dad abuses him."

"Did he tell you that?"

"I saw it."

"You saw it?"

"Don't worry Dad, I'll never go to Billy's house again."

"I'm glad. I don't want you to get hurt." Mark stopped at a red light. "Do you think Billy would talk to me?"

"When I asked him, he said maybe."

Mark turned right.

"Can we try right now? He's at the mall."

Mark looked at his watch. "Sure. Call your mom and let her know we'll be a little late...and why."

"I forgot my phone at home." Mark handed his phone to her. Carina called and explained the situation. She ended the call by apologizing.

"You left without asking?"

"Sorry, Dad."

"Tell me about Billy."

"I think he's scared. He believes no one likes him."

Mark listened, then several minutes later, pulled into the parking lot. Together they went inside the mall.

Carina went straight to the video arcade and saw Billy playing a game. "Dad, let me talk to him first."

"Okay, I'll be right here."

She went inside and, after a few minutes, returned with Billy. His hands were in his pockets, and his black hair hid his eyes.

"Hi Billy," Mark said with his hand outstretched.

Billy formed a fist and extended it.

Mark responded with a fist bump. "Carina said you'd like to talk with me."

"I might."

"Can I buy you a coke?"

"Sure."

Mark led the way. After passing a booth that sold art work, they cut across to the left side and entered a different hallway. The smell of cinnamon filled the air as they came to the food court. At

Subway, Mark ordered a coffee, then stepped aside for Billy and Carina. They each ordered a coke. After Mark paid, they took their drinks to an empty table.

"Tell me about yourself, Billy."

"Nothing to tell."

Mark waited a moment. That was all Billy planned to say. "Carina said your dad abuses you."

Billy lifted his head, moved the hair from his eyes and looked at Carina. He didn't seem upset with her, more like grateful.

Mark opened a creamer package and stirred it in his coffee. "Want to tell me about it?"

"I don't know. My dad's okay when he's not drinking."

"How often does he drink?"

"Every day." Billy moved the hair from his eyes.

"And when he's drunk he hits you?"

"Most of the time."

"Billy, that's not right. I'd like to help you...and your dad."

"How?"

"By giving him a chance to change," Mark said. "Let's go talk to him."

"No, we can't do that." Billy stood and gripped the back of the chair. "He'll, he'll…"

"It can't get much worse... right?"

"I don't know."

"There are people that can help you... and your dad."

"He won't let anyone help him."

"We'd never know unless we try. So how about it, would you allow me to talk to him?" Billy sat again, then nodded his head yes.

"Let's finish our drinks, then I'll drive you home."

***

Billy's hands fidgeted the entire way to his house. He played with his earrings, nose ring and the metal studs on his jeans. Twenty minutes later they pulled in front of his house.

"Is that his car?" Mark asked.

Yes." Billy didn't move.

"Are you ready?"

Billy nodded, yes.

"Let me do the talking." Mark turned.

"Carina, please stay in the car."

"Okay, Dad."

Billy led Mark inside the house.

A guy lifted off the couch. His shirt was open, and his hair uncombed. "Who are you?"

"I'm Mark Steele." He stepped closer to West and held out his hand. Since the guy wouldn't shake his hand, and had an icy cold stare, Mark went straight to the point.

"I'm here to talk to you about your son."

"My son is none of your business."

"I think your son is my concern because you've been abusing him, and that will stop."

"Is that what he's telling you? The boy's a liar."

Mark stared at the man. "Carina, my daughter, said you hit Billy. And on our way here, your son told me you punched him just this morning, and he has bruises to prove it. Here are your options. One, you pick up that phone and tell the police what you've done, and I'll stay here until they come. Or two, I will call the police and wait for them to get here. Bottom line — the police will be notified... It'd be better if you make the call."

The man spewed vulgar language.

"Billy, go to the car." Mark pulled out his phone and dialed as Billy left the house.

West continued to rant about how this was his home, and Billy was his kid. "Billy, get over here." He pointed at Mark. "And you get out."

Mark stepped out of the house and went to his car, still talking to the police. The man followed Mark and again called for Billy who was now standing by the car.

Mark turned toward West and blocked his path to the vehicle. "Stay by the car Billy. You don't have to be afraid."

Chapter 51

Mom, Dad's home," Carina yelled as they entered the house with her dad's luggage in hand. "Dad, what will happen to Billy?" On the way home, they had talked about how Billy confessed everything his dad had done to him to the police. Carina had also shared her version of the story.

"I'm assuming he'll go to a foster home," Mark said as he approached their home.

"That seems unfair."

"Why?"

"After his dad gets out of jail he can go home, but Billy has to leave." Carina set the bags down.

"I hadn't thought of it that way. Yes, it's a little unfair, but they couldn't let Billy stay there by himself."

"How long will Mr. West be in jail?"

"I don't know."

Kaitlyn removed her apron as they entered the house. "Don't know what?"

"Carina and I were talking about Billy's father." Mark hugged Kate, then with his arm around her, looked at Carina. "Let's pray Mr. West gets the help he needs so Billy can return home soon. By the way, I'm proud of you, Carina."

She beamed.

"Anyone hungry?" Kaitlyn asked.

"Something smells good... hamburgers?" Mark said as they went to the dining room.

"Close... It's meatloaf." Kaitlyn and Mark went into the kitchen and returned with the meatloaf, mashed potatoes and corn on the cob. They sat, then Mark blessed the food. After dishing a slice of meatloaf onto his plate, he looked at Carina. "Have you decided what we're going to do Saturday night?"

"If it's okay with you I'd like to find a movie on Netflix and watch it as a family."

"Movie?"

"Yes, Saturday night—my date night with my daughter." Mark winked at Carina. "She wants to family."

"Family?"

"Family is now a verb, meaning we'll do something together."

"That sounds like fun." Kaitlyn scooped a spoonful of potatoes on her plate and passed it to Mark. "Okay, tell us what happened."

"Yes, tell us." Carina looked at him.

"At the airport, my luggage, was on the conveyor belt going round and round." Mark took a corn on the cob and lathered it with butter.

"No Dad, get to the good stuff."

Mark laughed. "I was trying to build suspense. The first two days in Nashville, I went to the location where I initially met the bad guys. I got there while it was still dark, and throughout the day followed the cars that were on my list. I investigated the locations they went." Mark paused and then thought about how much detail he should include in his story.

He'd nearly been caught at one of the first locations. It was in a trashy neighborhood, and the house he was investigating looked abandoned. Mark had followed a guy there and watched him go inside. Mark had parked his car a block away before walking to the house and looking in the window. He saw a few girls inside, but none matched Brenda's description. After several minutes, someone yelled, "Who's there?" Mark dropped under a bush. At the same time, a cat jumped out of a trash can, redirecting the man's attention. It gave Mark a way of escape.

After investigating nearly ten different sites, on Wednesday afternoon, he found the place he was looking for. Mark had followed a vehicle from the adult book store. The blue sedan matched the description and plate number on his list. The driver, a guy in a muscle shirt, parked in front of room twelve of an old run-down motel then went inside.

Mark parked across the street and moved to the back seat to observe. He hoped the tinted windows would hide him. There were a dozen rooms, all in line, with doors facing a small parking lot. Weeds sprung up from every crack in the parking lot. A small office was on the other side of room one. There was a car parked in front, and someone in the office.

Five minutes later, the guy in room twelve left then went to rooms five and three. After several minutes in each room, he went to the office. Mark looked through his binoculars for a few hours. He caught a glimpse of a girl pacing back and forth in front of room twelve's window. The curtains were drawn in rooms five and three.

Mark continued speaking to his family. "Understand, when watching people, your eyes can play tricks on you. It looked like Brenda, but I had to know for sure, so I waited."

Mark wondered if this motel was ever used by the public. The sign in front said rooms were 150 dollars a night. Probably priced high to keep away any potential customers and leave the motel exclusively for their criminal enterprise. But that was something he didn't want to tell his family. He forked the last portion of his meatloaf, dipped it in ketchup, then into his month. After he washed it down with water, Mark continued his story.

The car was still in front of the office, but the guy wasn't visible any longer. He probably went to the area behind the office. And since the girl wasn't by the window any longer, Mark wanted a closer look. He ran behind the motel and discovered another window in the back. Looking in, Mark saw it was empty. Since the window was single-paned, Mark heard water flowing. *She must be showering.* The door inside the room had no knob. *Whoever's in there can't leave.* Mark tried the window and found it locked. He stayed still. She began singing.

Thirty minutes later, around 6:30 pm, the motel door opened. Mark lowered and peaked through the window. The curtain helped hide his face. The muscle shirt guy returned with a duffel bag. *Was this the one who....* Muscles unzipped the bag on the bed and pulled out a lacy blouse and white shorts. When he heard him speak, Mark knew this was the guy who'd shot him.

"Hey, get out here and put this on."

"Can I get something to eat?"

"Just get out here."

A few seconds later, the girl exited the bathroom wrapped in a towel, water dripping from her hair. *Brenda.* Mark's pulse increased. This time, he would get her and bring her home. She took the clothes and went back to the bathroom. If the guy laid a hand on her, Mark would forget his plan and jump in there now. He continued to observe.

The guy lifted a camera. "Hurry. We need pictures of you in these clothes."

"I'm hungry."

"You're always hungry. We'll talk about that after we take the pics."

A minute later, Brenda came out wearing a purple blouse with tight shorts.

"Smile like I taught you, and I'll get you something to eat."

A faint okay came from Brenda.

He looked through the camera. "No, no, it's not any good. Comb your hair. I want these pictures to be perfect."

Brenda left the room again and returned less than a minute later. The guy had her stand against the wall. He unbuttoned a few of her blouse buttons and unsnapped her shorts. Mark's muscles tightened. *He does one more thing.*

The man stepped back and raised the camera. Mark relaxed a little until he saw Brenda's seductive smile and poses. He felt sick to his stomach. The guy took several pictures, giving Brenda different commands of how to pose. Several minutes later he lowered his camera.

She re-buttoned her blouse and shorts. "Can I get some food now?"

"I suppose since you've been cooperating." He raised the camera and viewed the photos. "Since these pictures look... chu chu chu." The guy raised his eyebrows with each "chu." *This guy is an idiot.* Mark wished the guy's toothpick would get stuck in his throat.

Brenda lowered her eyes.

"I'll treat you. What do you want?"

"Anything."

"How about a quarter pounder and fries from McDonalds?"

"I'd like that."

Mark examined the window. Brenda could easily break it and escape. But she didn't. *She must be afraid.*

Mark ducked down when the guy turned toward the window. After hearing the door open and close, Mark ran to the corner of the motel, just in time to see the car leaving the parking lot. After looking around and seeing no one, he jumped into action.

Mark had spent part of the day studying the area on Google maps. McDonalds was about two miles away. Calculating the drive time and drive thru time, Mark figured he probably had fifteen minutes. He only needed three.

Mark ran to his rental, drove close to Brenda's room, and positioned the vehicle across from the motel door. He left the driver's door open and the engine running. Then he kicked in the motel door. Brenda, wide-eyed, jumped from the bed. Just as she was about to scream, Mark placed his hand over her mouth. Her eyes widened even more. "I'm here to help you. I'm removing my hand, please don't scream. She seemed to remember him and calmed down. Mark scooped her up and carried her to the car.

He shut the car door, but not in time. The guy in the office ran out with a gun in his hand. Mark accelerated. The car fishtailed, hit the street doing around thirty, then bounced over a pothole. Brenda moved to the passenger's door. Mark glanced at her. "It's okay."

The police station was almost twenty miles away. He had to get there fast but first had to lose the office guy, who was now behind him. He made several turns, each one slowed his speed. That wasn't a good plan, so he pressed on the accelerator and shot down a residential area. He'd accelerate faster, but there were kids in some yards. He needed to get out of this area.

Mark entered an industrial area. He checked his rear-view mirror. Office guy was a few blocks behind him, but still matching his speed. Brenda's occasional screams weren't helping. "Brenda. I'm here to help you."

Her body still shaking, Brenda looked at Mark for several seconds, then lower her voice. "They'll kill my dad."

"I'll call him, and you can talk to him. Would you like that?"

She nodded yes.

The car behind him was now a block away.

Mark fished out his phone and pressed Tony's number. It rang three times, and on the fourth, Tony answered. Mark said a few words, then handed the phone to Brenda. "Daddy?" She burst out crying. "I'm sorry, Daddy. I really am sorry." She continued to talk to him, at times being silent.

Office guy's vehicle was gaining on him. Mark accelerated. *Fifteen miles to go.* Mark remembered a residential area was just ahead that lasted about four more miles. That meant stop signs. *Can't do that. Think, Steele.*

A few minutes later Brenda put the phone on the seat. "He hates me."

"What? No, your dad doesn't hate you. Didn't he tell you he loves you?"

She wouldn't respond.

"Brenda, it'll be okay."

She stared straight ahead. She wasn't screaming any longer, and that was good. The car behind them came closer. Mark was now pushing ninety on a two lane divided highway, driving in the right lane. *Where are the police when you need them?* A deep ditch in the middle separated the streets, with a guard rail on the right. He knew there was one more mile until residential. There was a service road ahead connecting the two streets. It was the only chance of losing this guy. Mark slowed and moved to the left. Office guy approached Mark's right side and flashed a gun. Mark pulled to the far left, slammed on his brakes and fishtailed through the service road. He thought for sure he'd roll the car. If he missed the road by even an inch, he'd fly into the ditch. Dust flew in the air. By some miracle, the maneuver worked. Mark was traveling the opposite way, and Brenda was screaming, again. His pursuer couldn't make the turn. Mark accelerated going the opposite direction for a mile, then took several turns. When he was certain the guy was not in sight, he drove to the police station without incident.

Mark pulled in front of the station. "Please tell the officers everything that happened to you. Can you do that?"

Brenda nodded yes.

Her eyes were huge as they walked into the station.

***

Mark let his thoughts come back to the present. Both Kate and Carina were looking at him. He noticed their plates were empty. With his appetite gone, Mark pushed his plate back.

"Did she say what happened to her?"

"Carina, that's too personal," Kaitlyn said. "Would anyone like a cookie?" They both said yes.

"Will Brenda be okay?"

Mark took a deep breath. *I hope so.* He let the question hang in the air until Kate returned with cookies and glasses of milk. "She has a family who loves her. I think she'll be okay."

Mark grabbed a chocolate chip cookie and took a bite. "It has a happy ending."

"It does?"

"Yes, at the airport, Brenda was a little slow to greet her dad."

"Why?" Carina asked.

"She was probably ashamed of what happened," Kaitlyn said.

Mark dunked his cookie into his milk. "Like your mom said, Brenda was ashamed. Maybe she convinced herself her dad would reject her."

"Reject her?" Carina asked.

"Remember when you got lost at the zoo when you were younger. When we found you, you weren't happy to see me. In fact, you cried?"

"I thought I was in trouble and that you would yell at me."

"That may be what Brenda was going through. I'm sure she was happy to be rescued but also scared. Her captors probably made her feel ugly, especially around men. They had brainwashed her into thinking that if she escaped, her dad would be killed. And maybe she thought her dad wouldn't accept her back. Her captors filled her with many lies, so I'm not sure what was going through her mind. All I know is she became very withdrawn." Mark stared at the wall, remembering the terrified look on Brenda's face. "Brenda had left...voluntarily. She left home as an innocent girl, she returned with deep emotional scars."

No one spoke for a minute. Carina leaned closer. "You mean Brenda ran away?"

"Yes. She willingly went to Nashville. That's why we need to know where you're at and who you're talking to."

Carina lowered her head. "Yes, Dad."

"When Brenda saw her mom, she ran to her. And get this, she hadn't seen her for years," Mark said.

"Where was her mom?"

"I don't know. She ran away herself but returned. Now, they're a family." Mark smiled as he thought of Tony, Jane, and Brenda hugging each other.

"I'd love to meet her," Carina said.

"That may happen. In two weeks, I plan to invite Tony and his family for supper. If that's okay with you, Kate."

"It would be great meeting them. That reminds me, we have dinner with our neighbors tomorrow night."

"I look forward to it," Mark said, knowing it to be untrue.

"Me too," said Carina.

Chapter 52

Five years later

Mark opened the car door, and Carina stepped out. The spring air, chirping birds, and the aroma of garlic and tomato, made for a perfect day.

They went inside the Italian restaurant. "Two for lunch, please," Mark said..

A woman directed them to their table. "Would you like anything to drink?" They both ordered water with lemon, then opened their menus.

"Your mom and I come here often," Mark said.

"Mom said I'd like it."

After looking over his menu, Mark set it aside. "Tomorrow is the big day."

Carina had arrived from Phoenix five days ago to finish the preparations for her wedding.

"Yes. I'm so happy, Dad. And Ryan and I are so grateful for the honeymoon gift. I can't believe we're going on a Caribbean cruise."

Mark smiled. The glow on her face made him feel like the greatest man on the earth. "So I'll finally get to meet Ryan tonight?"

"Yes. He's flying in this afternoon. After I pick him up, we have a few errands to do, but we'll be home before supper. Dad, he's incredible. I know you'll like him."

The waitress put waters and a basket of breadsticks on the table. "Are you ready to order?"

"Spaghetti and meatballs for me," Mark said.

"I'll have the same."

The waitress wrote it down, collected the menus, and left.

"Your mom said you dropped out of the police academy."

"I did. Mainly to support Ryan. We didn't think two police officers in one family would work."

"I suppose not." Mark hid his disappointment.

"Dad, can I get the address of the resort?"

"Resort?"

"The one we visited when I was in tenth grade."

"You and Ryan can stay at our house."

"I don't mean to stay there. I just wanted to show Ryan. You know, for memory sake."

"Sure. I can get that for you when we get back home."

"Coming home for the wedding has made me think about how much my life has changed these past few years. It all started with that weekend at the resort five years ago."

"That weekend changed our entire family."

"Yes. I'm glad you included mom and me in your missions. I'll never forget the times when Brenda and her family came over to our place."

"I'm glad they came. It was great to see how that tragedy got turned around." Mark squeezed the lemon into his water and took a drink.

"I liked it even better when we went to their house." Carina opened her napkin and put it on her lap. "After her third visit, Brenda told me what happened. She didn't get real detailed, but she said enough. It was horrible for her."

"She opened up to you? You never told me that."

"She made me promise not to. I don't think she'd care anymore. I will never forget how she said all these horrific things without any emotions at all."

"What do you mean?"

"It's hard to explain. It was almost like she was reading from a script." Carina took a drink. "Until she talked about the person she called, *The Man*. She was terrified of him."

"I wish the police would have found him, but he got away. They busted many people, including the kid who lured Brenda to Nashville. When they raided the bookstore, they discovered and shut down a sex trafficking ring, but *The Man* escaped." Mark took a bite of his breadstick. "Have you kept in touch with Brenda?"

"I haven't. Have you?"

"I talk to Tony occasionally, and he mentions Brenda." Mark looked at his glass, then back to Carina. "For years, Brenda had night terrors. Those have finally gone away. The last I heard she's in college studying to be a social worker."

"I'm happy for her."

The waitress placed salads in front of them. "Do you want my tomatoes?"

"Sure." Mark forked the quartered tomatoes and put them on his plate. He poured extra thousand island on his lettuce, stirred it, then took a bite. For a few minutes, they ate without speaking.

After Carina had eaten most of her salad, she put her fork down. "Something else I just remembered...the limo ride. I'll never forget it. For several months, it made me so popular at school. Everyone wanted to know everything about it."

"That was fun. When your mom reminded me of how I won her heart, I figured I'd better go big with you."

"Well, it worked." They both laughed.

Carina held out her purity ring. "Dad, there's something I want you to know. You gave this to me on that weekend, remember? I'm not sure if you knew this, since I was acting so wild before that, but I have never dishonored this ring. On our wedding night, Ryan will be the first and only guy I've ever been with."

"That's wonderful."

"Dad, you're crying." Mark wiped the tears.

Carina took out a book from her purse. "I brought this with me, and I'd like to read a little to you." She opened it and read. "I want a guy with a strong personality, yet gentle. He must be brave, yet loving. And above all, he must think I'm important." Carina said. "I wrote those words after our resort weekend."

Mark looked at Carina. His "little girl" had become everything he'd prayed for and expected.

"You believing in me, changed everything. It didn't hurt when the judge dismissed all the charges. Thanks for saying all those nice things about me in court."

"Those words were all true."

Carina squeezed his hand. "There was something I should have added."

"What's that?"

"He must be like my dad and love Jesus."

It was difficult, but Mark controlled his emotions. "And I take it Ryan has matched that description?"

"Yes, all that and more. He actually tried talking me out of dropping out of the police academy but respected my decision. I think he realized it was the right thing to do for our relationship." Carina picked up a breadstick, then grinned. "And when he saw I wasn't about to change my mind."

Mark chuckled. Yes, his daughter had become just like him, stubborn. But he liked the word "determined" better. The waitress removed their salad plates.

"I'm curious, whatever happened to Billy?" Mark asked.

"As you know, he dropped out of school. Billy didn't like his foster home, probably because of the rules. I heard he went to a home for troubled kids until he was eighteen. I lost track of him until a year ago. On his Facebook, I saw he has a little baby. I'm not sure if he's married, but he seems happy."

Mark nodded and was about to say something when the waitress returned with their spaghetti. He twirled the noodles with his fork. "Did you know that I've joined forces with Tanasha and Roger?"

"I'm sorry, I don't remember them."

"They were the ones who had the ministry called Freedom Now." Mark waited for Carina's puzzled look to change. "We went to church and listened to her story?"

"Oh, yeah. Now I remember. I didn't want to go to church."

Mark laughed. "I kind of dragged you and mom there."

"I'm glad you did. Ryan and I go every Sunday now. So what do you do at Freedom Now?"

"Not as many rescues as before. Mom is happy about that."

Carina smiled.

"I mostly train others younger than myself how to find abducted children and bring them home. But, enough about me. I want to hear about your plans. Tell me more about Ryan."

For the next twenty minutes, Carina spoke about Ryan and how they met at the police academy. They planned to wait a year before starting a family. Carina wanted two children, a boy, and a girl, and since Ryan came from a big family, he wanted more. They decided they'd have three, but no more than four. Mark hoped for a lot of grandkids.

After they'd finished their meal, Mark paid, and they went to the car. "I still have twenty- four hours before I give you to Ryan, so you're still my little girl." He opened his arms, and they hugged. "Mom and I are very proud of you." He looked into her eyes. "I'm looking forward to meeting Ryan."

"He wants to join the special unit of the police department but isn't sure what division yet. Right now he's on the night shift."

"Where's his beat?"

"Downtown Phoenix."

"I suppose you'll be up at nights wondering if he's okay."

"I'll probably pray a lot." Carina chuckled. "But Mom taught me to let go of any fear and follow my heart."

"She taught you that?"

"Yes, she told me why she didn't want you in any dangerous job. She was protecting her own life. And she said that was wrong thinking."

"You have a very special mother."

"I sure do."

Once they entered the car, they continued to talk. Mark filled her in with his current project, and she talked about their new apartment.

***

Hearing the door bell, Mark took a deep breath and went to the front door. He wanted this meeting to be perfect.

"The words will come," he had remembered Kate saying. He took another deep breath and opened the door. *A rescue is easier than this.* His pulse increased. He'd rather be dangling from a patio. *Man up Steele.* He wondered why meeting this young man made him so nervous. Mark concluded that his plan to reveal his own weakness was the reason. After straightening his tie, he greeted Ryan. Ryan was an inch taller than him, had short brown hair, and looked like he didn't have an ounce of fat.

"Hello, Mr. Steele." Ryan extended his hand and made eye contact.

"Call me Mark." He shook Ryan's hand. His grip was firm. "Let's go to my office." Mark hugged Carina. "Mom is in the kitchen."

A firm handshake and eye contact, two things Mark liked about his young man. But this wasn't just any man, this was the person who'd marry his little girl tomorrow, the guy he'd give his daughter to in marriage.

They entered his office. Mark motioned toward a chair. Ryan took a seat. Mark sat as well. "I'm glad to finally meet you in person. We've talked a few times on the phone, but it's not like seeing each other face to face."

"Glad we could finally meet."

"This may feel a little awkward, but considering you guys are getting married tomorrow, there's something I wanted to share with you. Kind of man-to-man thing. I'm not sure where to start." He cleared his throat. "You may have already realized that Carina is a strong-willed girl." Mark stopped. *Why did I start with that?*

Ryan nodded.

Mark continued, "We were close as she grew up but then during her teen years we became distant. I became distant. I took her for granted and almost lost her and Kate. Did she tell you about that time?"

Ryan leaned closer. "Not a whole lot. She did say she had gotten into trouble as a teenager."

Mark stood and perched on the end of the desk. "I take some responsibility for that. I was so focused on my work, I let our relationship fall apart. But after Kate told me she was leaving me, I realized my mistake." Mark paused. "I had to work pretty hard to win Kate and Carina's hearts again, and get them to let me back into their lives... What I'm telling you...I hope you never stop courting my daughter, even after you're married. Strive to keep your hearts as close as they are right now." Mark allowed several seconds to pass. "After the honeymoon and when life becomes routine..." Mark directed his eyes to the desk, then back to Ryan. "What I'm trying to say is don't let what you do—your job, your work— ever become more important than your marriage."

"Thanks, Mr. Steel—"

"Call me Mark, please."

"Mark, I'll do my best. I love your daughter very much. She's a special girl. I'll always remember that."

"I know you will, son. I wouldn't be giving her away if I didn't believe that." Mark exhaled, then stood. "She told me a lot about you. You're on the night shift?"

"Yes, but I hope to get into a special unit, maybe the detective section. I'm not sure yet."

As they talked, Mark realized Ryan was much like himself. He wasn't afraid of taking risks, even if it meant putting himself in dangerous places. Ryan spoke with passion, similar to the drive Mark had many years ago and in some cases, still has. Time passed quickly, and the hour came to an end.

"It's time to eat," Kate called from the other room.

Mark stood, followed by Ryan. "And remember this above everything else." Mark paused. "Treat her well so you'll have happy ever after stories to tell my grandchildren." Mark smiled, put his arm around Ryan, and together, they went to eat.

***

Under the white flowery arch, Mark hooked his arm, and Carina placed her arm in his. They exchanged eye contact—time froze. A lifetime of memories paraded in Mark's mind. He saw the moment he brought his daughter home from the hospital. Then, pictured her on his lap after the accident. He remembered the red carpet at school and later listening to her graduation speech as valedictorian. The possession music started. "Ready?"

Carina patted his arm. "I love you, Dad." She removed the purity ring and put it in her dad's hand. "I won't need this anymore."

He tried to keep the tears from falling, but one escaped. "I love you, baby."

No one had to remind him to go slow up the aisle. Mark planned on taking in every moment, his precious daughter by his side. Sounds of clicking cameras and turned heads greeted them as they proceeded. Mark made eye contact with Kate and noted deep love in her eyes. For a moment, he flashed back to his own wedding. He loved Kate more today than ever before, and he knew she loved him. Mark stopped at his arranged spot.

The minister looked at Mark. "Who gives this woman to this man?"

"Her mother and I." Mark turned and hugged Carina. "You're beautiful," he whispered, "your prince awaits." He then released her. He really released her. Pain and joy flooded him as only a father could feel.

Carina smiled, then moved next to her husband-to-be.